FAÇADES

by
Alex Marcoux

Bella
BOOKS

2011

Bella Books, Inc.
P.O. Box 10543
Tallahassee, FL 32302

Printed in the United States of America on acid-free paper.

Originally Published by Alice Street Editions 2000, Harrington Park Press®
First Bella Books edition 2011

This first Bella Books edition has been augmented with substantial additional text and contains editorial changes from the original.

Cover designer: Judith Fellows

ISBN-13: 978-1-59493-239-7

About The Author

Alex Marcoux is an awarding winning novelist. Her novels are: *Façades, Back To Salem* and *A Matter Of Degrees*. She wrote the screenplay *Back To Salem – The Short Film* produced in 2008. Alex expanded on her novel writing experience in a forthcoming spiritual self-help book. She presents workshops on writing, creativity and spirituality, all of which encourage people to take their imagination to a new level.

A longtime resident of Colorado, she is often found hiking the foothills plotting her next suspense thriller. Visit Alex at www.AlexMarcoux.com.

Literary Awards:
Façades:
RMFW Pen Award

Back To Salem:
Lambda Literary Award Finalist Lesbian Mystery

A Matter Of Degrees:
Golden Crown Literary Award Finalist for Best Speculative Fiction
Gaylactic Spectrum Best Novel nominee.

This book is dedicated to all those who have been persecuted because of who they love.

Acknowledgements

There were many people involved the initial publication of this book, you know who you are, and I remain extremely grateful for your help. As "Façades" goes back to print I want to thank the publisher, Linda Hill and everyone at Bella Books, along with Michelle and Preston for their continued love and support.

Also by Alex Marcoux

Façades
Back To Salem
A Matter Of Degrees

Chapter 1

Sidney Marcum sat in her fourteenth-floor office, scheduling her week. Distracted by the sound of the rain beating against her window, she got up and stood looking down at the busy New York City street below. She watched the pedestrians as they hurried along Broadway. *People are always in such a hurry*, she thought. *They never take the time to do what really matters…Then it's too late.*

The buzz of her intercom interrupted her thoughts, forcing her back to reality. The softness in her eyes disappeared and was replaced with coolness, as if something solidified her heart. "Sidney, Mr. Jacobs from Global Records is on line two."

"Thank you Michelle." Sidney hesitated as she reached for the phone. She had not heard from David Jacobs in a long time. *Why is he calling?* She picked up the handset and candidly greeted the caller, "Did you know I've been fired by two people in my life, and I don't talk with the other guy. How are you, David?"

"Great Sid," the man laughed. "Are you still holding that

against me? I thought you forgave me for canning you, after I gave you *the Gang*."

Sidney kidded her long-time business associate, "My ego has never completely healed. To what do I owe the honor of this call?"

"I heard you're in the market for a new client. I have another lead."

Sidney was curious. The lead she got on *the Gang* literally put her in business. "Well, I am looking right now. I have two prospects. What do you have, David?"

"A once-in-a-lifetime opportunity."

"I've heard that one before."

"No really, it is a great opportunity. It's an established artist."

"You know I don't get excited about established artists."

"But Sid, trust me, she's bigger than big. She's having some problems with her existing manager, but his contract is up next month. She also has some minor PR problems. Sid, you're the best. I recommended you for the job and she wants to talk with you."

"Who is it?" Sidney asked.

David hesitated. "It's Anastasia."

"Some *minor* PR problems? Anastasia doesn't need a new manager; she needs to use a little discretion."

"Sidney, at least talk with her before you dismiss the idea." There was silence. "Sidney?"

"Of course I'll meet with her, but I won't make any promises."

"That's all I can ask, thank you." David added, "Jerry Benson is my top A&R person now. He's not as good as you were, but he's good. I'll have him call your office to arrange a meeting."

Sidney hung up the phone and once again approached her window. The glass reflected the tall and slender build of the thirty-eight-year-old. With her long fingers she brushed the bangs of her short brown hair away from her face. For those few who were fortunate to really know Sidney, they knew she had a natural beauty. When she smiled, her energy could light up a room. Her eyes could be beautiful, yet at times equally haunting; a small scar flawed her face near her right eye. Very few of her business associates ever saw the genuine side of Sidney. Most in the music business knew Sidney Marcum as a powerful woman who should not be crossed.

The walls of her office were lined with awards, plaques and pictures of herself with various entertainers. It was a spacious office, harboring a small bar in the corner of the room, along with a Bang & Olufsen sound system. A sofa was placed conveniently opposite her desk. As with many workaholics, her office supplied the essentials, including a private bathroom with shower to help her through those long after-hour sessions.

Sidney was the founder of Marcum Promotions, Inc. (MPI), which was approaching its tenth year in business. Her business had grown tremendously over the years. She attributed her success to good old-fashioned hard work, good connections and being in the right place at the right time. Through the lead of her former boss, David Jacobs, she became the personal manager of a pop group called *the Gang*. David knew the young group of boys had talent and needed a manager. He suggested that Sidney consider managing the group. To this day, Sidney believed that David passed the lead to her out of guilt after firing her from Global Records.

Personal managers function as the general managers of an entertainer's business. Generally, their responsibilities range from negotiating record company deals and coordinating tours and publicity campaigns to hiring and supervising personnel. Sidney had a talent for dissecting a market and identifying what was really wanted. Then she would re-package the entertainer or entertainers to meet market demands. She had the ability and the connections, and she successfully pulled it off. Although she enjoyed the challenge of making a star, she recognized that stars were different from hungry, young artists. Once the star was born, Sidney was happy to step aside and delegate the day-to-day interactions of her performers to her managers.

As Sidney stared out her office window, her thoughts returned to Anastasia. All her success stories did not compare to Anastasia's achievements. But Sidney knew that Anastasia's career was plagued with public relation problems. Apparently Anastasia was a lesbian, and in the last year she had made little effort to conceal it. It was Sidney's belief that the country was not ready for a lesbian superstar, certainly not the way Anastasia had been marketed to the public. Sidney searched her CD collection until she found Anastasia's second album, *Lovers*. This production secured her superstar status. The cover of the CD portrayed a beautiful, light-skinned black woman with long dark hair, dressed in a white T-shirt. She was kneeling on a beach, tee shirt clinging to her body, lips parted with desire in her eyes. To Sidney it was obvious that a large percentage of her following was young and male. A young man who found out his goddess was gay would probably stop buying her music.

Once again, her train of thought was interrupted by the intercom. "Sidney, Mr. Davis is here to see you."

"Thank you Michelle, tell Scott to come in."

A strikingly handsome man entered her office. He towered over her as he hugged and kissed her.

"How's the love of my life?" His deep blue eyes sparkled as he asked.

"I'm great, how are you?"

"Good! I want to know if we're still on for the Kramer Benefit next month. If so, I need to get my tuxedo tailored." The Kramer Benefit was an annual fundraiser held to honor the memory of Seth Kramer, a musician who had died from AIDS nine years earlier. The event was attended by people in the music business, including artists, producers, record company contacts, and agents. Sidney had attended the event every year, and Scott had been her escort the previous five years.

"I haven't decided who I want to go with yet," Sidney teased.

Scott smiled as he walked to the familiar bar and poured himself a Dewars and water. He glanced at his reflection from the mirror behind the bar and finger-combed his wind-blown hair. The dark hair was accented with graying sideburns earned from his forty-eight years. The two sat comfortably on the sofa.

"I heard from David Jacobs today," Sidney stated.

"Really? Why?"

"He wants me to talk with Anastasia about managing her."

Scott got excited. "Really? That would be quite a client. She's incredible. A gorgeous woman. Can I meet her?"

Sidney was surprised by Scott's reaction. "Down boy, I'm just going to talk with her." Over the years, Sidney had grown to trust Scott's opinion and confided in him. "You know, what Anastasia really needs is to exercise some common sense. She doesn't need me."

"Common sense? Regarding...her lover?"

"Yes."

Scott was silent as he studied Sidney, then he confronted her. "You don't want to represent her because she's gay."

"Is that a question or a statement?" Sidney asked.

"I guess an observation."

"That's not fair. Anastasia doesn't need me to dictate how she should live her life."

Scott smiled. "Isn't that what you do for a living?"

"Anastasia has already made it. She's more successful than most artists dream of being. Sure, her career will be damaged if she doesn't use some discretion, and soon. But she'll survive, just not as a superstar, and there's nothing wrong with that."

Scott was confused. "Well, then what's the problem?"

"I can't take her on as a client unless I can improve the product. I can't improve her unless she's willing to make some changes in her life, or at least changes that impact the way the market perceives her."

"What if she's willing to admit she's gay, and comes out of the closet?"

"Then I don't want her," Sidney coldly admitted. "She wouldn't be a good business venture. In this business, the more albums you sell and the more concerts you book, the more money the performer makes, and the more money I make. Believe me, the world is not ready for a lesbian superstar."

"What if she's willing to modify her image?"

"That's why I'm talking to her."

There was a knock at the door and an attractive black woman peeked into the office. "Excuse me, Sid, I heard Scott was here." The woman approached Scott and the two exchanged hugs.

"How are you, Natalie?" he asked.

"Fine." Even through Natalie's casual attire it was evident that she had an incredible build. In previous years she had competed in body building contests. Although she had stopped competing, she still could intimidate most men.

Scott turned to Natalie. "You're gay; what do you think about this Anastasia thing?"

Natalie looked at Sidney, obviously confused.

"I hadn't told her yet." She quickly filled Natalie in on her conversation with David Jacobs.

Natalie had been with MPI for about five years and was one of Sidney's road managers. She was Sidney's most loyal and dedicated employee and a good friend. Natalie listened to her friends debate whether MPI had any right to tell someone, like Anastasia, how to live his or her life.

Then Natalie responded, "I think you need to treat Anastasia as any other business venture. She could bring some serious money into this company."

After the small meeting broke up, Sidney returned to her desk to finish some work. Again, she found herself distracted with memories and started doodling on her calendar. *Ten years,* she thought as she circled the date on the March calendar. *This would have been our ten-year anniversary, if Charlie and I were still together.* As she remembered, her brown eyes softened with a sparkle.

The MPI employees, including Nelson Fryer, were excited about the possibility of working with Anastasia. "You know what this means, don't you?" Nelson asked Sidney before their meeting with Anastasia.

Sidney seemed preoccupied with documents on her desk. "No, Nelson. What does this mean?"

"If we get Anastasia, we'll be recognized as a significant player in the business. The income she has generated is incredible."

"That's the key word, Nelson, *has* generated. I just want to do what's best for us. There's absolutely nothing wrong with staying small and profitable."

Although all MPI's employees wanted to attend the meeting with Anastasia, Sidney limited the attendance to herself, Nelson and Natalie. Nelson had taken over direct management of *the Gang* five years earlier and had become a valuable asset to MPI. Sidney had recognized his merit and had promoted him to Vice President. Natalie had become her best road manager, and if Anastasia came on board, Sidney felt Natalie would do the best job.

The meeting was scheduled for ten o'clock. Sidney was irritated when Anastasia and company arrived at her offices twenty minutes late, offering no apology. Nelson escorted the trio to the conference room and offered beverages. Natalie soon joined the group.

Minutes later Sidney entered the conference room. "I'm glad to finally meet you," Jerry Benson introduced himself.

Anastasia and another woman walked around the large conference table to introduce themselves. Sidney and Anastasia shook hands. *Who does she remind me of?* Sidney wondered. Although the singer wore jeans, a simple oversized cotton top and little makeup, her natural beauty was evident. Anastasia was quiet; she even seemed preoccupied.

"Hi, I'm Stephanie Mitchell," the other woman introduced herself and offered her hand to Sidney.

"Sidney Marcum." Sidney took Stephanie's hand, noticing the overindulgence in jewelry which went along with the flashy skintight leather pants and bleached blond hair.

"I'm Anastasia's partner," the forty-year-old continued. "I also write her music and lyrics," she bragged. Stephanie was a hard-looking woman. She may have been attractive at one time, but now appeared weathered by the business.

Sidney quickly got down to business and started the meeting. She gave her guests some history on MPI. Ten years earlier she had started managing a young group of singers. Under her guidance *the Gang* became an overnight sensation. Within three years she formed a production company and started recording the group's music. When MPI was in its fifth year Sidney expanded the business by taking on a pop soloist, Jason Light. Once again, Sidney repeated the success story. For the last year, Sidney had been training a new manager to assume Jason's direct management and had *been* searching for another entertainer to manage.

Her presentation was professional, yet warm. As she concluded, she invited the group to discuss why they had gathered. "I'd like to think of this as an opportunity to get to know each other, and to see if we can work together, or not work together for that matter. I think it's important to discuss what we expect from each other."

There was an uncomfortable pause from the group, until Jerry Benson broke the ice, and started talking about what he expected from a personal manager. Nelson followed, discussing his expectations of artists. Then Natalie chimed in with her insight.

Finally, Anastasia turned to Sidney. "Assuming we contracted with MPI, I expect that you work for me." She glanced at Nelson, then said, "I don't work with substitutes or backups."

Sidney stared back at Anastasia and unexpectedly smiled.

"That's a start. What else?"

Gradually, Anastasia started opening up, initially talking about little things that may have irritated her with her previous manager. Then Stephanie joined in. Sidney listened carefully, occasionally taking notes.

The small group listened to Anastasia and Stephanie whine about minor points for about a half an hour, then they started discussing more serious issues. To Natalie's surprise, Sidney maintained her interest and encouraged the two to continue with their gripes.

"I don't know if you're aware of this," Anastasia continued, "but Stephanie has been my road manager for years. I see no reason to change this. She's done a good job."

"Does Stephanie perform any other responsibilities?" Sidney asked.

"Yeah, I told you. I write her music," Stephanie interrupted. "You know one issue we got to talk about is—us. We're lovers and I travel with her, and I don't want to be told that I sit too close to her, or I can't be seen going to our room together, or God forbid—I slap her ass. Affectionately, you know what I mean!"

This did initiate a response from Sidney. "Your public display of...affection, isn't this what has caused your PR dilemma?"

"Absolutely, and I'll listen to your advice, but I don't want any lectures. You're making the big bucks off of me, I expect you to fix the problems," Anastasia responded.

Natalie had known Sidney over ten years. She saw Sidney's jaw tighten and recognized the subtle sign of her irritation.

"Speaking of the big bucks," Stephanie continued, "I heard you demand a twenty percent commission. Twenty percent is outrageous for an artist of Anastasia's caliber." Stephanie seemed proud of herself as she raised the issue. "Also, in the next few years we're going to be paying a bundle to her previous manager. We're not going to put ourselves back in the same position. We'll require a sunset clause in the contract. Anastasia deserves some protection."

Sidney stood and smiled at the group. She turned to Anastasia. "Is there anything else?"

Anastasia looked at Sidney cautiously, but did not say a word.

Sidney walked toward the door and was about to leave; she hesitated, and turned to address the group. "There seems to be a misunderstanding." She could see the disappointment in her coworkers' eyes. "You see, Anastasia, I thought you needed a manager, not a puppet." She pulled the notes from her pad, "For the record, I will not allow a *key person* clause in any of my contracts. There comes a time when a change in direct management is better for the artist. For that matter, I will never sign a contract with a *sunset* clause."

Sidney approached the conference table again. "You know the expression, 'You get what you pay for'? Our commission is not negotiable. Our company is the best, and we deserve to earn top scale in this business." She hesitated again, then walked over to where Anastasia was sitting. "Anastasia, you don't need a new manager. You need to exercise some common sense.

"The way I see it, you have three choices right now. First, continue the way you're going, but you'll crash. As callous as this may seem, the world is just not ready for a lesbian superstar.

"Second, come out of the closet. You'd have to completely repackage yourself and reconstruct your marketing strategy. True, you'll never be the superstar you have been. But you're talented and I'm sure you'd earn a good living."

Stephanie sat quietly, fuming and avoiding eye contact with Sidney, while Anastasia held Sidney's stare, then asked, "And my third choice?"

Sidney hesitated. "You'd have to live your life as a façade, a front, an illusion. Then you'd have a chance to regain and, with some creativity, perhaps exceed your previous status."

"You mean—stay in *the closet*," Anastasia said.

Sidney shook her head. "No, it goes beyond *the closet*. You need to give your audience what they expect. *The closet* shelters the world from who you are. A façade gives the world what they want to see. To live a façade would require total sacrifice and commitment from you and Stephanie. Stephanie could no longer be your road manager. The two of you would have to limit your time with each other in any public situation. The two of you would need to establish separate residences. You would have to date men. Have you considered marriage or even children? And if you think that's enough, you're wrong. You'd have to be more dedicated and work harder than ever before."

Sidney left the table, opened the door, then turned back to the group. "Anastasia, as cold as this may sound, I have no interest in working with you on the first two options."

The group stood and started to exit. Tension saturated the room.

As Stephanie passed through the door she turned to Sidney and mumbled, "Homophobic bitch."

Anastasia was silent as she walked through the door, staring at Sidney. There was something about Sidney that seemed familiar to Anastasia, but she could not put a finger on it.

An hour later, Sidney was working in her office when Nelson and Natalie knocked at her door. "Do you have a minute?" Natalie asked.

"Come in."

The two entered her office and sat on her couch. Sidney noticed Nelson was slouching. "I guess you have something on your minds," Sidney stated.

The two looked at each other, as if encouraging the other to talk.

"You're upset with me," Sidney said.

"Not upset, just wondering if we did the right thing," Natalie answered.

"You mean if *I* did the right thing."

"No, we're a team, and we stand behind your decisions. But…

don't you think you were a little harder on her than you had to be?" Natalie asked.

"I just can't believe you made a decision of this importance, without discussing it with me," Nelson added. "Since when are commissions for a star of her class not negotiable? Or since when have we not considered getting creative with contract clauses?"

"I'm sorry if I disappointed the two of you, but I believe I made the right decision. Nelson, just because I made a decision without consulting you doesn't undermine your role in this company, but last time I checked I still had the authority to do it."

"You're right. I'm sorry; I was out of line. I guess I'm just disappointed at the way it turned out." Nelson excused himself and left the office.

Natalie also excused herself and started to leave. Then Sidney asked, "Do you really think I was wrong?"

Natalie hesitated, then, maintaining eye contact with Sidney said, "If you don't want to represent her because she's gay, yes. Then you're just as bad as the rest." She turned and left.

Chapter 2

The grand disco sphere sparkled as it rotated, and the colorful lights reflected off the ball, high above the dancers' heads. Strobe lights followed, simulating slow motion dance. The loud music made it difficult to think, and the bass from the speakers vibrated the room.

Tonight was the grand opening celebration for Alternatives, a lesbian dance club located in Essex County of Northern New Jersey. The club targeted professional women in their late twenties and older. Rochelle, the club owner, was watching the opening-night celebration. Most of the women were tastefully dressed, complying with her *no jeans* policy. It was only 11:45 P.M., and already a good-size crowd had gathered. Rochelle appeared agitated as she checked her watch. She was exhausted. She had prepared for this night for months, and she'd had limited sleep, especially the past week.

Rochelle seemed relieved when she saw Stephanie at one of

the bars. The friends exchanged hugs.

"How's it going, are you nervous?" Stephanie asked as she held her Absolut and water.

"I was getting nervous. I was starting to wonder if you were going to show," Rochelle admitted.

"I told you we'd be here, we're here." Stephanie continued looking around the room. "Good crowd."

Rochelle seemed pleased as she inspected the room. "Yeah. I've been working round-the-clock, ever since you said you'd help me out. I put up a bunch of opening night flyers in the Village." Rochelle pulled a flyer from her pocket and gave it to Stephanie. "I also sent flyers to gay-owned businesses in Northern Jersey and the city. I think it's paid off."

Stephanie just glanced at the flyer. There was a picture of Anastasia on it, advertising her special appearance during the grand opening celebration. Stephanie crumpled the flyer and shoved it back in Rochelle's pocket. "Don't let Anastasia see it." Then Stephanie slipped into the crowd.

"Where are you going? And where's Anastasia?" Rochelle asked.

Stephanie turned back to her friend and smiled. "I'm going to play for a while, relax. Anastasia's back in your office getting dressed."

Rochelle shook her head as she watched her friend work the room, flirting with just about everyone she ran into. "What a fool; she doesn't realize what she has," she whispered. But her voice was lost in the loud music.

At one o'clock, Rochelle addressed her audience. "I want to thank everyone for coming and celebrating the opening of Alternatives. As promised, tonight I have a special treat for you. It's my privilege to introduce to you one of the best performers of our times. Ladies, please welcome…Anastasia."

The audience seemed genuinely excited about Anastasia's appearance. She performed two songs, "I'm Here to Stay" from her first album and another from her second album.

After the performance, Anastasia joined Rochelle and Stephanie at the bar for a drink. Rochelle appeared less stressed and more relaxed and was grateful to Anastasia. "Can we have a picture taken together to commemorate the occasion?"

"Sure," Anastasia agreed. "The three women lined up in front of the bar, posing as shutters clicked.

An hour later, Anastasia was leaving the club by herself when she spotted a grand-opening flyer, boasting her picture. The advertisement was posted outside the main entrance of the club. Earlier, she had entered through the rear access and had not seen the flyer. *Shit.* Anastasia removed the flyer, stuffing it in her pocket. *I'll have to talk with Steph about it when she gets home.*

The following morning, Anastasia was awakened by a ringing telephone. "Who the hell is calling at seven on a Sunday morning?" Rolling over, she realized she was alone in the bed. "Steph?" she called out, but there was no response. Anastasia reached for the phone, "Steph?"

"Now you've really done it. I warned you; it's over. We're through," Jeffrey Simon, her personal manager, yelled. Then there was a dial tone in her ear.

Although Jeffrey's call confused her, Anastasia was more concerned that Stephanie was nowhere to be found. Anastasia's stately house in Bernardsville, New Jersey, was only about a forty-minute drive from Alternatives. Stephanie had planned to return home after she helped Rochelle close the club.

Around ten o'clock that morning, Stephanie finally called,

complaining about the work involved with closing a bar. Apparently, she had crashed at Rochelle's home, and planned to return home that afternoon.

Later that morning Jerry Benson called. "Have you seen the *New Jersey Gazette* this morning?" The *Gazette* was a newspaper that targeted the Northern New Jersey and New York Metro market. Although its circulation was modest compared to the larger metro papers, the paper was one of the oldest and most respected in the state.

"Is there a reason why I should see the *Gazette?*" Anastasia asked.

"This is one day you may want to get it," Jerry insisted. Then he hung up.

Anastasia dressed quickly in jeans and a T-shirt. She was accustomed to dressing in disguise when going out in public and stuffed her long dark hair under a baseball cap and put on sunglasses. She drove her Jaguar to her favorite coffee shop for breakfast.

"Good morning, Cindy." Anastasia greeted the waitress who filled her mug with coffee.

Cautiously, the waitress greeted Anastasia. "How are you today?"

Anastasia took a sip of coffee. "Better now. Thanks." She raised the mug to toast the waitress, then took another sip and pulled out the Sunday *Gazette*. As she unfolded the paper, her heart seemed to skip a beat. "Oh my God," she said, as she read *"Anastasia frequents lesbian bar."*

Sitting quietly, Anastasia read the article that started on the front page. The column was damaging; it portrayed Anastasia as deceitful, because she had not been honest with her fans. But the article was not what upset Anastasia the most. When she turned the page to continue reading, she found an enlarged picture of herself, Stephanie, and Rochelle at the club. The picture showed Rochelle and Stephanie kissing Anastasia while standing in front of a bar with neon lights spelling out *Alternatives*.

Anastasia's problems were just beginning. The following day, Jeffrey Simon's lawyer contacted her to discuss contract termination. A call from a Quench Soda product manager followed. The company had been talking with Anastasia about becoming the spokesperson for their product. Now they were no longer interested in her. Later that week, she learned that Global Records had frozen the funds for her new album. Jerry further explained that Global had no intention of releasing the new album after it was recorded.

Frustrated, Anastasia asked Jerry if Global would release her from her contract. Later that afternoon David Jacobs called and informed her that Global would not free her from her obligations.

The press ate up the *Gazette* article, and soon the newspaper reporter was being interviewed by every TV newsmagazine. She attributed good old-fashioned investigative reporting to how she broke the story.

Sidney was busy reviewing market research information on new candidates when Nelson knocked on her office door. He entered her office and placed the most recent edition of *The National Enquirer* on her desk. The cover showed the compromising picture of Anastasia with the headline "Anastasia Comes Out to Play." Sidney skimmed the article, then said, "That picture sure gets around."

"I need to apologize, you were right. She's a walking time bomb," Nelson added.

Chapter 3

That Friday evening, Scott picked up Sidney from her office. He looked handsome in his tuxedo, and Sidney looked equally beautiful in an elegant gown. As a principal for the New York City Public School system, Scott did not have many opportunities to rub elbows with celebrities. So each year, he enjoyed attending the Kramer Benefit with Sidney.

The attractive couple entered the formal ballroom of the New York Hilton & Towers. Sidney was radiant. She carried herself expertly among the crowd of entertainers and peers from the music business. Over the years, she had perfected her techniques of working the crowd. She manifested power, was poised, polished and confident. People went out of their way to be introduced to her or to greet her. Scott always enjoyed himself at this function, but knew this was Sidney's vocation and was quick to sense when she wanted him to leave so she could discuss business.

Shortly after they arrived, Sidney noticed that Jerry Benson accompanied Anastasia, and Stephanie was noticeably absent. Anastasia seemed reserved and spent most of the evening at an isolated bar, among friends, but away from the party's mainstream.

Later that evening, Sidney decided to make an effort and greet Anastasia. Seeing an opening, she walked to the bar that Anastasia had been frequenting. Warmly, she greeted the bartender. "Hi. Can I have a Perrier, please?" Then she turned toward Anastasia. "Hi Anastasia, how are you?"

Anastasia acknowledged Sidney by turning in her direction, but remained silent. She stared at Sidney with cold eyes. "Are you here to tell me 'I told you so'?"

Sidney shook her head. "I just wanted to say hello."

As quickly as she said it, Sidney turned to leave and was rejoining Scott when she heard Anastasia's voice behind her. "I'm sorry."

Sidney acknowledged Anastasia by nodding, then turned to leave with her escort.

"Can we talk?" Anastasia asked. Sidney continued to hold her escort's arm, signifying to Scott not to leave. "Please?" Anastasia asked calmly.

Sidney hesitated, then turned to Scott and introduced Anastasia. Scott briefly enjoyed his encounter with the celebrity, but quickly excused himself when he recognized the five-minute signal from Sidney.

The two women moved back to the secluded bar. "I need your help…," Anastasia started. "Will you manage me?"

"I'm sorry Anastasia; I don't think there's anything I could do for you. There's just been too much damage this time."

"I'll do what you tell me to do, you know, I'll live fucking Cinderella's life if that's what I need to do," Anastasia continued.

"Anastasia, it's not that I don't *want* to help. I just don't believe I *can* help. I can't take you beyond where you've been. To be honest, I don't think I could take you back to where you've been." Sidney studied Anastasia and realized how hard it must have been for Anastasia to approach her. "You're a talented person. With some creative marketing, you can still have a successful career as a mid-level performer, and be out of the closet. I would think you'd be happier that way."

"You're not even going to consider it?"

Sidney shook her head.

Anastasia pulled something out of her purse, and placed a folded piece of paper in Sidney's hand. "For the record, I didn't go to the club to socialize. I was performing."

Sidney opened the flyer that advertised Anastasia's special appearance the opening night of Alternatives.

Scott rejoined the women, but could see they were not finished. So he was surprised when Sidney took his arm, suggesting it was time to leave. The two turned to leave, then Sidney abruptly returned to Anastasia. "This isn't personal, this is business." She studied Anastasia. "I'm making no promises, but I'll run a new analysis bearing in mind the recent press. I don't believe the results will be favorable compared to my other options. Remember, no promises, but I'll look at it."

Anastasia smiled after Sidney left. Somehow, she did not feel quite as alone.

The following Monday morning, Sidney was in a staff meeting when she addressed the group. "I want another market analysis on Anastasia."

Nelson was surprised. "I thought that was a dead issue?"

"She expressed interest in MPI once again."

"That's because her manager ran out on her, with good reason," Nelson added. "You know I didn't agree with the way the first meeting was handled. But you were right; she's a walking time bomb. Let it go."

"I will, just as soon as I see the new report." She delegated the areas of research to her employees. Specifically, she wanted to know revenue projections considering the recent publicity. She also asked for an analysis, assuming the *Gazette* published a retraction and an apology to Anastasia. The group was given ten days to finish the work and report their findings.

An hour later, Sidney pulled out an old business card from her Rolodex and called Dimarto's Private Investigation Services.

"Yeah, this is Dimarto," a male voice answered the phone.

"Tony, this is Sidney Marcum. I need some research completed in a week or so. Do you have the time to do it?"

"Well, I am really busy right now. But, I suppose I can bump some of my work and squeeze you in," the man said.

The two agreed to meet at the Bethesda Fountain in Central Park at noon.

It was 12:10 P.M. when Tony arrived. Rather than greeting him, Sidney rose from the park bench and started walking away from him. He followed her until she believed no one was watching the two, then she spoke to the man. "I need you to check out the *New Jersey Gazette* and a reporter for the paper. Nancy Roberts."

"What are you looking for specifically?" Tony asked.

Sidney told the investigator that the paper broke the initial story on Anastasia. "I want to know about the reporter. What was she doing at the bar that night? Is she gay? I want financials on the newspaper and a list of their top ten advertisers. Who are their creditors? Who makes the decisions at the paper? What lawsuits have they been involved in over the last ten years? I also want to know about the nightclub, Alternatives. What was Anastasia doing there?" She handed the man a white envelope. "I need your report by next Wednesday. I know this is a lot of work for a short period of time. I've included overtime in your payment. Give me an accurate report, and I'll match what's in the envelope."

The man casually opened the envelope and counted the cash. Obviously satisfied, he pocketed the envelope. "I'll call you next week."

A meeting with Anastasia was scheduled on Friday of

the following week. Sidney expected to hear from Tony by the Wednesday before the meeting, but he did not call. On Thursday morning Sidney's staff gave their report. As expected, their recommendation was to contract with another group of entertainers, not Anastasia. Their recommendation was supported by good research. Sidney thanked her staff for responding to her request so promptly and dismissed the meeting.

The rest of the day dragged by. At three o'clock, Sidney called Tony, only to get his answering machine. At five o'clock she picked up her staff's report regarding Anastasia. For two hours she reviewed their report, concluding that their recommendation was sound and supported by the facts. Shortly after 7:00 P.M., she packed her attaché case and started walking to the garage. As she entered the multi-level parking facility, she thought, *It's just as well I didn't hear from Tony, after all, facts are facts and business is business. Anastasia is just not good business.*

She opened the trunk of her Mercedes and stored her briefcase. Then she sat in her vehicle, fastened her seatbelt and started the ignition. A disturbance from her backseat startled her and a cold hand collapsed her mouth. Her heart was racing, then she heard, "It's okay, it's me, Tony."

Sidney turned to find Tony sitting in her backseat. "Jesus Christ, Tony, you scared me. What the hell are you doing in my car anyway?"

Tony quickly apologized. "Sorry. My report's due today. I figured I wouldn't miss you if I waited in your car. Sorry…I must have fallen asleep."

Sidney's pulse was slowly recovering as she collected herself. "Yesterday. Your report was due yesterday, on Wednesday."

"It is Wednesday, isn't it?" He looked at his watch, and realized that he was a day off, but offered no explanation.

"Where is it?" Sidney insisted.

The man pulled out a large envelope from his jacket and gave it to Sidney. He left his hand extended, waiting for payment in return.

"I want to review this. You'll get paid in full, assuming the information is accurate."

Under the circumstances, Tony was not about to argue with Sidney. Besides, she had always been good to him in the past. "I'll be in touch," Tony said. Then he left.

The next morning, Sidney was not sure what she would tell Anastasia. She paced her office, thinking about the information in both her reports. Her secretary stepped into her office and informed her that Anastasia and her staff were waiting in the conference room.

Sidney greeted her guest, and asked everyone to take a seat. Stephanie was noticeably absent. To start the meeting, Sidney explained to Anastasia that MPI had conducted an additional market analysis as she had requested. She quickly summarized her staff's findings and recommendations.

As Sidney addressed the small group, she noticed that her staff could not look Anastasia in the eye. She was also aware that Anastasia held her head high, maintained good eye contact, and did not become agitated, even though the findings were unfavorable.

"Anastasia, I've spent considerable time evaluating my staff's recommendations. Their conclusions are sound, and I agree with them."

Anastasia stood and offered to shake Sidney's hand. "Thank you for taking the time to reconsider." She stood tall, smiled, then turned to leave.

"I'm not finished, please sit."

Anastasia appeared confused, but listened to her.

"I agree with my staff's recommendations, but their conclusions were based upon limited information."

Nelson and Natalie were puzzled and stared back at Sidney.

"I may be able to help you. But it will take a lot of work and sacrifice on everyone's part, especially your own."

"Does this mean you'll work with me?" Anastasia asked.

"For a handsome fee I'll give you six months. If I can't put your career back on track, I'll keep this generous fee, and we'll both move on with our lives."

Chapter 4

The legal contract between MPI and Anastasia awaited signatures. Sidney sat at her desk skimming through the agreement. When she reached the signature page she picked up her pen. Although she knew the agreement favored her company she hesitated as she placed the ink to the signature line. She stopped and put the pen down, resting it on the document.

Sidney ran her hands through her hair, contemplating the unexecuted agreement that rested in front of her. *I hope this is the right thing. What if it's not?* She rose from her desk and walked to the small refrigerator where she removed a diet beverage. As she took a sip of the drink her eyes met her bachelor's diploma from Yale University which hung on a wall. *This business has been very good to me.* Her eyes moved to her Master's diploma from New York University...*but certainly not without sacrifice.*

As Sidney contemplated the agreement with Anastasia, she recalled how she had made the transition into the music industry.

* * *

At twenty-one, Sidney Marcum left Yale University with a marketing degree, considerable debt and an employment opportunity with Whitman Industries, a large company with diversified interests. As an Associate Product Manager, Sidney became responsible for product management of a snack line, in the Food Division at the New York City headquarters. She also continued with her graduate work at New York University. Sidney knew she performed best when challenged and under pressure. Accordingly, she placed demands on herself, leaving little time in her life for friendships or social activities.

During her first year at Whitman Industries, her boss, Ted instructed her to attend the company Christmas party. "It's good politics. Although management won't notice if you're there, they always seem to notice if you're not. Plan on being there," he directed.

Sidney received a disapproving look from Ted when she arrived at the party late. The banquet room of the New York City Hilton was crowded. She walked to a bar and ordered an Amstel Light, then she turned to study the party. Although she did not recognize many people, there were two secretaries from her floor at the bar next to her. A stranger controlled the attention of the two women. They were flaunting their bodies at this man.

Sidney pulled out her cigarettes and was searching for a match in her purse, when the stranger offered her a light.

"Thank you," she said.

"Hi, I'm Michael," he introduced himself.

"Sidney Marcum. Have I missed anything?"

"Not really, just the boring Merry Christmas speech the chairman gives every year."

The women seemed to be irritated that Sidney was receiving Michael's attention. She politely excused herself and left the man with the attentive women.

Although Sidney hated office politics, she knew she needed to

26

play the game well to make it in the business world. She worked the party like a professional. Sidney had an effective presence; she was attractive, but it was her magnetic energy that drew people to her. With her street smarts and intelligence she could easily impress most. But it was her quick wit and sense of humor that enabled her to become the center of attention.

A couple of hours later, Sidney was preparing to leave the party when Michael approached her. "So what department do you work in?"

"Food Division."

"What do you do?" he asked.

"I'm a product manager. What do you do, Michael?"

"I'm…I work in the Securities Division, but I'd love to tell you more over a drink." He smiled warmly and offered to help Sidney with her coat.

"Thanks, but I really need to get home. It was nice meeting you." Sidney smiled at him. "Good night." She turned to leave and opened the door.

Michael called after her, "Dinner, Monday night?"

Sidney stopped and turned to look at him. Although he was not strikingly good looking, there was something about him. He was tastefully dressed in a black suit, complementing his nice build and dark hair. It was hard to guess his age; Sidney placed him in his mid-40s. She was aware that people were watching them talk. She held the door open wider and gestured for Michael to follow her into the hallway.

"I have classes Monday night."

"Tuesday?" His dark eyes flirted.

"Thanks for the invitation, but…I'm working on my MBA, I have classes every evening." Sidney smiled. "I'm sure you've been there and understand."

Michael smiled pleasantly. "Of course."

"Well, I've got to run. Good night Michael; it was nice meeting you."

Michael watched her leave and thought to himself, *She will be a challenge, I like that in a woman.* He smiled.

The week following the Christmas party, Ted came into Sidney's office. "Whitman wants to see you in his office, now."

"Who?" Sidney asked.

"Mr. Whitman, you know, of *Whitman Industries*," her boss said sarcastically.

Sidney was confused. "Why?"

"I don't have a clue, I thought you might."

"I've never met the man."

Sidney was deep in thought as the elevator traveled to the executive suites. *What did I do?* The elevator door opened and she was on the executive floor.

A receptionist greeted Sidney. "How can I help you?"

"Hi. I'm Sidney Marcum. I'm here to see Mr. Whitman."

The receptionist hesitated, then picked up the phone. She spoke to someone and hung up. Before the receptionist had a chance to say anything else, another woman entered the lobby.

"Hi, I'm Kelly, Mr. Whitman's personal secretary." She escorted Sidney to Mr. Whitman's office. "You can go in, he's expecting you."

As Sidney entered the office, she saw the back of Mr. Whitman's chair. He was on the phone. The secretary approached him and asked, "Do you want Ms. Marcum to wait outside?"

"No, I'll be off in a moment," the man said. Sidney could barely hear him because he spoke with his back to her. "Have her take a seat at the conference table." The man's arm pointed to the opposite end of the large office.

Sidney sat at the table, but she still could not see Mr. Whitman; the back of his chair obstructed her view.

"I'll be with you in a minute, Ms. Marcum," the distant voice said. Then he continued his telephone conversation.

The office was impressive. A polished marble floor, a

mahogany desk, custom built bookshelves lined with books, vases, awards and art. Three majestic portraits of men lined the office walls. A nametag identified each as a *Whitman*.

Mr. Whitman finished his phone call and continued sitting in the distant chair across the room. Sidney still could not get a good view of him. He appeared to be writing when he started speaking. "I guess you're wondering why I've called you here."

"The thought has crossed my mind," she admitted.

"I want to talk with you about your busy schedule…" The voice was vaguely familiar. Just as Sidney figured out who he was, Michael stood. "And how we can make the time to have dinner together."

Sidney could not believe this was happening. "It would seem you have me at a disadvantage."

Michael offered Sidney his hand. "I guess we were never formally introduced, I'm Michael Whitman."

Sidney had heard that Michael Whitman was brilliant. But she always assumed he was older. He represented the fourth generation of Whitmans to run the company and had taken control of the business ten years earlier, when his father passed away.

"So you're the chairman who gave the Merry Christmas speech at the party?" Sidney smiled.

"Guilty," Michael smiled back.

"I guess that should teach me never to show up late again." When Sidney returned to her office she found a single yellow rose in a vase, on her desk with a note, *"Thank you, Michael."*

Sidney had mixed feelings about her plans for dinner that Saturday night. On one hand she was excited; she had not had a date since she moved to the city. On the other hand, she felt guilty about taking an evening off from her studies and work, especially since finals were quickly approaching.

Michael picked her up promptly at 7:30 P.M., and Sidney was pleasantly surprised when he arrived without a chauffeur. At Le Cirque the two were ushered to the best table in the restaurant. Dinner was perfect and Michael was a gentleman throughout the evening. After dinner he brought her back to her apartment. As they stood awkwardly at the door, he took Sidney's hand, looked into her eyes and said, "Thank you for one of the most perfect evenings of my life." Gently, he picked up her hand, met it with a kiss, then left.

On Monday morning Sidney found her yellow rose had been replaced with a dozen red roses. The card read, *Thank you for your company. Lunch today? Michael.*

As Sidney sat looking at the roses, she tried to understand what she was feeling. *He's attractive, intelligent, even mysterious. Actually, it was refreshing not having to fight off an advance; he was a perfect gentleman.* She briefly thought about the age difference, estimating twenty-five years separated them, then quickly disregarded it as an issue. *As long as my work and studies don't suffer, I shouldn't be concerned about spending time with him.*

As finals approached and Sidney's schedule became a challenge, she suggested they limit their activities together. Michael agreed, but proposed that she join him for a ski weekend in Aspen following the holidays. She looked forward to a weekend away with no school to worry about during intersession.

Sidney had never been to Colorado. As the plane approached Stapleton Airport she could see the snow-covered peaks of the majestic Rocky Mountains. Michael was quick to play tour guide and showed her Pikes Peak, Mt. Evans and the Continental Divide. When they arrived in Denver, they learned the flights to Aspen had been delayed for three hours. Michael was spontaneous and suggested they rent a car and drive to Aspen.

As Michael and Sidney traveled west on Interstate 70,

Sidney became captivated with the greens of the evergreen trees contrasting with the snow-covered mountains of the foothills. The car climbed steadily to a plateau where a breathtaking view of the snow-covered peaks of the Continental Divide was revealed. The sky was crystal clear and bluer than Sidney had ever seen. She quickly fell in love with Colorado.

They arrived mid-afternoon and checked into the Hotel Jerome, located in the heart of downtown Aspen. Their luggage was sent to the suite. Then they ventured out to the shops and returned to the hotel to get ready for dinner. The penthouse suite was impressive, decorated with Victorian antiques, and offered a private bedroom and bathroom for Sidney. She was not surprised; their relationship had not progressed beyond a good night kiss.

The evening was delightful. They had dinner at a Mexican restaurant within walking distance of the hotel. During dinner, Sidney found herself staring at Michael. *I think I actually like this man. He's warm, affectionate, and powerful.* Sidney found this combination intriguing. As they walked back to the hotel, she found it comforting with Michael's arm around her shoulder.

Back in their room, Michael built a fire and poured after-dinner drinks. Sidney accepted one and sat on the floor, next to the fireplace. She was pleasantly surprised when Michael joined her on the floor. He raised his glass to toast. "To our weekend getaway, and the most beautiful woman in Aspen." His eyes flirted.

She smiled and raised her glass. "To our weekend."

As Sidney enjoyed the warmth from the fire, she found herself attracted to Michael, but she wondered if she was feeling the effects of the alcohol.

Michael pushed Sidney's long dark hair away from her face. He kissed her, gently at first and as their passion grew he pressed her to the floor. The couple lay together kissing, their tongues daring each other to explore further. His thigh gently found a comfortable place between Sidney's thighs, and he expertly negotiated his hand beneath her sweater, against her soft skin to feel her.

Sidney began to explore his hard body, and with every caress he responded with increasing intensity, until he abruptly stopped.

He lifted himself above her. "I'm not going to stop, unless we stop right now."

Without hesitating, she pulled him to her. He massaged her denim jeans against her skin and when he approached areas of her body which had longed to be explored, she moaned. Within seconds, there was of flurry of activity in which jeans were unzipped and stripped and sweaters removed. They both knelt in front of each other with the nearby fire illuminating their skin. With only underwear and bra concealing them, he skillfully unclasped her bra and took a nipple to his mouth while simultaneously reaching for her unfamiliar moist cavity beneath her underwear. A finger teased and entered.

Sidney moaned at his touch which excited him further, and in the moments to come he could not restrain from tearing the remaining clothing from both of them. He swiftly took her to him, penetrating her. Rhythmically he pressed, steadily increasing stride, becoming more and more excited until he could no longer control himself and released all, gasping for air as he collapsed onto Sidney.

Sidney could feel Michael's racing heart pounding as he lay on her. Gradually it slowed and he lifted his head and smiled. "Don't worry, I'm not finished." He kissed her lips, her breasts and made his way to where she craved attention and within moments his tongue brought her to climax.

For some time the two lay together, enjoying the aftermath of their encounter. As the fire dimmed the room cooled. Michael stood to tend to it and Sidney excused herself, dressed and stepped out on the private balcony. There was a chill in the air. Sidney could see her reflection in the adjacent window. Her clothes and hair were in disarray and she pushed her hair away from her face. She found her cigarettes in her coat pocket, took one out and lit up. She laughed at the thought of having a cigarette after sex, but as she inhaled the smoke into her lungs, she thought, *Damn that feels good.* Then she admitted to herself, *The sex wasn't bad, either.*

In the spring, Sidney fell in love with a property on the Jersey shore. It was a summerhouse on the Manasquan River, in Brielle, about an hour and a half drive from the city. The waterfront property was beautiful, but the house required work. Sidney bought the property and the two lovers used the house on weekends as their private getaway. Michael never really cared for the house; it did not meet his standards. She routinely scolded him, telling him to stop being a snob.

Sidney continued with her studies and full workload, which limited their time together. A little over a year into their courtship, Michael and Sidney were having a romantic dinner at Michael's penthouse apartment.

"How's your salmon?" Michael asked.

"It's wonderful. How's yours?"

"Delightful. I have a special dessert for you tonight. Save room," he instructed.

"You know I'm not a big dessert eater," she said.

"I think you'll like this."

After the main course was cleared, Michael excused himself from the table, then returned with a plate covered with a silver dome. He placed the small plate in front of Sidney.

"What's this? Dessert?" Sidney asked.

"Check it out."

Sidney smiled as she lifted the dome off the plate, anticipating a high calorie seven-layer chocolate cake. But what she found was a small box.

"What's this?" she asked.

"Open it."

Sidney hesitated, then picked up the box and opened it. It was a diamond ring.

Before she had a chance to respond, Michael dropped to a knee. "I know you probably find this terribly old-fashioned, but Sidney...would you be my wife?"

Sidney later regretted her initial response. She laughed. "You're not serious." But when she saw the hurt in Michael's eyes she realized he was serious.

Michael's smile disappeared. "I am serious."

"I'm sorry, Michael. We have a wonderful relationship right now. I don't want to screw it up."

"It'll make it better," he said confidently.

"Michael, I'm four months away from getting my MBA. I'm just starting my career. If we got married, it would change everything."

Michael only became more serious. "I'm forty-six years old; I've never been married. I'm in love with you Sidney. I'd like to eventually build a family together. Please reconsider."

Later that evening after Sidney returned home, she reflected on the events of the evening. She knew she loved him and had no interest in seeing others. She was glad to hear that Michael wanted children; she loved children but it was one subject they had never discussed before. Their age difference was never an issue, probably because she always felt older than her years. *But I know I would never be comfortable working for his company...if we married.*

The following day, Sidney visited the executive offices unannounced. She had never done this before. "Sidney Marcum to see Mr. Whitman," she informed Kelly.

"You don't have an appointment," Kelly said as she referred to Michael's calendar.

"Please let Mr. Whitman know I'm here. I believe he'll see me. Thank you."

Reluctantly, Kelly went into the office and was surprised when he graciously asked her to show Sidney in. Michael was also surprised by her visit. Sidney did not utter a word until Kelly closed the door, then she said, "I'll never be Mrs. Whitman. It makes me sound like your mother. Besides, I like my own name."

Michael smiled and took Sidney's hands in his own. "Does this mean you'll marry me?"

"You know I can't marry you and work for you."

"Consider yourself fired," he said, and kissed her.

Sidney started looking for new employment immediately. About a month into her search, she became frustrated with her prospects. Michael tried to be supportive and told her he would find her something. But she refused his help. It was important to her to be hired based on her qualifications, not because she was Michael Whitman's fiancée.

While reviewing some career publications, Sidney came across an interesting position for an A&R Manager. Curious about the position, she submitted her resume, which qualified her for an interview. The position was with the Artist & Repertoire department of Global Records. The A&R manager would be responsible for finding talent, signing them on with the record company, and guiding them to promote their careers. Sidney interviewed well. Later that evening, when she discussed the prospects of the position with Michael, she could not help sounding excited about the opportunity. That evening, Michael telephoned an old friend, the Senior Vice President of WABS, the network controlling Global Records. He called in a favor.

Sidney received her MBA that spring and the two were married. Shortly after the honeymoon, she started work at Global Records. Like everything she touched and loved, she excelled at her new career. It excited her to work with musicians and build stars. She was responsible to David Jacobs, a director at Global

Records.

The newlyweds became increasingly busy with their careers. It was customary for Michael to meet with business associates at home during the evenings. After dinner, he would routinely excuse himself from Sidney and retreat to his office with a guest. Sidney often wondered if the purpose of meetings was business or political.

Shortly after they married, Michael shared his political ambitions with his wife. He wanted to become New York Governor. Michael had compiled a detailed plan of action to achieve his political goal. The present New York Governor, Hugh Carey, had just started his term. Michael was posturing for the Republican nomination for the election in six years. He realized it would take years of networking, and was gaining support for his political aspirations.

Sidney also became obsessed with her new career. She established a good working relationship with David and connected with the artists. She worked aggressively to secure their contracts and build their careers. From David, Sidney learned the music business in and out, and displayed a natural ability to work with the producers, managers, agents and others involved in the industry.

Sidney knew her husband commanded a power that few possessed, and routinely studied him. This power went beyond his financial earnings, it was his natural presence and she was determined to understand it and master it.

About two years into their marriage Sidney realized the romance had dwindled from their relationship. Their lovemaking had become infrequent, and felt more like sex and less like love. Michael became increasingly less attentive to Sidney's needs.

On their two-year anniversary, Michael acknowledged the marriage had changed and vowed to work on their relationship, especially since he wanted to start a family. Their lovemaking became more frequent, though Michael seemed more interested in procreation than lovemaking.

Each month, Michael waited anxiously to see if Sidney was

pregnant, and when her period arrived, his disposition quickly deteriorated. One day Sidney approached Michael. "Maybe a child right now is not the best thing for us."

Michael responded abrasively, "Of course it is. Maybe it's time to find out what's wrong." The following day, the two met with a fertility specialist. The doctor scheduled a series of tests on Sidney to ensure that she was able to conceive.

"It just doesn't seem right. We've been married over two years, have always had unprotected sex, and she hasn't become pregnant," Michael informed the doctor.

"But Michael, we've only really been trying the last six months."

The doctor did not want to speculate until he saw the test results. He also wanted Michael to have a sperm count.

After a couple menstrual cycles the tests were completed, and all the results were normal. The doctor just encouraged them to relax and keep trying.

Sidney started to see a different side of Michael. He had become less patient and was quick to anger with her. Occasionally, Michael became agitated and would grab her, and she was not surprised the first time he hit her. Initially she blamed herself, thinking she must have provoked him. Then she realized that no matter what she did, he seemed to become agitated with her, and his frustrations often resulted in physical abuse. When Michael did take it a step too far, he showered Sidney with gifts and apologized for the indiscretion.

Michael and Sidney pulled away from each other, and both continued their obsessions with their careers. For Michael, it was politics, and for Sidney the music business.

* * *

Sidney returned to her desk, picked up her pen and signed the contract between MPI and Anastasia.

Chapter 5

Anastasia had just returned home from a meeting with MPI and her attorney. "Hello. I'm home. Steph, are you home?" But the house was silent.

Where is she? Anastasia wondered. She walked to the kitchen, poured a glass of water and sat at the counter where she went through her mail. She noticed a card she had mailed to Marian and Luther Hall had been returned, unopened. *Damn them. How long are they going to keep punishing me? I'm over this. This has to end, now.*

Anastasia picked up the phone and called.

A male voice answered on the third ring.

"Hello." Anastasia did not speak. "Hello? Is anyone there?" he asked.

"Daddy?" Anastasia whispered.

"Anastasia?" Luther Hall whispered back.

Anastasia hesitated before she answered. "Yes." Seconds later

Anastasia heard a dial tone. She wiped tears from her cheeks. *How did it ever get this bad?*

* * *

Anastasia was the only child of Marian and Luther Hall. Her father, Luther, was active in the black movement of the 50s. As a Southern Baptist minister, he preached at a small church outside of Macon, Georgia. There he met Marian, the daughter of a white community leader. Although the two initially fought admitting their feelings for each other, ultimately, they could not deny that they were in love. The prospects of a relationship between Marian and Luther enraged the white community. The two eloped, but when they returned from their honeymoon, they found Luther's church aflame. With the church destroyed, the newlyweds moved to Richmond, Virginia, where Luther started a new church. A year later, Anastasia was born.

As a child, Anastasia knew she was different from her peers. During her teenage years it became difficult for her to develop friendships. She felt as if she did not fit in, because she was either not white enough or not black enough. In actuality, her stunning beauty intimidated her classmates and alienated her from her peers.

As Luther watched his daughter grow into a young woman, he realized she was exceptionally gifted with her beauty and her voice. Although Luther encouraged her participation in the church choir, he refused to let her sing outside the church. Luther made every effort to shield his daughter from the world and isolated her.

In Anastasia's last year of high school, Luther became disheartened when she expressed interest in attending college. He encouraged community or local state colleges, while Marian recognized that her daughter should explore her options. Marian was supportive when Anastasia expressed interest in attending Rutgers University in New Brunswick, New Jersey. In her search to fit in, Anastasia chose a northern environment, hoping it would be more tolerant of biracial people.

Against her father's wishes, Anastasia left Richmond and moved to New Brunswick that fall. Initially she was overwhelmed with all the changes in her life. She soon realized that her father's sheltering had hurt her perceptions of life.

Her dormitory roommate, Amy, was a sophomore and very popular with other students. Amy was eager to help Anastasia adjust to her new life. A month after school started, Amy was invited to a fraternity party and extended the invitation to Anastasia. The freshman was excited; she had never been to a college party. Her roommate offered Anastasia a makeover and some clothing to wear, suggesting Anastasia's clothing was inappropriate.

After Amy applied the finishing touches of makeup, Anastasia walked to the dorm bathroom to inspect the makeup job, but she did not recognize herself in the mirror. The tight Jordache jeans and sweater accentuated Anastasia's sensual figure, her low-cut neckline boasting cleavage. As her eyes moved over her body, she could feel herself blush. Then her eyes met her face. Red lipstick outlined her full sensual lips and her eyes were accented. Her long black hair fell naturally around her flawless face. As if repelled by her looks, Anastasia backed away from the mirror.

Another woman had come into the sink area from the showers. She was dressed in a short bathrobe revealing her muscular legs. She started brushing her wet blond hair. As Anastasia caught the woman's eyes in the mirror, she innocently asked, "What do you think about my makeup? I'm going to a party."

The woman turned and studied Anastasia's face. "I know you have a beautiful face. I think it's a shame you put all that paint on it."

"You do?" Anastasia asked. "What about my clothing?"

Turning, the woman studied her. "You don't look comfortable. Are you?"

"Not really." Anastasia started removing the makeup from

her face with water and a paper towel. The waterproof mascara smudged over her eyes and cheeks.

The woman removed a jar of cold cream from her toiletry bucket and handed it to Anastasia. "Try this."

As Anastasia removed the stubborn makeup, the woman could not help but notice the disappointment in Anastasia's face. "Is it an important party?" she asked.

"Kind of. It's my first party and…I just want to fit in," Anastasia confided.

"First party here?"

"Actually, first party ever," Anastasia admitted. "I've had a pretty sheltered life, up until a month ago."

"Oh." The woman stopped styling her hair and turned toward Anastasia. "I'm Shelly, I'm in 207, down the hall from you."

Anastasia shook her hand.

"I hope I didn't offend you," Shelly said. "You're a very attractive woman; you don't need all that makeup. Maybe a little mascara and eyeliner, and just be yourself. You'll fit in just fine." The woman ran some mousse into her own hair, picked up her blow dryer and said, "Well, I've got to get ready for a party also."

"Are you going to the one at Delta Phi? That's where Amy and I are going."

Some mascara remained smudged on the side of Anastasia's face. Shelly took a face cloth and dabbed it with some cold cream, then held it up to Anastasia's face. "May I?" she asked.

Anastasia glanced in the mirror noticing the smudge. She nodded, and Shelly gently rubbed the cream on her face.

"No, I'm not going to the frat party. Amy and I don't exactly run in the same circles," Shelly said as Amy entered the bathroom.

"There you are, what…what happened to your makeup?" Amy glared at Shelly.

"It just seemed to be too much for me," Anastasia apologized.

Well, we've got to get moving." Amy hurried Anastasia out of the bathroom.

Anastasia hastened into the hallway. She turned back toward

Shelly and said, "Thank you." Shelly smiled as the door closed abruptly between them. Anastasia turned toward her roommate. "Amy, that was very rude."

"You should thank me. Did the lesbo touch you?"

"What?" Anastasia asked.

"Shelly is a lesbian. Do yourself a favor and stay away from her."

A lesbian? Anastasia pondered as she walked back to her dorm room. *But she seemed so nice.* Being the daughter of a fundamentalist minister presented Anastasia with little opportunity to meet people of diverse backgrounds, especially homosexuals. Heated words from her father's sermons, about the evils of homosexuality, echoed in her head: *"Homosexuality is evil; it's immoral. Sinners repent and save your soul."*

Back in her room Anastasia lightly applied some makeup and changed into more comfortable clothing; then she and Amy left for the party.

Beer, loud music, dancing and guys were prevalent at the party. To Anastasia's surprise, she found that she was the center of attention among most of the guys. Around midnight, a student named Ben seemed to claim Anastasia as his prize. The attractive junior had an incredible build and was a school football star. He brought Anastasia a beer, then asked for a dance. Initially, he seemed nice and interesting to Anastasia. Then as the evening progressed, and his drinking continued, he seemed to change. An hour after they met, the two were slow dancing and Ben's hands started exploring her body.

"Please don't do that," Anastasia pleaded.

Ben ignored her plea and continued to grope her body as he leaned heavily over her, kissing her neck.

She managed to peel herself away, grabbed her jacket and told Amy she was leaving. Anastasia hoped that Amy would come with her, but she seemed more interested in a senior. Feeling her first effects of alcohol, Anastasia wandered alone across campus.

When Anastasia reached the second floor of the dorm, she

heard an acoustic guitar and a woman singing the familiar gospel song, "Jesus Loves Me." The music was coming from the lounge. As she walked toward the sitting room she listened intently to the female voice, and for a moment, she became homesick. The door to the lounge was ajar. To her surprise, Shelly was sitting on the floor, eyes closed, picking away at the guitar. No one else was in the room. She sang softly and seemed at peace. Anastasia was about to leave her in her serenity, then opted to stay and suddenly found herself humming the tune. On the last verse she decided to join Shelly and sang the remaining lyrics with her.

When Shelly heard the powerful voice accompanying her, she opened her eyes and was surprised by Anastasia's entrance. At the end of the song Shelly smiled and said, "You have an incredible instrument there."

"Thank you. Your singing is very comforting."

"Thanks. How was the party?"

"Disappointing," Anastasia answered. "How was yours?"

"Disappointing." They both smiled.

When Shelly started singing another gospel song, Anastasia chose to stay and joined in on the familiar tune. She was fascinated that a lesbian was singing gospel music. The two spent close to two hours singing and chatting about themselves. Anastasia confided about her upbringing and desire to fit in. Shelly encouraged her to just be herself.

Shelly was a political science major in her third year. She admitted that she was gay and, sensing Anastasia's naiveté, she adamantly swore she would never touch her.

The following morning, Amy gave Anastasia a disapproving look when she heard the two women spent time together in the floor lounge. "You shouldn't hang around her, everyone is going to think you're a lesbian too. Then you're certainly not going to fit in."

But Anastasia found Shelly's company to be fun, stimulating and sincere; qualities she hadn't found among many of her peers. In spite of the discouragement, Anastasia continued the friendship.

Anastasia learned to embrace life. She frequented most parties and her popularity with the other students, especially men, grew. She experimented with alcohol and marijuana, and soon realized she did not care much for either one. She had little difficulty finding dates; rather, she routinely debated which offer to accept. It became customary for Anastasia to return from her dates and find Shelly in the lounge with her guitar. The two would spend hours singing and talking into the early mornings.

Each week, Anastasia spoke candidly with Shelly about the progression of her dates. Although she was still a virgin, she was curious about sex and interested in experimenting. Shelly was not surprised when Anastasia showed up upset at her dorm room early one Sunday morning.

Crying, Anastasia admitted she had had sex with her date the previous evening. "It was horrible. It was cold, aggressive, there was nothing affectionate or comforting about it."

"Do you feel anything for this guy? I mean…do you love him or like him?"

"I thought I liked him, but now I don't know."

Shelly tried to comfort her. "You may be one of those people who just can't have casual sex. That's how I am. It was your first time, Anastasia. Next time try waiting for someone you really care about. I'm sure it'll be a wonderful experience."

It was then Anastasia decided to wait for the right person.

Halfway through Anastasia's second semester, Shelly introduced her to a woman named Kim while the two were at the dining hall. Shelly had met Kim at a party the previous weekend and was interested in her. "So, what do you think?" she asked Anastasia, after Kim left the two women alone.

"What do I think…about what?" Anastasia naively asked.

"Kim. I met her last week."

Anastasia studied the attractive woman from a distance. "She's gay?"

"Yeah."

She continued to study the woman, then boldly asked, "What does she have…that I don't have?"

"She's gay, Anastasia."

"You don't find me attractive?"

Shelly was confused by the conversation. "Anastasia, you're the most attractive woman I have ever seen. But…you're an untouchable. You're not gay." As abruptly as the conversation started, the subject was changed.

Two weeks later, Anastasia returned to the dorm after a party and was surprised that Shelly was not in the lounge. She knew Shelly had a date with Kim that evening, and returned to her dorm room, feeling an unfamiliar ache in her heart. The pain haunted Anastasia for days.

An uncomfortable distance existed between the two as Shelly and Anastasia walked back to the dorm after an evening at the library. Shelly did not know what was bothering her friend.

"Anastasia, is everything okay?"

It was just after eleven o'clock, the campus was quiet and a cool spring breeze caused Anastasia to shiver. "Everything's fine. Brr, I just have the chills."

Shelly removed her sweatshirt, handing it to Anastasia. "Here, I have a long sleeve shirt on."

"No thanks." Anastasia abrasively pushed the sweatshirt away. "Anastasia, have I done something wrong? Are you upset with me?"

Ignoring the question, Anastasia continued her walk toward

the dorm in silence.

"Anastasia!?" Shelly pulled her arm to stop her.

With no place to go, Anastasia turned to face her.

"What's going on?" Shelly asked.

The women stood only inches apart, looking into each other's eyes. Shelly saw confusion and fear in Anastasia. She hadn't a chance to inquire about it because Anastasia abruptly kissed her, then backed away.

Anastasia's heart pounded as she waited for a response. She shivered, not knowing if it was because it was breezy, or because she had made such a bold pass at her best friend.

Shelly took her sweatshirt and draped it around Anastasia's shoulders, then tied the clothing's arms together gently against her breasts. She searched Anastasia's eyes, "Is there anything you want to tell me?"

"Why are you so quick to discard me?" Tears pooled in her eyes. "Is it because I'm black?"

A wisp of hair blew across Anastasia's face, obscuring one of her eyes. Shelly moved the soft strands away from her face, revealing a tear drop rolling down her cheek. She watched the droplet meet the edge of her lips. Shelly's lips met Anastasia's and they kissed.

For Anastasia, she had never had a kiss which increased her heartbeat. Where her breathing deepened, and every cell of her being was hungry and sensitive to the touch. She savored the slow, gentle feel of Shelly's lips upon her own, and the unfamiliar feeling from areas of her body which had never been aroused and ached for more.

It wasn't from the cold, but the surge of emotions and hormones which caused Anastasia to tremble. Shelly stopped kissing her and held her close to warm her. As she held her she whispered, "I had no idea."

For the remainder of the semester, Anastasia struggled with her feelings. It wasn't her feelings for Shelly which troubled her; it was her deep-seeded fundamentalist Christian upbringing. In the end, she never found the answer to one of her questions, *How could God disapprove of love just because it's between two women? Or two men?*

Anastasia and Shelly's relationship lasted for about a year. Then, Shelly moved to Africa for a Peace Corps position after she graduated. The two women continued to write to each other for about six months, then Anastasia's letters were returned, stamped *"Moved-no forwarding address."* She waited anxiously for another letter, but it never came.

Anastasia's studies remained her top priority in her junior and senior years. But to help with college expenses, she performed as the lead singer for a local pop band. Her schedule was demanding and consequently her visits to Richmond became infrequent.

After Anastasia graduated, she returned to her parents' home. While living under their roof she respected their way of life. However, her parents' views regarding homosexuality made her uncomfortable. A couple months after she returned from school, the subject surfaced during dinner one evening. Anastasia had forgotten how anti-gay her father was, and in anger she defended a person's choice of who they love. To Anastasia's surprise, she blurted to her parents that she was a lesbian. In anger, her father started quoting biblical verses reiterating the evils of homosexuality. In the weeks to come, it became clear that Luther Hall could not accept the fact that his daughter was a lesbian. An ultimatum was given to Anastasia: go *straight*, or leave home. She chose life.

During Anastasia's school years, she realized her dream was to sing. To explore her vision, with her life savings, she moved to The Big Apple and rented a studio apartment in Greenwich Village. She knew there were limited opportunities for someone with a bachelor's degree in music, so she took a job tending bar at a neighborhood bar and grill.

In her free time she searched the classified ads for auditions. By the time Anastasia responded to a vocalist-needed ad for a rock band, she had become accustomed to rejection. The four-piece band included a female lead singer, and apparently was searching for an additional vocalist. The lead singer, Stephanie, provided Anastasia with music to review before the tryout. During the audition Anastasia started singing the lead vocals rather than backup vocals. Other band members were surprised that Stephanie did not halt the audition. Rather, she listened intently to Anastasia's voice and knew she was gifted. She thought, *What a powerful voice in such a feminine woman... what a knock-out.* Although Stephanie knew Anastasia's performance would overshadow her own, she knew she could take their group to new levels.

Stephanie was far from stupid. Anastasia was hired as the lead singer. Although Stephanie remained a band member, she concentrated on writing new songs and managing the group. When she learned Anastasia was gay, she pursued her unrelentingly and eventually the two became lovers.

The band worked the club circuit for about a year before they got a break. They made a demo which had been circulating to many recording companies, and the group was excited when they heard from a Global Records A&R man. During a telephone conversation with Stephanie, Jerry Benson advised he would be at the Limelight the following Friday night when they were scheduled to perform.

Before the performance, Anastasia felt butterflies in her stomach and the rest of the group seemed equally nervous. Anastasia was aware that this performance could launch their career, and she felt responsible for the group. She sang beautifully, yet displayed a very subtle seductive style for the audience. Although her performance was truly extraordinary, the sensual aspects were unique and after the show Stephanie and the other band members were cross with her because of the change. They quickly ate their words when Jerry Benson expressed interest in her performance.

Global Records was interested in Anastasia but not the group. Although Stephanie appeared to be a good sport, she was quick to remind Anastasia where she would be without her, and that she had written the songs which got Global Records' attention. Stephanie was happy to accept Anastasia's offer to write music for her and become her road assistant.

A year later Anastasia's first album was released. The title track, "I'm Here to Stay," rose to the top and remained number one for 10 weeks. Two other songs on the album also became hits. She wrote the majority of the songs while Stephanie wrote two. Anastasia's music style was unique, crossing between rock and R&B. But what set her apart from other performers was her unusually powerful voice combined with a natural sensuality, often provocative. Global Records and her new manager, Jeffrey Simon successfully targeted the male audience and built the next diva.

When the Grammy Award nominations were announced the following year, Jeffrey Simon along with Jerry Benson and David Jacobs of Global Records celebrated. Anastasia had been nominated for Best New Artist, Album of the Year and Best Female Pop Vocalist. Later that year, Anastasia took all three awards.

Two years after her first album, *Lovers* was released. The sophomore album out-performed her first. She had a successful tour and produced three profitable videos. The following year she earned four additional Grammy Awards for *Lovers*. Global Records and her manager had been successful in marketing Anastasia as a sex goddess and every man's fantasy. Although she frequently felt she was deceiving her fans, she knew it sold records.

Two years later her third album debuted, but it was a disappointment. Stephanie had written the majority of the songs and Anastasia was unable to deliver an authentic performance since the songs' subjects were foreign to Anastasia.

Almost eighteen months passed and Anastasia was having trouble pulling everything together. The record company was pressuring her to produce another album. Stephanie insinuated that Anastasia's writing had become weak over the years, and compelled her to produce only Stephanie's songs.

Anastasia was also starting to realize that her partner was becoming a liability. In public, Stephanie would not hesitate about discussing their life together as a couple. Initially the indiscretions did not bother Anastasia, then she realized the publicity could destroy her career.

One day, Jeffrey, Anastasia's manager stormed into the recording studio. "When the hell are you going to get down to business?" His face red with anger.

Anastasia halted the recording session. "Excuse me? What the hell do you think we're doing?"

"I think you're blowing it." Jeffrey glared at Anastasia in rage. "You haven't recorded anything worth a damn in five years. Global's not interested in working with you, agents aren't interested in booking you this year. Why? Everyone is getting tired of seeing Steph kiss your ass. You're blowing it, Anastasia."

He pulled out a handful of envelopes, apparently fan letters, and started reading excerpts from some of them. "Dyke go home…" He threw the letter at Anastasia then started reading from a postcard. "You just haven't had a real man…" Jeffrey threw it at Anastasia and pulled out another, and another. "Repent or God will punish you…You're a lie to your fans, you should be punished."

Jeffrey threw the remaining envelopes at Anastasia. "My contract is up in six months. Unless you can pull yourself out of the toilet, I'm out of here. You're not taking me down with you."

Stephanie watched the whole scene and, after Jeffrey left, she said, "Good, let him go, who needs him?"

"I'm going to call Jerry and find out how bad it really is." Anastasia calmly left the recording session.

Anastasia learned that it was bad. The record company's confidence in her was shaken and most believed she was going to crash. For the first time in her life, Anastasia felt helpless and did not know where to turn. Her manager and A&R person seemed to have given up on her, and her relationship with Stephanie was not healthy. However, she refused to believe her career was over at the age of thirty-one.

Over the years, Stephanie mastered reminding Anastasia where she would be without her. Consequently, Anastasia lost confidence in her music. In her mind, her last album was a loser, and it had been years since she'd recorded successful music. Both Stephanie and Anastasia knew their relationship was not perfect, but both recognized they needed each other.

Over the next few months, Anastasia worked hard to turn her luck around. She spent most of her time in recording studios working on the next album, but never felt she was making significant progress.

She was surprised when David Jacobs called her at home one evening. "I understand that Jeffrey's contract is up in a month or so. I've heard the two of you are considering parting. Is it true?"

"We've talked about going our separate ways," Anastasia admitted.

"Can I offer some advice?"

"Sure," Anastasia reluctantly agreed.

"You need to make some decisions about where to go from here. If you're serious about maintaining your diva status, you need the absolute best manager." David continued, "If you're still serious, I'll try to get an appointment with the best manager in the business."

"Who are you talking about?"

"Sidney Marcum, she manages *the Gang* and Jason Light."

Anastasia was not impressed. "I'm familiar with her company, but—"

"Let me put it this way, I don't know any other manager who can get your career back on track."

"Assuming I work out a deal with a new manager, will Global release some funds so I can start doing some things?"

"You need to show us that you're in control of your career, and make some commercially satisfying music before Global commits any further. But without a solid manager, you'll get nothing. Shall I set up a meeting between you and Sidney?"

Later that evening, Anastasia told Stephanie about her conversation regarding Sidney Marcum. Stephanie told Anastasia, "I'll do some research on Marcum Productions."

Chapter 6

Natalie and Nelson were surprised by Sidney's decision to take over Anastasia's management. Both had learned, however, not to question her decisions and showed their support. Sidney called a staff meeting the following Monday to discuss the new assignments.

To her staff, Sidney identified key areas that needed to be resolved over the first six months. One of the key issues was the lack of cooperation from Global Records. An artist bound to a record company that was unwilling to release her music was worthless. Sidney also recognized that a complete retraction from *the New Jersey Gazette* was essential if Anastasia was to reclaim her superstar status. Another matter that needed to be resolved was Anastasia's concert bookings. Apparently the agents were not interested in booking her.

Sidney identified the issues to her staff, one by one. She

never addressed how the issues would be remedied, only how significant their defeat would be to her marketing plan.

Natalie and Sidney had been working for hours at the office. "Natalie, would you schedule a recording session with Anastasia? I want to hear her new material. Then call Antoine's and get on his schedule for a photo shoot."

Natalie surveyed the office then looked at her friend, and surmised that Sidney had been working overtime. "You've really put yourself out on a limb for this one, haven't you?"

"Well, let's just say I haven't chosen the easier path. You know I get bored when I don't have a good challenge."

"Well…I'm going to be leaving, do you need anything else, Sid?" Sidney had noticed that Natalie had been leaving work on time lately. She also noticed that Natalie had been more cheerful than usual.

"Hot date?" Sidney asked her friend.

Natalie smiled. "Sort of."

"What's her name?"

"Karen," she answered. "We've been seeing each other for about a month now. I'd rather not say too much; I don't want to jinx a potentially good relationship."

"It's been a long time since you've smiled like that around here. You have such a beautiful smile. I'm glad to see you're happy, Nat."

Natalie gave Sidney a hug. "Thanks, we'll have to work on your happiness next."

"I am happy, Nat."

David Jacobs had not been surprised when Sidney called his office and demanded to meet him for lunch at the Russian Tea

Room. "Sidney, you look great," he said as they embraced.

"I see the years have been good to you." They exchanged small talk, then Sidney got down to business. "I'm sure you've heard; I've taken over Anastasia's management."

He nodded. "Yes, I have heard."

"I understand that Anastasia is under contract for one more album. Jerry told me that Global has no intention of releasing the album, and I hear the funds are gone for her promotions. Is it true?"

He nodded again. "Sid, Global has taken too many chances on Anastasia. She hasn't been very profitable the last year or so. I've heard her new stuff is just like her last album, which was a major disappointment. Anastasia has become too much of a risk. It's time to put our money in another entertainer's career. I'm not saying we'll never release her album, just not until things smooth over."

"David, you were the one who pleaded with me to take over her management. Weren't you?"

"Yes, and I believe you are the best person for the job. Your timing is just impeccably bad."

"I'm going to ask you for a favor, David."

"What's that?"

"Replenish her operating budget and promise to release her work in a timely fashion."

"I'm sorry Sid, but I just can't do that."

"Then release her from her contract obligations," demanded Sidney.

"You know I can't do that, either." He was smiling.

Sidney stared at her former boss. "David, either work with me on a new album, release her from her contract, or—"

"Or what?" he asked smugly.

There was a chill to her tone as she spoke. "Or I'll drag your ass to court."

"On what grounds?"

"Courts don't like it when you interfere with an individual's livelihood. I even have some case law that supports the premise."

David was curious. "What case law?"

"Remember the artist Larry Coryell?" Sidney pulled out her notebook for reference. "The New York case noted that courts 'look critically on provisions which restrict the employee in his right to earn a livelihood by imposing unreasonable restrictions on his activities.' You won't let Anastasia go, but you won't release her album. Don't you think those restraints are unreasonable and harsh?"

David smiled. "You learned from the best. You do know that, don't you?"

"Are you talking about yourself or Michael?"

Sidney scratched a line through her first milestone on her "Anastasia objectives list." She had successfully resolved the contract issues with Global. David had agreed to generously support Anastasia's efforts and would release her next album when commercially ready. She was reviewing her objectives list when her receptionist buzzed her. "Yes, Michelle?"

"Jennifer Warren is returning your call. She's on line three."

"Thank you, Michelle." She referred to her list and circled the second task. Then greeted the caller. "Hi counselor, what are you doing for lunch tomorrow?"

"You had my secretary block out my calendar from ten to three o'clock tomorrow. I'm hoping you can tell me what we're doing for lunch."

"Are you upset with me?" Sidney laughed.

"No, I got used to your unconventional methods years ago," Jennifer answered.

"Is tomorrow okay?"

Jennifer rearranged her schedule to spend the time with Sidney.

As the Mercedes entered the Lincoln Tunnel, Jennifer asked

Sidney, "We're going to New Jersey? When are you going to tell me what's going on?"

"We're going to a little Italian restaurant outside of Newark. It's supposed to be pretty good."

Jennifer was skeptical. "At ten o'clock in the morning?"

"Of course not. Oh, I didn't tell you? I have a meeting with the *New Jersey Gazette* at eleven. Then we can have lunch."

Jennifer was trying to get some clarification. "Am I going to this meeting at the *Gazette?* And if so, am I representing you?"

"You're going to the meeting. You're my friend...who just happens to be an attorney."

Sidney quickly filled Jennifer in on her new client and her problems with the *Gazette*. She was still preparing Jennifer as they walked into the building. "Jennifer, when I give you this sign," she put her notepad in her inside jacket pocket, "I want you to excuse yourself from the meeting." She handed Jennifer her cellular phone. "Use my phone, call Natalie at my office and say hello. Okay?"

"What are you getting me into? Never mind, I don't want to know." The lawyer took the phone and stuffed it into her purse. Jennifer was in her late forties. She was the picture of professionalism. Her long auburn hair was pulled away from her face in a bun and she wore a business suit that concealed her full figure.

"Sidney Marcum to see James Palermo," she informed the receptionist. Both Sidney and Jennifer were escorted to the office of the newspaper's general manager, editor and principal owner. The receptionist opened the door to the office and a large man rose from his desk, frowning.

Sidney firmly shook the man's hand. "It's a pleasure to finally meet you, Mr. Palermo." Jennifer also offered a warm handshake.

"Likewise, I'm sure." The man appeared confused. "I'm sorry, I don't mean to be rude, but I don't know why we're meeting. My secretary didn't know how or why you got on my calendar."

Sidney pulled out her pocket notebook and offered the man

her business card. "MPI Artist Management." He shrugged his shoulders and turned to Jennifer. "Are you with MPI also?"

"No, Mr. Palermo." She offered her card, which got his attention.

"Jennifer Warren, Attorney at Law," he read aloud. "Well, ladies, to what do I owe the pleasure of this visit?" he asked insincerely.

"Well, James, may I call you James?" Sidney asked.

The man nodded.

"James, I've recently taken on a new client who has had a string of bad luck. Recently your paper printed something about her that is bordering on…well, let's just say slander."

"And your client just happens to be?" Palermo asked.

"Anastasia."

Palermo's voice rose. "That wasn't slander; that was a good piece of investigative reporting."

"It was reckless disregard of the truth," Sidney challenged.

"She's a lesbian, and freedom of speech gives me the right to print it."

"But if you knew the report was false, and you published it anyway, that would be reckless, wouldn't it?"

Palermo's neck and face reddened. "Where are you going with this?"

"If you publish something and you know it's false, then it would be reckless, right?"

He would not answer.

"What was your reporter doing at a lesbian bar? Is she gay?"

Palermo was irritated. "Absolutely not."

"Then what was she doing there? How did she know that Anastasia was going to be there?"

Again, he did not answer.

Sidney took a flyer from her notebook and slammed it in front of Palermo. The flyer advertised Anastasia's special appearance at the club. "This is how your reporter knew Anastasia would be at Alternatives that night."

"So. What if it was?"

"This says that Anastasia is to perform at a lesbian bar. You published that 'Anastasia frequents lesbian bar.' Anastasia didn't go there because she's a lesbian or to socialize. She went to the club to perform. Where in your article did it say that she performed?"

"That's your case?" He laughed, and looked over at Jennifer who was just listening to the conversation. "Thin. Very thin." He stretched his legs on top of his desk, clasped his fingers together to support his neck and leaned back in his chair.

Sidney leaned over him. "Maybe thin, but certainly not frivolous, and I can show some pretty substantial damages that directly relate to your article."

"So? You wouldn't dare sue me, you'd lose."

"Maybe I would lose, but the publicity would be good for Anastasia. She can afford the legal costs. Can you?"

Sidney turned away from Palermo and put her leather-bound notebook back in her pocket.

Jennifer interrupted the conversation. "Would you excuse me for a moment?" She left the room.

The discussion of money brought Palermo back to a conversation he had had that morning with his bank officer. He had been trying to refinance a loan that had a substantial balloon payment due later in the year. Although the newspaper had been doing business with Federal Union for twenty years, the bank denied refinancing of his loan.

"Can you?" Sidney persisted.

"Can I what?" he barked.

"The way I see it is—Anastasia has nothing to lose to file suit against you. The legal costs and expert fees alone to litigate a case like this would be in the six figures. That's a drop in the bucket for her, how about you? Can this paper afford that? James, do you have a good insurance policy?"

Palermo appeared uneasy and removed his legs from his desk. "What do you want from me?" he asked.

"A complete retraction and apology."

"You'll never get it," Palermo said.

The two were interrupted by his secretary's intercom page. Palermo picked up the phone and angrily said, "Not now." But his secretary said something that captured his attention. "No. I'll take the call." He turned to Sidney. "This will be a minute."

His tone changed when he greeted the caller. "Hi Henry, how's the wife?" There was a long pause, and then he became visibly upset; his forehead started to perspire. "Well, I'm sorry to hear that. Specifically which article did you find offensive?" Palermo looked up at Sidney, and continued the conversation. "Well, I hope we can do business again, someday." He hung up.

"That was our second largest advertiser; he apparently didn't like our report on Anastasia. He's ceasing business with the *Gazette*. I got a call yesterday from our third largest advertiser; they pulled their account. I suppose you had nothing to do with this."

"Well, you know James, I know some very influential people who might be able to get your business back, or perhaps make up for your losses."

"Federal Union. Are you responsible for my loan rejection?" he asked.

Sidney shook her head. "James, that would be blackmail. I do know some mortgage companies that may be able to help you out, though. Help me out, and I'll see what I can do about helping you out. Okay?"

The man sat at his desk, defeated. "What do you want me to say…in this retraction?"

Sidney pulled out a paper and placed it in front of him. "I've already written it for you. I want it on Sunday's front page, just like the original article. It can't deviate one word from what's written here."

There was a knock at the door, and Jennifer entered. "Oh, we were just finishing," Sidney said, and turned to James. "Run this. We'll talk on Monday. Okay?"

Sidney toasted her friend over lunch. "Thank you for being there when I need you."

"I don't know what just happened," Jennifer admitted, "and I don't want to know." The two women laughed.

Although Jennifer and Sidney had been friends for about ten years, they had not seen each other in over a year. The women spent their lunch catching up on old times.

"The only time I see you is when you're in trouble or need help. Do you think we can change that?" Jennifer smiled.

Sidney cracked a smile also. "I'll try to stay out of trouble, and I'll call you in a couple of weeks to do lunch again. How's that?"

"Has Michael given you any trouble lately?"

"No, actually he's been on good behavior."

"Good." Jennifer gestured toward a young couple that was having a romantic lunch. "Anyone special in your life these days?"

"No. I really don't have the time, right now." Sidney avoided eye contact with her friend.

Jennifer reached over the table and placed her hand on Sidney's. "Charlie is not coming back, Sidney. You should get on with your life."

"I have gotten on with my life. Really. My priorities have just changed," she tried to assure her friend.

Chapter 7

That Sunday morning, as Sidney sipped her first cup of coffee, she was pleased to read the *Gazette's* retraction. The article ran on the front page of the newspaper, unedited from her draft. She experienced a sense of accomplishment as she drew a line through her second objective on her list.

The following morning, her coworkers applauded her as she entered her office. "How'd you do it?" Natalie asked as she closed Sidney's office door behind her.

"The usual way. I just asked him nicely."

"Right. Anastasia's photo shoot is scheduled for Wednesday morning, nine o'clock at Gilgo State Park. It's just east of Jones Beach and west of Fire Island. Will that work?"

Sidney marked her calendar. "I'll plan on it."

That day, the media bombarded MPI. They demanded comments on the *Gazette's* retraction. As usual, Sidney wanted to be prepared and spent part of her day writing a press release.

The following day, Sidney called agents she frequently worked with. The timing seemed perfect. Because of the newspaper's recent retraction, most agents were eager to discuss booking the fallen superstar.

As Sidney drove out to Gilgo State Park the following morning, she realized she was getting excited about promoting Anastasia. Everything seemed to be falling in place: Global had agreed to release her next album; the *Gazette* had printed the retraction; and now, the agents were working with her.

It was going on ten o'clock by the time she arrived at the shoot location. Stephanie was in the parking lot chatting with what appeared to be groupies. A crowd had formed outside of the roped-off photo area. The bystanders were trying to watch the action on the beach, about eighty yards away. One of Antoine's security assistants recognized Sidney and opened a roped section, permitting her to pass. The majority of the crew was standing about halfway between the parking lot area and the water.

It was the week before Memorial Day, and the weather was perfect. The low eighties seemed appropriate for the beach shoot.

As Sidney approached the small group, she noticed that the photographer, Antoine, was upset. "That bitch won't take her fucking sunglasses off," he yelled at Sidney.

Anastasia was pacing rigidly in ankle-deep water, alone, about thirty yards from the camera crew. She was dressed in a bathing suit and had a towel draped around her shoulder, concealing most of her torso.

Sidney walked over to Natalie. "Is there a good reason why she's not cooperating?"

"Your guess is as good as mine." Natalie added, "She wouldn't let Andrea do her make-up, and she says it's ridiculous to shoot a beach scene without sunglasses on. Antoine, being equally stubborn, is demanding that she take them off."

Antoine was pacing and cursing about losing time, and rain was in the forecast. As Sidney walked down to the water, she saw threatening clouds in the distance. She removed her sandals and carried them as she walked into the cold water, approaching Anastasia.

"Do you want to tell me what's going on?" Sidney asked calmly.

"I already told them; it's absurd to shoot a beach scene without sunglasses."

"You're right," Sidney agreed as she studied the photo props that dressed the beach. "We also need beach umbrellas, a couple of beach balls, some of those blow-up floating devices and some beach blankets." Eyeing the beach towel cloaked over Anastasia's shoulder, she approached her and tried to remove it, "Here, let me use your towel—"

"No," Anastasia objected and tugged the towel back onto her shoulder.

Anastasia's reluctance heightened Sidney's curiosity. She approached her and tried to look into her eyes, but could not penetrate the dark glasses. Slowly, Sidney reached for the towel and removed it. But this time there was no resistance. Severe bruising was noticeable on Anastasia's right side and a nasty gash marred her upper arm. Calmly, Sidney circled Anastasia to see the bruises extend to her back. As Sidney looked toward the camera crew, she realized they were too far for the others to see her injuries. Without saying a word, Sidney draped the towel back over Anastasia's shoulder, once again concealing the injuries. Then slowly, she removed the sunglasses from Anastasia's face, revealing a black eye. Sidney calmly replaced the glasses.

Turning toward the parking lot, Sidney abruptly bolted, leaving Anastasia. Anastasia attempted to follow Sidney, but she was too fast.

"Sidney, stop," she cried. But Sidney continued her flight. Anastasia's cry got the group's attention; they soon noticed Anastasia chasing after Sidney.

Natalie was able to intercept her friend before she reached the parking lot. She bolted in front of Sidney. "What's going on?" Natalie saw that Sidney was upset; her jaw was clenched shut, and her face was deep red. "Sid, are you okay?"

Sidney ignored the question and continued toward the parking lot. Natalie turned back and saw that Anastasia was injured, as she held her side and winced from pain with each step.

"You've got to stop her," Anastasia yelled at Natalie.

Reconsidering her next step, Natalie chased after Sidney and tugged on her arm until she stopped.

Sidney turned back toward her friend. "Leave me alone, Nat."

Natalie saw the anger in Sidney's eyes. "Who did it? Stephanie?" Sidney remained silent. "What are you planning to do?" Again, Sidney ignored the question, then Natalie asked, "How can I help?"

Sidney could see that Anastasia was approaching. "Can you keep her on the beach?" she asked.

"And what are you going to do?" Natalie asked.

"I'm just going to talk to Stephanie."

"I wouldn't mess with her, Sid; I think she's bad news."

"I'm just going to *talk* to her."

Natalie hesitated, then turned back toward Anastasia. She was able to quickly stop Anastasia by turning her away from the parking lot and directing her back toward the water.

"You've got to stop her," Anastasia cried.

"It's okay." Natalie made a feeble attempt to comfort her.

"No, it isn't okay. She's sticking her nose where it doesn't belong." Anastasia tried to turn back but she was no match for Natalie. "She's just going to make things worse. God, Steph's gonna be so pissed off." Then, as if defeated, she sank to her knees on the beach sand.

Natalie sat next to Anastasia. "Even if I wanted to stop her, Anastasia, I don't think I could."

Sidney soon reached the parking lot, put her sandals back on, and searched for Stephanie. The groupies were still there and Stephanie was still talking to them. When she reached the group, she asked Stephanie, "May I have a word with you?"

Stephanie hesitated, then followed Sidney away from the crowd and through some parked cars. The hot sun beat down on the asphalt and added to the discomfort of the situation. Stephanie was the first to break the silence. "What's up?"

Sidney continued her pace and stared ahead. "I just saw Anastasia. Is there anything you want to tell me?"

"No!"

Sidney turned around to meet Stephanie's eyes. She calmly spoke. "I'm going to say this once, and only once. If you ever hit Anastasia, you'll never work in this business again. You'll never be allowed on her sets, shoots, tours, anything. Do you understand me?"

Stephanie's neck reddened and her anger erupted. "Who the hell do you think you are?" She yelled, "This is none of your goddamn business. This is between Anastasia and me." Her anger escalated and instinctively she raised a fist.

Sidney ignored the threat. "That's where you're wrong; this *is* my business. We have a photographer and crew over there that can't do their job because of you. We still have to pay them for the day. Any time you mess with the business, you're messing with me, and I don't like it, and I won't put up with it."

Stephanie's fist withdrew, but her anger visibly simmered. "If I were a man, we wouldn't be having this conversation."

"What?"

"You heard me. If a man hit her, you wouldn't dare say anything because you know it's none of your business. But I'm a woman...and she's a woman." Stephanie moved closer to Sidney. "You just don't like people like us."

"Excuse me?"

She was smiling as she strolled around Sidney. "You just don't like lesbians. Admit it," she taunted.

"This has nothing to do with your lifestyle. You hurt my business and Anastasia's. Damaged merchandise doesn't sell. Why is that so hard for you to understand?" Sidney continued, "I don't want to see you at any of Anastasia's functions for two months, no rehearsals, no performances, nothing."

"Bitch," Stephanie uttered and abruptly brushed past Sidney.

"By the way," Sidney said, "Anastasia never told me you hit her."

"Then who did?"

"You just did."

Stephanie quickly got in her car and peeled out of the parking lot.

As Sidney walked back toward the beach, she realized the altercation had gotten the attention of the photographer's crew and groupies. All eyes were on Sidney as she approached Natalie. Anastasia was sitting on the beach with her back to Sidney. Natalie followed Sidney's lead out of hearing distance from Anastasia.

"Are you okay?" Natalie asked.

"Yeah. How is she?"

"She's upset. She's afraid you're going to make things worse."

"That's not my intention."

"I know that," said Natalie.

"Take her in to see Thomas Phelps. I'll call and make the arrangements."

Sidney was in her car heading north, across South Oyster Bay. She pulled out her cellular phone and punched in the phone number.

"Dr. Phelps's office," a familiar voice answered the phone.

"Hi Nancy, this is Sidney Marcum. How are you?"

"Sidney? How are you? We haven't heard from you in ages. How have you been?" She continued to rattle off questions, not giving Sidney ample time to respond.

"I'm doing great Nancy, but I need a favor from you and Tom. Can you help me?"

"Of course. What's up?"

"I have a friend who needs medical attention today. Can you fit her in?" Sidney asked.

"Consider it done. Now what's her name?"

"How does Jane Smith sound?"

"Like you don't want me to know who she is," the nurse answered.

"This is the deal, Nancy, I can't afford to have her injury leaked to the press and made public. Would you and Tom be able to treat her, bill me, and I promise, I will personally take care of it?"

"She's not shot, is she?"

"No. I don't believe there's anything serious. It's just a sensitive situation. What do you think? Can you help me?"

"Of course we will."

"Can you update Thomas? Or I'll be happy to discuss this with him."

Nancy laughed. "You know I run this office. I'll tell Tom what's going on."

"If he has any concerns, have him call me. Natalie is bringing her in. They'll probably be there in an hour or so."

Anastasia bitched about Sidney all the way to the doctor's office. "I hope she knows what the hell she's doing. What's going to stop the doctor from selling the story to the press? Damn her, she should just mind her own business. Doesn't she realize she just made it worse for me? Steph is going to kill me!"

Natalie's patience was wearing thin. "I'm really getting tired of hearing you bitch about Sid. She's just trying to help. Take my advice, trust her. She knows what she's doing."

Anastasia remained quiet the rest of the drive to the doctor's office, which was located in New York Hospital. Natalie parked the car in the employee parking lot, then removed what appeared to be a parking permit from her glove compartment and placed it in the windshield. Before entering the building, Natalie handed Anastasia a scarf and sunglasses, "Put these on."

When Natalie and Anastasia entered the waiting room, Nancy smiled warmly at Natalie, and casually greeted Anastasia. "Ms. Smith? Right this way, please." Both followed the nurse into a private examining room. She handed Anastasia a robe. "Put this on and I'll be back in a moment."

Nancy and Natalie left the room, leaving Anastasia alone for a few minutes. Shortly after, Nancy returned to conduct an initial examination, then Dr. Phelps followed.

"Ms. Smith, it looks like you're pretty lucky," Dr. Phelps explained after the examination. "I was concerned that you broke a rib or two during your…fall. There are no breaks, but you're very bruised, and appear quite uncomfortable. We're going to dress the laceration on your arm, and give you some anti-inflammatory agents to help your ribs. If the pain doesn't subside in three days, call me."

Throughout the examination, Anastasia anticipated that someone would bring up her identity, or ask how her injuries occurred. But no one did. She was never asked to sign any documents. Just before Anastasia left the examination room, Nancy returned. Smiling, she said, "I understand you're a friend of Sidney's. We haven't seen her in years. How's she doing?"

"Sidney seems…to be the same as usual."

"She's such a sweetheart; please let her know we miss her and think of her often."

Anastasia agreed sarcastically, "Yeah, a real sweetheart." Before Anastasia opened the door to leave the examination room, she turned back to Nancy and asked, "Do you know who I am?"

"Of course we do, Ms. Smith," Nancy answered.

Chapter 8

Sidney left the photo shoot, and, as she reached the Southern State Parkway, she knew she was having difficulty concentrating on her driving. Her mind kept returning to her confrontation with Stephanie. The more she thought about Anastasia and Stephanie's situation, the more unsettled she became. When Sidney saw the sign for the Meadowbrook State Parkway, she decided to exit. She headed south, and quickly returned to beach communities, soon reaching Jones Beach.

A walk on the beach may take my mind off their situation and help me relax. She parked her car, rolled up her shirt-sleeves and removed her sandals. The warm sand ran between her toes. Shortly after, the warm sand was replaced by cold water from the breaking waves. Sidney's mind continued to race. She hardly noticed the other people playing, swimming, running and enjoying the unseasonably warm day. After she had walked about a mile, she realized the walk was not relaxing her and decided to sit and enjoy the beach. But as she sat there, her mind kept taking her back to more difficult times.

* * *

Eleven years earlier, Sidney had just celebrated her fifth wedding anniversary with Michael as well as her fifth year at Global Records. Her career had progressed wonderfully, but her marriage had become a façade. Michael was campaigning aggressively to become the next New York Governor. Although he realized their marriage needed work, he also knew he needed a loyal wife and a successful marriage to secure the Republican seat in the elections.

The two had come to an understanding: she would portray a loyal and loving wife; and he would release her from their marriage after the elections. On two previous occasions, Sidney had tried to leave Michael but had been unsuccessful. Both times her husband's hired hands had picked her up within forty-eight hours. She had reluctantly agreed to become Michael's pawn and played his game, envisioning her future freedom.

Michael's business had grown tremendously over the years, particularly the Securities Division. During the evenings, Michael had continued his private business sessions with Keith Connerly, Whitman Industries' attorney. Sidney suspected that Michael was involved in questionable security sales and purchases. Her suspicions were proven correct when she came across some of Michael's notes concerning a company named Vision Tech. She knew that Whitman Industries had previously acquired thousands of shares of Vision Tech stock. The notes indicated that Vision Tech had a problem with a new software product, and the company was planning to push back its introduction. The new product setback would be announced at the next shareholders' meeting.

From her previous employment at the company, Sidney was

familiar with the Whitman Industries network computer system. Over the years, she had learned how to access the company's Security Division information. *Michael's never been very creative,* she thought the first time she typed in his mother's maiden name and the computer recognized the password.

Sidney gained access to the Whitman Securities data through Michael's home computer. She learned that the company had sold all shares of Vision Tech the day after the date of Michael's notes. Almost one month later, Vision Tech announced the development problems at the shareholders' meeting. As expected, the stock plummeted, and Whitman Industries bought Vision Tech stock again at a bargain price.

Over the years, Sidney learned that Michael kept detailed notes of his discussions with Keith Connerly. She suspected the notes were about their insider trading activities. Although the papers were damaging to both men, she believed that Michael kept them to incriminate the lawyer in the event he ever crossed him. The documents were locked away in his home desk filing cabinet.

For years, Michael had blamed Sidney's inability to conceive and produce his heir as the reason for their marriage's difficulties. But Sidney looked at the situation differently. She was scared to death to have a child with Michael. His volatility had increased over the years, and her biggest fear was that he would vent his frustrations on a child. Sidney also wanted to minimize any attachment to him, knowing he would never divorce her if she had his child.

Sidney was almost ready for a formal dinner party. She was dressed, had her makeup applied, her jewelry on, and her long hair elegantly styled. Michael was dressed in a black tuxedo. As she stepped back to view herself in the full-length mirror, Michael voiced his opinion. "I like your other black shoes, the ones with the taller heel."

"I like those too, Michael, but these are more comfortable." Sidney studied herself in the full-length mirror. "Don't these look okay?"

Michael retreated to the closet through their master bathroom. He returned with a couple pairs of shoes. Sidney's heart skipped a beat when she saw the shoes he selected. "Try these on," he ordered, but as he said it a small case fell out of one of the shoes. Leaning over, Michael picked up the tiny case and opened it. "What the hell is this?" he asked.

"It's a diaphragm," Sidney answered.

"I know what it is. What the hell is it doing here?"

Sidney remained silent.

"Have you been using this?" Michael's tone was rising.

"Yes, I have."

Michael was losing his patience. "We've been trying to get pregnant, for…for what? Four years now? And you've been practicing birth control all along?"

"For the last two years."

Michael was expressionless as he stared at her. He slapped her face with the back of his hand. Sidney had expected it and remained calm. Then she said, "This is why I don't want a baby with you, Michael. I'd be scared to death you'd abuse your own child."

"You bitch. You know I want children. I thought you were sterile."

"Michael, we've had an agreement for over a year now, remember? I pretend to be your loyal wife through the elections, then we're getting divorced. A child would only complicate matters."

Michael laughed.

"May I ask what is so funny?" Sidney asked.

"You're so stupid." Michael was still laughing. "I'm never going to divorce you, especially now."

She could not believe what she was hearing. Her anger built to rage, and, with all her strength, she instinctively slapped him. He was taken off guard by her unnatural aggression but was quick to rebound and punched her squarely on her jaw. She was knocked off balance and fell to the floor.

Sidney held her face, then pulled her hand away, seeing blood on her fingers. "Okay, you've made your point; you're stronger than me."

Michael went to the mirror and inspected the red welt on his face. His rage grew. Methodically, he removed his tuxedo jacket, cummerbund and bow tie, and was unzipping his pants as he approached Sidney.

"Don't even think about it. The answer is no," Sidney said.

He picked her up roughly, and twisted her arms. "I don't need your consent to fuck you."

"Michael, that hurts. Stop it! I said no, and I mean it!"

Stopping was furthest from Michael's mind. He threw Sidney on the bed and jumped on her. As he struggled with lowering his trousers, Sidney repeatedly lashed out to strike him. A blow to his jaw enraged him further, and he punched her with increased force, numbing her momentarily. He pulled off his pants and climbed back on her, but she kneed him in the groin. He collapsed and groaned in pain as Sidney pushed him off of her. She was getting on her feet when he cried, "You bitch," and attacked her from behind, slamming her against the wall. When she turned, he struck her face, then repeatedly punched her stomach and ribs. A hard blow to her face took her down on the dresser. Her face crashed on a vase, and as she fell, the back of her head landed sharply on the pedestal of the full-length mirror.

Sidney would never completely recall what happened after that, as she struggled with consciousness. Enraged, Michael dragged her back to the bed, tore off her pantyhose, and raped her. Distracted by the damage he had inflicted on her face, he covered it with a pillow and brought himself to climax.

Chapter 9

It wasn't the light that brought her back to consciousness. It wasn't anything she heard or smelled, either. It was the nagging headache and throbbing from her side which brought awareness to her situation. She opened her eyes, but could not see much. It was as if she opened window with shutters obstructing her view.

With her hands she explored her face. She felt the stickiness of blood and torn tissue near her right eye, and her left eye was almost swollen shut. As she turned her head, she felt the damp and sticky carpet beneath her. The carpeting was saturated with her own blood.

"Michael?" She called out weakly.

There was only silence.

Her memory returned in bits and pieces. It felt more like a nightmare. Sidney was on her bedroom floor. She tried to sit up but was overwhelmed by a stabbing pain on her side. With her second attempt, she ignored the debilitating hurt and sat. There was no sign of Michael. His tuxedo jacket was gone.

Could he have gone to the party and left her? She wondered.

With all the strength she could call upon, she got on her knees and inched toward the full-length mirror. There was blood by its pedestal, and Sidney felt the wound on the back of her head, knowing that was where she had hit it.

Then something within her spoke. It wasn't a voice. It was a feeling. Something urged her to move and to be quick. From experience, she knew Michael's goons would be by soon to pick up the pieces. Her heart raced as she tried to muster up the strength and courage to escape. She retrieved and put on a long raincoat. She pulled a scarf around her face to conceal her injuries. Then she turned toward the antique secretary's desk that was in the front foyer. From a secret compartment, she removed Michael's emergency cash and pocketed the wad of bills in her raincoat.

As she approached the front doorway, she heard the faint bell from the elevator. Since the penthouse was the only apartment on the floor, Sidney knew it was either Michael or his goons. Seconds later, the door lock was being released. With barely enough time, she ducked into the front hallway closet. As she peered through the opening, she saw two well-dressed men enter and move toward the bedroom.

Carefully, Sidney emerged from the closet and approached the doorway. Her escape door creaked as she opened it, hastening her pulse. Quietly she stepped through the doorway and closed the door, hoping the men did not hear her. She approached the elevator but knew its bell would draw attention. Opting for the stairwell, she painfully managed to descend one floor before she found an elevator on the lower level.

In the lobby, the doorman, Clark, did not recognize her as she stumbled off the elevator. "Can I help you, Miss?" he asked.

"Clark, I need a taxi," Sidney managed to say. She carefully looked away from him, so he could not see her injuries.

The doorman obediently ran outside and flagged down a cab,

then returned to the lobby. He started to help Sidney outside, but his phone rang. "Excuse me, Miss, this should just take a minute." He left her at the entrance of the revolving glass door.

"Hello," he answered the phone. "Have I seen who?" Clark turned and watched as Sidney desperately tried to move the heavy revolving door. "Mr. Whitman's wife, Sidney?"

With the phone in hand, he walked toward the revolving door. Sidney's heart beat faster as she pushed the glass door to within a few inches of her freedom, and then it stopped. The doorman's foot was wedged in the opening preventing her escape.

Trapped and desperate, Sidney turned toward him and removed her scarf, revealing her injuries. "Clark...please," Sidney pleaded.

"Ms. Marcum, you mean?" The doorman continued his telephone conversation, as he stared at Sidney trapped in the revolving door. "No, I haven't seen her," he said as he removed his foot, enabling her escape.

Sidney entered the emergency room of New York Hospital. As she approached the admitting desk, her world started to spin. Initially the motion was subtle, then more intense. To steady herself, she raised an arm searching for the wall, but as she groped she aggravated the injury to her ribs. The pain brought her to her knees; her world clouded, and there was no more light.

On initial evaluation, the attending physician ordered a rape kit. This was standard protocol when rape was suspected. Evidence samples were gathered and pictures were taken before Sidney regained consciousness.

Some time later, a nurse woke Sidney. "Hi, I'm Julie, can you hear me?" The nurse repeated herself. "Can you hear me? You're at New York Hospital. You're in the emergency room. You're safe."

Sidney opened an eye, but did not respond.

"Doctor, she's awake," the nurse said.

A tall and slim woman introduced herself. "Hello, I'm Dr. Gray." The woman appeared to be in her late thirties. She jotted down something on the ER report then hung the clipboard on the wall next to the gurney. She turned to the nurse. "Would you leave us for a few minutes?" The nurse left.

Dr. Gray spoke softly to Sidney. "Can you hear me? Do you speak English?"

"Yeah," Sidney said. Instinctively she moved her hand to her right eye, finding the right side of her face masked in bandages. "How am I?"

The doctor smiled warmly but her eyes hinted at concern. "You'll be fine, you are a real mess, though. You have two broken ribs, a gash on your head that required fourteen stitches, and I'm sure you have a concussion. There are multiple bruises all over, particularly your face, thighs, arms and ribs. But most seriously, you have a severe laceration near your right eye.

"I think your eye is okay, but you require surgery to repair the damage to your face. Dr. Benoit is an excellent plastic surgeon; probably New York City's best. He's been called, but he's in surgery right now, and won't be here for another hour or two."

The doctor pulled a stool next to the gurney and sat. She pushed her long bangs behind an ear, enabling Sidney to see her crystal blue eyes. "What's your name?"

"Debbie. Debbie White," Sidney lied.

"Is there anybody we can call for you?"

Sidney realized just how alone she was. "No."

"Can you tell me what happened?" The doctor asked softly.

"I fell," Sidney lied.

"You fell?" The doctor raised an eyebrow, reflecting her disbelief.

"Yeah, I fell. Is there a problem with that?"

"Okay Debbie, you fell. But I should tell you something. If we treat a patient who appears to have been assaulted in any way, we are required by law to report it to the authorities. So, if someone walks in here and they look as if they were mugged or raped, a very specific protocol is followed, evidence is taken, and the information is turned over to the authorities. Do you understand this?"

"Do what you need to do."

The doctor continued to talk to Sidney in a gentle voice. "Look, I know you weren't mugged, we searched your coat to find some identification. The only thing we found was cash, and lots of it. You're certainly not homeless; you walked in here wearing what was left of a very expensive dress along with diamond earrings that probably cost more than my last car.

"It's pretty clear that you were sexually assaulted. We have physical evidence to support this." The doctor studied Sidney for a response, but there was none.

A moment later, Sidney changed the subject by grabbing the doctor's hand. "What's your name?"

"Gray. Charlotte Gray."

"Charlotte, please stitch up my face."

"I'm sorry, I guess I wasn't clear. You need plastic surgery, and even with that, there'll be scarring. Your face would be considerably disfigured without the proper care."

"That's okay. I don't want plastic surgery. Please do it," Sidney said.

"You don't understand," the doctor objected.

"Yes, I do understand, I'll look like Frankenstein. It's my choice, isn't it?" Sidney knew there was no real escape from Michael. She was hoping that he would release her from her imprisonment if she were damaged beyond repair. But if he did not, she wanted to spend the rest of their time together reminding him of what he did to her.

Reluctantly, the doctor agreed to care for her eye. Moments later a nurse came in to help the doctor with the stitches.

After Dr. Gray finished with the sutures, Sidney was taken to another area to accommodate triage evaluations. As the nurse wheeled the gurney down a new hallway she explained, "As you can see we have a lot of construction around here. They're almost finished with the new ER wing. We're so cramped for space. You're going to be resting in one of the new ER examination rooms for a while. Dr. Gray won't release you until we're sure that head injury is okay."

Sidney glanced at a marble plaque that decorated the wall of the new wing, but could not read it. "Could you back up for a minute?" she asked the nurse. The nurse pulled her backwards so she could read the plaque. *"In special thanks to Michael Whitman for making the Whitman Emergency Room a reality."* Sidney started laughing.

"Are you okay, dear?" the nurse asked as she wheeled Sidney into the new room.

"Yes, don't mind me. It must be the pain killer," she lied.

"Now remember, you have a head injury. If you fall asleep, we'll be waking you." The woman showed Sidney an alarm button. "Just press this if you need anything or feel like you're going to get sick. We're just down the hall and we'll be checking on you frequently." As the nurse left, she shut off the overhead light, leaving a night-light illuminating the room.

Sidney remained restless for a couple hours. It was about 11:30 P.M. when she convinced herself she felt better and decided it was time to go home. Sitting up, she carefully moved her legs off the gurney and slid to the floor, only to feel the familiar sharp pain in her ribs. In the dim lighting she noticed a locker next to a sink. Slowly, she walked to the locker and opened it, but her belongings were nowhere to be found. A wave of dizziness rushed over her. At the sink she soaked a hand towel in cold water. She squeezed out most of the excess and raised the cloth to her face. Sidney looked at her reflection in the mirror above the sink. She found her dark silhouette haunting and contemplated whether to turn the light on above the mirror. Mustering up every ounce of strength, she pushed the light switch up.

Initially, the light hurt her eye, until it adjusted to the brightness. She ran her fingers over her facial wounds and studied her reflection until she realized she was trembling. The right side of her face was completely bandaged, but there was no recognition for the left side. Her exposed eye was severely bruised and almost swollen shut. The white of her eye was red from broken blood vessels. Her lips were swollen and cut.

As she searched the mirror for some resemblance, she watched a tear form and drop from the corner of her uncovered eye. *Control*, she lectured herself. She returned her attention to her locker where an article of clothing was folded on the top shelf. Sidney reached up to grab it, but as she stretched, she became light-headed and her world darkened. She steadied herself on the locker door. *I must be moving too quickly.*

A noise from behind startled her. She turned to see who had entered, but her movements were too fast for the injured ribs. Between the excruciating pain and the darkness, Sidney was overwhelmed and collapsed.

When her consciousness returned, she found herself sitting on the floor, knees up, with her head between them. Someone was holding her in place. A woman's voice said reassuringly, "Take deep breaths."

After a few minutes, Sidney's world started coming back, and she realized that Dr. Gray was supporting her on the floor. Sidney rested her head on her knees and raised her arms, to hide her embarrassment. Dr. Gray remained by her side. In silence she gently stroked Sidney's back to comfort her. No matter how hard Sidney tried to remain in control, she could feel herself fall apart. The events of the day had overcome her and she no longer could hold on. The tears came and would not stop.

The doctor stayed on the floor with Sidney as she wept. At one point a nurse walked in, but the doctor motioned for the woman to leave. Sidney finally said, "Sorry. I don't usually cry."

"No apology necessary. Under the circumstances, it wouldn't be healthy if you didn't let it out." The doctor gave her some tissues. "Are you okay?"

Sidney nodded.

"You do know that what happened to you is wrong, don't you?"

"Yes, I know," Sidney answered.

"But you don't want to press charges against him?" Dr. Gray probed.

Sidney ignored the question.

The doctor suspected that Sidney's attacker was someone she knew. "It doesn't matter *who* did this to you, it's still rape, and it's wrong. If you're not willing to go to the authorities, there are some shelters or domestic violence groups that could help you."

Sidney just shook her head. "They're not options for me." She appeared frustrated. "I don't expect you to understand."

"Then help me understand," Dr. Gray suggested.

"Why? What does it matter to you? Trust me, he'll get away with it." *He always gets away with it.* For the first time in Sidney's life she felt beaten and did not know where to turn.

"He shouldn't get away with this," Dr. Gray said calmly.

"He will, though. A week from now the hospital will not even have a record of my visit tonight."

"That's impossible," Dr. Gray said. "There's an extensive trail of paperwork associated with assault victims." She helped Sidney back to her bed, where she spent the rest of the night.

Charlotte Gray felt sorry for the woman who walked out of the hospital the following morning dressed in hospital scrubs. She had paid cash for her services. Later that day, Charlotte copied the Debbie White ER report and placed a copy of it in her office file.

A couple weeks later Charlotte was looking through the main ER files, searching for the Debbie White original report. The report was missing. *My God, she wasn't lying. Who is she?*

Chapter 10

About ten weeks after Sidney's visit to New York Hospital, she and Michael were to attend a dinner party in Michael's honor. For political reasons, Michael had donated an exorbitant amount of money to a worthy cause. Sidney did not know, nor care, which organization benefited from her husband's donation. She was just told to be ready, and she was. Before the event, she was in the hotel rest room tending to last-minute makeup details.

She was just getting used to her new hairstyle. Michael had always loved her long hair. When her hairstylist suggested the short style to compensate for her hair loss from her head injury, she agreed.

As she studied her face in the mirror, she stared at the visible scar near her right eye. She recalled Michael's reaction when he saw her the day she returned from the hospital.

* * *

"You look like a monster; who the hell sewed you up?" Michael asked.

Within a couple of hours she was in the office of the city's leading plastic surgeon, Dr. Timothy Benoit. Dr. Benoit treated Sidney for several weeks, attempting to reduce the facial damage. On her first visit he told Sidney, "You're going to have some scarring, but we'll try to minimize it." Then he asked, "Did someone report the dog to the authorities?"

"Yes, the Doberman is being put to sleep this afternoon," Michael responded.

Sidney wondered if the good doctor believed a dog could have given her a black eye also.

* * *

As Sidney walked into the banquet room, Michael greeted her with a smile. Of course, she returned it, and he escorted her toward the center of the room, where she saw Dr. Benoit. "Timothy, what are you doing here?" she asked.

"I do some work for New York Hospital, besides this gives me an opportunity to show off some of my best work." Timothy smiled as he examined Sidney's face.

Sidney confided in Timothy. "I always get these events mixed up. Why is Michael the guest of honor this evening?"

"New York Hospital's new ER wing," Timothy answered. "Michael donated…well, let's just say he funded the majority of the project."

For an instant Sidney panicked, fearing the hospital staff might recognize her. Then she found comfort in the fact that her appearance had changed so much since that dreadful night.

Michael needed Sidney at his side, and as usual she played her role flawlessly. The two of them stood in the center of the room, and one by one the guests greeted both Michael and Sidney.

About forty-five minutes into the cocktail hour, Sidney noticed Charlotte Gray waiting to greet them. For a moment,

Sidney feared that Dr. Gray would recognize her and her heart quickened. Then she thought, *I did nothing wrong. I'm not going to play victim again.*

As Charlotte waited to speak with Michael, Sidney watched her. Charlotte was more attractive than Sidney remembered. The woman was fashionably dressed and surrounded by what appeared to be admirers.

Charlotte offered Michael a warm handshake and introduced herself. Michael returned the greeting, then introduced the doctor to Sidney. "Charlotte, this is my wife, Sidney Marcum."

Sidney smiled warmly and shook her hand firmly. Charlotte's handshake was equally firm, and although the two women's eyes met, there appeared to be no recognition from Charlotte.

"What do you do for the hospital?" Michael asked.

"I'm an attending physician in the ER. So I can see, firsthand, the difference your donation has made. We really needed the space. You'll never realize just how many people you will help." She thanked the two, then politely excused herself so that others waiting had a chance to greet Michael.

Sidney casually watched Charlotte retreat to another group of people. She never looked back. Sidney was confident she had not been recognized.

Later, Sidney was in the rest room sitting at a vanity mirror touching up her makeup. "Hello, Debbie White." Sidney caught Charlotte's reflection in the mirror, then stood to see if anyone else was in the rest room. "Relax, no one's here."

"I didn't think you recognized me," Sidney said.

"I almost didn't. Then I put two and two together when I heard Timothy brag about what a terrific job he did on your face. That is, after an ER doctor botched up the stitches from a dog bite." Charlotte walked closer to inspect her face. "He did a good job; I'm glad you had it taken care of."

"I didn't have a choice."

"It was the right thing to do." Charlotte seemed to be a little uncomfortable. "I just wanted to see how you're doing." She started to retreat, then turned and asked, "Is there anything I can do to help?"

"You would help me, even though you know who my husband is?" Sidney was curious.

"Yes. I would help."

Sidney hesitated, then she simply said, "No."

"Are you sure?"

Sidney studied Charlotte. "You may be able to help me with something. But I can't talk about it here. Can we meet tomorrow?"

They made arrangements to meet at a coffee shop the following morning. Then Sidney returned to her husband's side wondering if she could trust Charlotte Gray.

Both women arrived at the coffee shop promptly at nine o'clock the following morning. They sat at a booth away from the window. The waitress served Charlotte coffee, and Sidney had decaffeinated tea.

Charlotte finally broke the silence. "How can I help you?"

"I need to have some blood work done, but it's imperative that Michael not find out. I can't go to my own doctor; he'd tell him. I went to a clinic, but they said the results needed to be sent to a doctor." Sidney looked at Charlotte. "I don't know a doctor I can trust."

"You can trust me," Charlotte said.

"Can I? I don't seem to have a lot of choices right now," Sidney admitted.

"You can trust me. What type of tests do you need?"

Sidney hesitated. "A pregnancy test."

Charlotte stared at Sidney before responding. "I see. Why do you think you're pregnant?"

"Well, I'm late, and I also did one of those home pregnancy tests."

"They're usually pretty accurate," Charlotte said.

"I know, but I'm making some pretty big decisions with my life. It would help if I had some confirmation. I don't feel pregnant; I haven't had any morning sickness or put on weight."

"Would you know how far along you are?" Charlotte asked.

Sidney did not answer.

"If you're pregnant, how long ago do you think you conceived?" Sidney remained silent, seeming uneasy. She stared back at Charlotte hoping she would understand.

"But...but that happened close to three months ago."

"It's the only time he's...," Sidney was searching for the words. "It's the only time we've had sex in the last six months."

"I know this is none of my business, but is it possible that there could be another father?"

Sidney became irritated, then considered Charlotte's position. "No, I've been faithful to Michael for over six years now."

"When was your last period?"

"Maybe a couple weeks...before that night. I thought I had my period a couple weeks after that, but it was only for a day. At the time, I thought my period was light because of all the stress. Then I missed my next period. But I've been irregular in the past, so I didn't think much about it." Sidney paused. "Will you help me?"

The doctor took out a notepad and started writing, "I want you to go to the Holland Clinic; I'm writing down the address. Tell them that your name is Sandy Ambrose. They'll have orders for the blood draw and test. Pay them cash. After you leave the clinic, call my pager and leave me the time you had your blood drawn, and I'll follow up and get the results within a couple of hours. Then page me four hours after that. Leave me a phone number where I can call you. Don't call the hospital, okay?"

"Okay," Sidney answered.

"By the way, how old are you? If you're pregnant, they'll conduct a quantitative pregnancy test that should tell us how far along you are. They use your age, along with your hormone levels, to estimate due date."

"I'm almost twenty-eight."

That afternoon, Charlotte had the answers for Sidney. The page came as expected, and Charlotte took a break from the ER, returning to her office for some privacy. She punched in the phone number and a woman answered on the first ring. "Mrs. Ambrose?" Charlotte asked.

"Yes," Sidney answered.

"The results are positive. They also show you're at the end of the first trimester. They estimated 11-12 weeks."

Sidney remained silent, then finally said, "Thank you for your help."

"Wait! What are you going to do?"

"I have a plan, but I still need to finish some loose ends. Please promise you'll never tell anyone what you know."

"I told you, you can trust me. Is there anything else I can help you with?" Charlotte asked.

Sidney hesitated. "I need a good lawyer, someone I can trust."

"I know one, a buddy of mine from college. She has her own practice in the city; she doesn't work for a large law firm. You can trust her. Her name is Jennifer Warren."

A meeting was arranged the following day. Although Jennifer's offices were small, they were tastefully furnished. The secretary led Sidney into Jennifer's office. The attorney appeared to be around Charlotte's age with long auburn hair skirting her shoulders. There was a handsome picture of her with a man and two young children displayed on her desk.

Jennifer rose from her chair and greeted Sidney warmly. "Mrs. Ambrose, I'm Jennifer Warren." The lawyer shook Sidney's hand firmly. "It's nice to meet you. I understand you were referred by an old friend of mine, Charlotte Gray."

Sidney was aware that the secretary had left and closed the door of her office. She confided in the attorney. "Jennifer, my name isn't Ambrose. I'm Sidney Marcum, the wife of Michael Whitman."

Sidney got right down to business. She informed Jennifer that she wanted a quick divorce. She told her about the verbal agreement she had with Michael, about getting divorced after the elections, then explained that he recently retracted his offer. Sidney admitted that it was an abusive marriage, and she feared for her own life. She described her unsuccessful attempts to leave him, only to be dragged back by Michael's men.

Jennifer listened intently to Sidney's story before she responded. "Sidney, I'd love to help you, but I've got to tell you, there's nothing quick about a divorce, particularly when one of the parties disputes the issues."

"I think I know a way to speed up the process, and make Michael more...inclined. But I need to work out some details. Would you prepare the documents, and when I'm ready, we can take him by surprise?"

"What assets do you want from your marriage?" Jennifer asked.

"Nothing, I just want my freedom." Sidney considered further. "I bought a house in New Jersey before we got married. I haven't been there in years. Michael hated the house, so he wouldn't fight me on that...I want the house." She thought further. "I need my car, and some cash, not a lot, maybe $5,000, just enough to get me settled. I have a good job, so I know I'll be okay."

"I wouldn't be doing my job, if I didn't tell you this. You could become a very rich woman walking away from this marriage."

"I don't want his money, I don't want anything from him except my freedom, and what I had before I married him."

Jennifer knew Sidney's willingness to walk away from the Whitman assets could encourage a quick divorce. She wondered what other details needed to be worked out before Sidney was ready to move forward. "How soon do you think you could have your details ironed out?"

"How quickly could the papers be drawn up?" Sidney asked.

"A couple of days."

"Perfect."

Sidney was busy over the next couple of days. She packed a small bag of personal items and hid it in her car trunk. She confiscated the cash she found in the house and made two maximum cash ATM withdrawals. She had less than one thousand dollars, but decided it would be enough.

Her biggest hurdle was finding the key to Michael's home desk. She had searched their home unsuccessfully. Jennifer was ready, and the two had agreed to meet at Whitman Industries the following morning at ten o'clock. It was the evening before their confrontation with Michael, and she was not ready.

The following morning Michael went off to work as usual. After he left, Sidney called Global Records and told David she had the flu. After hanging up, a wave of nausea hit her and she ran to the bathroom and threw up. *Wonderful. Premonition? Nerves? Or first sign of morning sickness?*

Sidney spent the rest of her available time searching for the desk key. Everything was ready, except she desperately needed the incriminating documents. It was 9:30 A.M. and she was running out of time. *The hell with it.* She went to the tool closet where she retrieved a screwdriver and hammer. Within five minutes, the drawer was open and she quickly found the *"Connerly"* file. She grabbed the file and ran out, leaving Michael's office in disarray.

Sidney smiled at Jennifer as she greeted her in the Whitman building lobby.

"Are you ready?" Jennifer asked.

"As ready as I'll ever be." The two entered the elevator. "I may ask you to leave the room at some point, is that a problem?"

Sidney asked her lawyer.

Jennifer studied Sidney before she responded, "I don't like that idea." She hesitated further. "But I'll let you use your discretion."

"Mr. Whitman, your wife is here to see you." Michael was surprised when his secretary paged him on his intercom.

"Tell her she'll have to wait; I have a phone conference scheduled in a couple minutes."

Walking past his secretary, Sidney stormed into his office. "I think your telephone conference can wait, this can't." His secretary followed the two women into his office. Michael nodded at his secretary, who took the sign to leave.

"Michael, this is Jennifer Warren, my attorney."

"Mr. Whitman, I've been retained by your wife to represent her in divorce proceedings."

Michael quickly jumped in. "Well, I wouldn't waste any more of your time. I'll never divorce Sidney."

"Sidney has proven that her marriage is over. She has explained details that reinforce her belief. Just so you understand, she doesn't need your consent. There is enough evidence to start divorce proceedings."

"Then do it, but I guarantee you the biggest battle of your career, counselor." Michael appeared agitated. "This is very unorthodox, visiting my office without an appointment, without my attorney present."

"On the contrary, I believe this visit is warranted. If you fight this battle, Mr. Whitman, I guarantee you the press will destroy whatever political aspirations you have. Oppose this and Sidney will become a very rich woman, at your expense.

"Mr. Whitman, both of you can be winners. Against my advice, Sidney is willing to forfeit her interest in your assets. She wants her house in New Jersey, her car, and $100,000. She is also willing to release a press statement suggesting the end of the marriage was caused by irreconcilable differences. Fight this and I'm sure the truth about your relationship will surface."

Michael appeared to be considering the attorney's words. "I'll take this under advisement with my attorney, Daniel Schwartz. I'm sure you've heard of him. He'll be in touch. Don't ever come to my office uninvited again." He opened the door, gesturing to the women to leave.

Sidney's pulse was beating fast. The thought of leaving without an agreement scared her to death. "Jennifer, I'll be out in a minute."

"No, I think you ought to leave also. I'll see you at home," Michael objected.

Sidney was persistent. She took the doorknob out of Michael's hand, and closed the door. "Michael, I'm going to make this short and sweet. You have something I want, my freedom, and I have something you want."

"Really. What's that?" He laughed.

"The Connerly file."

Michael's smile disappeared. "You're bluffing."

"If you want a fight, Michael, I'll give you the fight of your life. I'll take half of your assets; I'll ruin your political career; and I'll watch the SEC put you in jail. But it doesn't have to be that way."

"Where's the file?" he demanded.

"It's in a lockbox, safe. Sign the divorce papers now, and the file will be returned when the state recognizes the divorce."

"That could take months."

"You have connections, use them." Sidney added, "By the way, should anything happen to me, I've left specific instructions for the file to be forwarded to the SEC."

"How do I know you haven't made copies?"

"You don't." Sidney opened the door, and gestured for Jennifer to come back in. "Jennifer, I believe Michael wants to sign the papers now."

The attorney pulled out a stack of papers and placed them on Michael's desk. She noticed that Michael's color had drained from his face.

Sidney came to the desk. "Where do we sign them?"

"I should have my attorney review them," Michael stated.

"This is not negotiable, Michael," Sidney reminded him.

Jennifer asked Michael's secretary to witness the signatures, then the couple signed the documents. As Jennifer packed her attaché case, Michael turned to Sidney. "The originals will be returned, right? How do I know I can trust you?"

"You don't Michael. I lived with you for six years." She smiled. "I've learned from the best."

As the women left the Whitman headquarters, Sidney paused outside the building. *I'm free.* To celebrate their victory, the two decided to have lunch. Over a glass of wine Jennifer stated, "Whatever you said to him was very effective." For the first time in years, Sidney genuinely smiled.

At the end of the lunch, Sidney placed an envelope in Jennifer's hand. "I need you to keep this in a safe place. Please don't open it, unless something happens to me. If something does happen...well, I've left instructions."

"A will?" the lawyer asked.

"Not really, more like insurance."

The following morning David Jacobs walked into Sidney's office and shut her office door.

"What's up, David?"

"Sidney, I don't know what the hell is going on, but I just got orders to fire you."

"Why?" Sidney was surprised.

"Damn if I know, it happened the same way I got instructions to hire you," David explained.

"What?"

"Before you were hired, instructions came from *upstairs* to hire you, and not to ask questions. I was just told to fire you and not to ask why."

"You mean I wasn't hired because I was the best candidate for the job?" Sidney was shocked.

"No offense Sidney, you weren't the most qualified for the position. But you've certainly proven over and over that you are the best person for the job. I just thought you asked your husband to put in a good word for you with Silverman, and you got the job."

"Who the hell is Silverman?" Sidney asked.

David was surprised at Sidney's reaction. "He's the Senior Vice President of WABS, the network that owns us. Your husband and Silverman have been friends for years. You didn't know?"

Sidney mumbled to herself, "I didn't get this job on my own merit. Touché, Michael."

Two men from security arrived to escort her out. She cleaned out her desk, hugged David and whispered in his ear, "Divorce can be a bitch."

David understood.

* * *

Raindrops on her face and a crash of thunder pulled Sidney's attention back to the present. It took a few minutes before she realized she was sitting on Jones Beach, and had just been to Anastasia's photo shoot. Now, the beach appeared deserted as the heavy rain beat against the warm sand.

Sidney knew she needed to focus her energy on the project at hand, Anastasia's music. She was mad at herself that Anastasia's situation had dragged her into her past. *The hell with her reality. She's put herself there*, she thought to herself as she ran back to the parking lot. *I can't let her circumstances drag skeletons out of my closet.* Another crash of thunder startled her as she approached the parking lot. *Focus on the business; stay the hell out of her life.*

Chapter 11

Sidney quickly learned she needed to play a more active role in Anastasia's music selection. After listening to her most recent work, she became concerned about the quality of her music. The new material was far from commercially satisfying.

Anastasia's music had changed after the success of her second album, *Lovers*. Her third album displayed a slightly harder rock style than her previous work, and her most recent work was more extreme. Sidney also believed her newest work lacked the sincerity of the younger superstar.

"Is it just me, or is her music getting worse each session?" Sidney asked Natalie during a recording session one morning. The two women were perched in the recording booth. A window separated them from Anastasia and the musicians. The music was starting to get on Sidney's nerves. She turned the recording room's volume down, took a couple aspirin from her purse and swallowed them.

"I think we should scrap all this stuff and start from scratch, what do you think?" Sidney asked.

"It's not all bad," Natalie responded. "It's not great, it's just not Anastasia. But you should feel good about all the things you've got going for her. Maybe you should focus on those things, and hope the music falls in place. Oh, by the way, congratulations on renegotiating the Quench Soda deal."

"Thanks, but we're dead if we can't get this new album off the ground. Let's start looking for some new music for her. We can't rely on it falling in place anymore."

Natalie observed the group wrapping it up. "It sounds like they're breaking for lunch." She reached for the control panel and turned the sound off. "You going out for lunch?"

"No, I think I'm going to stay right here and nurse my headache." Sidney lay down on a couch that occupied most of the small booth.

"Can I bring you back something?"

"Sure, surprise me."

Sidney closed her eyes and tried to rest. She had just fallen asleep when the bass vibration from the synthesizer awakened her. *That went by fast; I guess the band is back.* She looked at her watch; it was only 12:15. *They wouldn't be back this early.* Wondering who was in the room, Sidney turned the recording room volume up so she could listen in.

A woman was singing accompanied by background music from a synthesizer. Sidney remained on the couch listening to the singer for a few minutes, then turned up the volume more. The woman was singing a love song. Her music was original and enjoyable compared to what had started Sidney's headache.

The artist followed with another song, a tribute to a friend or perhaps a lover who died of AIDS. Then, a spiritual song followed, envisioning that evil could be abolished if everyone worked together.

As Sidney listened to this woman, she realized what Anastasia's music was missing. *Spirit. This person is singing about things that really matter to her. Anastasia's music lacks spirit, heart and sincerity. But most importantly—passion.*

She listened to the music more intently. *This woman is actually good.* She started to get up to see who was singing when the telephone in the booth rang. She turned off the volume for the recording room then picked up the telephone. "Hello, this is Sidney."

It was her secretary, Michelle. "Hi Sidney. I'm transferring Mr. Robbins, the producer of *The Sammy Lyons Show.*"

"Michelle, would you check the calendar and see who's scheduled to use the recording room now?"

"Anastasia is scheduled."

"They've broken for lunch and someone is in the recording room. Would you check the schedule and let me know who's on for the lunch hour?" As Sidney said it, she realized how lazy she must have sounded to Michelle. All she had to do was get up and look, and the mystery would be over.

"Sure, I'll check into it. I'm transferring Mr. Robbins now."

"Hi Brian, how are you?" Sidney greeted the caller. As usual, she quickly got down to business. She mandated ground rules for Anastasia's appearance on the talk show. Among the directives, the host was not to ask questions about Anastasia's sexual orientation. She also insisted that the talk show host's questions be submitted, in writing, two weeks before Anastasia's appearance. Every precaution was taken to protect Anastasia's business and her own. As Sidney finished her discussion with the producer, she realized the bass vibration had stopped.

"Brian, I have another call coming in, talk with you next month, got to go."

Sidney leapt to look out the window, but nobody was there. "Shit!" She opened the door of the recording booth which exited out to the hallway. She heard a bell and instinctively ran toward the it. But the elevator was in an adjacent hallway, and she was unable to see it until she rounded the corner. She turned the L-shaped hallway just in time to see the elevator doors close. "Wait," she called out, but it was too late and the vehicle descended.

When she returned to the booth, she called Michelle. "Hi, did you happen to find out who's in the recording room?"

"Sidney, there's no one on the schedule today, except Anastasia."

"Thanks for checking." *Why couldn't I have gotten off my ass to look?*

When Natalie returned to the booth with Chinese takeout, Sidney filled in her friend on the mystery vocalist. "Do you have any idea who could have been using the room?" Sidney asked.

"No, the room is usually locked. I guess we must have forgotten. I'll make sure it doesn't happen again, Sid."

"No, you don't understand. This woman is very talented. Her music has...depth. I want to know who it is and if she's represented."

"I'll do some checking around."

It was about 1:30 P.M. when Anastasia and the musicians returned to the recording session and got down to business. Sidney's headache resurfaced, making it difficult to concentrate on Anastasia's work. Her concentration was further handicapped by thoughts of the mysterious vocalist.

It was four o'clock when the group of musicians decided to break for ten minutes. It had been an unproductive session. Sidney paced the small booth as Natalie sat on the couch. "I think I'm going to use this as my opportunity to split," Sidney announced.

The two women continued talking, making plans to meet with Anastasia the following day. Sidney wanted to prepare Anastasia on how to handle sensitive questions from the press.

Anastasia's tour would start soon and so would significant press exposure.

As they spoke, Sidney became aware that one of the musicians was working behind her in the recording room. A vaguely familiar chord was repeated over and over again on the piano. Although Sidney maintained eye contact with Natalie, she found the musician's work to be distracting. Initially, she was unaware why, then as the musician started humming the tune and her heart beat faster. *It's the mystery singer.* Sidney turned around and looked through the glass that separated the recording room from the booth. To her surprise, Anastasia was sitting alone in front of the piano, stroking the keys and humming the tune.

"Natalie, come with me," Sidney directed, and the women entered the recording room.

Sidney silently approached the piano. Anastasia noticed the two approach and stopped playing. She took a drag from a cigarette, then rested it in an ashtray on the piano. "Is there a problem?" Anastasia asked Sidney.

Natalie just watched, oblivious to what was going on, then Sidney spoke and she understood. "You were in here at lunch today?" It was more a statement than a question.

"Yeah, what's the problem?" Anastasia looked annoyed.

"That was you singing?"

"Yeah."

"Who wrote the music and lyrics?"

"I did."

Sidney smiled at Anastasia, then looked back at Natalie. She was beaming. It had been years since Natalie had seen her friend smile so naturally.

"Why haven't you played the songs you worked on during lunch for me?"

"I didn't think you'd be interested in them."

"Why would you think that?"

"I've played them for Steph and Jeffrey. Both thought they were too different from my style."

"They are different," Sidney agreed. "Especially compared to your last album. But what I heard at lunchtime was good. Your new music is…," Sidney was searching for the word, "unattached."

"Jeffrey may have been right not to pursue this music in the past, but I think we'd be fools not to look at the possibility. Besides, many artists change their styles as their careers mature. How many songs have you written with this style?" Sidney asked.

"Oh, I don't know. Maybe a couple dozen."

Sidney smiled, but it quickly vanished from her face. "Have they been copy protected?"

"No. But I did the registered mail deal to establish dates of origin on most of them."

"Good."

The group of musicians had returned from their break and started taking their places in the studio.

Sidney addressed the group. "We're going to wrap it up for the day. Same time on Wednesday." As the group started to disband, Sidney turned to Anastasia. "Not you. When everyone is gone, would you play something for Natalie?"

After the group departed, Anastasia picked up a guitar and sang the ballad about searching for a love. The song described a person's quest for finding a love, knowing that they deserve it and are eager to return the love. Although it was a simple song, her performance was flawless but, more importantly, sincere.

At the end of her performance, both Natalie and Sidney stared at Anastasia, smiling.

Chapter 12

Excited about new possibilities, Sidney wanted to hear all of Anastasia's work. She asked her to perform privately the following morning for Natalie, Nelson and herself. After the performance, her staff became equally excited and agreed they could not ignore this softer rock or adult contemporary music style.

Although obsessed with the new challenge ahead of her, Sidney proceeded cautiously. She spent hours listening to Anastasia's new songs. She selected one, then directed Anastasia and the musicians to be prepared to record the song within one week.

Contemplating the next step, Sidney spent hours listening to Anastasia's recording of "The Light."

Have you ever wondered what the world would be like without evil?
Without negativity? Without darkness?

Can you imagine what it would be like with just the light?
Come with me on this trek of mine as I stroll through the
boundaries of my mind.
Visualize a world where abundance has satisfied hunger.
Can you see the cure?
No more cancer. No more AIDS.
Our medical advances have finally caught up with reality.

Now, travel with me further.
Journey with me to my deepest imagination.
Where evil no longer exists and the light shows us the way.

Can you see the light?
Can you feel it?
There's no evil or negativity or hatred, here.

Now that you've seen it—help me return to reality.
Because here is where we need to be.
We know our calling now.
Help me show that the light is the answer.
And the light is simply love.

Have you tried it?
It's hard, I know.
To confront adversity with love and kindness seems unfitting.
But, have you tried it?
It's infectious.

Try it in your world and your life will change.
Then you'll know just how blessed you are.
Can you imagine if we can get everyone on board?

The answer is simple—manifest love.
It's in our hands and up to you and me.
Stop making excuses and blaming others.

> If everyone sends the light instead of darkness,
> bliss would be reality.

Such a powerful message, Sidney thought. *But how should we proceed?*

Later that week, Sidney called a meeting with Natalie, Nelson and Anastasia to discuss their options on how to continue. To Sidney's surprise, Stephanie showed up for the meeting, but Sidney was in such good spirits, nothing could bother her. The meeting was held in Sidney's office. She went to her bar and pulled out five champagne glasses and a bottle of chilled champagne.

"I wanted everyone here to discuss an idea I have to test Anastasia's new work," Sidney said. She poured the champagne and handed around the glasses. "I've listened to the tape, over and over, and it's good."

"But?" Anastasia asked.

"No buts. The question is—where do we go from here?" Smiling, she raised her glass. "To our next step."

The group sang out, "To our next step," and sipped their champagne.

"I've heard the tape," Stephanie announced, "and it's good, but don't you think you're taking too big a risk releasing such different music? I mean, after all, she's gonna lose her followers."

"It's a risk," Sidney agreed, "that's why we need to act cautiously."

"What do you have in mind?" Nelson asked.

"We have two options. We can go the traditional route or completely unconventional. If we take the traditional path and the market doesn't approve of her new style, we'll lose a whole year. But if we get creative…"

Sidney smiled and held up the recording of "The Light."

"When I first heard Anastasia sing this song, I hadn't a clue who she was, and that created mystery, and mystery is exciting. If we release her music in any salable format, we automatically lose the mystery. But...what if we didn't run to market? What if we released "The Light" to radio stations anonymously? Why not nurture the mystery before we go to market? Why not exploit that excitement?"

Stephanie was losing patience. "I'm sorry, what the hell are you talking about?"

Nelson was starting to understand. "You mean release the song to the radio stations, anonymously, and hope they play it. You cultivate a mystery around the identity of the singer. If the song doesn't take, you don't lose a whole year, nor risk losing her existing market."

"Exactly." Sidney was excited. "First, you blitz the radio stations with the single from a mystery vocalist, but you tell them not to play it until...let's say 8:00 A.M., on a certain day. Her song will be played simultaneously on the majority of the rock, pop, adult contemporary and even R&B stations. Remember? Whitney Houston used a similar technique in the late 80s when Arista introduced one of her songs.

"Right up front, you tell the radio stations about a mystery vocalist contest. We tell the radio stations to play the song and suggest to their listeners to send in a postcard guessing the name of the vocalist, to qualify to win an outrageous prize. We also tell the radio stations they'll get a kickback if the postcards identify their favorite radio station, or perhaps their favorite deejay. So the radio stations will have incentive to play the song."

"Sounds like payola, though," Nelson cautioned.

"Not if the payments are disclosed. I'm not suggesting we do anything unethical. But you're right to be concerned; we'd run it by our lawyer first.

"The contest postcards come to us, which will help us gauge the song's acceptance," Sidney continued.

"Or at least the listeners' interest in the contest," Natalie laughed.

"We can also use *R&R's* top singles chart. Their top 40 songs are based upon airplay, not sales."

"But if you have no sales, where do you make money?" Stephanie asked.

"That's the initial drawback, you don't," Sidney answered. "Not until her new music is released, anyway. But one of the advantages is, if the song is a dud…we bury it and walk away, and nobody finds out who sang it. But it's not a flop; I'll stake my reputation on it. Everything about it is right: It's haunting, it challenges us; and her music style is unique. I think this unconventional introduction could be an effective way of introducing her new style," Sidney smiled.

"Okay, and if there's interest in it?" Anastasia asked.

"You capitalize on it. We don't release your identity until your album is ready to hit the shelves. And we'll unveil you at a live performance at some major event, like the Grammys or MTV Music Awards." Sidney continued smiling as she walked around her office brainstorming.

Anastasia seemed to be getting excited now. "Okay, but can we do this? Are we capable of pulling off something like this?"

"If we can get Global Records behind us, we can," Sidney answered. Then her attention returned to the bottle of champagne and she topped off everybody's glass.

Sidney easily convinced David Jacobs the mystery idea was a great way to proceed. David loved the music and was eager to work out the details to execute her plan. Global was finally committed to Anastasia again.

The mystery vocalist plan was executed without a flaw. Radio stations were quick to support Global Records' efforts, and by the end of summer, postcards started arriving. "The Light" quickly climbed *R&R's* Contemporary Hit Radio chart. Everything suggested that the song was going to be a hit. MPI and Global Records moved forward with the plan to produce Anastasia's new music style.

Anastasia worked endlessly to get the album ready for market. She was also busy making appearances on talk shows. Although Sidney screened most of the questions prior to Anastasia's appearances, she knew there would be times when compromising questions would surface. With Sidney's help, Anastasia became prepared to handle tough questions about her own sexuality and issues involving the *Gazette's* story. Sidney had carefully constructed responses to these sensitive questions that would not reveal their secret nor compromise Anastasia's integrity. Anastasia's responses were polished, demonstrating thought and a mature side that her fans had not seen before.

Anastasia's tour that summer was choppy. In previous years she toured with her crew by bus. But this year her bookings were scattered, so she flew in and out of New York frequently. She worked this to her advantage by frequenting the recording studio between concerts, continuing her work on the new album.

At the end of Sidney and Anastasia's six-month trial period, "The Light" had been number one on the *R&R* chart for five weeks. The mystery vocalist was the talk of the radio stations. Both women agreed to extend their contract an additional year.

By the end of the year, Anastasia had written and recorded her first soda pop jingle for Quench Soda. She also made her first commercial appearance for the soda manufacturer.

Anastasia's efforts were relentless, she never objected to what Sidney asked of her and never complained. She was determined to live up to Sidney's expectations. Early into her representation, Sidney told her, "I'm not a typical personal manager. Most managers are friends with their artists. I'll never be your friend, Anastasia. Never cross me, work hard for me and I'll be your best ally." And she was.

Global Records hosted a lavish Christmas party each year. In the past, Anastasia attended the party with Stephanie, but this year a man escorted her. While Sidney was dancing with her partner, Scott, she smiled and thought *I'm happy to see Anastasia is playing the game well.*

As the song ended, Sidney directed Scott to the side of the dance floor, near David Jacobs and his wife. She greeted both of them, then asked if she could talk with David for a minute. Scott naturally acquainted himself with Mrs. Jacobs, giving Sidney the opportunity to speak with David.

"David, I know what I want for Christmas," Sidney hinted. How much is this going to cost me?"

"I would say a few favors."

"What do you want?"

"The Super Bowl."

"Is that all? I think I can arrange that. How many tickets?"

"No, David. I want Anastasia to perform at half-time."

"Look, I know that Anastasia's working really hard to turn things around, but I just don't think the timing is right. We'll see next year."

"You're right, they probably wouldn't book her. But they might book the mystery vocalist."

David stared at Sidney. "Wouldn't that be good business?" He appeared deep in thought, then shook his head. "I think that's beyond me, Sidney. I don't think I could pull it off. I'm sure they already have someone under contract to do the show."

"You told me once that Global is a subsidiary of WABS. Did you know that WABS is airing the game? I bet you they would be willing to book the mystery vocalist if they knew Global had the recording contract with the artist, and an album ready to be released two days after the Super Bowl."

"You have an interesting way of getting your point across. Assuming I got it, you're sure the album will be ready for release?"

"Consider it done. Do we have a deal?"

"I'll do my best."

"Just remember, when you talk with WABS, leave my name out of it," Sidney reminded him.

Both David and Sidney returned to their partners, but their thoughts were with the challenge at hand.

It was New Year's Eve when David called Sidney at her office. "Merry Christmas. You got it."

"I got what?" She smiled.

"The Super Bowl," he answered proudly.

"Did they ask who the mystery vocalist was?"

"Sure, but don't worry, I didn't tell them. We've been successful keeping our secret so far. I don't see any reason to set us up for a leak now."

"Thank you. By the way, Christmas was last week."

"What do I know? I'm Jewish," he laughed. "How close are we to wrapping up?"

"Let's plan on getting together on Monday; we can't afford to fall on our faces now."

Sidney picked up the phone to call Anastasia, then hesitated. *This news is too good to share over the phone.* She glanced at her watch. Two o'clock on New Year's Eve. *I'll surprise her with the news personally.* Before leaving her office, she called Scott to let him know her plans, and told him she would meet up with him at the shore later.

Sidney had been to Anastasia's home a couple of times. Although she was going out of her way a little, she decided it would be worth it. At the security gate, a voice asked, "Who's there?"

Sidney looked into the video camera, "Sidney Marcum to see Anastasia." The gate opened and she drove up to the stately house.

She was not out of her car when the front door opened and Anastasia walked outside. She was dressed in jeans and a sweatshirt, and was barefoot. "Is something wrong?" Anastasia asked.

Sidney walked casually to the grand entrance, handing her a bottle of wine. "Happy New Year. May I come in for a minute?"

"Sure."

Stephanie soon joined the two in the foyer. "What are you doing here?"

"Can't I come just to wish the two of you a Happy New Year?"

"That would be uncharacteristic of you," Anastasia answered.

Sidney smiled. "You're right, it would. I got some news and I wanted to share it with you."

"Well, what is it?" Stephanie asked impatiently.

"We have a plan and date for your unveiling. I thought you might want to know."

"Damn right we want to know," Stephanie said. Stephanie had been getting on Anastasia's case for the last month. She kept saying to Anastasia, "This mystery stuff may be fun, but when it comes down to it—you haven't sold any records."

"When and where?" Anastasia asked.

"Super Bowl Sunday, half-time, on the fifty-yard line."

Both Anastasia and Stephanie shrieked with excitement. They danced around the foyer like two children, completing their dance with an embrace. Then Anastasia turned to Sidney and hugged her affectionately. "Thank you," she whispered in Sidney's ear.

Sidney left the two of them to celebrate, and headed toward the shore to ring in the New Year with Scott.

Chapter 13

The weeks that followed went by too quickly. Everyone was involved with last-minute details for the release of *The Light*. Sidney spent most of her time involved in the production of the Super Bowl half-time show. She was happy to see the generous budget Global set up for the show along with the liberal advertising allowance to publicize it.

On the Friday before the Super Bowl, Global Records shipped the unmarked corrugated boxes to record distributors all over the country. Orders for the album *The Light* had been placed weeks earlier. Timing was perfect. *The Light* would reach the distributors Tuesday morning, two days after Anastasia's unveiling.

Pasadena's Rose Bowl was bulging with 98,374 football watchers. Garth Brooks and Vanessa Williams sang the National Anthem before the Dallas Cowboys and Buffalo Bills took the field.

Anastasia was pacing in her dressing room, waiting for half-time to approach. Her heart was pounding so hard she was beginning to feel weak.

"Relax," Stephanie told her as she took a drag from her cigarette. But Anastasia could not relax and continued to pace.

Natalie stuck her head in the door. "They're down to the two-minute warning. I guess that means you'll be on in about twenty minutes." She laughed at her own humor, then closed the door.

Five minutes later, Sidney knocked on the dressing room door. "How are...," but she did not finish her question. It was obvious that Anastasia was quite nervous; she looked green. Sidney went to Stephanie. "Steph, would you be able to give me a couple minutes alone with Anastasia?"

Stephanie considered saying no, but realized it would be best all around if she left quietly.

Anastasia was still pacing. Sidney took Anastasia's hand and directed her to sit in a chair. The entertainer had a distant stare. Kneeling, Sidney tried to make eye contact with her, knowing she had less than ten minutes to snap her out of it.

"Anastasia talk to me," she said calmly. "Anastasia—"

"I've never been this scared in my life," Anastasia said faintly. "It's not just the hundred thousand people out there. How many are watching on TV?"

"This is a *very* large audience," Sidney agreed.

"I've never performed to a crowd this large with so much at stake. I keep wondering what if I freeze? What if Steph's right and this is too much of a change? Am I going to lose my existing fans?"

Sidney knew she had to work fast. "Anastasia, I'm not going to lie to you. This is the biggest show of your career. As far as your fans are concerned, for every one you'll lose, you'll gain two. Anastasia, you're going out there and you're going to blow them all away." She paused, then continued, "I know this, do you know how?"

Anastasia nodded distantly.

"Because you're the best, Anastasia. You're the most talented performer of your generation. The last thing you're going to do is fall apart out there. This is your business, and you're damn good at it. You've got to trust me, Anastasia. I know this business better than most. And I'm also damn good at what I do. What we're doing is right; I have absolutely no doubt. This is going to put you back on top."

Natalie knocked on the door and entered, but she could see that the two women were not finished. She whispered to Sidney, "The players are off the field. They're setting up the stage. Will she be ready in five?"

"I'll let you—"

"Yeah, I'll be ready." Anastasia stood up. "How do I look?" she asked Sidney.

Anastasia was conservatively dressed in a white suit. It was elegant, stylish and feminine. She wore fashionable pumps with moderate heels. Sidney wanted to promote an image of seriousness to be consistent with "The Light" theme.

"You look great," she handed Anastasia a black cloak. "And you're going to be great; you know that don't you?"

"Yes. I do," Anastasia answered as she swung the cape around her shoulders and walked out of the dressing room.

The fifty-yard line was transformed into a state-of-the-art stage and a voice came over the speaker system. "May I have your

113

attention please?" The plea was repeated over and over again, and gradually the roar of the crowd subsided as their attention was drawn to the replay projection screen where the announcer addressed the audience.

"For almost five months now, we've listened to 'The Light.' It has remained the number-one song for almost three months. Up until now the artist has remained anonymous. But tonight, for the first time ever, our mystery singer will appear in person to perform 'The Light.'"

The applause from the stadium was thunderous, and remained steady for close to three minutes before it fell to a level that would enable the show to continue. Liquid nitrogen was released around the base of the stage, forming a large cloud that encompassed the stage. Then the chemical formed a cloudy hallway running from the stage to the sideline.

The music began, and from the sideline a figure entered the cloud, walking toward the stage. A camera followed the ghostly figure through the cloud as she sang the first verse, broadcasting her performance on the replay monitors. When she ascended the stage, the audience could see she was wearing a black hooded cloak and sunglasses, obscuring her face.

The lyrics were synchronized perfectly. Her performance was truly moving and the audience seemed reflective. Anastasia could feel her excitement build, and her confidence grew as she heard the audience respond to her performance.

When the song came to the end, Anastasia's attire was still concealing her face. The audience cheered with satisfaction and Anastasia bowed appreciatively. Without missing a beat the music started again, but this time playing one of Anastasia's most successful songs, "I'm Here to Stay." She removed the hood and flung her cloak, then her sunglasses, off the stage, revealing her identity to the crowd as she began to sing. Anastasia felt goose bumps and the hair rise on her back as the audience responded with a thunderous show of approval.

While Anastasia performed the choreographed number,

a stagehand placed her guitar and a stool on the stage. When she finished the number, Anastasia moved the stool and guitar to center stage. The cameras caught her flawless smile as she began strumming the initial chords of one of her new songs, a love ballad titled "I Deserve." As she finished the lyrics of the song, she was aware that the crowd was standing and cheering. She remained sitting and smiled to the crowd as she finished the final chords with her guitar, then she stood and bowed to the audience.

It was then that Anastasia knew she was back. The crowd remained standing, cheering in satisfaction. She smiled and blew a kiss to the camera, then waved to her audience as she was escorted off the stage to the sidelines, where security attempted to control a large crowd. Anastasia could feel the tears form as she made her way through the crowd.

In the dressing room, Natalie and Stephanie hugged and congratulated Anastasia. Natalie handed her a tissue.

"Where's Sidney?" Anastasia searched the dressing room.

"She's setting up a press interview, and we have five minutes to get you ready." Natalie pulled the chair out in front of her dressing mirror, and Andrea, the make-up person, quickly tidied up her hair and makeup. A few minutes later, the door opened and Sidney walked in. She smiled and said, "Congratulations."

Anastasia embraced her. "Thank you for believing in me," she whispered. She quickly backed away, but Sidney saw the tears in Anastasia's eyes.

"Are you okay to do this?"

"Yeah." She reached for a tissue.

"They've been prepared with a bunch of ground rules. Basically they can only ask questions about your performance tonight, nothing else. Do you understand?"

Anastasia nodded.

They quickly went over some signals to each other, in case Anastasia felt uncomfortable or Sidney wanted to abort the interview.

He watched the half-time show from his home projection television, and was impressed with Anastasia's performance. *So far, it's better than the game*, he thought as he turned the volume up to hear the interview. Clearly, the press was also impressed and supportive of the artist's new style.

"Anastasia, how did you do this? How did you pull all this off?" a persistent reporter asked.

"I didn't do this. This was a team effort. We did it. And we wouldn't be here without the head of our team," Anastasia stated.

"And who is that?" the reporter asked.

"Sidney Marcum," Anastasia answered. Then she reached out of the camera's view to where Sidney was standing and hugged her. Sidney was caught off guard and blushed as the cameras caught the embrace.

When Anastasia's interview was finished, he flicked off the TV with the remote. *Interesting*, the man thought. Then he reached for the telephone handset, and pressed in the numbers.

"This betta be good, the game's not over," a man answered.

"This is Michael Whitman. Is this Joey?"

"Yes, Mr. Whitman. How can I help you?"

"Is this a good time to talk? I have a job for you."

"For you, any time is a good time, Mr. Whitman."

Chapter 14

Four songs from *The Light* quickly climbed the charts in the months that followed. The album went platinum in no time. Sidney worked overtime to effectively manage Anastasia's schedule. Contrary to the previous year, requests for product endorsements, concerts, and special appearances cluttered Anastasia's calendar.

Sidney also initiated discussions with a movie producer to cast Anastasia as the leading actress in an upcoming movie. The producer, Timothy Clausin, was searching for an actress with singing experience to effectively play the role. Brett Pillar, the hottest actor on the screen, had already been cast as the leading man. It was a long shot but Sidney left no stone unturned.

In April, Anastasia popped into Sidney's office unexpectedly.

"What's up?" Sidney asked.

"We need to talk about my tour this summer."

"What about it?"

"We're scheduled to perform in Denver, I think in August. I want to boycott Colorado.""

"You want to what?"

"You know—boycott Colorado. A lot of entertainers are boycotting the state. Streisand, Liza, Madonna, Whoopi, to name a few."

"Since when have you become political?"

"What's happening in Colorado is just wrong, Sidney."

Sidney had become familiar with the boycott on Colorado. Apparently a gay activist group had promoted boycotting the state to oppose the recent adoption of Amendment 2 to the Colorado Constitution. The amendment was put on the ballot after Colorado for Family Values, a Christian fundamentalist group, lobbied hard for the measure. It surprised the nation when the amendment won in the election the previous November. The effect of the amendment legalized discrimination of gays and lesbians. Immediately following the election a lawsuit was filed alleging that Amendment 2 was unconstitutional. Denver District Court issued an injunction against the amendment, stopping it from being enforced, until arguments were heard. Trial was set later that year.

"Look Anastasia, we've had the commitment in Denver since last year and—"

"Fuck the commitment, Sidney. This is important to me," Anastasia interrupted.

"Would you let me finish?" Sidney was irritated. "Let me look into this boycott and Amendment 2. I've heard mixed reviews about whether the boycott truly helps...," Sidney appeared to be searching for the words, "whether it helps your cause. Don't worry about it, and whatever you do, don't say anything to the press. Okay?" Sidney searched for a response. "Okay?"

"Okay," Anastasia reluctantly agreed.

"Is there anything else?"

"Well, actually yes. I've been thinking about a way to show everyone how grateful I am for what MPI has done for me. In May it'll be one year with your company. I want to do something special to show my appreciation and say thanks."

"You just did." Sidney returned her attention to the papers on her desk.

"Why do you have to make this so difficult?" Anastasia's voice rose.

"Excuse me?"

"I'm trying to talk to you and you're blowing me off."

Sidney rested her pen on her desk, giving Anastasia her undivided attention. "What do you have in mind?"

"I'd like to take everyone out for a night on the town. I want to treat everyone at MPI along with his or her partners. I'll rent a limo or two and make sure everyone has transportation, and gets home safe." Anastasia looked for a response. "Well?"

"This sounds important to you. Just do it."

Anastasia smiled at her small victory. "Do I ask Michelle to check your calendar, or do you keep your own calendar?"

"Don't worry about my calendar, set it up. If I can make it—great, otherwise I'm not going to lose sleep over it."

Anastasia was pissed. "You know Sidney, sometimes you're just a plain asshole." She turned and stormed out of the office.

A couple weeks later Natalie approached Sidney at her office. "I understand you've upset Anastasia."

"So what else is new?"

Natalie knew how to handle her friend. "Sidney, this party is Anastasia's way of trying to be nice. She wants to show her appreciation to everyone, but mostly you. You're not making it easy for her."

"She doesn't need to thank me; I'm just doing my job.

Remember, she hired us?"

"Why do you fight these social events so much? Are you afraid you might have a good time and enjoy yourself? Or is it because you don't want to get to know the people you work with? Or God forbid, perhaps you're afraid they'll get to know you."

Sidney was annoyed. "Are you through?"

"No." Natalie knew she was pushing it. "This is important to Anastasia. Go to this party, if not for her, for yourself." She walked around Sidney's desk and rested her hands on her shoulders. She leaned over and whispered in her ear, "Sid, I love you...it's time to get on with your life." Sidney did not see the tears in Natalie's eyes as she kissed the top of her head, then left the office.

Anastasia and Stephanie seemed to be in a feisty mood when Natalie arrived at the village bar and grill. Before Natalie had a chance to sit, Anastasia asked, "Well, did you talk with her?"

Natalie looked toward a waitress as she approached their table. "What can I get you, honey?"

"Draft beer, please," Natalie answered. She sat between Stephanie and Anastasia.

"You two ready for another round?" the waitress asked Stephanie and Anastasia.

"Sure," Stephanie answered.

"Since when have you been hanging out here?" Natalie asked as she checked out the pub.

"It's convenient to Steph's apartment. We occasionally visit when we stay in the city," Anastasia answered.

"So, did you talk to HB?" Stephanie asked.

"HB?" Natalie asked.

"You know—homophobic bitch," said Stephanie.

Anastasia poked her. "Stephanie, relax." Then she turned her attention back to Natalie. "Did you talk with Sidney?"

Natalie pulled out her cigarettes and lit one. "I saw her."

"Is she coming?" Anastasia asked.

"I don't know. Maybe…maybe not."

"What is wrong with that woman?" Anastasia asked.

"The woman's homophobic, that's what's wrong," Stephanie said.

Natalie just shook her head at Stephanie's speculation.

"No, she's a bitch, but I don't think she's homophobic," Anastasia said. "Natalie…is it true about Whitman?"

Natalie was curious. "What about Whitman?"

"Michelle told us that Sidney was married to the man," Stephanie answered.

"Really, what else did she tell you?" Natalie wondered what Michelle knew. She had only been with MPI three years.

"Sidney lives with a younger man," Anastasia said. It sounded more like a question than a statement.

"And her heart was broken when a guy named…Chuck or Charlie dumped her," Stephanie added.

"Why the sudden interest in Sidney?" Natalie asked.

"Sidney knows everything about us and we know squat about her," Stephanie started.

"We know you've known her longer than anyone at MPI, and she dates a high school principal named Scott," Anastasia continued.

"Even though she's shacking up with Mr. Jail Bait," Stephanie said.

"And she lives in New Jersey," Anastasia finished. "So, tell us. Are we right?"

Natalie saw a curiosity in Anastasia's eyes that she had not seen before. "Okay, I'll clear up a few points, but when I'm finished, that's it. No more gossip. Do I make myself clear?"

The two nodded.

"Sidney *was* married to Michael Whitman shortly after she got her MBA. They were married about five years, and from what I understand, they divorced about…twelve years ago."

"From everything I've heard about Whitman, he's such a great guy. What did he see in Sidney?" Stephanie pried.

"Well, let's just say people aren't always what they seem." Natalie was getting frustrated with Stephanie. "Sidney's not the enemy here; she hasn't done anything to you. Why do you always have to slam her so much?"

"She hasn't done anything? What about turning our lives upside down?" Stephanie seemed bitter. "I don't live with my lover anymore. I can't travel with her. If we go out together, I can't even sit next to her. We don't do the bars anymore. Our life sucks and it's all because of that—"

"Leave it alone, Steph. I've told you, those were my choices. We did what we had to do." Anastasia was getting irritated.

The waitress finally returned and served their drinks.

"What about the rest?" Anastasia asked.

"The rest?"

"The younger man and the man that broke her heart," Anastasia continued.

"Remember, this goes no further." Natalie looked for a response from the two before she continued. "She does live with a guy who happens to be younger. His name is…Justin. And yes, Charlie did leave her and broke her heart. And that's it. I've said enough." Natalie was eager to change the subject. "So did you set up an appointment with Celeste?"

"Yeah, I have one tomorrow evening," Anastasia answered.

"Who's Celeste?" Stephanie pried.

"She's a psychic. Natalie has used her for years," Anastasia answered. "I haven't had a reading in a couple of years. I thought it was time."

"Are you going to start with that hocus-pocus stuff again?"

"Stephanie, I just want a reading."

The scent of freshly burned incense permeated the candlelit room. As Anastasia sat across from Celeste a chill ran up her spine. The older woman wore an indigo sweater with extravagant

122

jewelry. Her long hair hung naturally, encompassing her face, making it difficult for Anastasia to see her eyes. Celeste placed a tape in her tape recorder.

"Before we begin, is there any area you want me to focus on?" she asked.

"My career," Anastasia answered.

The woman closed her eyes and remained silent for what seemed forever. She opened them and pulled her hair back, permitting Anastasia to make eye contact for the first time. Celeste reached over to the tape recorder and pressed "record." Smiling warmly she said, "You don't need a psychic to tell you that you've done well with your career." The woman stared back at Anastasia. "But…you are at your peak."

"So it's downhill from here?"

"I wouldn't put it that way. But I do see a change for you in one…no, about two years. It affects your career. But I feel this is a positive change for you personally and even spiritually. Perhaps your priorities just change."

"Wonderful," Anastasia responded sarcastically.

"There is something else about this change." Celeste closed her eyes and appeared to be concentrating. "You don't like being judged."

"Are you asking or are you telling me?"

"You are very…what's the word? Reserved? You put up a wall or perhaps a front. Yes, that's what it is—a front. Do you know what I mean?"

"No," Anastasia lied.

"You hide yourself from people. You don't let them see the real you but a fake you. Do I need to give you an example?"

"No."

"This all goes back to a past life you had in ancient Egypt. I don't know if you play on the game board of past lives, so you can take this or leave it. Have you done any past life work?"

Anastasia shook her head. "No."

"Can I share what I saw in your past life?"

Anastasia nodded.

"It was in ancient Egypt. You were a servant or a slave to a high-ranking politician. You were considered an untouchable because of your social class and judged for what you were. During this lifetime you were a man and fell in love with your master's wife.

"In this relationship you found true love. But the two of you could not be together, except for exchanging brief periods of affection. There were complications in her life that did not permit her to abandon what she had to be with you. I believe it was…children. Yes. Two children. The two of you planned to be with each other when the children grew, but…it was too late. Somehow her husband found out that she was unfaithful. He punished her for being with an untouchable, by imprisoning her.

"She eventually died, alone in prison, before the two of you could be with each other again."

"And I'm supposed to learn something from this?"

"Yes. Otherwise I wouldn't have shared this with you."

Chapter 15

Anastasia's celebration event was scheduled for the Thursday before Memorial Day weekend. She remained secretive about her plans. Arrangements were made for two limos to pick up the employees and their partners that Thursday evening at MPI.

That morning Natalie entered Sidney's office. "And how are you today? It is a lovely day, isn't it?" She was beaming.

"Okay Natalie, what's going on? Are you okay?" Sidney asked.

"Wonderful, absolutely wonderful," she smiled. "Sidney, I made a decision last night about my relationship with Karen. Not to change the subject, but did you know that we've been seeing each other for over a year now?"

"Should I congratulate you?" Sidney asked, trying not to sound too sarcastic. "Now what did you decide last night?"

Natalie sat in the chair in front of Sidney's desk, forcing eye contact. "I decided to take our relationship to the next level."

"You guys moving in together?"

"Hell no. I want her to meet my family. So I'm going to bring her tonight, to meet you."

"I should have known you were up to something. Is that thing tonight?"

"Yes, like I told you on Monday, Tuesday and Wednesday. It's tonight. You're not going to be a brat now, are you?"

"You'll still love me, won't you?"

"Don't ask stupid questions." Natalie was losing patience. "Are you taking Scott?"

"No, he has another commitment."

"Would you please do this for me?"

"To meet Karen?"

"No, because it's important to Anastasia and it would mean a lot to me."

Sidney remained silent, then confided in Natalie, "I've heard about the limo parties. Do you think you could find out where dinner is? I'll join you there. Then I'll be able to leave when I feel like it."

"And I'm supposed to trust you?"

"Natalie, you have my word, I will join the party for dinner. Have I ever lied to you?"

Natalie left the room and returned in a half-hour. "That was harder than I thought it would be. You promise you'll join the party for dinner and dancing?"

"No, that wasn't the deal. It was dinner," Sidney said flatly.

"But I just spent a half-hour negotiating with Anastasia to get this information. Dinner, after-dinner drinks, and you'll at least consider a dance. You can drive yourself there and home."

"Deal." Both women shook hands, then laughed.

Natalie and Sidney were surprised to learn the restaurant was in New Hope, Pennsylvania. Apparently, Anastasia thought getting away from the city would be fun. The limousines were to be stocked with drinks and appetizers for their two-hour trek to the restaurant. Apparently the restaurant was closed to the public to cater the private party.

Sidney looked at Natalie. "You're not going to let me out of this, are you?"

"Absolutely not. And I've been threatened with death if we tell anybody about her plans."

"You can trust me." Sidney looked at her watch. "What time is dinner?"

"Eight sharp."

"I think I'll leave work early. Justin is going away for the weekend. I'll try to spend some time with him before he leaves. I'll meet you at the restaurant."

Sidney arrived at her shore house about three o'clock that afternoon, but Justin was nowhere to be found. She did find Lynette, her domestic helper, in the kitchen. She appeared to be preparing dinner. "Hi Lynette."

"Hello Ms. Marcum, you're home early."

"Yeah, I was hoping to spend some time with Justin. Do you know where he is?"

"He's down by the pool," she answered.

"Thanks." Sidney opened the rear patio door that overlooked a below-ground pool. She walked down the path to the pool level. The property extended past the pool and pool house and dropped another level to a private beach area on the Manasquan River.

As she walked around the pool, she could see Justin's muscular back in a chair. He appeared to be fixing one of the crab traps. "Want to go out for a sail?" Sidney asked.

Justin smiled warmly at the sight of Sidney. "Hey Mom, what are you doing home early?" The eleven-year old put down the crab trap and stood almost as tall as Sidney, to embrace her.

"I have a business dinner tonight. I thought I'd come home early and play this afternoon. How was school today?"

"Good, but I can't wait for vacation."

The two spent a couple of hours together, cruising the river in their 27-foot Hunter sailboat.

Later, as Justin finished his dinner, Sidney asked, "What are your plans for the weekend? Have you packed?"

"Dad's sending the car for me tomorrow, after school. I think we're going to the East Hampton house. I'll be back on Monday, probably late. I'll pack after dinner."

"Lynette is staying tonight. I'm sure it's going to be a late evening. But I'll see you in the morning before you leave for school."

Sidney was showered and dressed when Justin knocked on her door and came into her room. He studied Sidney's attire. "Where are you going tonight?"

"To a dinner party at a restaurant. Anastasia's hosting it."

"When are you going to introduce me to her?" Justin asked, then entered her large walk-in closet.

"What are you doing?"

"Mom, you're dressed like you're going to a staff meeting." He inspected the clothes in her closet, then selected something that Sidney had not worn in years. "Try these on," he instructed her.

Sidney started to object, but knew it would be useless; she could never argue with her son. He left her alone and closed the closet door. She put on the black pants, then the white silk blouse. Such a simple outfit, but even Sidney admitted the combination was striking. She tried to recall the last time she wore them together. Then she remembered, *It was with Charlie.*

"That's better." Justin showed his approval as he opened the closet door again. "Try these," he instructed, then handed Sidney a pair of Chanel shoes, a scarf and belt.

"Is this your way of telling me you want to be a fashion designer or something?"

Justin laughed. "No. I just want you to go out and have fun, Mom."

As Sidney drove west toward the Delaware River, she thought about Justin's comment, *"I just want you to go out and have fun, Mom."* He was such a great kid. It had been a long time since she went out for anything other than work. The thought unnerved her; then she reminded herself that she was going out for business, and she felt better.

She crossed the river, and traveled north on a winding road into the little town of New Hope. *New Hope*, she thought. *What a great name.* Sidney followed the directions to the restaurant, but almost missed it. Two limos in the parking lot of the large house signaled she was in the right place. She glanced at her watch; it was 8:10 P.M. A sign for the restaurant entrance directed her to the front of the building.

The entrance led into a small piano bar. Anastasia was sitting at a piano and everyone appeared to be enjoying themselves in a sing-along. Natalie saw Sidney enter, and was the first to greet her. "You made it," she said with a warm smile.

"Did you have any doubt?"

Are you serious? You...you look great." Natalie grabbed Sidney's hand and pulled her toward the bar. "What do you want to drink?"

"Chivas and water," Sidney said to an attractive woman tending the bar.

The bartender quickly returned with her drink. "Can I get you anything else?"

"No, thanks." Sidney turned her attention to Natalie. "How was the limo drive?"

"I know you don't want to hear this, but it actually was great. Everyone enjoyed it. Do you want to meet Karen?"

"Sure, where is she?"

"She's at the piano with the group; let me see if I can get her."
A few minutes later, Natalie returned holding a woman's hand.
"Sidney, this is Karen. Karen, this is Sidney."

Sidney shook the hand of an attractive white woman in her
mid-to-late forties.

Karen smiled. "It's nice to finally meet you, I've heard so
much—"

"Don't worry, I only told her about your good traits," Natalie
interrupted.

Anastasia had finished a song on the piano and noticed that
Sidney had arrived. She hugged Sidney, taking her by surprise.
"Thank you for coming."

The remainder of the group greeted Sidney, then retreated
to the dining room. Two large round tables were set for the
party. The dining room decor and atmosphere were perfect. The
windows in the room were lined with lace curtains. Two windows
viewed outside, while two looked into a dark room that appeared
not in use. Sidney took a seat next to Natalie and Karen, then
Anastasia followed and sat next to Sidney. Nelson and Michelle
also sat at Anastasia's table, along with their spouses. Soon
everyone was seated, and Sidney was surprised that Stephanie
was sitting at the other table with the rest of the party.

The woman who had tended the bar came into the dining
room with wine menus. She asked Anastasia if she wanted to
order wine for the group. To Sidney's surprise, Anastasia turned
to Sidney. "Would you order the wine?"

The woman handed Sidney the wine menu. Sidney reviewed
it, then selected a chardonnay and a cabernet sauvignon for each
table, to start. As Sidney handed back the wine menu, the woman
clutched the menu where Sidney held it, holding Sidney's hand
along with the menu. The woman's touch caught Sidney by
surprise. The waitress smiled at Sidney before she released her
grip.

"Hello, my name is Carol and I will be your server this
evening," the woman introduced herself to the two tables. "I

know this is a special evening for you, so if there is anything we can do to help make your evening more enjoyable…," she turned and smiled at Sidney, "please ask."

"Ms. Carol seems to have a little crush on you, Sidney," Natalie whispered.

"A little?" Anastasia joined in.

"Somebody must have told her I'm picking up the tab." Sidney blew it off.

To Anastasia and Natalie, however, it was obvious the waitress was interested in Sidney. She remained attentive to Sidney's needs throughout the evening. Every time Sidney's wineglass was about half-full, the waitress quickly refilled the glass.

After the appetizers were served, Anastasia stood away from the table and raised her wineglass. "I want to take this opportunity to spoil the fun and say something serious." She quickly got the group's attention. "This has been such a wonderful year for me. And I know it's because of this group that I've been able to get back on my feet." Anastasia raised her glass. "To a great group. Thank you for everything, and I'm looking forward to another great year."

Sidney found the dinner enjoyable. The food was excellent, and the company was surprisingly fun. Halfway through the dinner, she realized she could not remember the last time she laughed so much. At some point, lights began flickering through the lace curtains that looked into what appeared to be a dance floor. Sidney could feel soft vibrations from the music, but it was not objectionable.

As the group finished dessert, Anastasia announced that after-dinner drinks would be served in another bar at the establishment. The group left the dining room and moved to a bar area that joined the disco. Like all bars, the club was dark and loud. A crowd appeared to be forming quickly.

Sidney sat in a love seat and was surprised when Natalie sat next to her. "There's something I need to talk with you about."

"What's that?"

"We're in a gay bar."

Sidney laughed, then realized her friend was serious. She looked around but could not tell by the gathering of people in the bar. Sidney reached for her liqueur and took a sip. She carefully replaced the glass and picked up Natalie's pack of cigarettes. Removing one, she asked, "May I?" But she didn't give Natalie a chance to answer. The smoke she inhaled felt good. *Why did I ever quit?* she wondered. *Oh yeah, I got pregnant.*

Sidney observed the group of people from her company. *They seem to be enjoying themselves.* Anastasia was entertaining them. She now wore a baseball cap and her hair was pulled back. Stephanie remained at a bar, talking to a female bartender.

"The rest of the group, do they know?" Sidney asked Natalie.

"They do. It was explained to them in the limo. They're okay about it, or at least they appear to be. After all, we're here for a private party. Anastasia told them that as soon as anyone feels uncomfortable, the limos will return to the city."

"Since when do you smoke?" Anastasia suddenly asked as she sat across from Sidney. "Did Nat tell you? We're in a gay bar."

"I don't smoke, and yes I know." Sidney continued to smoke the cigarette.

Sidney and Natalie talked about work, while Karen danced with Nelson and his wife. Natalie knew that Sidney would try to leave as soon as her drink was finished. When the deejay started playing decent dance music, the rest of their group visited the dance floor, except for Natalie and Sidney.

Natalie turned to Sidney. "Come on, let's dance."

Sidney remained seated. "I don't think so, Nat. I think I'm going to be taking off."

But Natalie insisted, she took Sidney's hand and led her to the dance floor.

Once on the dance floor, Sidney felt less tense. *Relax,* she lectured herself. *So far, I've had some harmless fun. Maybe Nat's right, a couple dances, then I'll head home.* She danced with Natalie, then Nelson, and even ordered another drink.

Carol, the waitress from the restaurant, walked over to Sidney. "My turn." When Sidney hesitated, the woman whispered, "I'm just asking for a dance, nothing else."

Sidney sipped her new drink, "Okay!" But as soon as she said it she started second guessing herself.

Shortly into their dance, Carol started small talk with Sidney. But her chatting became more personal. "I love those earrings. They're so pretty. They go well with your eyes." She moved closer to Sidney, "You have beautiful eyes."

Sidney avoided Carol's eyes and backed away with a dance move. When Carol closed the gap between them again, she turned her back to Carol, not anticipating the move was an invitation for Carol. Within seconds, the Sidney felt hands on her waist. With the song coming to an end, she turned, nodded at Carol and started to leave the dance floor. Without missing a beat, Carol grabbed Sidney's hand and led her into a slow dance.

Sidney stiffened and was about to give Carol a piece of her mind when she heard a familiar voice from behind, "Here you are, honey. Carol I hope you don't mind if I cut in."

Anastasia took Sidney's hand from Carol's. She laced her long fingers through Sidney's and with her other hand on her slim waist Anastasia led her toward the center of the dance floor, away from Carol. "We told you she had the hots for you." Anastasia smiled, but could feel Sidney tense by her touch. "Relax, I'm not gonna bite."

But relaxing was the furthest thing from Sidney's mind. She was ready to leave the dance floor when Anastasia slowed almost to a stop.

"Sidney, women dance together all the time."

"Look, thank you very much, but I didn't need you to come to my rescue."

Anastasia wasn't looking for a fight. The beat had picked up so she introduced more space between them, but continued in a partner dance. She directed dance moves reminiscent of the old disco songs, and twirled Sidney around and back. As she whirled

Sidney around the dance floor, she could feel her relax.

"Truce?" Anastasia asked.

"Truce."

Anastasia asked seriously, "Do you tango?"

Sidney thought she was teasing, but without given a chance to respond Anastasia reversed the baseball cap on her head, so the rim pointed backwards. She firmly took Sidney's hand and waist, pulled her close so that they were inches apart, and eye-to-eye. Sidney didn't know what her outer shell revealed, but Anastasia looked into her eyes with a deadpan expression. With an anticipated increase in beat from the familiar tune, Anastasia led Sidney into the tango.

A part of Sidney was amused by the situation as Anastasia expertly led her through the dance. Anticipating her moves, Sidney intuitively followed her lead. They became so wrapped up in the tango, they hadn't noticed the other dancers clearing the floor, watching them and clapping. Sidney was oblivious to the camera flash, camouflaged by strobe lights, and Anastasia was unaware that Stephanie drank incessantly as she watched from a nearby bar.

The song climaxed with Anastasia dipping Sidney, leaving her vulnerable as she held her parallel to the floor. Anastasia's deadpan expression disappeared and transitioned into a smile as she looked into Sidney's eyes. Lost in the moment, Sidney returned the smile as Anastasia helped her stand.

Sidney left the dance floor. It was time to leave. She gathered her belongings wished members of her group a good evening and swiftly made her way to the exit with Natalie on her heels.

"You okay to drive?" Natalie asked as she Sidney cleared the entrance of the club.

Sidney got a rush of fresh air as she emerged from the smoky building. "Yeah, I'm fine." She turned to Natalie and smiled. "Go back and have a wonderful time. It was nice meeting Karen. She's charming." Sidney hugged her friend and was gone.

Natalie watched her leave, thinking, *God, it's nice to see her smile again.*

The cool night air hit Sidney as she wandered the parking lot, and she began to feel lightheaded. *How much did I drink?* she wondered. Looking out into the full parking lot, she tried to remember where she had left her car. She was displaced and confused. She glanced at her watch, revealing it was 1:30 A.M. *Oh my God, I can't believe it's this late. Where are the limos? I parked near them.* Sighting one of the vehicles, she started walking toward it.

"Sidney?" She heard a familiar voice call her from behind.

She turned to see Anastasia running toward her. "Is everything okay?"

"Yeah," Anastasia answered. Then she tried to catch her breath. She pulled the baseball cap off her head, ran her fingers through her hair, pushing it away from her face. Beads of perspiration glistened on her face. "Thanks for coming tonight. I know you didn't want to, and Natalie practically begged you. But…well, I'm just glad you came."

"I'm glad I came too. I had fun."

"Well…goodnight, and drive carefully." Anastasia turned and started walking away. Sidney continued searching for her car.

Seconds passed, then she heard "How come we're not friends?" Anastasia yelled from 30 feet away.

Sidney walked back toward Anastasia and asked calmly, "Excuse me?"

"Most performers are friends with their personal managers. It, like, goes with the job." She continued to walk toward Sidney.

"I'm not like most managers."

"Right from day one, you've been…unapproachable." Anastasia was getting upset. "You have this attitude like you're better than me or you don't want to have anything to do with me, personally anyway."

"Anastasia, it's not personal. Over the years I've just found it easier to maintain business-only relationships with artists I work with. That's just the way I work. It's less complicated that way, and easier to be…unattached. Besides, friends usually have things in common," Sidney continued. "Anastasia, I don't see the two of us sharing similar interests."

"Well, maybe that's the problem."

"What?" Sidney asked.

"This is a one-sided relationship. You know me and I know nothing about you. The way I see it is—we're both women, we both work in the music industry, and we're both obsessed with our careers. Those are things in common. Just because I'm gay and you're straight doesn't mean we don't have enough in common to be friends."

"Your sexual orientation has nothing to do with the fact that we're not friends. I consider Natalie one of my closest friends. Friendships require a lot of time and work. I just don't have the time to invest in one new friendship, never mind all the artists I work with."

"With an attitude like that, you'll go through your life missing out on a lot of friendships."

"Probably so, but everyone sets their own priorities. I'll respect your life, if you respect mine." Sidney offered a handshake, then smiled. "Truce?"

Anastasia smiled weakly, then shook Sidney's hand. As she walked back to the club she thought, *I can't put my finger on it, but ... somehow I feel connected to her.*

Chapter 16

The morning following the party was business as usual for Sidney. Her staff, however, was not as dedicated. She was glad to see that someone had made arrangements for a temp to answer the phones, since Michelle did not arrive until nine o'clock. Slowly after that, the remainder of the staff arrived, discussing events from the previous evening.

At 2:35 P.M. Michelle interrupted Sidney on the intercom. "Sidney, Timothy Clausin is on line two."

"Thanks Michelle." She picked up the phone. "Hi Timothy, how are you?"

"Sidney, I've watched Anastasia's tapes," the producer started. "The camera likes her, but she needs acting lessons. Filming starts in three months; get her prepared. Plan on having her meet Brett before filming starts. I'll have a contract sent out on Tuesday."

Sidney was thrilled. It was her first movie deal and she wanted to share her news with someone. She went out to the reception area where she found Michelle swallowing a couple of aspirin.

"Anastasia got the leading role in Clausin's next movie, *The Rivalry*."

"Congratulations,"but Michelle seemed less than enthusiastic about it.

Sidney wasn't about to let Michelle's hangover dampen her spirits. This was a major accomplishment and she wanted to share it with someone who would appreciate it. Both Nelson and Natalie had left early for the holiday weekend.

"Michelle, would you call Anastasia and find out if she's going to be home the rest of the afternoon? Be discreet. Don't tell her about the movie."

Ten minutes later, Michelle entered Sidney's office. "Well, she's not at home. She's at Stephanie's apartment in the Village. I guess they just went there after the party last night. She wanted to know what was up. I told her we needed to send over a courier with some paperwork. So, how'd I do?"

It was 4:15 P.M. when Sidney left work, intending to surprise Anastasia with the news. But as she drove to Greenwich Village, she started having second thoughts. She had never been to Stephanie's apartment and was feeling uneasy about crashing their personal space.

I'll leave it up to fate, she decided. *I'll see how easy it is to find a parking space.* Minutes later Sidney rolled into a space in front of the building. *Must be because of the holiday weekend*, she thought. She walked toward the apartment building's secured lobby, and a woman holding the door for her.

As the elevator door opened to the fifth floor, Sidney heard loud heavy metal music. *People can be so inconsiderate*, she thought as she walked the hallway searching for Stephanie's apartment. As she neared apartment 504, the music got louder.

The entrance door to Stephanie's apartment was ajar and the

deafening music came from inside. Sidney knocked loudly on the door and it opened. "Steph?" She yelled into the apartment. There was no response. Sidney continued to knock as she walked into the apartment entry. "Anastasia," she yelled. Still there was no response.

Sidney couldn't see anyone from the foyer so she ventured into the kitchen and dining area, still found no one. As she looked into the living room, she saw the room was in disarray. Overturned plants and a broken vase cluttered the floor. Although the blinds were closed and the room was poorly lit, the carpeting and furniture were light in color, emphasizing the disorder.

Sidney's heart began to race, but she was not sure if it was because of the blaring music or the apprehension from her surroundings. Something dark was on the carpeting about five feet from her. She felt the carpeting. *Wet. Blood.* It formed a trail. With her eyes she followed the blood to the couch, but the couch was empty. A broken frame lay on the floor and Sidney picked up the smashed picture of Stephanie and Anastasia. When she reached to place the picture on a shelf, she saw the body curled up between the corner wall and the couch.

Sidney inched fearfully toward the body. *Oh my God,* she realized it was Anastasia. Blood had soiled the carpeting around her. Anastasia's head was tucked between her knees and her back was against the couch.

Gently, Sidney placed her hands on Anastasia's shoulders, but she was not prepared for the eruption. Anastasia struck out blindly with one fist while protecting herself with her other arm. She caught Sidney squarely on the jaw. Sidney wrapped her arms around Anastasia and restrained her. "It's me, Sidney," she shouted.

The deafening music muffled her voice and Anastasia's eyes remained closed as she squirmed from Sidney's hold. Sidney knew her grip would not last long. She started to gently rock her, back and forth, hoping the action would calm her. Anastasia's resistance weakened and Sidney also loosened her grip.

There was a deep gash on Anastasia's forehead. Blood had trickled into one eye, obstructing her vision, while the other eye was swollen shut. Finally, Anastasia attempted to open her eyes. When she saw Sidney and not her assailant, her resistance vanished, and she embraced her.

Sidney gently lifted Anastasia's chin, enabling eye contact. She yelled, "Where's your receiver?"

"What?"

"Your amplifier, where is it?"

"Dining room," Anastasia shouted back.

Sidney gently repositioned Anastasia against the couch, then left to search for the sound system. She found a built-in unit in the dining room wall and turned it off. The sudden quiet drew Sidney's attention to her pounding heart. She returned to Anastasia.

"Do you know where she is?" Sidney asked.

Anastasia shook her head.

"Could she be in the apartment?"

"Anything's possible with her."

Sidney quickly looked through the apartment but found no sign of Stephanie. Then she returned to Anastasia with some towels and a cold, wet facecloth. She placed the dressing on Anastasia's forehead wound.

"Can you walk?"

"Yeah." Anastasia pulled herself up on the couch.

"Do you have clothes here?"

"Bedroom closet, on the left side."

Sidney worked fast. She rummaged through the clothing, found a pair of jeans, a baseball hat, sunglasses, a T-shirt and a large cotton shirt. She helped Anastasia into the oversized shirt to hide the bloodstained clothing. Sidney loosened the baseball cap and placed it on Anastasia's head and finished the disguise with the sunglasses.

Tucking the extra clothing under one arm, she grabbed hold of Anastasia's hand. "Come on, let's get out of here."

The two hurried as they exited the building, trying to be inconspicuous among the pedestrians. When they reached the Mercedes, Sidney opened the passenger-side door, allowing Anastasia to enter. As she turned, she saw Stephanie walking down the sidewalk toward the car. *Shit. God...please don't let her see me.* Calmly she closed the car door, casually walked to the driver's door and got into the vehicle. She ignited the engine and pulled out of the parking space. In the rear-view mirror, Sidney watched Stephanie continue her stroll down the street, oblivious to their escape. *Thank you.*

Sidney put distance between herself and Stephanie, then glanced at Anastasia. "You look like shit."

"You look like you went a round, too." Anastasia raised the towel to Sidney's lip and gently rubbed it. "Sorry."

Sidney looked in the vanity mirror above the visor. Blood ran from her mouth down to her jaw. With a tissue, she rubbed the blood from her face. *I must have cut the inside of my mouth when she hit me.* She pulled out her cellular phone and pressed the numbers. "Hi Nancy, this is Sidney Marcum. I'm on my way to you; is Tom in?"

Sidney headed uptown and took Anastasia to New York Hospital to see Thomas Phelps. His nurse, Nancy, recognized Sidney as they walked in and immediately escorted the two to a private examination room. She exchanged a hug with Sidney, then turned her attention to Anastasia's forehead.

Within minutes, Dr. Phelps entered the examination room. "Why Ms. Smith, I see you've fallen again."

Sidney set the clean clothing on a chair, then left the room while Anastasia was being examined.

At the nurses' station Sidney called Natalie. She was disappointed when she was greeted by her answering machine.

"Natalie, it's Sid. Call me as soon as you get this message. Please. It's about six o'clock on Friday evening. Call my cell."

Sidney tried Natalie's cellular phone, but the phone was either out of range, or off. *Shit. As she disconnected the call, she saw the low battery indicator on her phone flashing.*

Dr. Phelps invited Sidney into his office. "I stitched up her head. It was a clean cut; there shouldn't be any scarring. The biggest concern is whether she has a concussion. Call me if she starts vomiting or has diarrhea. Tonight, wake her every couple of hours. Make sure she's alert, then let her go back to sleep."

"Otherwise, she's okay?"

"Hell no, until she stops…falling, she'll never be okay."

Anastasia changed into the clean jeans and T-shirt, and the two returned to the car. Before they left the parking garage, Sidney took out her cellular phone and tried to reach Natalie, but there was no answer. She left a message on her voice mail, "Hi Natalie, call me on my cellular." She wondered what to do with Anastasia.

"Anastasia, do you have any friends you could stay with tonight? Perhaps someone that Stephanie wouldn't know about." *She knew it was a long shot.*

"Just take me home, Sid."

"What about Stephanie?"

"I can't run from her the rest of my life. If she wants to find me, she will."

"Why put yourself back in the line of fire? Give yourself time to think, or at least heal."

"I'll be okay. Just take me home." She rested her head back and closed her eyes.

Sidney headed toward the Lincoln Tunnel. Traffic getting out of the city was heavy because of the holiday weekend. While heading south on the New Jersey Turnpike, memories of Michael's abuse crept into Sidney's reality. *No, you don't,* she lectured herself.

Anastasia seemed to have fallen asleep. At the Garden State Parkway exit Sidney contemplated, *What do I do? Nat, please call.*

She stared at the phone, but it did not ring. Waiting to pay the toll, she pondered, *Sidney hated the thought of bringing her to her home. But she knew someone was supposed to watch her that night and what if Stephanie was at Anastasia's? God…what do I do?*

She paid the turnpike toll, then turned left at the fork, south on the parkway toward *"Shore Areas."* As she merged into heavy traffic she turned off her cellular phone. Traffic was heavy most of the way. Anastasia slept for much of the trip, except when Sidney poked her to see if she would wake up. Then she said, "Go back to sleep," and Anastasia did. By the time she arrived home, it was close to ten o'clock.

Sidney was surprised that the noise from the garage door closing did not wake her. She got out of the car and opened the passenger's door. "Anastasia, wake up. Anastasia?"

"Yeah?" She opened her eyes. When her eyes became accustomed to the surroundings she asked, "Where are we?"

"My house, for tonight anyway."

"I told you to take me home."

"Someone has to wake you up tonight, doctor's orders."

Sidney escorted Anastasia into a guestroom with a private bath. She went to the dresser and pulled out hospital scrubs. "You can use these for pajamas. In the bathroom you'll find a toothbrush and other toiletry items; make yourself comfortable. If you need something, I'll be in the kitchen."

In the kitchen, Sidney checked her phone messages. There was a message from Scott, one from Justin and two from Natalie. Natalie had left an unfamiliar phone number.

Sidney called Natalie first.

"Hi, it's me."

"Sidney, what's going on?"

She quickly filled her in on the events of the afternoon and evening.

"So, Anastasia is with you now?" She was surprised.

"Yeah."

"I'm sorry I couldn't help."

"Where are you?"

"Karen and I are at Fire Island for the long weekend."

"I completely forgot. I thought you were in town. It would have been easier bringing her by your place."

"Actually, it's probably best this way. Steph knows where I live. She hasn't a clue where you live."

"You're probably right. Go back to your weekend and have fun."

"Call me if you need help."

"Good night."

Sidney made a quick tour of the living area and removed some personal items, particularly photos. *I can't believe I'm doing this. This is my home. God, I feel invaded.* As she placed her personal possessions in a hall closet, she had to remind herself, *This is a good thing I'm doing. Right?*

Then she turned to the refrigerator, she was hungry, she had not eaten since noon. She was pulling leftovers out when Anastasia joined her in the kitchen, dressed in the hospital scrubs.

"Hungry?" Sidney asked.

"Yeah, I'm starving."

Sidney prepared a couple of plates then zapped them in the microwave.

"You should have taken me home."

"Yeah…then it would be on my head if Stephanie beat on you tonight." *Realizing she sounded insensitive,* "If you want me to take you home tomorrow, I will… but maybe you need some time to think about things."

"You mean I should think about Steph."

"I didn't say anything about Stephanie."

"But you thought it. Everybody does. They think it's so easy and wonder why I don't leave her. Unless you've walked in my shoes, I don't want any of your advice." Anastasia continued rambling on, "Where would I be today if she hadn't given all of herself to help me out? I owe her, and she does love me, you know."

"Look…I didn't mean to upset you. I don't know what you're going through," Sidney lied. "It's late. Get a good night sleep. I'm sure things will look different in the morning."

Chapter 17

The following day came too quickly for both of them. Setting her alarm every two hours, Sidney looked in on Anastasia, assuring herself there were no complications from the head injury.

It was ten o'clock when Anastasia finally got up. There was a note in the kitchen, *"Coffee and Danish on the back deck, make yourself at home, Sidney."*

From the kitchen, Anastasia walked into a sunroom that opened to a deck. She paused momentarily, admiring the view of the water. The evening before, she had not realized the house was on the water. She walked through the sunroom and opened the deck screen door. The deck overlooked the river. She found a thermos of coffee, pitcher of water and assorted pastries on a patio table and made herself at home.

As Anastasia sat and admired the view, her thoughts returned to Stephanie. *She knew she had procrastinated long enough. She needed to do something. But Stephanie's sacrifices had always triggered guilt within Anastasia and clouded her judgment. How could I break up with her after all she's done? Then she feared what Stephanie would do to her if she broke off their relationship.*

Rustling from some nearby trees interrupted her thoughts. Somebody was pruning near the pool. Anastasia did not recognize Sidney at first. She had never seen her dressed casually before; she wore shorts and a tank top. Sweat stained the back of her top, near her shoulder blades. *It must be hot in the sun.* As Anastasia stared at Sidney, she found herself admiring Sidney's body. She hadn't seen her toned, muscular arms and legs before. Anastasia watched Sidney putter around her yard, weeding and pruning the bushes and trees. *There's something else that's different about her,* she thought. It took Anastasia a few minutes to figure it out. *She's almost smiling.* She heard the faint music playing from a boom box in the pool house. *She's humming, too.* When a new song started on the radio, Sidney started singing along. Anastasia strained to hear her voice, then smiled. *Don't give up your daytime job.* She had never seen this side of Sidney before and was a bit intrigued.

Sidney had always projected an all-business attitude and regularly lived up to her reputation of being a bitch. *I've never seen her so happy, and she's doing manual labor. What's wrong with that woman?*

As Anastasia studied Sidney, she became embarrassed. After all she was invading her privacy. "Good morning," she called to Sidney, announcing her presence.

Sidney turned toward the house and climbed the deck stairs to join Anastasia. "How'd you sleep?" she asked as she sat and poured herself a glass of water. She wiped the beads of perspiration from her face and chest with a towel.

"How would you sleep if someone woke you up every other hour?"

"Probably about the same as the person who woke you."

"You're right. Thank you," Anastasia replied.

The swelling on Anastasia's eye had gone down, but she was

sporting a black eye. "You look better," Sidney said.

"I feel better."

"Anastasia…about last night, I'm sorry if I upset you; it wasn't my intention." She poured herself another glass of water, then changed the subject. "I laid out some clothes for you in the living room. They should fit. I have some chores I'd like to get done today, but I need another three hours or so to finish them. Unless you have an objection, I'll take you home later."

"That's fine."

"Enjoy the pool and the beach. Help yourself to any food; sandwich makings are in the fridge. Okay?"

"Thanks, Sidney."

Anastasia found the clothing on the living room couch. As she pulled on the shorts, she thought, *I wonder whose clothes these are. The shorts seem to be larger than what Sid would wear. Maybe she's lost weight.* After getting dressed, Anastasia visited Sidney's library and selected a medical thriller. She ventured down to the beach, set up a chaise lounge and umbrella, opened the book and enjoyed the day.

Sidney was still working on the property when she heard Anastasia come up from behind her. "Do you actually enjoy this work?"

"Yeah, I do."

Anastasia touched Sidney's shoulder. "You're getting burned."

Sidney could feel her shoulders starting to sting. "Do you know what time it is?"

"A little after three."

"Oh, I'm sorry. I guess time got away from me." Sidney left the weeding and went into the pool house, opened the refrigerator and pulled out a diet soda. "Would you like something to drink?"

"Sure, one of those would be great."

"Shouldn't you be drinking Quench Soda?" Sidney teasingly asked.

"I won't tell, if you don't."

Sidney took the two beverages to a cafe table by the pool. As she sat, she realized how hot and tired she was. *She shouldn't have sat down.* She glanced at the front of her soiled clothing. *I need a shower.*

"Your property is beautiful. It's obvious you spend a lot of time working on it."

"I do enjoy it," Sidney said, then asked, "Bored?"

"No, not at all. I've been relaxing and enjoying the peace and quiet."

"Would you excuse me for a minute? I need to cool off."

"Sure."

Sidney returned to the pool house. Within a few minutes she came out dressed in a one-piece black bathing suit. She walked to the diving board and stood for a moment while Anastasia admired her stance. She dived into the cool water. Moments later, Sidney returned to the table wearing a large man's shirt over her bathing suit. She ran her fingers through her short hair, brushing it away from her face.

"Sorry. I must have gotten overheated."

"Feeling okay?" Anastasia asked.

"Much better, thanks. Do you like to sail?"

"I haven't sailed since I was a kid."

Sidney reached over and rotated Anastasia's wrist, so she could see the time. Then she looked out on the river. "Do you have time for a sail?" Sidney smiled.

"I'm stranded," Anastasia smiled back. "I'm at your mercy."

"Great. Follow me." She got up and walked down to the private beach. "Would you help me get the dinghy into the water?"

The two dragged the small boat off the beach and into

the water. Sidney rowed the dinghy about fifty feet out to her sailboat, which was tied up to a buoy.

She helped Anastasia onto the sailboat first, tied the dinghy to the buoy, then skillfully climbed onto the sailboat. The boat swayed as Sidney climbed on top of the cabin and removed the protective cover from the rolled-up main sail. She returned to the pit and started the engine. As the engine idled, she released the boat from the buoy. The boat started to drift, but Sidney returned to the pit and motored away from the shore.

She was steering the boat with the tiller when she asked Anastasia, "Do you think you can keep the nose in the wind, while I put the sail up?"

"You want me to what?"

"I need you to steer the boat straight into the wind, so I can put up the main sail."

Anastasia took the tiller and said, "Did I tell you the last time I sailed I was on a 14-foot Sunfish?"

"This is the same thing, just a little bigger."

Anastasia took control of the helm, while Sidney climbed back on top of the cab. At the mast she stood tall above Anastasia, reached for the sheets and started pulling. Anastasia was distracted by Sidney's stature as her body effectively raised the main sail. Although the boat continued to sway, Sidney had a feel for the breaking water. Soon the main sail was up and Sidney returned to the pit and turned the engine off. Taking the tiller, Sidney turned the boat, allowing the wind to fill the sail. The sailboat gently leaned and started moving forward.

"Would you like to put the front sail up?" Sidney asked. Anastasia looked at the front of the boat. "You want me to go to the front of the boat, and put a sail up?"

"No, you can do it from here." She handed Anastasia a rope. "This is the jib sheet, when you pull it the front sail will come out. You just keep on pulling it until the sail is full. Okay?"

"Okay." She pulled on the rope and the jib started to come out.

As the sail billowed, the boat heeled further and Anastasia was caught off guard. Not anticipating the incline, she clumsily lost her footing and was about to fall on her face when Sidney grabbed hold of her waist. Anastasia steadied herself and continued pulling the sheet, then Sidney showed her where to tie it off.

Anastasia smiled after she accomplished her task. "How's that, captain?"

"Would you like to sail the boat?"

Anastasia was hesitant, so Sidney reviewed sailing fundamentals with her. After she seemed more comfortable, Sidney introduced heeling. She positioned the sails for optimum wind, causing the boat to lean considerably. The speed of the boat also increased. Sidney saw fear in Anastasia's swollen eyes as the boat heeled.

"Here, sit next to me," Sidney gestured.

Anastasia moved closer, then Sidney took Anastasia's hand and placed it on the tiller, next to her own. "By steering the boat, you control the amount of wind on the sail. If you're uncomfortable with the incline, you just remove the wind from the sail." Sidney moved the tiller slightly, and the lean and speed decreased. "You see? Try it."

Anastasia moved the tiller back toward the original position and the lean and speed increased. She continued to test her ability to control the heel, then within a few minutes she laughed and settled into a comfortable lean.

Sidney studied the surrounding river and boats. "I need to go in the cabin for a few minutes, are you okay?" Sidney asked.

"I'm fine."

Minutes later, Sidney surfaced from the cabin, carrying cheese and crackers along with a couple cans of soda. She also had changed into sweats and handed Anastasia a sweatshirt.

"Getting hungry?" Sidney asked.

Anastasia looked at the snacks. "I am now."

The excursion was enjoyable for both. Sidney was pleasantly surprised that boat traffic was reasonable for a holiday weekend. It was close to seven o'clock when the two returned to the house.

As Anastasia walked away from the beach, she thought, *I can't remember the last time I had so much fun.* "Thank you, Sid. I really enjoyed that," she said as she looked back at the sailboat.

Sidney could hear the phone ringing as they passed the pool and approached the house. She flew up the stairs and answered the portable phone that sat on the patio table. "Hello...Hi, how are you?" Sidney sat speaking with the caller. She laughed, then smiled.

Anastasia was curious about the caller. Sidney seemed captivated by the conversation. Casually, Anastasia passed Sidney and entered the house, leaving Sidney alone on the deck with her caller. As Anastasia inspected some photographs in the living room, she heard Sidney's voice getting louder.

"I love you too, sweetheart. Have fun tomorrow and I'll see you Monday night...Yeah, we'll do something special...Miss you too, bye." As Sidney rested the phone in its cradle, she noticed Anastasia looking at photos over her fireplace mantel. "Hungry?" she asked.

"Yeah, I am," Anastasia said.

"You've got a choice. I can take you home or I can feed us. Since I'm hungry also, I vote for dinner. What do you think?"

"Dinner sounds good."

"There's a good Italian restaurant not too far from here. It's casual, want to try it?"

"Do you think I could borrow a shirt?"

Sidney set Anastasia up with an assortment of blouses and a couple pairs of pants to choose from. Within an hour the two of them were showered and ready to go. Sidney was checking the weather channel when Anastasia came out of the guestroom dressed in one of Sidney's blouses. Sidney glanced at Anastasia in her blouse. *That blouse doesn't look like that on me.*

The two exited through the garage. Anastasia was getting into the Mercedes when Sidney said, "No, I don't drive that on weekends."

She followed Sidney out of the garage, toward another vehicle. *This woman is just full of surprises*, Anastasia thought when she saw the doorless and topless Jeep Wrangler.

Anastasia had not seen this side of the house before. The house sat away from the road and was landscaped so that it was not seen from the street. As the Jeep pulled out of the driveway, Anastasia said, "I've been meaning to ask you...where are we?"

"The Jersey shore, we're in Brielle."

"Where's that?"

"We're about twenty minutes south of Asbury Park." The wind gust through the open vehicle as they drove along. Anastasia held her hair away from her face. "There's a hat in the well if you'd like to use it."

"Thanks." Anastasia put the baseball cap on. Aware that the vehicle offered little protection from the elements she asked, "What do you do when it rains?"

Sidney looked at Anastasia, then laughed. "I get wet."

The two were wind blown by the time they got to the restaurant, but quickly pulled themselves together. Sidney was surprised that Anastasia kept the hat on. The restaurant was crowded, and the hostess told them there was an hour wait. Sidney put her name on the list, then asked, "Is Steve around tonight?"

"Yeah, he's in the back. Who should I tell him is here?"

"Sidney."

"Want a drink?" Sidney turned to Anastasia.

The two squeezed up to the bar and Sidney ordered for them. The rim of Anastasia's hat seemed lower to Sidney. Then she realized people at the bar had recognized her. Some were pointing at her and whispering.

"Hi Sidney," a large man greeted her. "Where's Justin?"

"He's away for the weekend," she answered. Then she turned to introduce Anastasia. "Steve, this is Anastasia."

The man immediately recognized her and smiled. "Hi…it's an honor to meet you." He nervously turned toward Sidney, "I have a table now, but if you can wait five minutes, I'll have a more private one."

The two opted to wait for the better table, and once settled there, Anastasia felt comfortable enough to remove the hat. The waitresses and bus staff all greeted Anastasia and asked Sidney where Justin was.

"Is Justin your significant other?" Anastasia asked.

That wouldn't be my first choice of words, Sidney thought. "I guess you could call him that," she answered.

The food, service and relaxation were just what Anastasia needed. She was enjoying her wine and salad when she got serious. "Sidney, I need to thank you."

"No, you don't."

"No, I do. I can't remember the last time I've had such an enjoyable day. I think I needed the rest." She ran her fingers through her hair, felt the stitches on her forehead, and was reminded of how the weekend began.

"Why did you come over to the apartment yesterday, anyway?"

Sidney's eyes softened, then she smiled.

"What?" Anastasia asked.

Raising a glass of cabernet, Sidney proposed a toast, "To Brett Pillar's next leading lady."

"I got it? I got the role?" Anastasia's face lit up.

"Congratulations."

Anastasia was excited. "I want the best bottle of champagne you have," she told the waiter.

"I can't believe you waited this long to tell me."

"I can't either, I guess I just forgot about it after…everything that happened."

"Thank you, I owe you big time."

"Just my percentage," Sidney said with a straight face. Again, Anastasia was reminded of how cold Sidney could be at times. Then Sidney started laughing, and the two returned to their celebration.

During dessert, Sidney changed the subject. "I told you last night I wouldn't meddle in your affairs, and I don't intend to. But you said something last night that troubles me."

"What's that?"

"You implied that you wouldn't be where you are today if it wasn't for Stephanie."

"That's right, she sacrificed everything for my career. She gave up her band; she wrote literally hundreds of songs for me. She was my road manager for years—"

"Anastasia, believe me when I say this…you would have made it, whether you met Stephanie or not. I don't mean to underestimate her role in your career, but your success snowballed because of you, not Stephanie."

"But she gave up so much—"

"Yeah, I'm sure she made some sacrifices. But believe me, her rewards far exceeded what she gave up. You shouldn't feel like you owe her a thing. Stephanie's been compensated immensely for the services she's provided you. More than she would ever have made as a musician."

Anastasia became quiet and Sidney wondered if she had stepped out of bounds. "Anastasia?" There was no response. "I'm sorry, I guess I should have stayed out of it."

"No, I'm glad you said something." Anastasia was upset. "I guess I just don't know how to respond to you."

"What do you mean?"

"I know I need to talk about this, but I get mixed vibes from you. One minute you're a cold fish and I sense you don't want anything to do with my personal affairs. The next minute, you act like a real person and show a sensitive side."

"I'm sorry if my actions confuse you. I know you need help…I just don't believe I'm the best person to give you advice." Sidney reached for Anastasia's hand, hesitated, then placed her hand on top of Anastasia's.

Anastasia was surprised at how warm Sidney's touch was.

"I'll listen." Sidney tried to be sensitive. But Anastasia remained quiet, and Sidney could feel Anastasia's hand tremble beneath her own. Sidney removed her hand and the silence thickened.

"Are you still in love with her?" Sidney asked.

"No, the love has been gone for a long time." Anastasia paused. "Aren't you gonna ask why I stay with her?"

"No, that's none of my business."

"There's the cold fish again," Anastasia sneered. "Well, it's gonna become your business."

"What do you mean?"

"You think the *Gazette* gave me problems before? You've seen nothing yet."

"Has she threatened you?"

"For years she's threatened to go to the press if we broke up."

"Are you ready to take the first step, Anastasia?"

"I think so. I just don't know how to do it. I know I can't live like this anymore. But can my career handle another scandal? I don't want to go down the toilet again."

"It will be costly, but I can take care of her threat."

"I don't care about the money."

"You have to be ready to walk away from the relationship."

"I'm ready. But I can't do it by myself," she admitted. "Will you help me?"

As Sidney drove away from the restaurant she could feel the effects of the alcohol. She took the Jeep east, then parked the four-wheeler a block from the ocean. The dimly lit street was lined with stately homes, impeding their view of the beach.

"Where are we?" Anastasia asked.

"The town? It's Bayhead."

"What are we doing here?"

"I've had too much to drink. I shouldn't be driving right now." She turned off the ignition.

"Do you want me to drive?"

Sidney stared at Anastasia, then laughed. "You've had more to drink than I have."

"Well, what are we doing here?"

Sidney detected a note of concern in Anastasia's voice. She smiled at Anastasia's uneasiness, then laughed again.

"What's so funny?"

"You don't trust me."

"What am I supposed to think? It's almost midnight and you park the car on probably the most secluded, dimly lit street in New Jersey. I trust you, but what are we doing here?"

"One of my favorite pastimes is a moonlit walk on the beach. Since I really shouldn't drive right now, and we're so close to the ocean, and the moon's out, I thought it would be a nice way to end the day. Okay?"

"You mean, begin a new day." Anastasia looked at her watch.

Sidney led Anastasia to a path that separated two properties. As they approached a dune sandwiched between two homes, they could hear the waves crashing on the beach nearby. The two climbed over the dunes, and saw the whitecaps on the waves. The moonlight was their only source of light. The beach appeared empty as they ventured toward the water.

"How often do you do this?" Anastasia asked as she removed her shoes.

"Two to three times a week."

"Always at night?"

"Are you still nervous? Most of the time I come at night, but I've come during the day."

"Do you ever walk alone at night?"

Always. "Once in a while," she misled her.

For Sidney, the walk was peaceful. After Anastasia relaxed, she seemed to enjoy it, too. For the most part, the women remained silent, in their own thoughts and meditations. Within a half-hour they returned to the Jeep. "How's your head feeling?" Sidney asked.

"It's okay. She's given me worse headaches."

"Can I ask a personal question?"

"What?"

"Why does she beat you?"

"Usually it's because she's possessive and jealous."

"And this time?"

"Because she's possessive and jealous." Anastasia paused. "She saw the two of us dance the other night, and…she thought I was flirting with you. She just went off."

"Because of me? The homophobic bitch?" Sidney chuckled as she said it.

Anastasia stared back at Sidney. She could feel herself blush. "How did you know—"

"How'd I know my nickname is homophobic bitch?"

"It's actually HB, for short," Anastasia admitted.

"I know everything. Everything that's important, anyway."

The following morning the two drank coffee as they watched the boats pass the house on the river. They discussed their day, and decided Sidney would take Anastasia home that afternoon, after she'd had a chance to work on her speedboat. Anastasia planned to relax by the pool and read her book.

Sidney wanted to get her ski boat ready for the season. After cleaning the boat, she told Anastasia she was taking it to the marina to fuel up. While she was gone, her phone rang.

I wonder if I should answer that? Anastasia debated. *No, I'd better not. Sidney's very private. I'm sure her answering machine will get the message.*

Anastasia was absorbed in her book when she heard an

unfamiliar voice. "Hi! Where's…hey, you're Anastasia. How are you?"

Anastasia smiled at the boy. "Well, I'm just fine and how are you?" *Who are you?* she wondered.

The boy eased into the chair next to Anastasia. "I've been wanting to meet you for some time. I think your new music is awesome."

"You do? Well, thank you. I seem to be at a disadvantage. You know who I am, who are you?"

"My friends call me JP."

"JP, is that for Jean Pierre?" Anastasia asked with her best French accent.

"No, it's for Justin Paul," he answered.

Justin? Anastasia did not have time to respond. Sidney had returned and was approaching the pool. Justin greeted Sidney with a hug.

"What are you doing back so early?" She smiled as she embraced him.

"I called from the car and left a message."

"I take it you two have met?" Sidney asked.

"Well, not formally," Anastasia said.

"Anastasia, this is Justin. My son."

"Your son?"

Chapter 18

Sidney was starting her last trimester when Charlotte Gray called her to discuss Scott's pig roast. "Scott's party is this weekend. He asked me to pass along the information. Do you feel up to going?"

"Yeah. Actually it would be nice to get out."

Charlotte seemed reserved when she gave Sidney the directions to the Long Island house. "I'll see you there," she said.

As Sidney drove to the party that Saturday, she could not help but wonder, *Am I doing the right thing? What if someone Michael and I know is at the party?* This unsettled her. Except for Charlotte's occasional house visits, Sidney had not socialized since she left Michael, about three months earlier.

Charlotte seemed a little distant with me when I told her I wanted to go to the pig roast. As she crossed the Verrazano Narrows Bridge, she continued to think about Charlotte. Sidney recalled the day Charlotte first introduced Scott. *She seemed distant when she and Scott helped me paint the nursery.* She recalled Charlotte's arm around Scott when she introduced him. *Maybe Charlotte's interested in Scott and thinks I'm interested in him,* Sidney speculated. *Of course, that's got to be it. I've got to clear this up. I'll pull her aside and set her straight when I get there.*

Finding Scott's house was not difficult, but finding a parking spot was a challenge. The street was lined with cars on both sides. As Sidney walked toward the house, she noticed a few cars displaying bumper stickers with pink triangles. *Must be some type of club.*

Music blasted from the rear of his house. Party balloons were tied to the mailbox and a rainbow-striped flag hung on a wraparound porch. Sidney followed party balloons that led her to the rear of the house.

Charlotte had been watching for her and was the first to greet her. "How was your trip?"

"Long, does it show?"

"No, you look great."

Sidney wore a new maternity outfit for the occasion. It was obvious that the pregnancy agreed with her. She looked healthy, happy and even radiant. Her tan contributed to her pregnancy glow. The weight she had put on showed only in her belly. With the exception of the scar near her eye, there was no physical reminder of the rape seven months earlier, except of course, the pregnancy.

"Charlotte, do you think we can talk a minute?" Sidney decided to get right down to business.

"Actually, I would like that. I need to talk with you about something, too." Charlotte led her away from a crowd that had gathered by the back deck. They sat on a bench in a private corner. "You go first," Charlotte suggested.

"Maybe I'm way off on this Charlotte, but I sensed some…

reservation from you when I told you that I would like to come to the party—"

"That's what I wanted to talk with you about," Charlotte interrupted.

"I think I know what you're going to say."

"You do?"

"Yeah. You're interested in Scott…right?"

"I'm interested in Scott?"

"Aren't you?"

Charlotte laughed, then realized that she had not let her friend in on the humor. "I'm sorry, Sidney." She tried to regain her composure. "Scott and I have been good friends for years, and that's as far as it will ever get."

"Then why didn't you want me to come today?"

"It's not that I didn't want you to come. I just wanted to share some things with you before the party. But I didn't feel comfortable discussing it over the phone."

"Then what is it?"

"Well…for starters, Scott is gay." Charlotte studied Sidney's reaction.

"Scott's gay?"

"Yeah, and there are a lot of gay people at the party. Then again, there are a lot of straight people here, also." Sidney remained quiet, which concerned Charlotte. "Does that bother you?"

"I don't think so. I'm just surprised. He seemed so…straight. I guess I just haven't known anyone personally who's gay."

"Sure you have. A lot of gay people are in the closet, so if you're straight it's harder to tell. But I'm sure you know people that are gay."

"In the business, yeah. I would come across gay people all the time, but they seemed so…what's the word?"

"Stereotypical?"

"Yes. Thank you."

"Not all gay people are stereotypical," Charlotte said. "Are

162

you okay with this, Sid?"

"Yeah, I'm okay."

Charlotte spent a good portion of the afternoon introducing Sidney to people at the party, including Scott's boyfriend, Gary.

"It's a pleasure to meet you, Gary," Sidney offered him her hand.

The man made good eye contact with Sidney and smiled warmly. "The pleasure is really mine." Sidney thought him to be about her age, about ten years younger than Scott.

"Gary is a very talented actor," Charlotte said.

"Really? Are you working now?" asked Sidney.

"Just about every night. I wait tables at the Blue Moon," Gary laughed. "My passion is acting, but I can't earn a living at it. I do some off-Broadway stuff on the side."

"You can't make a living at it, yet," Charlotte encouraged him.

Minutes later, Charlotte introduced Sidney to another friend.

"Sidney, this is a good friend of mine from school, Natalie. Natalie, this is Sidney."

Natalie smiled warmly at Sidney then offered her a friendly handshake. "Hi, Sidney. It's nice to meet you."

Sidney exchanged greetings with the attractive black woman. *"Hunter Mountain"* was prominently displayed over her shirt pocket.

"Sidney, I'm going to give Scott a hand with the buffet. I'll be back in a little while." Charlotte excused herself, leaving Natalie and Sidney alone.

"Do you like Hunter?" Sidney pointed to the Hunter Mountain logo on the shirt.

"It's convenient. It's close to the city, but too crowded," Natalie answered.

"Yes, it has gotten crowded over the years," Sidney agreed.

"You've skied Hunter?" Natalie asked.

"Yes. I grew up in the Catskill Mountains. Not too far from Hunter."

"Do you still have family there?"

"My parents passed on when I was younger. But I have an aunt and uncle in Middletown."

"I'm sorry about your parents."

"That's okay. It was a long time ago. My mom passed away when I was a baby, so I have no recollection of her. And my father passed away when I was in high school; then I moved to Middletown to be with my aunt and uncle."

Sidney found Natalie's company enjoyable and interesting. She had gone to school with Charlotte, and Jennifer Warren, her lawyer, and now worked at New York Hospital, in administration. Fifteen years earlier she had competed in body building contests, but found she could not compete with the women who took steroids, and she retired. Feeling very pregnant, Sidney found herself envying Natalie's figure.

"Hi," a woman interrupted Natalie and Sidney's conversation. She nodded at Sidney.

"Hi Joyce," Natalie said.

"Nat, I haven't seen you in ages. I heard you and Stacey broke up, is it true?"

"Yeah, a couple months ago." Natalie was aware that Sidney was following the conversation.

"Is that Gray over there?" Joyce pointed at Charlotte, who was setting up the buffet on the deck. "It's about time she started getting out again. That bitch really screwed up her head." Joyce excused herself and left to greet Charlotte, leaving Natalie and Sidney alone again.

Sidney turned to Natalie. "Charlotte…Charlotte is gay?"

"You didn't know?"

Sidney shook her head. "Why didn't she tell me?"

Natalie was aware that Charlotte had been struggling with telling Sidney. "Maybe this is her way of telling you."

Sidney then changed the subject, and it was not brought up the rest of day. She enjoyed the day and the company of her new friends Natalie, Scott and Gary.

After the buffet dinner, Sidney said goodbye to the group. As

Charlotte walked her to her car she asked, "Are you up to driving back?"

"Yes. I want to get back at a decent time. Thanks again for the invitation." She gave Charlotte a brief hug, then got in her car to head home.

When Charlotte returned to the house, she found Natalie waiting for her on the porch. Natalie tapped the bench she sat on, suggesting Charlotte take a seat. "She knows," Natalie said as Charlotte sat.

"She knows what?" Charlotte asked, even though she knew what her friend meant.

"She knows you're gay."

That explains the cool hug I just got, Charlotte thought.

"I know this is none of my business, Charlie, but you're getting in over your head."

"What are you talking about?"

"She's delightful. She's attractive, intelligent, has a great sense of humor, but very straight."

"Meaning what?"

"Meaning…you're on the rebound. Don't put yourself in an unattainable situation with her. I know you, Charlie, you're going to fall in love with her."

"Not that this is any of your business, but my friendship with her is strictly platonic, and I have no interest in changing that."

The following morning Charlotte made an unexpected visit to Sidney's shore house. When Sidney answered the door Charlotte lied, "Hi, I just happened to be in the neighborhood. Can I come in?"

Sidney backed away from the doorway, permitting Charlotte to pass. "I was just preparing breakfast, want to join me?"

"Sure, what can I help you with?" Charlotte set up the patio table that overlooked the river and carried the pastry and coffee out toward the water.

The two sat quietly at the patio table, both sensing a distance between them. Charlotte finally started, "Are you surprised I'm gay?"

"Yeah, very surprised." Sidney remained distant. "Why didn't you tell me?"

Charlotte was silent for some time, collecting her thoughts. "I don't know."

"You're not even going to try to do better than that?"

"I didn't think my sexual orientation was relevant to our friendship. Part of me still doesn't."

"You don't think honesty is relevant to a friendship?"

"You know that's not what I said." Charlotte paused and stared out at the river, collecting her thoughts. "You're not going to make this easy for me, are you?"

Sidney continued staring out at the water, remaining distant.

"To be honest, Sid, I was scared to death you wouldn't understand, and you'd terminate our friendship. And our friendship means a lot to me, but that's it. I have no hidden agenda. I'm not here to corrupt your life, Sid. I just enjoy our friendship, that's all."

Sidney shook her head. "I don't understand it, Charlotte. I've never really thought about it as an option." She paused, then asked, "Does this make me homophobic?"

"You're not homophobic. Maybe a little unaware."

Sidney remained quiet for some time, then asked, "Why do you think you're gay?"

"Oh, I don't know. Some people believe it's biological and others believe it's psychological. Me? I'm just more comfortable with women sexually, than with men." Charlotte was trying to read Sidney. "Are you okay with this? Can we still be friends?"

"Yes, I'm okay. But do you have any other little secrets?" Sidney smiled, then confided, "One of the things I was surprised at yesterday, was that a lot of the gay people seemed...what's the word? Unstereotypical?"

"What do you mean?"

"You know, you always hear about the butch or dyke women and men who are queens."

"Yeah, and whips and chains and uniforms, and so forth." Charlotte laughed before continuing. "Gays and lesbians come in all shapes and sizes, Sidney. They can be stereotypical or not. You have to understand, a lot of people could lose their housing, employment, even their children if their lifestyles were made known. That's why so many people stay in the closet."

"If all these people are in the closet, how do you know they're gay?"

"Gaydar."

Chapter 19

Two weeks later, Charlotte, Natalie, Scott, and Gary were finishing the final coat of paint in the nursery while Sidney prepared dinner. The nursery was starting to take shape; the carpeting was going in the following week.

Sidney quickly learned that Scott and Gary were warm and caring men. She also found it amusing that Charlotte and Natalie nagged each other all the time. During dinner that evening, Sidney asked, "Do you realize the two of you sound like an old married couple?" The two women looked at each other and laughed.

After dinner, Natalie asked Scott and Gary if they wanted to take a walk to the waterfront. Scott grabbed a sweatshirt for Gary. "Put this on, there's a chill in the air."

When Sidney and Charlotte were alone, Sidney asked, "Have you and Natalie ever...ever been involved?"

"No."

"Why not? It's obvious the two of you love each other."

"We talked about it once. There's definitely an attraction there, but we've become such good friends. We realize we have too much to lose if it didn't work."

"That's a pretty unattached way to look at it."

"Besides, we've known each other for so long, it probably would be like sleeping with a sister, or something."

"How long have Gary and Scott been together?"

"Going on five years."

"Gary looks tired. Is he okay?"

"No." Charlotte paused momentarily. "He has AIDS."

"I wondered." Sidney was quiet for a while, then said, "This must be very difficult on Scott. Is he okay?"

"He's not HIV-positive, if that's what you're asking. The two of them entered the relationship practicing safe sex, but Gary had already been infected. They learned he had AIDS the beginning of the year."

"I'm sorry your friends are going through this." Then Sidney changed the subject, "I signed up for Lamaze this week; it starts Wednesday. "

"That's great. I'm glad you're doing it."

"My doctor said I would get more out of it if I had a Lamaze partner." Sidney looked at Charlotte. "Would you?"

"Would I...would I be your Lamaze partner?" Charlotte was beaming.

"Yeah, would you?"

"Of course."

At times Charlotte had forgotten Sidney's history. Sidney had committed to stay out of work until the baby was born, and had isolated herself from everyone she knew, maintaining the secrecy of the pregnancy. Charlotte was the only person who knew the truth, and she was Sidney's only close friend.

"Sid, do you think you'll ever tell Whitman about the baby?" Charlotte changed the subject.

"You sure know how to kill a mood," Sidney remarked. "I

don't know. I just want the baby to get here, be safe and healthy, and then I'll think about it."

Moments later, Natalie and the guys returned to the house. In the foyer Gary removed his sweatshirt and Sidney noticed a striking pendant fall gracefully against his chest. It seemed familiar, somehow, as she stared and admired it.

Sidney went to the foyer, away from the rest of the group. Eyeing the pendant she said, "That's beautiful, Gary."

"Thank you."

"May I?" she asked. As she reached for it, Sidney looked deep into Gary's brown eyes.

"Sure."

Sidney picked up the golden pendant to examine it. It had a loop on top of a T cross. "It seems so familiar. I must have had one of these when I was a kid, or something. What's it called?"

"An ankh."

"An ankh? What does it signify?"

Gary smiled. "The general meaning is 'life.' But there's a lot of disagreement about what the symbol represents. Its origin is ancient Egypt. Some believe it means immortality, or man and woman or the key to the Nile River. But my favorite meaning is not life—but resurrection."

"Resurrection?"

"Yeah. Some believe that it symbolizes reincarnation and is the key to the gates of life and death." Gary smiled warmly as his hand enveloped Sidney's hand holding the ankh. "That's what I'm banking on."

Sidney smiled back at Gary. "It's beautiful, Gary. Thank you for sharing that with me."

Charlotte rearranged her work schedule to make all the Lamaze sessions. As Sidney's due date approached, Charlotte spent more time at the shore house helping Sidney. When she was unable to help out, Natalie filled in. Charlotte also saved her vacation and personal time so she could take time off to help when the baby arrived. The baby's due date came and went and both Charlotte and Natalie appeared more eager to have the baby than Sidney.

Charlotte was at work when she received the page, and her heart began to race when she read "911" on the beeper display. *It's that time.* She knew the baby was on its way and immediately called the house.

"Hello," Sidney answered.

"It's me. What's going on?"

"I'm heading out to the hospital. The contractions are about two minutes apart. Will you be able to join me?" Sidney asked calmly.

"Two minutes apart? Get to the hospital. I'm leaving now; I'll see you within two hours. I'll have my mobile on if—" Then she heard a thump. "Sidney? Sidney?"

She heard a muffled noise from the telephone handset, then a familiar voice came on. "Hi, it's me. She can't talk now, she's having a contraction."

"Natalie, thank God you're still there. Take her to Monmouth Med. I should be there within two hours. I'll have my cell on. Call me if anything changes."

Charlotte was a nervous wreck all the way to the hospital. Although she had practiced the commute on two occasions, she made two wrong turns. Sidney was about seven centimeters dilated when Charlotte arrived, and six hours later Justin Paul was born. As Charlotte cut the umbilical cord, she could not hold back the tears.

Both Natalie and Charlotte stayed at the hospital that night. They shared an uncomfortable Murphy bed in Sidney's room. Sidney was up most of the night, breast-feeding Justin. The following morning, Charlotte was rocking Justin when a nurse came in and wakened Sidney.

"Is that necessary?" Natalie asked. "She just fell asleep after being up for forty-eight hours."

"No, it's okay," Sidney said. "What do you need?"

"I need this filled out for the birth certificate," the nurse stated.

"I'll take it," Natalie said, and the nurse handed her the form. She filled in the easy answers, talking to herself as she did it. "Name of mother, Sidney Marcum. Sidney, do you have a middle name?"

"Ann," she answered.

"Name of father?" Natalie asked, but there was no response. Natalie glanced at Sidney who was looking over at Charlotte. She repeated the question. "Name of father?"

"Unknown," Sidney replied.

Although Natalie wrote "unknown," she whispered to herself, "There's more to this story than that."

Sidney stared at Charlotte. *My God, Charlotte knows so much about me. More than anyone.* The morning light had filtered in through the Venetian blinds. Charlotte appeared tired, but peaceful as she held the newborn. *Where would I be today, if it weren't for her? Probably still with Michael.*

Charlotte was admiring the new arrival and smiling. *You are so precious, young man.*

Sidney and Justin were discharged the following afternoon. Charlotte and Natalie took them home. After settling in, Natalie announced she had to get back to work the next morning, and soon left.

Charlotte had made arrangements to stay on a few weeks to help Sidney out. After she went back to work, she returned to the shore house on her days off for another three weeks. Justin was a little over six weeks old when Charlotte told Sidney, "Some things at work have been slipping. I'll need to spend more time there, so I won't be able to visit for a while."

Initially, Sidney felt bad that her life had interfered in Charlotte's job. She showed her support by not calling and bothering her. Charlotte called every other day initially, and then she started calling weekly. Sidney found that she looked forward to her calls, and soon realized she missed her.

About two weeks had lapsed between phone calls, then Charlotte finally called. "Hi Sidney, how's the little one?"

"He's wonderful, you wouldn't recognize him. Do you realize he's three months old tomorrow?"

"Really?"

"Has work lightened up for you at all?"

"Not really. It's been really around here. I did seventy hours last week. This week I'll probably beat that." Charlotte sounded tired.

"Do you see any light at the end of the tunnel? It would be nice to see you before I enroll Justin in kindergarten."

"I'm hoping next month's schedule lightens up, then I'll come down and visit."

"Well, I miss you. Please take care of yourself," Sidney said.

"Got to go, bye." Charlotte hung up.

Sidney was troubled by Charlotte's telephone call. *Is it my imagination? Or did she sound distant?* Now she felt guilty. *She's probably putting the extra hours in because of all the time she took off because of me.*

She picked up the phone again, then punched in the numbers.

"Hi, Natalie. It's me."

"Hi Sid, how's my favorite nephew?"

"Great."

"Is everything okay?" It was unusual for Sidney to call Natalie at work.

"Yeah, I just wanted to make sure we're still on for Saturday."

"I'll be there."

It had become customary for Natalie to visit Sidney and Justin every other Saturday. Natalie arrived at the shore house promptly at eleven o'clock. She took the two out for shopping and lunch. Justin slept through lunch while they talked at the restaurant.

"Natalie, how's Charlotte doing?" Sidney asked.

"What do you mean? You two are talking to each other, aren't you?" Natalie asked.

"We talk, but she seems preoccupied. I know she has a lot of pressure at work, and she's putting in a lot of time. Did she get in trouble for taking time off when JP was born? Is her job in any way threatened?"

"I think you should talk this over with Charlotte, not me."

"I'm sorry, I didn't mean to put you in a compromising situation. I'm just worried about her."

Natalie studied her friend. "Sidney, Charlotte is going through something right now. It wouldn't be right for me to talk about it. Why don't you go into the city sometime and surprise her?"

"Maybe I'll do that."

As Sidney drove into the city, she was rehearsing what she would tell Charlotte when she surprised her. *Hi! Just happened to be in the neighborhood and...Right.* It had been over seven weeks since she had seen her. She knew something was wrong and she feared the worst. *What if she's sick? I'll get myself sick, if I don't stop worrying about her.* Then another thought crossed her mind. *Maybe she's met someone.* As she thought it, she felt a flutter of jealousy. *Ouch. Now why did that bother me?* Then her attention was drawn back to Justin, in the carrier on the seat next to her. He giggled as he stared at the swaying charms hanging from the carrier's handle.

She had not been to New York Hospital since the night she was raped. Memories of that dreadful night came fleeting back. As she walked blindly down the fifth floor corridor a woman's voice brought her back. "Can I help you find someone?" a nurse asked.

"I'm looking for Charlotte Gray's office," Sidney responded.

The nurse looked at the baby. "He is just beautiful." Then she introduced herself. "I'm Nancy, I work with Dr. Gray. Her office is right around the corner, but she's not back from lunch yet. Is she expecting you?"

"Well, no. This is kind of a surprise. I'm a friend, and she hasn't seen her nephew in close to two months, so I thought I'd surprise her."

"Come back to the waiting area, you'll be more comfortable there."

"Thank you."

Within twenty minutes, Charlotte rushed through the waiting area. "Nancy, could you pull the Schmidt and Greenburg charts? Thanks." Charlotte was preoccupied with what she was reading. Oblivious to her surroundings, she never looked up and never saw Sidney waiting for her. Her hair was longer and she appeared thinner.

Oh, no. She is sick, Sidney thought as Charlotte walked passed her.

Sidney picked up the infant carrier and went to the nurses' station. Justin was asleep. "Nancy, can I take those in?"

"Sure." She handed Sidney the charts.

When Sidney opened the door to Charlotte's office, she was surprised at how dark it was. The blinds remained closed.

"Just put the charts on the credenza," Charlotte almost barked.

Sidney did so, and said, "Don't you ever say 'please' when you ask people to do things for you?"

Charlotte appeared stunned. "Sidney? What…what are you doing here?"

Sidney rested the baby carrier on the floor next to the credenza, and Charlotte changed the subject. "Oh my God, look how big he's gotten."

As Charlotte admired the baby, Sidney continued to assess

175

the situation. She opened the vertical blinds. There were a half-dozen empty Styrofoam cups around the office. The trash basket overflowed with the remains of fast-food meals. A couple pairs of soiled hospital scrubs were tossed on the sofa. Charlotte pulled the reading glasses from her face. Dark circles under her eyes blemished her attractive face.

"What the hell is going on here?" Sidney demanded in a hushed voice, so she would not wake the baby.

"I don't know, you tell me."

"What is wrong? Why won't you come visit us?"

Charlotte remained silent.

"Did I do something wrong?"

Charlotte avoided eye contact by staring out the window.

Sidney pulled Charlotte's face so her blue eyes met her own. "You look like hell. Are you sick?"

"No."

"Please tell me what's wrong."

"You won't understand, Sid."

Sidney reached for Charlotte's hand. "Then help me try to understand."

Charlotte appeared uncomfortable and released Sidney's hand, then picked up the phone. "Nancy, I'm going to be a little while…could you hold my calls? Thank you." She hung up. "I don't know where to start." Charlotte paused. "I crossed the line, Sid. I didn't intend to, I don't even know when it happened. But, it happened."

Sidney could see tears in Charlotte's eyes. "You're scaring me, Charlotte, what the hell are you talking about?"

"Sid, I've fallen in love with you."

Sidney remained silent.

"I'm sorry. Between Lamaze and JP's birth, then spending the vacation time with the two of you, I fell. I didn't realize it until I came back to work. I thought the best thing I could do was to stay away for a while and hope my feelings subside or get under control."

Sidney was quiet for a long time. "Were you ever going to tell me?"

"That wasn't the plan. I was hoping I could get through this by myself."

Sidney remained silent, staring out the window.

"Our friendship means the world to me, Sid. I don't want to lose it. I know how upset you got when you found out I'm gay. I knew you wouldn't take kindly to this. Are you mad?"

"No. I don't know what I am," Sidney admitted. "I know I miss you." She approached Charlotte, her friend's eyes now pooling with tears and took one of her hands. Charlotte cried, and her pain was more than Sidney could stand. She wrapped her arms around Charlotte's neck, and hugged her to comfort her. Sidney whispered, "Maybe we can work this out together."

But Sidney's sensitivity seemed to intensify Charlotte's pain. She stiffened at Sidney's embrace; her tears fell and would not stop. Sidney loosened her hold and saw Charlotte's anguish. Gently, she wiped a tear from her face with a thumb. *Her skin is so soft.* Another tear fell, and instinctively she kissed the tear away. Then she repeated the kiss for another tear, closer to Charlotte's lips. Before she had chance to understand her feelings and actions, her lips met Charlotte's.

For a split second, the two women kissed until their minds caught up with their feelings. Sidney backed away from Charlotte.

"Oh my God. I'm so sorry." She checked on Justin. The baby was still asleep. "I've got to go." She quickly picked up the baby carrier and was gone before Charlotte had a chance to object.

As Sidney drove the Garden State Parkway toward her home, she reflected on what had happened in Charlotte's office. Sidney always knew that Charlotte was an attractive woman. The fact that she kissed Charlotte was not what disturbed her. What bothered her was that she found herself attracted to her. She recalled her feelings while they kissed. *My God…I wanted more. Sidney wanted to wrap her arms around her and hold her. She wanted Charlotte's moist lips upon her lips.*

Over the past three months, Sidney had wondered if her thoughts of Charlotte went beyond friendship. Their kiss answered her question.

Sidney's struggles with homosexuality were deep rooted by her Catholic upbringing. As a child, she had been led to believe that homosexuality was sinful. Although she was not a practicing Catholic, the years of parochial schooling could not be easily forgotten.

How could this be happening to me? Sidney asked herself. Homosexuality was never an option she considered before. She always believed it was one of those things that only happened to others, not herself. She had been married and had sex with men, some of it was even enjoyable. *Why the hell am I thinking about a woman?*

Sidney knew she was getting herself upset. She looked in the mirror and saw tears forming. At the next exit she pulled off the road and sought out a private area to park. Justin was waking and looking for his lunch. She enjoyed feeding him and it calmed her.

I'm getting upset over nothing; it was just a kiss. It doesn't mean I'm gay, she tried to convince herself. *Oh my God. She told me she was in love with me, and I kissed her. How insensitive could I have been?*

After Sidney put the baby down that evening, her thoughts returned to Charlotte. A couple times she picked up the phone and called her, but hung up before the phone rang.

Then she called Natalie. "I took your advice and went to the hospital to see Charlotte."

"You did? How did it go?" Natalie asked.

"Well, she told me she was in love with me, and I kissed her."

Sidney sounded upset and Natalie knew she was troubled.

"Girl, you better tell me what happened, and don't leave out any details." Natalie was concerned for both her friends. After Sidney filled her in, Natalie asked, "How are you?"

"I'm worried I hurt Charlotte even more."

"But how do you feel about her?"

"I'm scared, Natalie. In retrospect, I knew I had feelings for her, but I can't be…I can't be a lesbian." *God, I hate that word. Lesbian. It sounds like a disease.* "I just don't know. I feel like such an idiot."

"Tell her," Natalie encouraged.

"Tell her what?"

"Tell her what you just told me. It sounds like you're confused. Just don't stop talking to each other."

The following day Sidney paged Charlotte. It took Charlotte fifteen minutes to call.

"Hi, it's me," Charlotte said. "You called?"

"We need to talk. Can you come down to the shore, or should I go up there?"

Charlotte hesitated, then said, "I can be there around five."

A distance separated the two when they met again. Justin was interested in playing, which helped break the ice. "I can't believe how much he's changed," Charlotte said as she picked him up. The two women exchanged small talk until the baby was tired out, fed, and fast asleep in Charlotte's arms. Sidney took the infant from her and laid him down in his crib.

"Thanks for coming down. I know you're busy," Sidney started. "Did you have a hard time getting off from work?"

"No, I was due. The extra work hours I've been putting in have been self-inflicted, to get my mind off things."

"Charlotte…I don't know how to say this."

Just do it Sidney. I'm a big girl. Let me get on with my life.

Charlotte had come prepared for the worst and repeated what she was thinking. "Just say it, Sid. I'll be okay. Believe me."

"I'm so sorry for kissing you yesterday. I was way out of line. It was insensitive of me to do under the circumstances."

Here it comes. Charlotte prepared herself.

"I wish I could explain why it happened or how I felt after our kiss…but I can't. Except it scared the shit out of me."

Slow death. Is that my punishment, Sid?

"I've had feelings for you for some time, Charlotte."

What? "What?"

"I was too scared to admit them or try to understand them. It was easier for me to just pretend they didn't exist, because the thought of being gay just…just scares me."

"What are you saying?"

"I'm not sure." For the first time Sidney laughed. "I don't know if I'm gay. But I know I love you and would like to see where this could go. But I also know this is a big risk for you."

I wasn't prepared for this. Charlotte smiled for the first time in months.

Sidney smiled back and laughed. "So, do you want to date or something?"

The following weekend, the two agreed to have their first date. Charlotte and Sidney planned to go out for a quiet dinner, while one of Sidney's neighbors babysat Justin. It was Sidney's first time being separated from her child. She found it difficult to relax during her evening out and excused herself twice during dinner to telephone the sitter.

When the two returned to the house they found Justin crying in the babysitter's arms. "I don't know what's wrong with him. He just keeps crying," she said as she handed Justin to Sidney.

Heartbroken that her child was distressed, Sidney unbuttoned her shirt and took the baby in her arms. Justin did not settle down easily. Sidney turned to Charlotte, "I know this hasn't been a relaxing evening. I'm sorry."

"Don't apologize. I know your priority is JP. It should be."

"This might take a while. The guestroom is made up; why don't you go to bed? We can visit in the morning."

Charlotte kissed Justin on the forehead, then squeezed Sidney's arm. "Good night," she said.

After Charlotte left, Sidney admitted to herself, *It's probably just as well JP is up. The thought of being alone with her...scares me.*

Sidney's thoughts and fears of Charlotte and the possibility of being gay haunted her. Once in bed, she tossed and turned, checking the display on her clock over and over. At 1:25 A.M. she gave up and decided to find refuge in a book. She dressed in her bathrobe and slippers and went downstairs. Stealing her novel from the living room end table, she moved into the sunroom. But before she turned the lights on, she became captivated with the river, and went to the window to view its beauty. A full moon illuminated the sky and lit up the river with millions of twinkles.

In awe, she whispered, "It's beautiful."

"It is," a familiar voice said from behind her. *You are too.*

Sidney turned to find Charlotte curled up on a couch behind her, covered with an afghan. The moonlight reflected her delicate image.

"Sorry, I didn't mean to startle you," Charlotte said.

"You didn't." Sidney maintained her stance at the window. "What are you doing up?"

"Got things on my mind. What are you doing up?"

"I thought I heard JP," Sidney lied. "What's on your mind?"

"You," Charlotte admitted.

Sidney's heart seemed to skip a beat. *Why did I have to ask her that?*

As if reading her mind Charlotte said, "Sorry, I don't want you to be uncomfortable."

"I couldn't sleep," Sidney admitted, then she looked back out on the water. "I'm scared, Charlotte."

"We both are."

"Would you believe I was actually relieved when JP acted up tonight?"

"I know."

"You do?"

"Yeah." There was an uncomfortable pause. "Sidney, I'm not going to push you into anything. If it's your choice, someday you'll have to make the first move."

"And you're okay with that?"

"Absolutely."

"What do we do in the meantime?" Sidney asked.

"Be friends." Charlotte could see Sidney smile. "Can I hold you?" Charlotte lifted the cover, gesturing for Sidney to join her on the couch. "I promise, I won't bite."

Sidney approached the couch and lay down, resting her head on Charlotte's shoulder. Charlotte covered her with the afghan, and gently cradled her. Initially, Charlotte felt Sidney stiffen up, her body trembling slightly, and it took forever for her to relax, and when she did, Charlotte whispered, "Thank you."

"For what?"

"Trusting me."

Sidney turned so that she could see Charlotte in the moonlight lying on her back, her eyes closed. They were inches apart. As she lay in her arms, Sidney had mixed feelings. She felt safe, and yet there was an underlying current of nervous energy. Her heart beat faster and her touch was more sensitive. She heard the shift in Charlotte's breathing, which deepened with each breath. Charlotte had fallen asleep. As Sidney lay in her arms she felt her friend's breast against her own.

As Charlotte slept, Sidney analyzed her feelings. Nervous? Yes. Anxious? Yes. Excited? Yes. As Charlotte held her, she realized how natural it felt. With her free hand, she rested it upon Charlotte and held her closely.

Charlotte stirred. "Are you okay?"

Sidney released her hold on Charlotte. "I thought you were

asleep."

"I nodded off." She turned her body so they could look into each other's eyes. "Are you okay?"

Sidney didn't know what to say, or what to do. But she knew how she was feeling. She wanted Charlotte's lips upon her to answer the questions which had been haunting her, though she was terrified to learn the answer.

It was Sidney who brought her lips to Charlotte's. Heart pounding from the fear of learning, she kissed Charlotte gently. Charlotte was careful to apply only the same amount of eagerness. To Sidney, it seemed that every cell in her body was sensitive to touch, and as she applied the tiniest bit of increasing desire upon Charlotte's lips, what came back to her was a kiss which caused her to yearn for even more.

The slow and gentle kisses grew, becoming more urgent and passionate until each was taxed by not touching the other and they were sitting upright, kissing. Sidney knew the next move was hers and she followed her heart, she lifted the nightgown over her head, leaving her body exposed to Charlotte's kisses.

Charlotte hesitated just a bit for Sidney to reconsider. As the two gazed into each other's eyes, Sidney unbuttoned Charlotte's shirt.

Damn it, Sidney thought. She had her answer.

Chapter 20

Charlotte and Sidney's relationship blossomed. Sidney quickly realized she had fallen in love. Charlotte absolutely adored Justin. Although Charlotte kept her apartment in the city, she essentially lived in the shore house. Soon her mail started coming to Sidney's house.

One day a letter was delivered to "Charlie Gray."

"Charlotte, who's Charlie?" Sidney asked.

"Who's who?"

Sidney dropped the letter addressed to "Charlie Gray" in front of her.

Charlotte recognized the return address of a college friend. "That's me," she answered. "Charlie is a nickname I got when I went to college."

"Charlie? I like that."

Sidney was surprised when she received a letter from David

Jacobs. The letter was sent to her post office box in the city. David wrote, *"Please call ASAP."*

When Sidney called, he bragged about a great new group Global Records had just signed. "They call themselves *the Gang*. They don't have a personal manager yet," he said.

"So?"

"So? *You* can do it," he said. The rest became history.

Among Sidney's new challenges were balancing her new business, Justin and her relationship with Charlotte. Initially, she worked out of her home, but her business quickly grew, and she needed to move it to the city. Although Charlotte was wonderful helping Sidney with Justin, she soon realized she needed a nanny and, hired Lynette Floras. The Hispanic woman had impeccable references with years of experience as a nanny and housekeeper.

Sidney knew from the start that she needed to establish ground rules regarding her business activity. Historically she had become obsessed with her work, and other facets of her life were compromised. But this time she refused to allow her career to control her life. *My top priority is JP and Charlie, and nothing is going to change that.*

As the three approached their first Christmas together, Charlotte convinced Sidney to spend the holidays at her house in Vail, Colorado. The contemporary house sat at the base of Vail's eastern slope, offering spectacular views of the surrounding mountains. They hung stockings from the stone-faced fireplace in the great room and decorated an eight-foot Douglas Fir in white lights, angels and ribbons. A dusting of snow on the deck, seen through the sliding glass doors of the great room, contributed to the festivities.

Justin, who was now one, sat in the middle of the room playing with one of his new toys, while Sidney and Charlotte relaxed, enjoying the fire and their hot apple cider.

"How long have you had this place?" Sidney asked.

"I had it built about ten years ago, before Vail became so popular," Charlotte answered.

"It's a lovely place. This is a great way to spend the holidays."

"It is," Charlotte agreed. She moved closer to Sidney, placed her arm around Sidney's shoulders and kissed her gently. "Let's make this our tradition. Let's come here for the holidays each year."

"That sounds like a wonderful idea."

Charlotte changed the subject. "Have you given any more thought to telling Michael about JP?"

"You sure know how to kill a mood, don't you?"

Sidney's biggest fear was that Michael would try to take Justin from her. Charlotte tried to remain optimistic. "You can't hide him the rest of your life. It could be disastrous if he found out about JP from somebody else."

"Charlie, you're the only one who knows. Who's going to tell him?" Sidney was getting upset.

"It's public record that you were married to the man. Justin was born six months after your divorce. Any cruel reporter could have a field day. I think you should talk with Jennifer and see what you can do to protect yourself."

Reluctantly, Sidney agreed.

"Did you know you were pregnant before the divorce?" Jennifer asked Sidney.

"That's why I needed a quick divorce, Jennifer," Sidney admitted. "He would never have let me go if he knew I was carrying his child."

Jennifer agreed with Charlotte. The threat that Michael could learn about Justin through an outside source was too dangerous. She was also concerned that a court would look unfavorably on Sidney, since she had hidden the pregnancy from Michael during

186

the divorce proceedings.

"I think we should go on the offensive and tell Michael he's Justin's father," Jennifer recommended. "Then negotiate an agreeable visitation arrangement. That's if Michael wants to be involved in raising him."

Sidney strongly objected, but Jennifer was able to convince her that if Michael ever found out and went on the offensive, there could be serious repercussions.

Michael and his attorney were contacted regarding Justin, but his response surprised them all. Michael denied the possibility that he could have fathered the child, then accused Sidney of attempting to extort support from him. Sidney knew that Michael had remarried, and his wife was expecting a child. She decided his need to procreate had been satisfied.

But one month later, Michael demanded a genetic test on Justin to determine if he was his son. Neither Sidney nor Charlotte was prepared for the roller coaster of emotions that followed. Sidney refused to put Justin though any unnecessary blood work. Months of legal posturing followed before Michael accepted the premise that Justin was his son, and a preliminary visitation arrangement was agreed upon.

Sidney's heart broke the first day Michael and Beverly, his new wife, took Justin for visitation. Both Michael and Beverly picked up Justin at the shore house for their first weekend visit. Justin was almost two years old, and Beverly was eight months pregnant. Before they left with Justin, Michael looked around the house. Charlotte and Sidney had renovated the house and built on an addition.

"The bungalow looks good," Michael said.

Then Justin was taken from Sidney, crying as the strangers pulled him from his mother's arms. When the limousine departed and was out of sight, Charlotte came out of hiding and joined Sidney.

"I hope this doesn't backfire on us," Sidney said as the tears came.

Charlotte could feel her pain. She put her arms around Sidney and held her close.

Sidney noticed what appeared to be a needle mark on Justin that Sunday evening. "Damn him," she uttered to Charlotte, "I bet you he had blood taken."

A month later Jennifer received formal papers demanding visitation every other weekend. The documents proposed a $200 per week child support, with generous increases as Justin got older.

"I don't want his damn money," Sidney complained.

"Just take it and don't worry about it. Unless you feel there's a threat to JP, I recommend that you agree to the visitation proposal," Jennifer said.

Sidney had a mutual fund set up in Justin's name and had the support money forwarded directly to the investment company. *I don't want anything from that man*, she thought.

"You were married to Michael Whitman? *The* Michael Whitman? And JP is his son?" Natalie was digesting what Sidney and Charlotte had told her.

"Political analysts say his failed marriage destroyed his campaign for governor," Natalie laughed. "You're the one that dumped him?" She sat back, trying to comprehend everything. "How come I'm the last to know?"

"Natalie, you're one of few who know. And I want to keep it that way. Can you keep our secret?" Sidney asked.

Over the years, Natalie maintained a close friendship with Charlotte, Sidney and Justin. She knew Charlotte and Sidney were in love and saw that they were doing a wonderful job raising Justin.

Charlotte eventually started looking for employment closer to Brielle and took a position at Monmouth Medical Center, an easy twenty minutes from the house.

Sidney's business took off, requiring her to spend more time in the city, away from Charlotte and Justin, who was now about three and a half. Natalie and Sidney started working out at a gym together about three times a week. Generally they worked out at lunchtime, but occasionally during the evenings.

One evening at the gym, Sidney was stretching on a mat while Natalie was working with free weights. "What made you get involved with body building?" Sidney asked, as she admired her friend's body.

"Why?"

"Just curious." Then Sidney added, "It's obviously time consuming, never mind hard work. Just wondering what drives a person to that level."

Natalie continued with her repetitions, but casually looked around to see if anyone was within hearing distance. "Well…I've always been openly gay. I've never been in the closet and hid who I am."

Natalie finished her reps, then started a different exercise. "When I was in my last year of college, some guys decided they would teach me what it was like to be with a *real* man." Natalie finished her set of repetitions then returned the weights to the rack. She sat on a mat near Sidney, and started stretching.

"Well, to make a long story short, they didn't convert me. But I vowed that no man would ever touch me again without paying for it. I started self-defense classes, which led to weights and eventually body building."

"I'm sorry, Nat. I didn't know," Sidney apologized for bringing up her experience.

"That's okay. Most of the anger is gone." Natalie smiled, then returned to the weights. "I see *the Gang's* second album is doing well. Business must be good."

"It is," Sidney admitted. "My production company is off and running also."

"Well, if you're ever in the market for a good person, keep me in mind."

"I didn't realize you were interested in something new." Sidney was surprised. Natalie had a good position at New York Hospital in Administration Management.

"It won't be too much longer before I hit the glass ceiling. I'd rather find something else before I hit a dead end."

"I understand. I'll definitely keep you in mind."

After their workout, the two returned to the locker room. "I'm going to take a ten-minute sauna, want to join me?" Natalie asked.

Sidney looked at her watch. "It's going on eight o'clock. I'm heading for the showers. I want to see Charlie before she goes to bed."

Charlie is a lucky lady, Natalie thought.

Sidney showered and left the gym, taking the elevator to the parking garage. *That must have been tough for Natalie. I wonder why Charlie never said anything.* While in the garage, she thought she heard footsteps. She stopped and looked around the dark structure. Everything was still. The November night air was chilly. She zipped her jacket, then continued toward her car. *I must be seeing too many movies with scary parking garage scenes.* She laughed at the thought.

Sidney searched in her handbag for her car keys. As she pulled the key chain from the bag, a cold hand clutched her mouth. Her heart began to race, and then she felt what seemed to be a gun barrel in her ribs.

"Don't turn around; let's take a walk," an agitated voice instructed. The man shoved Sidney forward, maintaining a hold around her throat and mouth. "If you value your life, don't scream," he said.

Sidney's heart pounded as the man shoved her into a hallway, about twenty feet from her car. Sidney could see a dumpster and what appeared to be a truck-loading area. She was pushed along past a light and a minute later she heard a crash from behind her, then the light faded. The next light broke in the same manner. *There's more than one person*, Sidney realized.

The man shoved Sidney's face up against a masonry wall and held her mouth with his hand. "Where's your money?" Sidney's bag was still draped on her shoulder. "Where's the money, bitch?"

She slipped the bag from her shoulder, letting it catch at the elbow.

A second person snatched the bag. A minute later, a different voice said, "The bitch only has thity-nine bucks."

"Where's your money?"

"That's all I have."

The man holding her seemed increasingly agitated. The gun barrel was removed from her ribs and he started groping her. "What else do you have? Take off your watch and jewelry," he ordered as he padded down her jacket. From behind, his grubby hands reached for the jacket's zipper pull. He yanked the zipper down and groped her pockets.

Sidney removed her watch and handed it to him. "You've got what you want, now let me go."

The man pressed her harder against the wall. His mouth to her ear, his breath reeking as he spoke, "Maybe I want more." One of his arms reached over her other shoulder and he roughly grabbed one of her breasts.

Enraged, Sidney bit her assailant's arm through a filthy sweatshirt. He screamed in pain and released her, giving her the opportunity to face him. As she turned though, the back of his hand struck her mouth and she fell against the wall near a dumpster.

"The bitch bit me!" He told his counterpart.

The other man laughed. "Let's take the money and run."

"Nobody bites me and gets away with it."

Sidney was getting on her feet when the man took a gun out

of the back of his pants and placed it against her head. "You're going to pay for that. Get her arms," he barked at his companion.

A smaller man, wearing a NY Yankees baseball cap obscuring his face approached her. He went behind her, grabbed her arms roughly and pulled them back until they hurt.

With Sidney, now restrained, the thug tucked his gun in his pants behind him and cockily approached her. There was no expression on the bearded man's face. A sense of vulnerability swelled within her; it was that feeling she had when Michael had taken his hand to her. That lack of control and uncertainty that crept into many of her nightmares over the years. She didn't know what to make of the beady dark eyes glaring at her. Without warning, he struck her in the abdomen, and she fell to her knees, the man behind her struggled to hold her up.

A blood curdling cry pierced Sidney's ears. Almost simultaneously, the man who had been restraining her released her arms. While she hadn't a clue what was going on, she seized the opportunity and sprung to her feet. The man who struck her had his back to her. She turned to the man who had been pinning her arms and in an instant kneed him in the groin. He fell, holding his genitals.

The situation was becoming clearer to Sidney; someone had come to her aid. They must have struck her attacker, who now stood with his back to her. The fuming man reached behind him for the gun tucked in his pants. With the move, she saw Natalie standing in front of him.

"He's got a gun," Sidney screamed as she jumped on his back, preventing him from firing his weapon. The large man bucked to rid Sidney from him, but she latched on tight. He ran backwards into a nearby dumpster, using Sidney's body to cushion the collision. Sidney fell limply off his back sliding beside the dumpster onto a pile of trash.

Natalie followed quickly with a blow to his face.

"You bitch, you broke my nose," he screamed.

With another blow Natalie disarmed the man, his gun falling

to the ground. She quickly recovered the weapon and tossed it into the dumpster. The smaller man charged at her, but after receiving a couple calculated blows, he was soon doubled over in pain. Within seconds, both men quickly left the area cursing and nursing their wounds.

Natalie ran to Sidney's side where she lay motionless in debris. "Sidney? Sidney?"

She moaned. Then blacked out.

"Sidney, where are you hurt?" While kneeling beside her, she realized she was in a dark fluid. A dab with her finger alerted her that it was blood. A lot of blood. Oh my God. Natalie uncovered a broken beer bottle was protruding from Sidney's lower back.

"Oh God…Help!" she screamed. "Help! I need an ambulance." Natalie rolled Sidney to her side. She removed her jacket and placed it under her head. She looked around the area, searching for Sidney's purse knowing she had a cell phone, but didn't see it.

Nobody had responded to her cries. "Sid, I need to go for help. I'll be right back. I promise." She bolted.

As Natalie reached the parking lot, she ran toward a passing car. "Help! I need an ambulance." But the car took off.

Another car was turning the bend, and heading in her direction. Natalie wasn't going to let this car get away. She waited on the side until the car was ever so close, then bolter in front of it.

The car stopped short of hitting Natalie, and a woman got out and screamed, "Do you have a death wish?"

The ambulance responded in seven minutes, but it felt like an hour to Natalie. Sidney slipped in and out of consciousness during the drive to the hospital. At one point, in a barely audible voice, she asked Natalie, "How bad is it?"

Natalie had learned from the EMTs that Sidney's condition

was critical. She had difficulty concealing her tears.

"Am I gonna make it?" Sidney whispered.

"Of course you are. You don't have a choice…We have some unfinished business."

At the hospital, Natalie telephoned Charlotte. "Charlie, we're at New York Hospital. Sidney's hurt, bad. You better come right away."

When Charlotte arrived, she found Natalie pacing outside an operating room. Natalie's blood stained clothing amplified her fear. They embraced. "How is she? What happened?"

"They took her into surgery about an hour ago. I haven't heard."

"Natalie, what the hell happened?"

Natalie told her friend what she knew.

"You two weren't together?"

"No, Sidney left the gym earlier. She wanted to get home and see you before you went to bed. I was driving down a level in the garage when I saw her car was still there. It didn't feel right, so I started looking around. They took her to a truck-loading area." Natalie paused momentarily. "One of the guys was getting ready to shoot me and Sid…Sid stopped him, that's when she got hurt."

"Charlotte?" A man's voice interrupted them.

Thomas Phelps, an old friend, approached the two women. He could see the concern in Charlotte's eyes. "What's going on?"

Charlotte told Thomas about Sidney, and asked if he would check to see how she was doing. Within a half-hour, Thomas returned with the surgeon. "Sidney's a lucky lady," the surgeon said. She had severed an artery and lost a lot of blood, but no major organs were permanently damaged.

"Can I be with her while she's in recovery?" Charlotte asked.

Against hospital policy, Charlotte sat with Sidney while in recovery.

When Sidney woke up, she found Charlotte by her side. "Hi sweetheart, you're going to be fine." Charlotte smiled and tears ran down her face. "How're you feeling?"

"Okay. Just weak." Sidney shut her eyes again to rest, then opened them. "Is Nat okay?"

"She's fine, she's right outside the door."

Sidney shut her eyes and slept the rest of the night.

When Charlotte brought Sidney home from the hospital, she was surprised with a welcome home party by Scott, Gary and Natalie. Justin and Lynette were also there. Sidney was more interested in spending time with Justin, but she did not make her guests feel unwelcome.

Natalie seemed quieter than usual, even a little preoccupied. Sidney cornered her, alone, in the sunroom. "You okay, Nat? You don't seem to be yourself."

"Yeah, I'm fine."

"I haven't seen a lot of you since…it happened. Thank you for everything you did." Sidney hugged her. "Sometimes I have nightmares about what could have happened if you hadn't found me."

"Maybe you should talk with someone about it."

"I'm talking with you."

"You know what I mean," Natalie said.

"So, what unfinished business do we have?"

"What?" *Oh God. She remembered.*

"In the ambulance, you said we had unfinished business."

"I said a lot of things in the ambulance. I was just giving you another reason to hang in there and not die on us. I didn't mean anything by it," she lied.

After her guests left and Justin went to bed, Sidney mentioned to Charlotte, "Gary doesn't look good."

"You're right, he doesn't."

Moments later Charlotte took Sidney's hand, "Come with me. I have a surprise for you." She led her to a spare bedroom that had been converted to a gym. The walls were lined with mirrors, a rack was set up with free weights, there were mats and a stand-alone multifunction gym unit. Part of the walk-in closet had been converted to a sauna. Sidney was overwhelmed with the surprise.

Charlotte sat on a mat and tapped the mat next to her. Sidney took the invitation and slowly sat down.

Charlotte took Sidney's hands. "Sid, I've never been so scared in my life. I almost lost you. I will never tell you how to live your life, but would you consider working out at home during the evenings?"

Sidney smiled. "I think I can manage that." She leaned forward and they kissed. Sidney found it surprising that the passion in their relationship had never diminished. If anything, it grew over the years.

Charlotte became serious. "Sid, would you marry me?"

Sidney laughed, then realized her partner looked hurt. "Charlie, you're not serious. Are you?"

"Yeah, I am."

"A marriage without state recognition isn't a marriage," Sidney said. "Besides, I've been married before, and believe me it's not what it's cracked up to be." She leaned over and kissed Charlotte again, but Charlotte still wanted to talk about it.

"A marriage between same-sex partners is a union. There are churches that perform union ceremonies. Then there are couples that do their own ceremony, without an administrator."

"Are you questioning my commitment to our relationship?"

"No, I don't think so. Well, maybe I am. We've never really talked about it."

"Charlie, as far as I'm concerned, we're going to be together forever. What we share goes beyond a marriage certificate." She pulled Charlotte's hand to her chest. "You have my heart and soul, Charlie, I want to spend the rest of my life with you…and then some. I hope you feel the same."

Charlotte's lips approached Sidney's. "I do. Forever."

Six months later Gary passed away following complications from pneumonia. At his request, he was cremated, and plans were made to have a celebration of his life, rather than a traditional wake and funeral. Charlotte helped Scott with the preparations for the celebration. They decided to do their annual pig roast to honor Gary's memory.

Sidney was looking forward to seeing Natalie at the celebration. She was not working out with her anymore and their lives had become so busy, she had not seen her in over three months. Sidney was also aware that a strain had developed between Charlotte and Natalie. A couple of months earlier, Charlotte had mentioned that she did not want to have anything to do with Natalie. When Sidney questioned why, Charlotte would not talk about it.

The day of the celebration, Sidney saw Natalie talking with some people on the porch. Sidney greeted and embraced her, but was surprised at the cool reception she received. Natalie immediately stiffened at Sidney's touch and would not look her in the eye.

Later that day, Scott cornered Sidney. Although the man appeared exhausted, with dark circles under his eyes, he offered her a warm smile and hug. "I have something for you," he said.

"What's that?"

Scott carefully placed a small box in Sidney's hand. "Gary asked that I give this to you."

Sidney opened the box to find Gary's gold ankh and chain.

"I can't accept this," Sidney said. "This should be yours."

Scott removed the pendant. "Gary was adamant about this, Sid. He wanted you to have it. He said, 'This belongs to Sidney and her alone.'" Scott opened the clasp and put the chain on Sidney.

Sidney felt warmth from the pendant as it hung around her neck. *It still has Gary's energy*, she thought. She embraced Scott.

Later that day, as they drove home, Sidney looked in the rear seat to check on Justin. He was fast asleep. "Charlie, this should teach us that life is too short. You and Natalie need to work your problems out."

"It's not that simple, Sid."

"That's where you're wrong; it is that simple," Sidney was annoyed. "Natalie used to be our best friend. I get warmer receptions from my enemies than I got from her today."

"Sidney," Charlotte hesitated. "Natalie and I made a vow to each other a long time ago. She broke a promise. It's going to take some time before I can trust her again. I know this is hard to understand, but the two of us need some time away from each other. Please trust me."

"How do you know she broke this promise?"

"She told me."

"The woman's honest with you...and now you punish her. What if she never told you?"

Charlotte concentrated on driving and appeared to be ignoring her.

"I think I know what promise she broke."

"Really? What?"

"She's fallen in love with you. Right?"

Charlotte did not answer.

"You guys have been friends with each other forever, but you place unreasonable expectations on each other."

"What do you mean?" Charlotte asked.

"You let each other into your lives, but then say you can't love each other...because God forbid if it doesn't work out, you'll lose a friendship."

"I thought I was in a monogamous relationship, are you suggesting otherwise?"

"Absolutely not. I just miss our friendship with her and hope the two of you can get beyond this."

Charlotte reached over and held Sidney's hand. "I miss her too. Natalie and I have spoken about this, and we believe that distance is the best thing right now."

Chapter 21

Sidney's a mother? Anastasia could not believe it, even after meeting Justin. *She doesn't strike me as having a maternal bone in her body.*

Later that week, Sidney negotiated an arrangement between Stephanie and Anastasia. Stephanie agreed to move to Los Angeles and not discuss with anyone her past relationship with Anastasia. She would continue to receive a modest monthly allowance from Anastasia, unless she opened her mouth. At which time, all support would cease and any music business prospects would be threatened.

The weekend after Memorial Day, Sidney was enjoying her pool with Justin when the phone rang. "Hello," she answered.

"Sidney, I told you I want to boycott Colorado," Anastasia said. Sidney was caught off guard. "How'd you get this phone number?"

"What?"

"My phone number, how did you get it?"

"Sid, I stayed there last weekend, remember?"

"It's an unpublished number; it's not listed on any of my phones here, and I certainly don't remember giving it to you. How'd you get it?"

This woman can really be a bitch, Anastasia thought. "If you must know, when I was at your home, I called the operator and asked what number I was calling from."

There was a long pause on the phone. "I don't take business calls at my home. In the future, call my office. If you want to discuss Colorado, come by my office Monday afternoon."

Anastasia heard a dial tone, fueling her anger.

Anastasia slammed her tour schedule on Sidney's desk that Monday afternoon. "I told you—I don't want to perform in Colorado. I want to support the boycott." She was scheduled to perform at Fiddler's Green, just outside of Denver, in August.

"And I told you I would look into the boycott, and I did. I don't believe the boycott is effective and I think it's in everybody's best interest to go."

"Go? Have you seen the list of performers boycotting? I'll be the embarrassment of the entertainment world."

"You will be if you go and don't make any noise," Sidney agreed.

"What?"

"There are two philosophies regarding protesting Amendment 2. Even the gay community is split on it. Some people boycott, others make noise."

"And I want to boycott," Anastasia said stubbornly.

"Do you understand the politics involved in this?"

"Enough to know that it's time to stand up to those narrow-minded right winged bigots in Colorado. This is wrong, Sid. By boycotting I can at least bring attention to the matter."

"But that's my point. Not all of Colorado is so conservative and narrow-minded. Did you realize that Denver, Boulder, and Aspen all have city ordinances that prohibit discrimination based upon sexual orientation?"

"Yes, it it was these gay-friendly laws which angered Colorado Springs' Christian activists to form Colorado for Family Values. And it was this group which lobbied to get Amendment 2 on the ballot. But what it comes right down to is-these city ordinances are going to be null and void if Amendment 2 is enforced," argued Anastasia. "Don't try to tell me that Colorado is progressive. Fifty-three percent of the population voted for this amendment!"

"True, but I can't believe that all of those Coloradans understood what they were voting for. The actual language of the amendment is very misleading. Have you read it?"

"No," Anastasia admitted.

"Colorado for Family Values campaigned that the amendment's purpose was to prevent homosexuals from enjoying *special rights*. They neglected to explain that these so-called *special rights* were really equal rights. They also neglected to tell people that the effect of the amendment would legalize discrimination against gays and lesbians."

"Okay, but I still don't understand why you're objecting to the boycott."

"Anastasia, most people who are boycotting Colorado are boycotting the populated or tourism areas, like Denver, Boulder or Aspen. These areas are gay-friendly and have the heaviest gay populations in the state. By boycotting Denver, you're punishing your gay fans, and we both know you've developed a very strong gay following."

"But not everybody sees it your way, or there wouldn't be a boycott."

"You're right. I don't disagree with those entertainers and businesses choosing to boycott. Their boycott has brought attention to the issues. In their way, they have made a political statement: Amendment 2 is wrong. That's important."

"Then why can't I do the same?"

"There's more at stake here than just gay rights, Anastasia. Amendment 2 attacks the Fourteenth Amendment, the right to equal protection. If you can take constitutional rights away from one group, do you think it will stop there?"

"Then what do you want me to do?"

"I think you should go to Colorado and make some noise," Sidney smiled. "And I'll help."

Anastasia's summer concert schedule was demanding, but whenever the opportunity to return home emerged, she took it. During her home breaks, she frequently visited Sidney and Justin for sailing excursions. Initially she popped in without an invite, which annoyed Sidney. Then she managed to befriend Justin, who was quick to extend her an invitation to the shore.

On Anastasia's first uninvited visit she arrived with pizza and soda from the pizzeria in town.

"What are you doing here?" Sidney asked, as Anastasia handed Justin a soda.

"It's nice to see you too, Sid."

"I told you, I don't do business in my home."

"Who said anything about business?"

Anastasia and Justin bonded quickly. Sidney was surprised at how good she was with him. *I wonder if she wants children one day.*

Anastasia knew Justin was gone most weekends and assumed he was with his father. Occasionally, she asked Justin about his father, but Sidney had prepared him not to discuss his father or their life with anyone, especially Anastasia.

During one of Anastasia's visits, Justin was washing and waxing the ski boat at the dock while Anastasia and Sidney sat by the pool, enjoying a cold drink. Sidney watched Justin and noticed that the river seemed to be getting choppy, and the wind was picking up.

"How are the acting lessons going?" Sidney asked.

"I think well. That's the feedback I'm getting, anyway." Anastasia changed the subject, "So, who's Justin's father?"

"Aren't we getting direct."

"You're obviously not interested in responding to the subtle approach."

"It's personal."

"And we're not good enough friends to share that information with me?"

"That's correct," Sidney answered.

"Bitch," Anastasia said.

"Absolutely," Sidney agreed, and the two laughed.

"Is it Michael Whitman?"

Sidney was surprised at the question, but did not show it. "Is what Michael Whitman?"

"You know. Is Whitman JP's father?"

"What do you know about Whitman?"

"I heard you were married to him. Just wondering if he was the father."

The wind had intensified and Sidney found herself pulled between the conversation and watching Justin as he worked on the boat. "JP," she called down to the dock.

"Yeah, Mom?"

"There's some weather coming in. Wrap up what you're doing."

"Okay, Mom," he yelled back to Sidney.

Sidney returned to her conversation with Anastasia, and for the first time, Anastasia saw concern in Sidney's eyes. "Anastasia… Michael is his father. But this needs to stay between us, do you understand?"

Anastasia did not have a chance to respond. There was a thud, then a splash. Sidney looked back to the boat, but Justin was nowhere in sight. She ran toward the dock.

"JP?" she called out. But there was no response and the two women bolted to the river.

Sidney was almost in a panic when she reached the boat. *Oh God. Where is he?* Justin was not there. A storm was moving in and the water was rough. Sidney desperately searched the water for a sign of him. "Justin?" she cried. A crash of thunder startled them.

"JP?" Anastasia called out. Each cry became more frantic.

Anastasia was the first to spot him, and she dived into the white caps. Justin was floating face down about twenty feet out. Sidney dived in behind Anastasia. Reaching the boy first, Anastasia pulled his face from the water. Moments later the women pulled Justin onto the beach and laid him on his back. Sidney cried, "Oh God, he's not breathing."

It was Anastasia who took control and began CPR. Sidney knelt next to her son and watched helplessly as Anastasia worked on him. *Oh God, please let him be okay. Please.*

Within a minute Justin started coughing and spitting up water and soon was breathing on his own. Sidney cradled the boy and rocked him as the rain came down, camouflaging her tears.

"Let's get him to the doctor; he's got a bump on the back of his head," Anastasia said.

Sidney continued rocking him, afraid to let him go.

Anastasia drove Sidney and Justin to the emergency room. Justin required five stitches on the back of his head, but otherwise he was fine.

Later that evening, Justin told Sidney, Anastasia and Lynette what happened. "I was working on the boat and the waves started getting big. I lost my footing and fell. I must have hit my head and fallen overboard, but I don't remember." The boy felt the bandage on the back of his head, then blushed and continued, "The next thing I remember, Anastasia was kissing me."

"In your dreams," Sidney laughed.

Later, after Justin had gone to bed, Sidney and Anastasia were talking about the events of the day. Lynette was picking up the dishes after their late dinner on the porch.

"It's all my fault," Sidney said.

"What are you talking about?" Anastasia asked.

"The accident. I should have had my eye on him, but I didn't."

"It was an accident, Sid."

"As soon as the wind started to pick up, I should have pulled him out of that boat. What kind of mother am I?"

"Ms. Marcum, perhaps you're being a little hard on yourself," Lynette said. She picked up the remaining dishes and returned to the kitchen.

"Sidney, it was an accident. It wasn't your fault. From what I've seen, you're a wonderful mother." Anastasia added.

Sidney got up and went to the screened window overlooking the river. The river was quiet after the storm. "I keep thinking about what could have happened if you weren't here." Sidney's back was to Anastasia and her voice was almost a whisper.

Anastasia joined her by the window.

"I almost lost him."

Anastasia saw the light reflect tears in Sidney's eyes. Gently, she put her arm around Sidney's shoulders, then followed her gaze to the river. "But we didn't lose him, Sid."

"You were the one who found him in the water. I didn't even see him…" Sidney turned to face Anastasia, looking into the familiar eyes. "What if you weren't here?"

Sidney wrapped her arms around Anastasia and hugged her. "I don't know how I can ever thank you enough," she whispered.

"You just did."

Anastasia paced back and forth in her hotel room of the Denver Marriott Tech Center. As she paced the floor, she practiced the speech she was scheduled to deliver later that evening. *I have to admit, itsn't bad,*, she thought.

One month earlier, Sidney had issued a press release, indicating Anastasia would give a statement regarding Amendment 2 before her scheduled performance at Fiddler's Green. Sidney wrote the speech and worked with Anastasia for days helping her refine her performance.

She glanced at her watch. *Three o'clock. I have four hours until*—A loud knock disrupted her thoughts. At the door she glanced through the peephole, but did not see anyone.

There was no one in the hallway, but she found an envelope on the floor. *"Anastasia"* was handwritten on it. She picked up the envelope and took it in her room. Inside, she found six printed brochures. As she read the titles of the brochures, her heart began to race. *"Medical Consequences of What Homosexuals Do," "What Causes Homosexual Desire and Can It Be Changed?" "Child Molestation and Homosexuality," "Psychology of Homosexuality," "Violence and Homosexuality,"* and *"Born WHAT Way?"*

Anastasia spent the next two hours reading the brochures. She was outraged by the blatant lies and distorted facts outraged by the brochures. The leaflets were professionally produced. They each had different color themes, a picture, illustrated graphs or tables. *These must have cost a fortune to print.* The brochures were produced by Family Research Institute, which meant nothing to Anastasia. Then she turned over the green brochure and read *"Colorado's Choice on November 3 Proposed Amendment 2."* Reality hit Anastasia. *Colorado for Family Values is going to be there tonight in full force.*

At 6:30 P.M., Anastasia joined Sidney and Natalie in the lobby of the hotel. As the three walked outside toward the limousine, Anastasia handed the envelope to Sidney. "I got a delivery from our Christian Fundamentalist friends."

In the limo, Sidney opened the envelope. "They're trying to spook you. Are you okay?"

"I'm nervous," Anastasia admitted.

When they arrived at the service entrance to Fiddler's Green, the women noticed a crowd of people had gathered. A news camera team was filming their arrival and the crowd's reaction. Security guards pushed the line of people away from the limo, allowing Anastasia, Sidney, and Natalie to get out of the vehicle.

One side of the crowd started yelling at the sight of Anastasia. A demonstrator held a sign high, saying *"No compromise on the word of God."* Another waved a sign saying *"Homosexuals repent-sin no more."*

The opposite side of the crowd cheered at Anastasia and waved signs saying *"Undo 2,"* and *"Hate Is Not Our Family Value."*

As the three women entered the dressing room, Sidney noticed that Anastasia was pale.

What *the hell am I doing?* Anastasia asked herself. *I'm not a politician. I've never made a speech to a crowd before. What if I look stupid?* She sat in front of the dressing room vanity mirror and stared at her reflection. *What the hell was I thinking?*

It was 6:50 P.M. The opening act was scheduled to start at 7:00 P.M. Natalie recognized Sidney's sign to leave her alone with Anastasia, and left the room.

Anastasia was still in her jeans and tee shirt. She looked at Sidney in the mirror. "I'm nervous, Sid. What if I freeze? I've never done this before."

Sidney pulled a chair next to Anastasia, then turned Anastasia's swivel chair so their eyes could meet. She recalled Anastasia's stage fright the night of the Super Bowl. "You're not going to freeze because this is too important, to you and a lot of other people. You're going to do great. The material is good. Just do it the way we practiced. Remember, you're not here to change the world. You're here to be heard. Do you trust me?"

With my life, Anastasia thought as she looked into Sidney's familiar eyes. "I do," she said. She left the dressing room and walked backstage where the opening act performers were getting ready to go on. Anastasia stood silently for a moment, collecting her thoughts. She turned to Natalie and Sidney and smiled, then she picked up the microphone and ventured through the curtain to the large empty stage.

Her presence on the stage initiated a mixed reaction from the crowd. There were cheers of encouragement and heckles of disapproval. Anastasia casually tapped the microphone to see if it was working. She stood there waiting for the audience to settle but it didn't happen. The demonstrators were harassing each other.

What the hell do I say to shut them up? I don't think, Thank you. Glad to be here tonight,' is appropriate. How about, 'Shut the fuck up?' Sid would love that. "Excuse me Colorado, can I have your attention? A little quiet please? Can we get on with the show?"

The crowd did simmer down a little, giving Anastasia an opening. She took a deep breath, then started. "Last November's election was one of the saddest days for civil rights for our country." She was immediately heckled with calls of disapproval. "Because on November 3rd the people of this state—" The noise level from the crowd quickly rose and her voice was soon lost in the demonstrators' jeers. *Oh God. What do I do?*

The demonstrators were harassing each other again. When a fight broke out in the crowd Anastasia walked back to an amplifier in the rear of the stage. She intentionally created feedback. The reflux of sound from the speakers to the microphone generated a piercing noise from the loudspeakers. She increased the volume on the amplifier, boosting the obnoxious noise. Soon she had the attention of her audience. She stopped the piercing noise and silence remained.

"You know you've really pissed me off," Anastasia said to the crowd.

Oh God, Anastasia, stay with the speech, Sidney prayed.

"This is the deal, Colorado. I came here tonight to be heard. So, if you don't shut up, I'll have security remove you. For those of you who don't want to hear this, I invite you to leave now, peacefully."

She paused and looked for departures. But there were none.

"If we can't do this peacefully, I'll shut this show down, and there'll be no concert tonight." Anastasia's train of thought had been broken. She stood in silence in front of the crowd and did not know where to begin. Oh God, don't let me freeze, she prayed.

Sidney knew Anastasia had been shaken. *Relax Anastasia, you can do this.*

Then, a little voice in Anastasia's head said, *"Just be yourself and speak from your heart."*

"About four months ago, I told my manager I wanted to boycott Colorado. But she wouldn't let me off that easily.

"Since last year's election, it's bothered me that the people of this state could pass such a hateful law. Colorado, if you knew the implications of Amendment 2 and voted for it, shame on you. But Colorado for Family Values, shame on you. You have turned this state upside down. You brought this hateful initiative to your home by misleading good citizens into believing Amendment 2 was something other than it is.

"And you know the litigation is not going to stop in Denver District Court, this is going all the way to the United States Supreme Court. And do you know why? Because each side has too much to lose."

Anastasia was starting to relax. She appeared poised and walked tall across the vast stage, attempting to reach each person in the large crowd.

"Colorado, Amendment 2 is not just about gay rights. All of our constitutional rights are being threatened. If constitutional rights of one group of people can be threatened and taken away, what will stop groups like Colorado for Family Values from threatening the rights of other people? You've got to ask yourself, what is their real agenda? People of Colorado-ask them. Ask Colorado for Family Values. If gays and lesbians are stripped of their constitutional rights, who's next?

"Or maybe they've already told us...Traditional Family Values. They claim homosexuals don't deserve equal rights because they don't fit traditional family values. What the hell do they mean by traditional family values? Do they exist?

"According to their definition a traditional family is a wage-earning husband, a subservient housewife, two kids, a dog and a house. Traditional means one career, one marriage, one house and two kids. I certainly can see how gays and lesbians don't fit the mold of traditional. But what about the rest of you out there? How many of you really have traditional families?

"What about you unmarried couples 'living in sin'?

"How about you working women? I don't think so."

"Single parents?"

"How about families without children? Where do you fit in"?

"How about those on your second marriages"?

"Interracial marriages? I can go on forever."

"My point is this. Our families today are innovative, maybe twenty percent of families fit their definition and are *traditional*. Maybe twenty percent."

Anastasia walked confidently across the stage as she addressed the audience.

"What do Christian fundamentalist leaders mean when they promote *traditional* values? What are they promoting? I'll tell you. They're promoting a lifestyle that hasn't existed since the post World War II era. A period of white male supremacy, conservative politics, heterosexual relationships, and Christianity. Oh happy days. That's what they're talking about. The fifties.

"I don't know about you, but as a black woman, I certainly don't want to go back there. How many of you want to go back there?"

"So my point is—if constitutional rights are stripped from

one group of people, what's to stop them from attacking another group?"

"Is it possible that the Colorado for Family Values campaign against gays is really a crusade against modern America? Ask them. The question really is—if they prevail *here*, with gays and lesbians, who's next on the list?"

"Christian fundamentalist. That's what they call themselves. They preach what's printed in the Bible, verbatim, word for word, with no interpretation for today's society. Women, do you know where that puts you? Ask them. They hide behind their Bibles and printed propaganda of lies and distorted facts about gays. And you take it as truth. Shame on you."

As Anastasia paused between thoughts, mixed signals of cheers and hisses could be heard from the audience. She remained focused, determined to get her messages across.

"Is it just me, or do these Christian fundamentalists sound like neo-Nazi groups or the Ku Klux Klan? Do you know what the differences are? There are differences, but they are more alike than different. They're all racist, sexist, homophobic and anti-Semitic. They all threaten our democracy. They all impose their narrow white supremacist agenda on society. But most importantly, Colorado, they all gain power by arousing people's emotions and prejudices. That's how they win. That's how Amendment 2 passed."

"I know I've gotten off the subject, and for that I apologize. These are the facts about Amendment 2—it's wrong. The effect of the amendment would legalize discrimination because of a person's sexual orientation. The so-called special rights, which Colorado for Family Values claims homosexuals have been earning, aren't special; they're equal rights."

"By stripping gays and lesbians of their constitutional rights of equal protection under the Fourteenth Amendment, you undermine all of our constitutional rights. You are setting precedents, a prelude of what could come for others."

"When Colorado for Family Values approaches you for

your support, and they will, say no. But more importantly ask questions. Demand answers."

As she finished her speech Anastasia looked to the audience with uncertainty. Although part of the audience heckled her and gave obscene gestures, the majority whistled and cheered.

Anastasia's real indicator was always Sidney. She always told her the truth no matter how painful it could be. As she walked off the stage she thought to herself, *I changed Sidney's speech. She worked so hard on it. I hope I got most of her points across.* When she saw Sidney's face lit up she knew she must have done well.

Sidney hugged her. "Congratulations."

"Did I do okay? I know I didn't follow your speech."

"It was better than my speech. You spoke from your heart."

In the concert that followed, Anastasia's performance was electrifying.

Anastasia, Sidney and Natalie planned to spend some time in the mountains before Anastasia and Natalie journeyed on to San Diego for another performance. Sidney rented a car and the three women headed west. They arrived in Vail early that Saturday afternoon and settled into Sidney's mountain home.

After exploring the house, Anastasia said, "This is a wonderful place. How often do you come out here?"

"Usually just Christmas." Sidney was quick to change the subject. "Your meeting with Brett Pillar is scheduled for the second week in September. Filming starts shortly after. Ready?"

"I believe so."

The three women spent the rest of the afternoon walking the town of Vail, then enjoyed dinner at Uptown Grill. When they returned to the house, it was close to ten o'clock.

"I'm beat," Sidney said as they arrived. "I'm going to bed. I'll see you in the morning."

Natalie and Anastasia migrated to the great room that opened to a deck. The mountain night air was cool, but refreshing. The women sat on the patio where they could view the mountains of Vail in the brilliant moonlight.

Anastasia had been humming a tune most of the evening. She would frequently jot down notes on a pad.

"What are you doing?" Natalie asked.

"Just working on a new song. I wish there was a piano around."

"Would a guitar be helpful?"

"Yeah, that would work."

Natalie went into the house and returned with a Gibson.

"I didn't realize Sid played."

"I never said she played. I'm going to have a glass of wine, would you like one?"

"Sure."

"Chardonnay or Cabernet?"

"Whatever you're drinking." Anastasia tuned the guitar and by the time Natalie returned, she was working on her new tune.

"So what are you working on?" Natalie asked.

Anastasia took a sip of the Cabernet. "It's a love song. I'm calling it "My Untouchable.""

"Will you play it?"

"Sure. But it's far from being finished." Anastasia picked up the guitar and sang a few verses of the unfinished melody. The song was about falling in love with an untouchable, and choosing to love the person from afar.

> *But, I need you. Can't you see it?*
> *I want you. Can't you feel it?*
> *From afar, like an angel*
> *I'll be there to hold you*
> *when you're hurting,*
> *or just need a friend.*

> *I see you,*
> *but I know I can't have you.*

I've loved you
but I know I can't love you.
You're my untouchable.
From afar.

Anastasia finished the song, then turned to Natalie for feedback. "I think it's too…two-dimensional. It needs work, I know. But what do you think?"

"Have you fallen in love?" Natalie smiled.

"No," Anastasia seemed annoyed. "The songs I write aren't always about things that I experience."

"I know, just the good ones."

"The song should have good market appeal. People fall in love with untouchables all the time."

"Untouchables?"

"Yeah, untouchables. A secretary who falls in love with her boss, a parishioner who falls in love with her priest, and a gay man falls in love with his heterosexual male friend. That's what my first girlfriend called me when she thought I was straight, an untouchable." Anastasia was on a roll. "So, has it ever happened to you?"

Natalie hesitated. "Yes, it has."

"See? It happens all the time. So what's your story?"

"It's personal."

"Oh relax. Did you ever tell her? It was a her, wasn't it?"

"Yes, it was a her. And no, I never told her," confided Natalie.

"Did you ever wish you had?"

"Sometimes—"

"So why don't you tell her?" Anastasia interrupted.

"You didn't let me finish. Sometimes I've wished that I told her. But most of the time, I'm glad I never said a word. Besides, it's too late anyway."

"If you could do it all again, would you do it differently?"

"Maybe," Natalie admitted.

He's looking forward to spending more time with you."

"Really?"

"Yes. Very impressed."

"What are you trying to tell me, Sid?" Anastasia knew the conversation was going someplace.

"While you guys are working together, it wouldn't hurt to be seen socializing with him," Sidney commented.

"You mean date him?"

"No. I would never tell you who you should date. I'm just saying the two of you are going to be spending a lot of time with each other. It could benefit both of you to be seen together. You can give the appearance of dating, without actually dating."

The filming got off to a good start. Anastasia showed a lot of promise, considering this was her first serious acting job. Brett and Anastasia took a liking to each other, so Anastasia was not surprised when he asked her to lunch one day.

"I need to ask you a personal question," Brett said.

"Okay."

"Are you a lesbian?"

"You don't beat around the bush, do you?"

"Not usually," he admitted.

"Between you and me? Yes, I am."

"You just haven't been with the right man."

Typical wounded male ego response, Anastasia thought. "There's no right man for me. But I was kind of hoping we could be friends."

"We are. I'm just a little disappointed."

"Don't you have a girlfriend? Cheri, isn't it?"

"Yeah, you interested in her?" He laughed.

"No," she laughed also. "I just want both of us to be honest with each other." Anastasia paused, then continued, "Actually, my manager suggested we might want to spend time together, socially."

"I like your manager's idea, but why?" Brett asked.

"A little PR. You see, if we gave the press the appearance that the two of us are dating…well, let's just say it wouldn't hurt my reputation. You never know, it might be good for your too."

Brett studied Anastasia and was silent for a long time. "Don't you feel like a traitor? I mean…being gay and not admitting it?"

"Every day of my life."

"Why do you do it?"

"I almost lost everything because the public wasn't ready for me to be gay. I was given a second chance and I took it. I'm not ready to give it all up yet."

Brett asked with a boyish grin, "So, you want to go on a date? I better have a talk with Cheri."

Over the next couple months Brett and Anastasia were together at restaurants and nightclubs. They always put on a good show for the press.

The filming broke in mid-December for the Christmas holiday. Brett returned to Malibu for the holidays and Anastasia faced her first Christmas alone, without family or a lover.

Chapter 23

Sidney was at her office, trying to tie up some loose ends before the holiday break when Anastasia entered unannounced.

"So what are you and JP doing for Christmas?" Anastasia asked.

"JP spends Christmas with his father. I believe they're going to St. Moritz this year."

"What about you?"

"I go to Vail every Christmas."

"Is Scott going? Or are you going by yourself?"

"I'm going by myself."

"It must be nice there this time of the year. Are you going to ski?"

"I usually do some skiing."

"Skiing sounds great. I can't remember the last time I went skiing." Then she hinted, "I don't have any plans for Christmas this year."

Sidney remained silent, hoping Anastasia would take the hint. "What do I have to do? Invite myself?"

"I usually go by myself, and enjoy the quiet." *She's not going to let this rest.* "Anastasia, you wouldn't enjoy it, I just play lazy most of the time."

"I could use some rest."

"I leave Monday, United Airlines around ten o'clock out of Newark, into Denver." *I can't believe I just invited her. But she probably won't be able to get tickets this late.* "Good luck getting tickets."

"I'm surprised you're leaving Monday, and not Saturday."

"Scott and I have plans for the weekend."

"Oh. When are we returning?" she asked.

"The following Monday."

The plane landed at 12:20 P.M. Mountain Time, that Monday afternoon. Sidney rented a four-wheel-drive vehicle and they headed west. They were making good time until they reached the Continental Divide. Snow flurries started as they approached the Eisenhower Tunnel, and when they emerged on the other side of the mountain, there was a whiteout. Their travel into Dillon was slow, and when they pulled over to use the rest rooms they learned that Vail Pass was closed because of an avalanche. They found a motel room and spent the night in Dillon.

They were back on the road by ten o'clock the following morning. As the car got back on the interstate Sidney asked Anastasia, "Did Brett go back to Malibu for the holidays?"

"Yeah, he was looking forward to seeing Cheri."

"The press has been having a field day with the two of you."

"Aren't you proud of me?" Anastasia laughed.

"The two of you have an understanding?"

"Yeah, pretty much. We both agree it's good PR. I think the only one who's unhappy about it is Cheri. Brett says she's okay.

She came out for a couple of weekends last month. We met once, and boy did I get a cold shoulder."

"Do you like him?" Sidney pried.

"Of course I like him…or do you mean, do I *like* him?" Anastasia asked.

Sidney just laughed.

"I just like him, if you know what I mean. He is an arrogant son of a bitch sometimes."

The two arrived in Vail before eleven, and spent the rest of the day food shopping, unpacking and getting settled. The rest of the week, the two spent on skis. Anastasia took private lessons in the mornings, giving Sidney time to ski alone, which she enjoyed. During the evenings they played lazy and stayed in. Each night they enjoyed their own home cooking, some wine, and relaxation by the fire, telling war stories from their day on the slopes.

On Christmas Eve, Anastasia was rummaging through some of the closets looking for something.

"What are you looking for?" Sidney asked.

"Your guitar."

"My guitar?"

"Yeah, I played with it this summer. Natalie gave it to me."

Sidney got up and disappeared down the hallway. She returned and handed Anastasia the guitar. Anastasia tuned the instrument, then began playing some Christmas carols. Sidney relaxed and enjoyed the fire, wine, and music.

At the end of the first song, Anastasia asked, "Was this Charlie's guitar?"

Sidney was once again surprised. "What do you know about Charlie?"

"Just what I've heard. He's an ex. He dumped you and broke your heart."

"Really? What else have you heard?"

"Just that you haven't gotten over him and you live in the past."

"Remind me to have a chat with Natalie."

"Actually, I didn't hear it from Natalie. Well, is it true?"

"I'll make you a deal, Anastasia. You don't ask about my past lovers, and I won't ask about yours."

It was about ten o'clock when the phone rang that Christmas morning. Sidney rushed to answer the call. The sound of the phone reminded Anastasia how isolated they were. It was the first call all week.

"Merry Christmas," Sidney greeted the caller.

"Hi Mom, Merry Christmas," Justin said.

The two talked a long time about their vacations, and how much they missed each other. Then he changed the subject. "Mom, Dad is staying in St. Moritz through New Year's. He says I can stay with them if it's okay with you."

Sidney remained silent. She was crushed to hear her son express interest in staying with his father on her holiday.

"Mom? Are you there?"

Sidney was trying to be understanding, "JP, what would you like to do for New Year's?"

"Of course I'd like to be with you, Mom. It's a shame though; if I come back early I'll be shortening Sean's vacation too."

"Who's Sean?"

"He's Dad's new chauffeur. Dad would have me travel back with him, if I go back early."

"When would you come back?" *I can't believe I'm asking.*

"On the third," he said, "Is it okay, Mom?"

"If that's what you want, it's okay." Sidney was crushed.

"Thanks, Mom."

"Sweetheart, put your father on so I can wish him a Merry Christmas."

"Okay. Bye, Mom. I love you," Justin said, then there was a long pause.

Michael got on the phone. "Yes?"

"You son of a bitch," Sidney was furious. "This is the second year in a row you've kept him through the New Year. I don't have him for that many holidays as it is."

"Now Sidney, it's not my fault he wants to spend New Year's with me." Michael was almost laughing. "Oh, by the way, you better not step out of line, if you know what I mean."

"No, I don't know what you mean. What the hell are you talking about?"

"I know you have a *friend* with you. You better not step out of line, because I'll own him, do you understand? You'll *never see* him." Then in a much heartier voice he said, "Merry Christmas to you, too."

Sidney heard the dial tone in her ear. In fury, she pulled the phone out of the wall and threw it across the room. If Anastasia had not seen it with her own eyes, she would not have believed it. When Sidney saw Anastasia staring at her, astonished, she apologized. "Sorry." Then she walked to the hall closet and pulled out her ski apparel.

"Are we skiing today?" Anastasia was surprised.

"I'm going out for a couple of runs. You stay here. It's pretty frigid."

Anastasia had never seen Sidney this upset before. *I better not let her go out by herself.* "That's okay. I'd like to take a couple of runs," she lied.

The two were dressed and had the car packed within fifteen minutes. It was cold. With the wind chill it was 18 degrees below zero. Anastasia got in the car and said, "Brr."

"Why don't you stay here? I'll be back in a couple of hours."

"No. I want to go."

Between the weather and the holiday, the slopes were empty. Initially, Sidney was silent on the gondola. Anastasia did not dare to bring up the telephone conversation. But about halfway up the mountain, Sidney started talking. "How can I compete with him?"

"Compete with who?"

"Michael."

"I'm lost Sid, what are you talking about?"

"How can I compete with him for JP's affection?"

"This isn't a competition, Sid. JP loves you, you don't need to compete for his love."

"Don't I? Then why is he spending New Year's with Michael and not me?"

"He's not coming back for New Year's?" Anastasia was starting to understand.

"I can't compete with him. Michael always seems to find a way to do it bigger and better, no matter what it is. His presents are always bigger and his vacations are always better. How can I compete with that? He has JP for weekends and holidays. I'm the one who nags him to do his homework and chores. Last week I heard JP say he wanted to go to his father's alma mater. Then he wants to work with his dad to take over Whitman Industries."

"Sidney, I really think you're overreacting. I've gotten to know JP pretty well this year. He adores you."

The gondola swayed in the wind as it approached the top of the mountain. The two exited the lift and Sidney turned to Anastasia. "Look, this weather isn't the best to ski in. Why don't you go in the lodge and warm up? I'll take a run and come back to get you."

God. It is cold out here, Anastasia thought.

"I'll be fine, really," Sidney tried to convince her.

Anastasia dropped her skis and stepped into her bindings. "I want to take at least one run before I break."

They selected an intermediate trail and agreed to meet halfway down the mountain, at a junction they were familiar with. Sidney quickly headed downhill.

The wind was bitter and did not ease as they descended the slope. The run had a modest grade and circled the mountain offering entrances to other trails, many of which were more advanced. It was hard-packed and fast, narrow with many bends, and lined with trees on both sides.

Although Anastasia was a good intermediate skier, Sidney was more advanced and soon was out of Anastasia's sight. This would not have concerned her any other day, but today was different.

As Sidney skied down the trail, her mind kept racing. She heard Michael's voice say over and over, *"It's not my fault he wants to spend New Year's with me…He wants to spend New Year's with me…"* Sidney felt the tears freeze on her eyelashes as she heard Michael's voice in her head. *"You better not step out of line, because I'll own him…I'll own him…I'll own him…"*

As her mind wandered, skiing conditions quickly deteriorated. The wind caused blizzard-like conditions. Sidney realized she was skiing too fast, and made an effort to slow down, but it was too late. The tip of her right ski caught an edge and she lost her balance and fell hard. Sidney's left ski released but her right one remained fastened. Her right leg snapped as the ski twisted around. She slid down the hill face first, attempting to stop with her hands, but she could not.

She never saw the "trail closed" sign and rope that tied off the expert trail. She slid right under the yellow warning rope, and was propelled into the vertical trail. *Oh shit*, she thought as she flew, looking at the vertical mogul field below her. Sidney landed hard on a mogul. The impact to her shoulder caused its dislocation, and intense pain. She slid from mogul to mogul down the steep terrain, until the backside of a large mogul stopped her body.

Oh God, this hurts. Sidney lay facing the mogul that had stopped her. She tried to look behind her but the pain from her shoulder intensified with every movement. Sandwiched between two moguls, she was unable to see the top of the trail. When she tried to move her legs, she felt an overwhelming pain in her right leg. She knew her leg was broken. A wave of dizziness overwhelmed her, and she passed out between the giant mounds of snow.

Anastasia continued down the trail at a more conservative speed. Visibility was poor, so she stayed alert to the changing conditions. She almost hit Sidney's ski as she swept by it, and stopped ten feet downhill of the ski. Then she climbed up the hill to investigate and recognized the Rossignol ski. It was Sidney's.

"Sidney?" she called out. "Sidney?"

Anastasia picked up the ski and slowly traversed the trail, searching for signs of her friend. About twenty feet down she found a Scott ski pole. She searched the trees that lined the trail. "Sidney?" But she was nowhere to be found. About thirty feet downhill, the trail came to a "Y." The right side continued the natural course of the ski run, while a yellow rope tied off a left bend.

Anastasia traversed to where the trail split. Standing at the point where the trail curved, she looked back up the mountain. *What happened to you, Sid?* "Sidney?" She continued to call, but the only thing she heard was the trees blowing in the wind. She glanced at the "trail closed" sign and yellow rope, then made her way to the restricted entry and peered down the closed expert trail. Below the steep initial descent was a dangerous mogul field. She looked quickly over the area and was about to leave, when something caught her eye near a mogul about twenty feet down. She stared at the object, trying to figure what it was. *It's small. Maybe goggles.*

Quickly, she removed her skis and stuck them upright in the snow, forming an X at the entrance of the closed trail. She studied the initial drop. An eight-foot vertical wall descended to a steep mogul field. *If I go down, I'm not sure I'm going to be able to climb back up.* Anastasia sat on the lip of the cliff and let herself fall off the initial vertical. She slammed hard into the first mogul, then moved to the next mound and next, until she reached for the object. Her heart skipped a beat as she pulled the partially buried object. *It was Sidney's goggles.*

"Sidney?" she called with more urgency. Again, there was no response. Anastasia moved from mogul to mogul, combing the challenging terrain. She was about thirty feet down when she heard someone calling from above, "Do you need help?"

Anastasia looked up to see a kid at the top of the slope. "Yeah, I think my friend is down here." The boy started removing his skis, then Anastasia yelled back to him, "No. Don't come down, you won't be able to get back up. Go for help. Please." The boy waved, then skied away.

Anastasia continued to descend the steep terrain. She saw an object partially buried in snow, about twenty feet away from her. Her heart started beating faster when she realized it was Sidney.

"Sidney?" she called, but the body lay motionless face down in a mound of snow. "Sidney?" She slid to Sidney's side, but she was motionless.

Anastasia gently pulled the snow from her face. *She was breathing.* She saw that her right leg was badly twisted. The ski was still attached. "Sid, can you hear me?" she called in the wind, but there was no response. Anastasia was afraid to move her in case her back or neck were injured. She looked up the trail but could not see the main trail. *I hope that kid gets help.*

Anastasia felt lost. She didn't know what to do. She prayed the kid who stopped would send help. But thoughts like, *What if he doesn't get help?* troubled her. She turned to Sidney, "Sidney can you hear me?" She didn't budge.

She glanced at her watch and decided to hang tight, for a half hour. As the minutes crept by, the wind picked up, the temperature plummeted and the sun disappeared behind the mountain. All the while, Anastasia chatted with Sidney.

"Now why did you go do something stupid like this, Sid? We were having such a fun trip. Damn it. JP loves you, that's all that matters." Anastasia looked away from her friend, as she admitted to herself, "I do too."

"I know your secret," she continued, "You pretend to be such a hard ass, but you're not.

She rubbed her hands briskly together. "Have I ever told you that you remind me of somebody I once knew? The funny thing is—I can't place when and where I knew her. But I know she was a lot less stubborn and pig-headed than you are."

Anastasia was concerned. The temperature felt like it had dropped ten degrees. Then she thought she heard a moan from Sidney, but it was so faint, she wasn't sure. "Sidney? Sidney, can you hear me?"

Sidney's eyes fluttered. "Anastasia?"

"Yeah, it's me." *Oh God, thank you.* "Sid, where are you hurt?"

"My shoulder…and I think I broke my right leg."

"How about your back and neck?"

"I think they're okay. Where are we?"

"Some closed trail. I saw a kid some time ago and asked him to get help. But no one has come."

"What time is it?" Sidney asked.

"It's almost three o'clock."

"Anastasia, you have to go for help."

"I'm not going to leave you here alone."

"You don't have a choice. In another hour the sun will go down. If we lose the light, nobody will find us."

Anastasia knew she was right. "Okay, I'll go. I promise I'll be back as soon as I can." She gently rubbed Sidney's back, "Hang in there." *God, please take care of her.*

Anastasia started her climb back to the top. After repeated falls she finally made her way all the to the top - to the initial precipice. *How am I going to get up there?* She studied the vertical wall above and decided the left side offered a better climbing face. As she climbed she thought, *The cold must be getting to me now. I'm starting to hear voices.* Anastasia was hanging on the wall face when an arm from above swooped down and pulled her to safety.

"God, am I glad to see you," she said when she saw the ski patrol.

"Are you okay?" one of the men asked.

Anastasia nodded. "I'm fine, but my friend needs help. She thinks she broke her leg, and her shoulder is hurt. She's down there." She pointed down the steep ski trail.

It was dark by the time Sidney arrived at the medical facility at the base of the mountain. She was taken into a small examination room where a nurse immediately started removing and cutting away her ski apparel.

Then a young, good-looking man walked in and introduced himself. "Hi, I'm Dr. Waters."

"You're a doctor?" Anastasia asked.

He detected disbelief in Anastasia's voice. "Yeah, I graduated and everything." He was obviously annoyed. Then he turned to the patient and started examining her. The ski patrol had splinted her leg and immobilized her upper left side. Although the doctor was young and green, he seemed thorough.

After his initial exam, he said, "Your shoulder is dislocated. I'm going to have to reset it."

"Have you ever done that before?" Anastasia asked.

"No," he admitted. "Would you like to do it?"

Sidney interrupted the bickering. "Doctor, would you please reset my shoulder, so I can go home?"

Sidney's arm was carefully removed from the sling. The doctor eyed the gold chain around her neck. "We should remove your necklace," he clumsily tried to undo the clasp.

"Here, let me try." Anastasia was losing patience with the doctor. She removed the chain and pendant and put it in her ski jacket pocket.

Moments later, they were ready to reset the shoulder. "I wish I could say this isn't going to hurt, but I can't." The doctor turned to Anastasia, "It might be better if you step outside."

"Absolutely not." Anastasia reached for Sidney's free hand.

The doctor suddenly jerked Sidney's shoulder and she shrieked in pain. Her grip on Anastasia's hand tightened as her shoulder was reset.

Anastasia felt heartbroken and lost seeing her friend in so much pain.

Hours later the two returned to the house, with a list of instructions and pain medication. Sidney wore a sling on her injured shoulder and had a cast on her right leg. Anastasia helped her into a La-Z-Boy recliner, then set out to build a fire to get the chill out of the great room.

"What can I get you?" Anastasia asked as the fire strengthened.

"A glass of wine would be nice."

"I don't think you should mix alcohol with pain pills."

"I haven't taken any pills."

When Anastasia hesitated, Sidney complained, "The pills are in that bag over there. Take them, I won't use them. May I have a glass of wine now, please?"

Anastasia poured two glasses of Merlot and carried them to the great room along with cheese and crackers. Sidney saw the broken telephone lying against the wall and was reminded of her conversation with Michael.

"I was a real asshole today," Sidney admitted.

"You won't get an argument from me."

"I'm sorry, and thank you for saving my butt."

Anastasia smiled warmly. "You're welcome. I guess this means we're even.

Sidney finally smiled.

The two women sat silently for a long time, enjoying the fire, snacks and wine.

"Oh, I almost forgot. I have your pendant in my jacket." Anastasia rose and went to the hall closet. Moments later she returned to Sidney. As she opened her hand she could not help but admire the gold pendant. "It's beautiful. Very unusual," she said, as she held it up to inspect it. "What is it?"

Sidney stared at the ankh she had worn since Gary passed away. "It's called an ankh."

"An ankh? What does it symbolize?"

"Life."

"It's unusual. What's its origin?"

"Egyptian. I believe ancient Egyptian," Sidney answered.

Egyptian?

Sidney took the pendant and set it on the table. "I probably shouldn't wear it until the sling comes off."

After Sidney's second glass of wine, she decided to get up. With a sling on her left arm and cast on her right leg she attempted to get up. Although the recliner was not in the recline position, the chair was angled enough to make rising impossible.

"Where are you going?"

"I'd like to use the bathroom," Sidney tried to wiggle forward in the chair.

"Here, let me help you." Anastasia moved to Sidney's right side and tried to help her up, but her leverage was not good enough.

"This won't work." Carefully, Anastasia moved in front of Sidney, avoiding the injured leg. She leaned forward and wrapped her left arm around Sidney's back. "Put your arm around my neck," she instructed.

For a moment, as Anastasia held Sidney close, steadying her, their eyes met. Sidney could not comprehend the feelings which surfaced, or why Anastasia's touch was familiar. She didn't understand why her heart swelled with warmth.

For Anastasia, images of a distant past came flooding back; imagery of ancient wonders, heartache and a long lost love.

Sidney was the first to divert her eyes, grounding herself from the intimate connection. *What the hell am I doing?* She scolded herself. Anastasia released her hold, and Sidney reached for her crutch and hobbled toward the bathroom.

"Here, let me help," Anastasia said. But as she took her arm she felt Sidney's body tense.

Sidney closed the bathroom door behind her and Anastasia leaned against the door, lost in her thoughts. *My God. I know I've looked into those eyes before…Egypt? I can't believe it. I've fallen in love with an untouchable. She remembered, last time I was the untouchable.*

On the other side of the door, Sidney ran cool water from the faucet. She splashed the water on her face, then wiped her face with the towel. She studied her eyes in the mirror's reflection. *I can't let her into my space. She's too dangerous.*

Chapter 24

Sidney and Anastasia extended their visit in Vail until after New Year's. The extra days of rest helped Sidney's healing. During the week, Sidney encouraged Anastasia to ski, but she chose to work on some music she had put on hold. The week went by fast. Soon, Sidney's shoulder felt better, and she was able to get around more easily.

On New Year's Eve morning, Sidney approached Anastasia with an idea. "You've been such a good sport this week. Can I treat you to dinner tonight? I have reservations at Latour's."

"If you don't mind, I'd rather just stay in. I've been planning a wonderful dinner for us. Can you handle it?"

"Are you sure? You've been cooking all week." Sidney was surprised.

"I'm sure. I enjoy cooking, and I don't get the chance very often."

Anastasia prepared filet mignon and lobster tails. The dinner was prepared to perfection and impressed Sidney. After dinner, the two retired to the great room.

"I've been working on some new music," Anastasia announced. "Would you like to hear it?"

"Sure."

Anastasia picked up the old guitar and played "My Untouchable."

Do you know who I am?
I've come to you in your dreams,
I've loved you on a different dimension.

But as I sit here, looking at you,
I can't help but wonder if you can see who I really am.
Can you see beyond my façade?
My veil? My disguise?
Or do you just see me as your friend, your partner in crime.

Do you know who I am?
I've kissed your sweet lips and held your heart so close...
but in another time, in another place, in another reality.

But here, things are not so clear.
The fuzziness clouds our minds.
And here, I am not who I appear.
I'm a façade and you're my untouchable.
Here, I'm your friend, and our friendship means everything.
I would never risk losing it.
Here, life's complications stop our reuniting.
You're my untouchable and to you, I'm trivial.

Do you know who I am?
I have been with you before.
Don't you remember our promise?
We'd meet here, as before.
Don't you recognize me?

Can't you see it in my eyes?
Don't you remember my spirit?
Don't be fooled by my disguise.

Here, it is hard; this blessing is a curse.
I can't have you, my love.
You're my untouchable.
Look into my eyes, the windows to my soul.
If you still cannot see it, you'll remain my untouchable.

I will find you again, next time
And then, I pray you'll remember me.
I'll keep searching until we reunite.
That's my promise to you.
Until then you'll remain my untouchable.

Sidney remained silent and thoughtful. "So you believe in reincarnation?" she finally asked.

"Yes, I do. More so than the alternatives, you know—heaven and hell. How about you?" Anastasia asked.

"Haven't given it much thought," Sidney lied. "Your song is good. Maybe you should get stranded in Vail more often."

"I've been working on it for a while now. I just needed the quiet time to finish it." Anastasia continued playing the guitar, listening intently to each chord. "This guitar has a good sound and feel." She continued strumming the strings of the instrument. In Sidney's mind, the music changed from its contemporary style to a more traditional love song. Each note bringing her back to a different time and place.

* * *

It was the Saturday before Sidney and Charlotte's fifth-year anniversary, and Charlotte was strumming her guitar on the shore-house porch. Justin was playing with his Matchbox cars in the great room, and Sidney watched him from the porch as she worked at a table.

Charlotte finished the love song and sat at the table next to Sidney. "Guess what week this is?"

"I don't know," Sidney lied. "What week is it?"

"You don't know?" Charlotte smiled. "Anything special about Friday?"

"Is it payday?" Charlotte pouted and Sidney laughed. "It's hard to believe we've been together five years."

"What do you want to do to celebrate?" Charlotte asked.

"Be with you."

"I have that conference in Boston this week. I leave on Tuesday and return on Friday morning. Want to meet for lunch?" Charlotte asked.

"You coming into the city?"

"Sure, we can meet at Nat's." Charlotte suggested her favorite Italian restaurant. "Then, I can kidnap you for the weekend. JP will be with his father next weekend."

Sidney smiled at the idea. "Where are you going to take me?"

"It's a surprise." Charlotte tried to sound mysterious.

"I'm game, what do I pack?"

"I'll make the arrangements and let you know later." Charlotte examined what Sidney was working on. "What are you doing?"

"I'm writing a help-wanted ad for a road manager. I'm going to need someone new for Jason Light."

Charlotte paused. "Why don't you talk with Natalie about the position?"

"I'd love to, but the two of you haven't spoken in over a year. I don't want to put anyone in an uncomfortable position."

"Let me call her and see how she's doing. Can you hold off on the ad a week?"

"I'll wait." Sidney looked into the great room and saw Justin's back to them. She leaned over to steal a kiss from Charlotte. "Thanks."

"For what?" Charlotte asked.

"For making an effort with Natalie."

As Justin got older, Sidney and Charlotte chose not to show their affection in front of him. Sidney feared that if Michael found out, it would cause problems. Although Sidney knew she would eventually need to tell Justin, she wanted him to be old enough to understand her choice.

For months, Sidney had pondered the perfect gift for Charlotte to celebrate their fifth year together. She decided on a ring to symbolize their commitment to each other. While previously she had opposed union ceremonies since there was no societal recognition, she knew it was important to Charlotte. Sidney realized she was ready.

Sidney had it all planned. While she hadn't a clue where they were going, she'd be ready with ring in hand and propose to her. The more she thought about the weekend, the more excited she became.

Charlotte left Tuesday night for Boston. Sidney had been given specific instructions about what she should pack. She planned to take the train into the city that Friday, Charlotte would drive into the city from the airport, and meet her at the restaurant. Charlotte told her they would return to the shore by three o'clock Sunday afternoon. That was all the information Charlotte gave her.

On Wednesday, Sidney picked up an attractive diamond-laced wedding band from the jewelers.

Thursday night, Charlotte gave Sidney some last-minute instructions. "I'll see you tomorrow. Noon at Nat's. I love you, Sid."

"I love you too, Charlie."

As Sidney walked toward the restaurant, she caught herself

236

smiling in the glass reflection of the stores she passed. She knew she was blessed having Justin and Charlotte in her life, and felt warmth in her heart at the thought of her family. As she ventured toward the restaurant, she experienced an overwhelming sense of gratitude for her relationship with Charlotte. To her surprise, she wiped a tear from her eyes, then thought, *it must be the bitter wind.* It was cold, and Sidney pulled her coat collar around her face to protect it from the wind.

She was a block away from the restaurant when she saw Charlotte walking on the opposite side of the street. She stared at her and smiled. *She's approaching forty five, and she looks great.* Sidney watched her walk along the busy street for a few minutes and realized she had no reservations about their weekend or their union.

"Hey Charlie," Sidney yelled.

Charlotte turned and smiled back at Sidney across the busy street. "Hi stranger," she called back. The two walked parallel to each other on opposite sides of the street, approaching an intersection. Charlotte stood at the light waiting for the traffic signal to change, while Sidney stood in front of the restaurant. When Charlotte realized she just missed the pedestrian walk signal, she yelled to Sidney, "Get us a table, I'll be there in a few minutes."

Sidney acknowledged Charlotte by smiling and throwing her a kiss. Then she went into the restaurant. As the hostess was seating her, there was a disruption at the door. Apparently someone stormed into the restaurant to call an ambulance. The bus boy was placing garlic rolls on the table when Sidney asked, "Is everything okay outside?"

"I think there's been a car accident." The boy seemed uninterested.

Sidney waited a couple minutes for Charlotte, but she did not show. *Knowing Charlotte was a doctor, she figured she was helping with the accident.* She left her coat and small overnight bag at the table and peeked through the window. A group of people had formed a circle in the street, but she did not see Charlotte.

She left the restaurant and walked toward the crowd. "Charlie?" She searched the faces but did not see or hear her. Sirens blared from an approaching ambulance. "Charlie?" she called louder. Sidney pushed through the crowd but had not been prepared for what she found. There was a small clearing, and in the center lay a body.

"Oh God," Sidney ran to Charlotte's side where she lay on the cold street, her head resting in a pool of blood. Sidney kneeled next to her and saw that Charlotte's eyes were fixed in a distant stare. Although she knew it was too late, she asked, "Charlie? Can you hear me?" Sidney sat on the ground and cradled Charlotte's body. "Charlie, can you hear me?" She whispered in her ear. "You can't leave us, Charlie. We need you."

The police and EMTs arrived. The bystanders were moved to the curbside. A paramedic approached Sidney. "What is her name?"

"Charlie...Charlotte Gray. You can help her, can't you?"

The paramedic knew Charlotte was gone, but he searched for Charlotte's pulse, anyway. "I'm sorry. There's nothing more we can do for your friend." The man hesitated then asked, "Could you come with me? We'll need some information."

"Give me a minute, please." Sidney tucked her face next to Charlotte's and rocked her back and forth. She was numb. *Oh God, how could this happen?* Fifteen minutes earlier, her life could not have been better. Now, her happiness and gratitude had all slipped away. The warmth in her heart was replaced with emptiness, and the flicker of light in her eyes...vanished.

Moments later, a police officer and EMT separated Sidney from Charlotte and escorted her to a police car. An officer informed her Charlotte had been the victim of a hit and run. As the officer took pertinent information from Sidney, she felt like she was going to be sick. "I need to go," she abruptly stood to leave.

"We're not finished," the younger officer objected.

The other policeman was more understanding. "How can we reach you if we have more questions?"

Sidney jotted her name and phone number down. She turned and left. Charlotte's body had been taken away, leaving a pool of blood saturating the street and tape where her body had been. A woman tried to get her attention as Sidney blindly walked down the street.

"Excuse me."

Sidney turned and stared at the vaguely familiar face. "Yes?"

"I believe these are yours." The hostess from the restaurant handed Sidney's coat and overnight bag to her. "I'm terribly sorry about your loss."

"Thank you," Sidney managed to say. Then she continued to walk aimlessly down the busy city street.

She walked for blocks before it hit her she didn't have her car. It was at the train station and she didn't know where Charlie had parked. For the first time since the accident, she was cold. She dropped her bag and put on her coat over her blood-soiled clothing. Then she continued down the street, not fully believing Charlie was gone.

Moments later, she blindly walked into an intersection and a passing car almost hit her. The driver of the car honked his horn, then shouted obscenities and gestured the finger. *She knew she wasn't in control and needed help. But who could she turn to?*

Returning to the curb, she withdrew her phone from her pocket and punched in numbers. The phone rang four times before it was answered. "Miss Springer's office." Sidney remained silent on the other end. "Hello? Hello?"

Sidney cleared her throat. "Is Natalie there, please?"

"I'm sorry, she's in a meeting. May I take a message for her?"

"No…" She almost hung up the phone, then said, "I need to speak with her, would you get her for me, please?"

"Is this an emergency?"

"Yes."

"Can I tell her who's calling?"

"Sidney Marcum."

"I'm going to put you on hold. I need to pull her from the meeting."

To Sidney, it seemed as if she was on hold forever. She was about to hang up when Natalie picked up the phone. "Sid? What's wrong?" Sidney could not talk. "Sidney, are you there?" Natalie could hear someone breathing on the other end. "Is that you, Sid?"

"Yeah, it's me."

"What's wrong?"

"I have terrible news, Nat. It's…it's Charlie."

"What about Charlie?"

"There was an accident…Natalie, she's gone." Natalie remained silent. "Natalie, I'm sorry to tell you like this, I don't know what to do."

"What happened?" Natalie tried to remain calm.

"Hit and run."

"When?"

"I don't know, maybe an hour ago. They took her away…"

"Sidney, where are you?"

"I don't know."

"Are you in Manhattan?"

"Yeah. We were supposed to meet at Nat's…that's where it happened."

"Sidney, I'll come and get you. But you need to tell me exactly where you are."

Sidney looked around for street signs. "I'm at the corner of Fifth and 21st."

"I'll be right there, don't go anyplace. Do you understand?"

"Yeah."

Within twenty minutes Natalie found Sidney pacing the sidewalk. "Sidney?" Natalie called.

She was unresponsive. Natalie rested her hands on her shoulders, placing herself in Sidney's line of vision. "Sidney?"

Sidney finally recognized Natalie and they silently embraced.

"I don't know what to do. We never spoke about this. I don't know her family at all. My car…it's at the train station on the shore. I don't have any way—"

"Don't worry, I'll help. The first thing we need to do is contact Jennifer."

Like Natalie, Jennifer was shocked by the accident. But Natalie was right; Charlotte had left instructions with Jennifer in the event of an accidental death. In a handwritten letter, Charlotte had outlined her wishes. Her family had disowned her twenty years earlier because of her sexual orientation. In her letter she specifically requested that her body not be taken back to her family's hometown for a burial. Rather, she requested a small party among friends to celebrate her life. She asked that her body be cremated and her ashes spread in the mountains of Vail.

Both Jennifer and Natalie helped with the arrangements. Jennifer contacted Charlotte's family and informed them of her death along with her burial request. Her father only asked when her will would be read. Natalie called friends and contacted people at Monmouth Medical Center and New York Hospital. The small memorial celebration was scheduled for Sunday afternoon at the shore.

Late that afternoon Sidney called her housekeeper, Lynette, and gave her the news. Lynette told her that Justin had been picked up by his father's limo after kindergarten, as scheduled. Justin would not return until Sunday evening.

Sidney knew she would have been lost without Jennifer and Natalie's help. She spent the night at Jennifer's home on the Upper East Side, and Natalie picked her up the following morning to take Sidney to her house. This was one time Sidney was in no hurry to get home. As Natalie's car exited the Garden State Parkway, Sidney said, "We should do some food shopping for the gathering tomorrow."

The two spent a good part of their day shopping, running errands and picking up Sidney's car at the train station.

They retired early that evening, having good intentions, but neither was able to sleep. At two o'clock that Sunday morning, Natalie strolled into the sunroom and found Sidney in the dark. The porch felt ten degrees cooler than the house. Sidney was bundled up in a blanket on the couch, staring out at the moonlit water.

"You should be sleeping."

Sidney continued to stare into the night. "I can't. What are you doing up?"

Natalie stood near the doorway and was rubbing her arms from the cold. "Just got a lot on my mind."

Sidney threw half the blanket off, inviting Natalie to sit with her. She rested next to Sidney, who covered her with the blanket. The two continued to stare out into the night.

"I just can't believe she's gone. I keep expecting her to walk in. I can't sleep in our…" Sidney hesitated, "in my bed."

Natalie reached for Sidney's hand, but was surprised when she found it clutched in a fist. She opened the fist and found a wedding band. Sidney allowed Natalie to inspect the band in the dim lighting. "Is it from Charlie?" Natalie had known Charlotte wanted to marry Sidney.

Sidney shook her head. "No…I was planning on proposing to her this weekend. It was our fifth-year anniversary, but I didn't even…"

"I'm sorry," Natalie said, then replaced the ring in Sidney's palm and delicately folded her fingers back over the band.

Sidney noticed tears forming in Natalie's eyes. *I'm so selfish. I'm not the only one in pain.* "I'm sorry. I've been wrapped up in what I'm feeling; I've forgotten what you must be going through."

"We didn't exactly…part on the best of terms," confided Natalie.

"Charlie didn't call you this week?" Sidney asked.

Natalie was surprised. "No, should she have?"

"Last Sunday she told me she would, but she must have gotten busy with the conference." Sidney hesitated. "I know you were in love with her, Nat, and that's why the two of you agreed to stop seeing each other."

"Charlie told you that?"

"Yeah, more or less. Last Sunday, I was writing a help-wanted ad. She suggested that I talk with you about the job. She said she would call you. Charlie missed you terribly. She asked me not to place the ad until she spoke with you."

"She didn't seem concerned about us working together?"

"No. I know she missed you and wanted your friendship back. She was hoping you were ready."

Natalie remained quiet for some time. "Thank you for sharing that with me."

The two nestled together on the couch until the sun peeked over the horizon, broadcasting the new day.

People started arriving at the house to pay their respects. An entourage, including Nancy and Dr. Phelps from New York Hospital, showed up first. Another group from Monmouth Medical Center arrived shortly after.

When Scott arrived, he embraced Sidney and would not let her go. He whispered in Sidney's ear, "I know Gary is taking care of her." Sidney smiled at Scott, finding some comfort in that thought.

Jennifer's husband Bill and children also came to the gathering. Bill was a big help. He offered guests drinks, passed out appetizers and picked up after those who had left.

It was close to four o'clock when Natalie approached Jennifer. "I'm going outside for a while."

"Are you okay?"

"Yeah. I just need a little air," she said as she grabbed her jacket.

At 4:10 P.M. the doorbell rang and Scott went to the front door. A man stood at the door with Justin.

"Hi, Uncle Scott!"

Scott opened the door and exchanged a hug with Justin in the foyer. "Hi, sport." Scott's attention returned to the man outside the doorway. Although Scott had never been introduced to Michael Whitman, he recognized him. "Hi, I'm Scott Davis. Would you like to come in?"

"No. Would you tell Sidney I'll be down by the water? Goodbye, Justin." Michael abruptly turned and left the front door.

Arrogant son of a bitch, Scott thought.

Justin made his entrance into the great room where Sidney spoke with some of Charlotte's friends. He ran to his mother and gave her a hug. "I didn't know we were having a party," he said. Then he went to play with Jennifer's two children.

"Excuse me, Sidney, can I talk with you?" Scott interrupted.

"Yes. What's up?"

"Sid, Michael brought JP here. He's down by the water waiting for you."

"Great, just what I need." Sidney pulled a jacket from the hall closet. *I wonder what's going on. Michael doesn't usually bring JP back, and he never wants to see me.*

Natalie was surprised when she saw Michael Whitman stroll down the keystone walkway toward the water. She sat behind the tall junipers that landscaped a private sitting area. He stopped about ten feet from her, but did not see her.

Sidney approached and greeted him coolly. "Michael."

"Sidney," he returned the cool greeting.

"To what do I owe the honor of your presence?" she asked.

Natalie felt terrible that she was sitting so close and could hear them. She looked for an escape, but there was none. She remained quiet.

"I heard some news this weekend, and wanted to see if it was true. I heard your…roommate passed away."

How'd he learn that so quickly? Sidney remained skeptical. "Why are you so interested?"

"I'm always interested in events that impact my son's life."

Sidney hesitated. "It's true. Did you say anything to him?"

"No. I am sorry," he said.

Sidney stared at Michael in disbelief. "Why? Why are you sorry, Michael?"

"I think it's a shame when anyone is struck down prematurely." Then he turned on her. "Besides, I was this close," he illustratively pinched two fingers together, "to nailing your ass."

"What the hell are you talking about?"

"I know you're a lesbian, Sidney, and Charlotte was your lover."

Sidney did not admit nor deny it. "And your point is…?"

"I will not have my son raised by a dyke."

"Meaning?" Sidney tried to remain calm.

Michael walked around Sidney taunting her. "We've prepared a motion to the court to get full custody of Justin, on the basis that his mother's a homosexual. Your lover's death is very untimely for both our sakes. But I'm sure there'll be other lovers for you, Sidney, and all it will take is for you to step out of line once, and I'll own him. Do you hear me? I'll own him."

"You'll never have full custody," Sidney said angrily.

"Yes, I will," Michael said smugly. Then he turned and left.

Sidney's world seemed to be collapsing. She walked toward the beach, then sat on a bench and gazed over the water. *I can't believe you left me, Charlie.* Moments later, she felt someone sit next to her.

"Sidney, I'm sorry," Natalie apologized. "I was in the juniper garden when Michael came down. He didn't see me." She hesitated. "I heard everything."

Sidney remained silent, but rested her head on Natalie's shoulder. Natalie put an arm around Sidney and held her closely as she wept for the first time since Charlotte passed away.

Sidney spent that evening with Justin. She tried to explain, as best she could, that Charlotte was not coming back. Sidney stayed by his side as the five-year-old cried himself to sleep. When she finally left his room, she was drained. She found Natalie looking through a photo album next to the fireplace. "I'm surprised you're still up," she said to Natalie.

"I'm surprised you're still up. You must be exhausted."

"I am," Sidney admitted, then sat on the carpeting next to her.

"Can I ask you a personal question?" Natalie asked.

"What?"

"What are you going to do about Michael's threat?"

"What threat?"

"You know, if he catches you in a relationship…"

"It's only a threat if I'm in a relationship."

"Meaning…you'll be careful not to get caught?"

"No. No more relationships for me."

"You're a young, beautiful woman, Sid. You're going to close yourself to any opportunity of sharing your life with someone?"

"Absolutely."

"Sidney, you're not serious."

"Yeah, I am. No relationships. At least not until JP is old enough to understand and be able to choose who he wants to live with." Sidney stated calmly, "I lost Charlie. I won't put myself in a position to lose JP, *ever.*"

Sidney was exhausted when she retired that evening. *She didn't think she'd have any difficulty falling asleep.* But as she climbed into bed she immediately became aware of the void beside her. Like the previous evening, she tossed and turned for hours.

It was early morning when she became aware of a dripping sound coming from her bathroom. First the noise was subtle. Then it became louder and more continuous as if water was running. Sidney got out of bed and headed for the bathroom. The water was running from the faucet in her sink. She turned the handle and the water stopped, but within seconds, the trickling started again. Sidney turned the light on to study the faucet. The light hurt her eyes. She turned the handle again, but this time the water would not stop and started to discolor. The water appeared rusty, then darkened and eventually turned red. *Oh my God.* Sidney backed away from the sink and watched blood trickle from the faucet.

The sound of a siren from behind her startled her, and as she turned, her bathroom transformed into a busy city street. Sidney saw Charlotte lying on the cold pavement surrounded in her own blood. Instinctively, she went to her side and cradled her body, reliving her worst nightmare. Sidney held her head close to her breast and whispered, "Why did you leave me?"

"Don't remember me that way," a familiar voice said.

The voice startled her. "Who said that?"

"I did," Charlotte stood next to her own lifeless body. "You need to let go, Sid. I don't want you to hold onto this memory. We've shared plenty of happy ones."

"Charlie?" Sidney stared at her in disbelief. Gently, she placed Charlotte's body back on the cold pavement, then stood in front of her. *I'm dreaming,* she told herself. Cautiously she approached Charlotte. She was wearing hospital scrubs and a radiant light surrounded her. "This is just a dream, right?" Sidney asked.

Charlotte smiled warmly. "If that's what you're comfortable believing, this is a dream."

Sidney reached for her, and as Charlotte took hold of her hand, the scene transformed once again. The two were on a mountaintop, surrounded by wildflowers, the warm sun beaming down on them. "Why did you leave me, Charlie?"

"It was my time. I did the lesson I set out to do."

"And where are you now? Can I come with you?"

"No, Sidney," she smiled again. "You haven't done what you're here to do."

"But...I want to be with you, Charlie."

"You will. One day."

"When? In heaven?"

"No. It's not that simple. We'll be together again, in another reality, in another lifetime."

"Another lifetime? Will I know you? Will I remember us?"

"It's possible, but probably not. But we will find each other, again. I promise."

"I love you, Charlie."

"And I will always love you, Sid. This is how I want you to remember me." She leaned forward and their lips gently met.

As Sidney woke, she sat up in bed and called, "Charlie?" Then reality hit. *My God. It was just a dream. It seemed so real.* She heard the trickling of water from her bathroom. *Deja vu?*

Sidney went into the bathroom and found the faucet dripping. She shut the faucet off, but this time the water stopped. As she turned to leave, she realized she was standing on something. She leaned over and picked up some clothing that had been lying on the floor. *What's this?* She turned the light on to see. She trembled when she saw the hospital scrubs in her hand. She rubbed them against her face and smelled Charlotte's perfume.

Chapter 25

The months that followed Christmas in Vail were busy. Anastasia worked on a new album as well as the movie. All the feedback Sidney got from Clausen regarding Anastasia's performance was favorable.

Sidney was busy negotiating with Global on a new contract for Anastasia. She used new recording demos of "My Untouchable" to bait Global into another year's contract with four years of options. Working with agents, Sidney also finalized the tour schedule for the year.

Although Anastasia's and Sidney's schedules were demanding, they always seemed to find time to spend with each other. Typically, Anastasia would visit the shore house a couple weekends a month, as a result Justin and Anastasia's friendship grew. Anastasia took the initiative to get Sidney out to exercise her leg. After her cast was finally removed, the two spent many evenings walking a favorite beach.

Brett continued to escort Anastasia throughout the filming. He was quick to deceive the tabloids about their passionate affair and easily justified the deceit. "I'm just giving the public what they want to hear." To Anastasia, Brett admitted on more than one occasion his attraction to her. Initially she was able to maintain distance and even suggested that they stop seeing so much of each other. But Brett would not hear of it.

When the filming was finished, there was an elaborate wrap-up party. Anastasia and Brett arrived together. Brett was very attentive to Anastasia's needs and the press ate it up. At one point during dinner, Brett leaned over and planted a kiss on Anastasia. The press was on top of them to capture the moment on film.

Anastasia remained calm, smiled at Brett, then whispered, "Do you want to tell me what that was all about?"

"I kissed you," Brett said with a boyish grin.

"Why?"

"I think it's time we took the next step," Brett admitted.

"Which is?"

"Dating. But I mean really dating, though. The two of us are good friends. I'd like more. Do you see a problem with that?"

"Well, yeah. Cheri for one, and maybe you forgot—I'm gay." Anastasia remained calm, frequently smiling, aware that eyes were on them.

"You don't have to worry about Cheri, it's over," Brett replied. "You're not gay, you just haven't been with the right man yet."

Why do they flatter themselves so? Anastasia thought.

"Can you honestly say you're not attracted to me?"

"Brett, you're obviously a very attractive man." Anastasia was agitated. "But don't ever tell me you know me better than I know myself."

"Are you seeing anyone right now?" Brett asked.

"No."

"We're both adults with no attachments. I find you very attractive and you admit that I'm attractive. Don't tell me you're so closed minded, and bigoted, that you wouldn't see where this friendship can take us." Then he continued, "I'm going to be in New York a lot over the next year. I've taken a role in a Broadway show."

When Anastasia left the party that night, she was deep in thought. It had been almost a year since she had been with Stephanie. *God, I'm lonely. I wonder...what would it be like with Brett?*

A couple days later, Michelle brought to work the *Planet Gossiper*. She dropped the tabloid on Sidney's desk and said, "I know you don't usually read these, but I thought you might be interested in this."

Sidney picked up the paper. The cover page depicted Brett and Anastasia kissing. To Sidney's surprise, she felt a nagging ache in her heart as she looked at the picture. Could she be jealous?

Anastasia drove down to Sidney's shore house late the following Saturday afternoon. She was disappointed when she learned that Justin was at Michael's for the weekend. Later that evening the two women got into Sidney's Jeep and headed out to dinner.

They arrived at the restaurant and were seated at their favorite table. The owner, Steve, always made sure the two were taken care of.

During dinner, Anastasia was quiet and Sidney noticed that she was drinking more than usual.

"Is there anything wrong?" Sidney asked.

"No. Just got a lot on my mind."

"Anything you want to talk about?"

"No," Anastasia replied, then poured herself another glass of wine.

They left the restaurant and a full moon greeted the women. It was warm for a March evening. "Are you up for a walk?" Sidney asked.

"I didn't bring a jacket with me," Anastasia started to object.

"That's okay, I have an extra one in the Jeep."

When they arrived at the beach, Sidney gave Anastasia a jacket and put on a sweatshirt. They walked over the moonlit dunes to the beach. The full moon illuminated the shoreline and the gentle breaking waves. For the first time since they left the restaurant, Anastasia spoke. "What a beautiful night." The sound of the water swelling against the beach was relaxing.

They walked silently for about a quarter of a mile before Sidney spoke. "You seem preoccupied tonight."

"Sorry, I guess I'm not good company."

"Your company is fine, I'm just concerned. Is there anything I can do? Maybe just listen?" Sidney started walking away from the water and headed toward the dunes. Anastasia followed and the two women sat side-by-side on the sand.

Anastasia remained silent for a long time. "I've been seeing someone for a while now. We haven't been dating or anything, we're actually just friends..." Anastasia stopped.

"Go on," Sidney encouraged.

"Well, I've found that my feelings have gone beyond friendship. I like this person, and I'd like to see where it could go."

"And how does...this person feel?" Sidney asked.

"To be honest, I haven't a clue. Sometimes, I think they feel more than friendship, then other times—I just don't know."

"You don't know how they feel?" Sidney was surprised.

"No, it's not exactly the type of person I would normally pursue." Anastasia remained silent for a minute then asked, "You do know who I'm talking about, don't you?"

"Well, I think we're talking about Brett, but Anastasia, I think it's pretty obvious how Brett feels toward you."

Without warning, Anastasia took Sidney's hand into her own. Sidney was surprised and confused by her touch. She found Anastasia's eyes searching hers. There was a connection Sidney couldn't describe; the same connection she had felt that night in Vail when their eyes met. It was as if their souls had found each other after searching for lifetimes, she couldn't avert her eyes and her heart warmed. Anastasia delicately brushed Sidney's wind-blown hair from her face, her touch intensifying the feeling of reuniting. Sidney's eyes settled upon Anastasia's lips which were slowly approaching, coming ever so close, lingering by her lips. She could feel the warmth of Anastasia's aura upon her face. It was Sidney who ultimately surrendered and met Anastasia. They kissed, gently and slowly, stirring feelings and emotions which had been dormant for centuries.

Sidney's heart beat faster and faster. She was so distracted by their kiss she did not hear the surf beating against the beach, nor the subtle movement of footsteps in the sand.

Consumed by the kiss, Sidney needed every ounce of strength to take back control and pulled herself from Anastasia's lips. "Oh God…Anastasia, I can't do this."

Anastasia backed away and got to her feet. "I'm sorry…" She turned and rushed off.

Sidney sat on the beach alone, trying to sort out what had just happened. She had feelings she didn't understand and there were desires that had been long forgotten. . Oh God, she thought as she watched Anastasia disappear in the shadows, This can't be happening.

As she sat on the beach, she contemplated what to do. She considered pretending their kiss never happened. Then she recalled how Anastasia's lips felt upon hers. How could she pretend it hadn't happened? She could lie and tell her she wasn't interested in women, but she thought her response to Anastasia's touch betrayed her. Then of course, she could trust her and tell her the truth. I could explain why I can't get involved with woman, she thought. That the risk is too great ... no matter what the temptation is. Knowing that Anastasia knew how important Justin was to her, surely she'd understand.

She got to her feet, brushed the sand off her jeans and headed back to the car. When she arrived she found Anastasia leaning against the Jeep. "We need to talk," Sidney said.

"I'm really sorry," Anastasia said.

Sidney leaned against the Jeep also. "I'm sorry Anastasia, but I can't..." She searched for the words, "I can't love you, but I'd like you to know—"

"I am so sorry," Anastasia interrupted. "I don't know what came over me. Maybe the wine, maybe the moonlight, maybe both." She paused. "Believe me, I'm not in the habit of making passes at straight women. It'll never happen again, I promise."

Sidney listened as Anastasia rambled on. "I know this is no excuse, but I've been getting a lot of pressure from Brett. I think I'm ready to take the next step with him," she lied. "It's just confusing thinking about being with a man. Maybe I'm going straight or something. I don't really know what I'm saying, except, I didn't mean anything by it. I'm sorry."

Sidney didn't know what to say. She hadn't expected this, "Apology accepted."

As Sidney drove back toward to the house, there was a nagging ache within her. It took her only seconds to process it. She was jealous. Here she thought their kiss had been as stirring to Anastasia as it had been to her. How could she have been so wrong?

At Sidney's house, Anastasia abruptly said, "I'm going to be heading home."

"Why?"

"I have a lot of things to do tomorrow, and I'd like to get a jump on them."

It was obvious to Sidney that Anastasia would not change her mind. Sidney had mixed emotions as she watched Anastasia drive away from the house that night.

Anastasia's tears would not stop as she headed north on the parkway. She couldn't remember the last time she had kissed someone so passionately. It had felt so right. And I thought she felt the same...*how could I have been so* wrong? She wiped the tears from her eyes. *I needed to know. Now maybe I can get on with my life.* But the tears continued to flow. *How am I ever going to be able to face her again?*

When Anastasia approached the exit for the New Jersey Turnpike, she found herself debating which way to go. *I hope I'm not making a mistake*, she thought all the way to Manhattan. She quickly found Brett's apartment building. It was close to midnight when he opened the door and let her in.

"It's about time you came to your senses," he said as she walked in. Then he kissed her firmly on her mouth and took her to his bed.

Two weeks later, Natalie noticed a strain between Anastasia and Sidney during a photo shoot. When Brett arrived to pick up Anastasia, Natalie could have sworn she saw pain in Sidney's eyes, if only for a second. Later that week, Sidney met with her staff and told them she wanted to spend more time with her son. She asked Nelson to start getting involved in Anastasia's direct management.

Sidney called a meeting between herself and Anastasia. She wanted to advise Anastasia of the management change. Brett arrived with Anastasia at her office and the two were openly affectionate toward each other as they waited for Sidney. Sidney and Brett did not know each other very well, so Sidney was surprised when he gave her a cold shoulder as she introduced herself. Then the two women went into Sidney's office, alone.

"What's up?" Anastasia asked, getting right down to business.

"I'm planning on taking some time off this summer to travel with JP. I'm turning over your direct management to Nelson, starting next week."

"Is that all?"

"Your campaign is in good shape, Anastasia. You'll still work with Natalie, but it's time my efforts are concentrated elsewhere."

"I'm sure Nelson will do fine, he was trained by the best."

"So you're okay with the change?" Sidney did not expect this reaction.

"Absolutely," Anastasia said.

Chapter 26

Three months later, Anastasia was a guest on *Late Show with David Letterman*. Since Nelson had a personal engagement, Sidney attended the taping in his place. Both Natalie and Sidney stood backstage and watched Anastasia perform "My Untouchable."

As Sidney watched her performance, she thought, *there's something wrong. She's lacking energy and stage presence.* Sidney and Anastasia had been running in different circles for months. This was the first time Sidney had seen her in. But as Sidney watched her perform, she knew something was different. Anastasia was only halfway through the song when she abruptly stopped singing, then exited the stage and ran into a nearby rest room. Both Sidney and Natalie followed her to the bathroom. Natalie went in while Sidney waited outside the door. The MPI staff gathered outside the rest room while David Letterman ad-libbed until they knew if Anastasia was able to continue.

Within a couple minutes, Natalie came out of the rest room and turned to the TV show's production manager. "She's pretty sick, she's not going to be able to continue."

"Should we call a doctor?" Sidney asked Natalie.

"Oh, I think this is pretty typical for this trimester," Andrea said.

Sidney nodded, acknowledging Andrea, Anastasia's make-up person, then casually strolled down the hall to the makeup room Anastasia had been using. Natalie followed her into the small room. Sidney did not want her friend to see her pain. She stared away from her, avoiding eye contact.

"You didn't know?" Natalie asked.

Sidney shook her head. "Am I the only one who didn't know?"

"You guys used to be so close. I just assumed you knew."

"How far along is she?"

"I think about fourteen weeks."

The door opened and Anastasia abruptly walked in. Her face was pale and seemed to get paler when she saw Sidney. Natalie said, "I've got to go reschedule the show, excuse me," and she was gone.

An uncomfortable silence penetrated the room. "How come you didn't tell me?" Sidney asked.

Anastasia ignored Sidney's question. She walked to the closet and pulled out her clothes, then started unbuttoning her blouse.

"Anastasia, why didn't you tell me? I seem to be the only one around here surprised. Everyone else knows."

"Why the hell are you surprised? You're the one who suggested I date Brett."

Sidney was not prepared for Anastasia's anger. "Date him, maybe. I never told you to sleep with him."

There were tears in Anastasia's eyes as she screamed at Sidney, "Get out."

Sidney walked to the door and reached for the doorknob. While looking at the back of the door, "I'm sorry; I was out of line. Your relationship with Brett is none of my business."

"You're right about that."

Sidney couldn't look her in the eye, "When you get back from Hartford, come to the office. We need to make some plans."

"My plans are to keep the baby!" Anastasia was almost crying.

Sidney finally turned and her voice softened. "I would be surprised if you didn't. We need to reschedule some of your concerts toward the end of your pregnancy."

Sidney had just wished Justin good night when the phone rang. She looked at the clock. *Who could be calling this late?* "Hello."

"Sidney, it's Nat," there was concern in her voice.

"What's wrong?"

"It's...it's Anastasia."

Sidney felt her pulse race. "What's wrong with her?"

"She started hemorrhaging after the concert. We're at Hartford Hospital."

Sidney was afraid to ask. "The baby?"

"It doesn't look good. They think she'll miscarry."

"How is she?"

"Her blood pressure was very low when we got here. They're probably going to hold her tonight and watch her, then release her in the morning."

"Have you called Brett?"

"Yeah, I just got off the phone with him."

"Is he going up to Hartford?"

"No. He's flying to LA in the morning to read for a role."

"How is Anastasia otherwise?"

"She's alone. She needs a friend, Sid."

"Did you tell Brett that?"

"Brett is hopeless." Then Natalie instructed her, "I'm telling you Sid, she needs a friend. I don't know what's going on between the two of you. But you might want to swallow your pride and be there for her."

259

"If I go, I might make things worse."

"But you'll never know if you don't go."

"I need to make some arrangements for JP. It should take about four hours to get there. Keep your cellular on and I'll call you back when I've made arrangements."

Lynette could not come over for about an hour, so Sidney arranged for one of her neighbors to stay at the house until Lynette arrived. She made a pot of coffee and had a cup while she discussed the arrangements with her neighbor. Then she poured the rest of the coffee in a thermos and left in her Mercedes.

It was close to two o'clock when Sidney arrived at the hospital. She found Natalie curled up on a bench outside of Anastasia's room.

When Natalie saw Sidney, she stood and hugged her. "In case she doesn't tell you, thank you for coming."

"How is she?" Sidney asked.

Natalie shook her head. "She miscarried about two hours ago."

"Is she sleeping?"

"I don't know. She asked me to leave some time ago."

"Why don't you go back to the hotel? I'll stay," Sidney said, but Natalie hesitated. "Please. Go to the hotel."

The small hospital room was dark. Sidney had difficulty seeing but went to the bed. She was surprised to find it empty. She whispered in the dark, "Anastasia?" There was a stir in the corner. When Sidney's eyes adjusted to the darkness, she saw Anastasia curled in a ball on a chair. Sidney approached the chair, but stopped short of her. Even in the darkness, Sidney could tell she had been crying. "Anastasia, I'm so sorry."

Without saying a word, Anastasia stood and approached Sidney. The two hugged silently. She whispered, "Please take me home."

The attending physician assured Sidney that Anastasia was free to go. They got in her Mercedes and headed west. Sidney called Natalie's hotel and left a message that she was taking

Anastasia home.

Anastasia was quiet most of the trip, occasionally changing the radio station. They were close to Anastasia's house when she asked, "How come you're always there for me? Even when I treat you like dirt."

"I thought we were friends."

"I'm sorry I didn't tell you I was pregnant."

"Don't worry about it."

The radio started playing Anastasia's newest hit, "My Untouchable."

But as I sit here, looking at you,
I can't help but wonder if you can see who I really am.
Can you see beyond my façade?
My veil? My disguise?
Or do you just see me as your friend, your partner in crime.

Anastasia abruptly changed the radio station. "I'm getting burned out on that one."

Sidney was surprised to see Brett's Jaguar at Anastasia's. "Do you want to come in?" Anastasia asked as the car idled outside the house.

A light came on inside the house, then the front entry lit up. "No, I want to get back before JP wakes."

The front door opened and Brett walked outside, rubbing his eyes. He was dressed in a robe and slippers. "Hi babe, how you doing?" He exchanged a hug with Anastasia as she got out of the car. Then he turned to Sidney, who was still sitting in her car. "Thanks for picking her up for me."

Anastasia walked around the car to the driver's side, and Sidney opened the window. Anastasia leaned over and the two looked into each other's eyes for the first time since the beach. She reached in and squeezed Sidney's shoulder. "Thank you."

Sidney smiled. "Good-bye." In the rear-view mirror, she watched the two embrace, then slowly walk into the house.

During the trip home, Sidney was unable to take her mind off Anastasia's eyes. She had once heard someone say the eyes were the windows to the soul. She didn't understand what that meant, until now. Every time she looked into her eyes, she saw something so familiar, but she couldn't put a finger on it.

Sidney called her office the following day and apprised Nelson of what had transpired the previous evening. "Clear her calendar for the next couple of weeks," directed Sidney. "She needs to put on a strong appearance next month at the Central Park Concert."

The Central Park Concert was being promoted as one of the largest concerts in history. Sidney knew the event would be crucial for MPI. *The Gang*, Jason Light, and Anastasia were all scheduled to perform.

The stage set up at Central Park was expansive.. Large tents were erected behind the stage, with private sections for dressing rooms and staging areas for the evening's productions. The concert started at five o'clock that evening and was anticipated to run until eleven. Twenty-five artists were scheduled to perform. Some would perform one song, others up to four. Sidney and the MPI staff were at the park early, since *the Gang* was scheduled to perform at 6:20 P.M., Jason Light was going on around 8:05 P.M. and Anastasia at 9:40 P.M. *The Gang's* and Jason's performances were good. The evening had been going smoothly, until Anastasia's makeup person called, and said she had the flu.

"Now what am I going to do?" Anastasia asked Sidney and Natalie in a panic.

"Relax," Natalie instructed, "I'll help."

"What do you know about applying my makeup?" Anastasia

asked.

"Nothing. You're beautiful, what do you need makeup for?" kidded Natalie.

"Are you serious?" Anastasia was getting upset.

"Of course not. Relax and come with me. I've done this before."

The two women went to their designated dressing area. They had about an hour to prepare Anastasia for the show. Natalie was able to get her to relax fairly quickly. She started talking about her relationship with Karen as she applied her makeup.

"Are you still seeing her?" Anastasia asked. "I like her."

"Yeah, she's pretty cool," Natalie admitted, and her face lit up. "Actually, I've been thinking about giving her a ring for her birthday next month. We've only been seeing each other about two years. Do you think that's too soon?"

"She makes you happy, Nat. Do it. Where did you find her? All the good ones are always taken."

Sidney poked her head into the tent. "Excuse me. Ten minutes to show time." Then she disappeared.

Anastasia continued her train of thought, "...or straight."

"Excuse me?" Natalie asked.

"All the good ones are taken...or straight."

Natalie concentrated on her makeup application. *I knew it. She is in love with Sidney.* When she finished the makeup, she picked up a brush and started working on her hair. "You know Anastasia, sometimes people aren't always as straight as they seem." Natalie could not believe she was saying it as the words came out.

Anastasia stared at Natalie's reflection in the mirror. "What are you saying?"

"You heard me."

"Are you talking about Sidney?"

Natalie ignored the question. "You're finished."

Anastasia turned her swivel chair so that she could see Natalie's eyes. "Nat, are you talking about Sidney?"

"I didn't say anything about Sidney. I only said that sometimes people aren't always what they seem."

"Is Sidney gay?"

Natalie ignored the question.

Anastasia interpreted the silence as an affirmation. "Sidney is gay."

"I never said that."

"You didn't deny it." Anastasia left the tent, leaving Natalie with her thoughts.

As Anastasia searched for Sidney, she got more upset with each passing minute. She finally found her standing backstage talking with the production manager. The man recognized Anastasia as she approached them. "Two minutes, Anastasia." He quickly ran off, leaving Sidney and Anastasia alone.

"I need to ask you a question," Anastasia started. "And...I need you to be honest with me."

It was obvious to Sidney that Anastasia was upset. "What's wrong?"

Anastasia maintained eye contact with Sidney. "Are you gay?"

Sidney felt her heart move up to her throat. "What?"

A production assistant yelled over to Anastasia, "One minute."

"Sidney, are you gay?"

"Anastasia, this isn't the time or the place to discuss this." Sidney was unable to make eye contact with Anastasia.

"You're right. It's well past the time, and I don't give a shit about where we are."

The entertainer who had been performing finished, and the MC was introducing Anastasia. Sensing something was wrong, the production assistant peered nervously over at Anastasia. The MC's voice penetrated the backstage, "...we are pleased to have with us tonight...Anastasia." Anastasia and Sidney could hear the applause.

"I'm not moving until I get an answer."

Sidney looked around. Everyone was staring anxiously at the two, waiting for Anastasia to perform. Her eyes finally met

Anastasia's. "Yes, I am but—"

Without warning Anastasia slapped Sidney's face, then turned and walked to the side entrance where the production assistant directed her to the stage opening. No one saw the tears in her eyes as she ran out on the stage to perform "I'm Here to Stay."

Sidney knew everyone was staring at her. She left the backstage and returned to the dressing tent. Her attention turned to the small television in her tent that was tuned to the broadcast of Anastasia's performance. *How the hell did she find out I'm gay?*

Natalie poked her head into the tent. "Can I come in?" Deep in thought, Sidney did not hear her. Natalie entered the tent and placed herself in Sidney's line of vision. "Sidney, what the hell happened out there?"

"I don't know. Somehow she guessed I was gay."

"And then what?"

"And then she slapped me." Sidney felt her red-blotched face. "Hard."

"I would have expected a number of reactions from her. But not that one. What else happened?"

Sidney shook her head. "Nothing."

Natalie took a folding chair and moved it to face Sidney. "Sid, what happened between the two of you? You used to be friends, now the two of you treat each other like strangers."

Sidney thought back to her walk with Anastasia on the beach. *It was that kiss. Things haven't been the same since.* Then she confided in her friend. "One night, about four months ago, Anastasia and I were walking on the beach…"

"And?" Natalie asked.

"We kissed."

"And?"

"When I realized what was happening, I stopped."

"What did you tell her?"

"Nothing. I was going to explain everything, but before I could, she apologized and said it was the wine and that she didn't mean anything by it."

"And you believed her?"

"Of course. She didn't give me any reason to believe otherwise. The next thing I knew she was seeing Brett, and whatever friendship we had seemed to disappear."

Natalie sat digesting the information that Sidney gave her. Sidney watched the television. Anastasia had finished the first song and started another. Her energy level and stage presence were great.

"Anastasia didn't exactly guess that you are gay," Natalie admitted.

"What do you mean?" Sidney glared back at her friend.

"Well, we were talking and—"

"You told her I was gay?" Sidney's voice rose in anger.

"Kind of."

Sidney got to her feet and started to pace the small tent. Occasionally she looked at Natalie but did not say anything. Natalie knew Sidney was about to blow; her jawbone visibly tightened and her face was red.

"Go ahead, get it off your chest," encouraged Natalie.

"I don't know what to say." Sidney continued to pace. "Natalie, I can't believe you told her. Of all people, you know what I can lose if that information gets in the wrong person's hands. I don't know what to say to you."

Natalie remained calm, letting her friend go off on her. Then Sidney challenged her, "Damn it Natalie, I thought you were my friend?"

Natalie was quick to defend herself. "Don't you ever question my friendship to you." She was visibly upset. "I told her you were gay…because I *am* your friend. I'm tired of seeing you go through the motions of life, without living it.

"Anastasia is in love with you; it's obvious to everyone except you." Natalie continued, "It's like you go through life with blinders on. You are by far the most brilliant woman I know, Sid. But sometimes you don't see beyond the tip of your nose." Natalie wasn't holding back now. "Sid, I've known you for a long

266

time. When you're around Anastasia, there's a sparkle in your eyes that hasn't been there since Charlie. Can you deny you have feelings for her?"

Sidney remained speechless. Her face was still red, and she stared at the floor.

"Do you realize you suck people into your life? You give them a taste of what you're all about. But before they realize you're such a damned...untouchable, it's too late..." Natalie's voice cracked as she finished, "they've fallen in love with you. But then you keep those damn blinders on and you're oblivious to that person's feelings." Tears fell from Natalie's eyes as she finished.

Sidney was shocked by Natalie's display of emotion. "You're not talking about Anastasia, are you?"

Natalie shook her head. "I was never in love with Charlie; I fell in love with you. That's why I dropped out of your lives, not because of Charlie...because of you."

"And Charlie knew?"

"Yeah."

"I had no idea."

"My point exactly."

"Why didn't you tell me?" Sidney asked.

"What good would that have done? You made it quite clear when Charlie died that you wouldn't put yourself in a compromising position. Initially, I respected your decision and I wanted to be supportive. Then as time went on, I could see life slipping by, for both of us. I've worked really hard to get over you, Sid. Karen has taught me that living life is a lot more fun than going through the motions."

Sidney remained speechless, trying to digest everything.

"Anastasia's in love with you, Sid. I don't want you to lose something that could be special."

They both turned to the monitor. Anastasia had finished an electrifying performance, and left the stage. The audience was screaming for an encore.

Anastasia came back on the stage. Rather than singing, she picked up the microphone to talk to the audience. "Thank you, New York. I always enjoy performing at home."

The audience cheered her on.

"You know, this audience has made me feel right at home tonight, and I'd like to share something personal with you. You see—I've been seeing this guy for some time. Some of you might know him, his name is Brett."

The audience roared, acknowledging the torrid affair the papers had been exploiting.

Anastasia smiled. "Brett asked me to marry him last week."

The audience continued to cheer.

"I haven't given him an answer yet."

There was an eruption of whistling, screaming and applauding.

When the audience settled down, Anastasia continued, "I understand this concert is being televised in California as we speak." Anastasia turned to the camera, "I hope you're watching, Brett; we've got a lot of plans to make."

The audience roared in satisfaction. Anastasia gave a signal to the band members for her encore, and she started singing "I Deserve."

In the tent, Sidney turned the television off. "If that woman is in love with me, she sure has a strange way of showing it."

"It's time for you to be honest with her," Natalie said.

"No, it's not. My son is my first priority. Nothing will change that." She hesitated as she turned to leave the tent. "I trust you will *never* say anything about me again." Then she left.

Chapter 27

On Monday morning a certified letter arrived at MPI's office. Natalie signed for it and brought the document to Sidney's office. "I just signed for this," she said as she dropped the envelope on Sidney's desk.

Sidney realized the letter was from a law firm. Natalie stayed as Sidney opened the letter and reviewed it. "What is it?" Natalie asked.

"Anastasia is firing us."

"She can't do that. Can she?"

"Actually, she's proposing to terminate our contract by buying us out," Sidney stated dryly.

"What are you going to do?"

"The offer looks reasonable. I'll run some new numbers, but I don't see any reason why we'd want to fight this."

Later that afternoon, Jennifer Warren telephoned Sidney. "We need to talk, can you come by my office?"

Sidney made a point of stopping by Jennifer's office before she left the city. Jennifer got right to the point, "I received a letter from Michael's attorney. He's petitioned the court for full custody of JP."

"On what grounds?" Sidney was furious.

"Although parts of the complaint are vague, it implies that you're a lesbian and an unfit parent."

Sidney sank into the soft chair next to her friend's desk. *My biggest nightmare is becoming reality.* This was not the first time Michael had challenged her for custody, but it was the first time he demanded it on the grounds she was a lesbian. The first time the parties settled on visitation rights for Michael every other weekend and selected holidays. When Justin was six, Michael sued for custody on the grounds that Sidney was an unfit mother. Although Michael was unsuccessful, he was awarded three weekends a month for visitation, and most holidays.

"Sidney, we need to prepare ourselves for perhaps the biggest fight of your life. I need to know what we're up against."

"What do you need to know?"

"For starters, I need to know about all your intimate relationships since Charlie."

Sidney shook her head. "There are none."

"What do you mean?"

"I haven't had a romantic relationship, with a man or a woman, since Charlie."

Jennifer stared at Sidney in disbelief.

"You don't believe me?"

"I do believe you. It's just that you're young and attractive, and I wonder what the judge will think."

"Jennifer, the day we had Charlie's memorial gathering at the shore, Michael told me he knew I was a lesbian. He said he had been preparing a petition to sue for custody. He threatened that when I got in another relationship, he'd take JP from me. I swear I haven't had an intimate relationship with anybody since Charlie. I took his threat seriously." Sidney admitted, "There was somebody I liked, but we never dated or anything. We were just friends and eventually she just got out of my life."

"What about Natalie?" Jennifer asked.

Sidney was getting agitated. "What about Natalie?"

"She's gay, the two of you work together. Did anything ever happen between the two of you?" Jennifer knew that Natalie had been in love with Sidney.

"No." Sidney was losing patience. "Jennifer, I haven't had a relationship since Charlie."

"Would you still characterize yourself as a homosexual?"

"Yes."

"But you haven't had homosexual relations since Charlie. Correct?"

"Yeah. Does that help, even though I'm gay?"

"I don't know, but unless you can say you're not a lesbian, I think that's the position we need to take. Michael will be calling an expert witness who will testify that homosexuals are unfit to be parents because they're promiscuous, child molesters, and have sex in front of their children."

"That's ridiculous."

"I know, but that is what's going to happen. Don't worry, we'll get our own expert to testify that homosexuals also make good parents. It will disarm some of their testimony."

"So it will be one person's word against the other?"

"True, but if their only argument is that you had a homosexual relationship seven years ago, their case is weak and their expert's testimony shouldn't impact the judge's decision very much. We still should get the best expert we can find."

"Do you have someone in mind?"

"Yes, Timothy Lewis. He's the leading psychiatrist in the tri-state area. From what I've heard, he's an excellent expert witness. If we can get him, we'll be in good shape."

A custody hearing had been scheduled. Jennifer and Sidney were busy over the two months preparing for the hearing. The two women met frequently to discuss the case information and review disclosure and witness information. Jennifer was disappointed to learn that Dr. Lewis could not be their expert witness because of a previous commitment. She was furious when she saw his name disclosed on the witness sheet as Michael's expert.

Sidney did not recognize most of the people on Michael's witness list, including two people who were to testify that she and Charlotte were involved in an inappropriate lesbian relationship. The only person that Sidney recognized was Lynette Floras, her domestic helper, who had abruptly quit a couple months earlier.

The hearing was a little over a week away, and Jennifer and Sidney were meeting to help prepare Sidney for cross-examination. "Have you told JP about the hearing?" Jennifer asked.

"Yes, he's aware that his father wants custody."

"Does he know that you're gay?"

Sidney shook her head. "No, at least I haven't told him. I've just said that both his father and I love him, and Michael thinks he can do a better job raising him than I can."

"You may want to tell him about your relationship with Charlie."

"I plan to. I just want to get a little closer to the hearing."

"You're right. We don't need him to leak anything to Michael." Jennifer continued, "Michael has subpoenaed one other witness for his case."

"Who is it?"

"Anastasia. Perhaps you may have some insight into what she

can offer."

"Anastasia?" Sidney could feel her heartbeat hasten. "I don't know what she would testify to, Jennifer. What does the disclosure say?"

Jennifer pulled out a document and started reading. *"Ms. Anastasia was a witness to a boating accident in which the Petitioner's son was hurt. She has knowledge of the relationship between the Respondent and her son. She knows facts relevant to the case that demonstrate Ms. Marcum is an unfit mother."*

All week Sidney had been debating whether or not to attend a charity event that benefited New York City domestic abuse shelters. One of the sponsors for the event was Broadcast Music Incorporated. She knew it would be a good opportunity to network for a new client.

While she felt strongly about supporting the cause, but she had heard that Brett and Anastasia were attending. Sidney had been avoiding her since the night of the Central Park Concert. She had recently read in *People* magazine that Anastasia and Brett were to be married later that month.

There was a knock at Sidney's office door. "Come in," Sidney said. She turned off a new prospect demo tape and Scott came into her office.

"Hi," he said. "What's this I hear about our date tomorrow night? You can't change your mind, my tuxedo is ready to go."

"I'm sorry Scott, I have the hearing on Monday. I could use the extra night to prepare my testimony," Sidney lied.

"Well, I'm not going to let you out of our date that easily."

"You can still go; Natalie will be there. I'm sure you'll have a lot of fun, even without me."

Scott called her bluff. "Do you want to tell me why you really don't want to go?"

Sidney smiled at Scott. "I'd rather not."

"Sid, let's go for a couple hours, and then I will personally escort you home." Sidney hesitated. "Great, I'll pick you up here tomorrow after work, and we'll go to dinner first."

The following evening Sidney was having difficulty concentrating on Scott's conversation during dinner. Scott knew Sidney's mind was someplace else. "May I say how beautiful you look tonight?" he asked.

Sidney smiled, "Thank you, and I'm sorry. I know I'm not good company. Would you like to do this some other time?"

"Nice try. Sidney, I've never known you to run away from anything," he boldly stated, "until now."

"I'm not running, Scott. I just don't see any reason to put myself in a situation involving conflict."

"The Sidney I once knew used to thrive on conflict."

Scott and Sidney arrived at the event around ten o'clock that evening. The party was packed, and Sidney seemed to relax as her peers and associates greeted her. She quickly displayed her power and control as she worked the crowd. The anxiety she had been feeling vanished and was replaced with confidence and radiance.

An hour had quickly passed at the party. Sidney and Scott were working their way through the crowd when they saw Brett, who held Anastasia close to his hip. Sidney was the first to offer her hand to Brett. "Congratulations on your engagement, Brett." She smiled warmly as she turned to Anastasia. "Congratulations, Anastasia."

Brett said coolly, "Sidney."

"Brett, I don't think you've had the opportunity to meet Scott Davis. Scott, this is Brett Pillar." Sidney turned to Anastasia, she was stunning. Her heart warmed just thinking of her. Until now Sidney hadn't realized how much she missed their friendship.

Anastasia shook Scott's hand and smiled warmly. "It's nice to see you again, Scott."

"If you'll excuse us, we were just on our way out," Brett was quick to say.

"Goodnight," Sidney said.

Sidney turned to continue their trek through the crowd, but stopped abruptly when she heard Brett curse. "Shit, you idiot. Couldn't you have been a little more careful?"

The front of Brett's tuxedo was wet, and Scott was apologizing profusely. "I am terribly sorry, Brett," he said. "Quick, come with me. We need to get that out before it sets."

As they moved through the crowd, Scott stopped at a bar and asked for a bottle of club soda.

"Come in here, Brett." Scott suggested that he follow him into the rest room.

Brett hesitated and looked back at Anastasia.

Scott found it amusing that Brett seemed intimidated by him.

Mustering every bit of his feminine side, he raised one wrist and let it fall limp. In his best queen impersonation he said, "I promise, I'm not going to bite."

The two men disappeared.

Sidney laughed at Scott's humor, then sat in a soft chair away from the rest room. Anastasia also smiled at the comment, but quietly paced outside the rest room waiting for her fiancé to return.

"Why don't you relax, and take a seat?" Sidney pointed at a chair next to her own. "I don't bite, either."

Anastasia asked, as she sat near her, "Do you want to tell me why you've had me subpoenaed?"

Sidney shook her head. "I haven't subpoenaed you. Michael has."

"He has? What's this all about?"

"He wants full custody of JP."

"What do I have to offer him?"

"The way the disclosure was written, you were a witness to the boating accident last year, and you have information that supports that I'm an unfit mother."

"That's ridiculous."

"I'm sorry you got dragged into this."

"I can't imagine anything I would say would be damaging for you, Sid." She paused. "How's JP?"

"He's fine. He's growing like a weed."

"Tell him I said hi."

"You should tell him yourself," Sidney started coldly, then softened. "He misses you. Just because we don't exactly run in the same circles…we shouldn't punish him."

"You're right. I'll call him."

Sidney hesitated. "I miss our friendship, too."

Anastasia hesitated. "Do you think we could get together to talk sometime?"

"Call us after your wedding."

Before Anastasia could respond, Brett opened the rest room door and looked for her. "I'll call you," Anastasia said, then she returned to Brett's side.

Sidney remained seated and Scott joined her.

"You did that on purpose, didn't you?"

"Hell yes. And I'd do it again, to get another look at those pecs."

Sidney laughed, but she knew wasn't the reason he had spilled his drink.

Chapter 28

Sidney anxiously awaited Justin's return from his weekend visit with his father. It was the evening before the hearing. She had rehearsed what she planned to say to him over and over in her mind, but she was still nervous. This was the evening she planned to tell him about her relationship with Charlotte.

The phone rang and Sidney answered it. "Hello."

"It's Michael."

"Michael? Is JP okay?"

"He's fine. I'm keeping him tonight, and I'll bring him to court in the morning."

"You're what?"

"I'm keeping him overnight. I'll bring him to court in the morning," Michael repeated.

"You will not. JP doesn't need to be in court. Why put him through it? Besides, this is my time with him. Bring him home."

"He's almost thirteen; he's old enough to learn the truth

about his mother. It's settled, you'll see him in the morning."

"It's not—" Sidney heard dial tone in her ear. *Oh my God.* She had never even considered having Justin attend the hearing. *She was horrified at the thought that he could learn she was gay in court.*

Sidney called Jennifer and explained Michael's phone call. Jennifer was surprised that Michael was so bold as to pull a stunt the evening before the hearing, but could not ease Sidney's concern. "Sidney, I'll request that JP be removed from the courtroom, if that's what you want. But I can't make any promises about how the judge will rule. The judge *will* want to talk with him in private at some point during the hearing."

"He doesn't need to sit through a custody hearing," Sidney said.

"I'll try, Sidney. Please relax, everything is going to work out."

"Jennifer, I haven't told him about Charlie and me."

"I thought you were going to."

"I was planning on telling him tonight."

The following morning, Justin arrived at the courthouse dressed in a new suit and tie. *He looks so much older than his years,* Sidney thought when she first saw him.

"Hi Mom," he said. "Hi Aunt Jennifer, how are you?"

"I'm great JP, how are you today?"

"Good," he replied and asked, "Mom, how do I look?" as he modeled the new suit.

"You look very handsome. Can we talk, JP?" Sidney asked. She directed him away from others in the hallway, including Michael. "JP, I don't agree with your father. I don't think you should sit in on the hearing. Jennifer is going to ask to have you removed from the courtroom. I didn't want you to be surprised…or hurt."

"Dad asked me to come to court," Justin said.

"I know that—"

"Sidney, we need to go," Jennifer interrupted.

"Do you want to come in with us?" Sidney asked Justin.

"I'm gonna hang out here for a while. I'll be in, in a few minutes."

Sidney hugged Justin and noticed Michael waiting for him. "No matter what happens in there, please remember that I love you."

"I love you too, Mom," he whispered back. Then he backed away and returned to his father's side.

Sidney and Jennifer sat at a table in the front of the courtroom. Michael and his attorney, Kyle Clancy, sat at a table next to their own. At one point Sidney looked behind her and was surprised by the number of people in the courtroom. Then she noticed that Justin was sitting behind his father and not her.

Sidney turned to Jennifer and whispered, "What are all these people doing here?"

Jennifer looked back. "It's an open hearing, anyone can attend. It is unusual though, that this many people would sit in on a custody hearing."

"All rise." The court clerk announced the entrance of Judge Hastings. Everyone stood as a man entered and sat at the high bench.

The judge put on his glasses and appeared to be referring to the docket. "In the matter of *Whitman versus Marcum*, we're here to determine the custodial arrangement for the minor child. Any pending motions or matters before we begin, Mr. Clancy?"

Clancy stood. "Your honor, we are requesting that the witnesses be sequestered."

The judge turned to Jennifer. "Any objections?"

"No, your honor."

"Granted. Counsel, please review the gallery and have all potential witnesses removed to the witness room down the hall."

Clancy's paralegal directed a couple of people out of the courtroom.

"Any other matters, Mr. Clancy?" the judge asked.

"No, your honor."

"Mrs. Warren, any matters before we begin?"

"Yes, your honor," Jennifer stood. "At this time we ask that the court remove Justin, the minor child in this case, from the courtroom. We feel it's in the child's best interest not to be subjected to a confrontation between his parents."

"Any objections, Mr. Clancy?"

Clancy stood. "Yes, your honor. We feel Justin is a mature young man and has expressed interest in being here. We feel he has every right to hear the events which will influence this court's decision about his future."

"Will the child...Justin Marcum-Whitman, stand?" Judge Hastings asked.

Justin stood, noticeably behind his father.

"Do you understand what this hearing is all about?"

"I understand that you will decide who I should live with," Justin replied.

"Do you want to sit through a long boring hearing?" The judge smiled.

"I do, your honor."

"I assume this child will not be a witness," the judge said.

"That's correct, your honor," chorused the attorneys.

"Counselor, any other reasons why I should remove this child from the hearing?" the judge asked Jennifer.

"No, your honor."

"Motion denied. The boy is free to stay." The judge took out his calendar. "I want time to talk with Justin. Tomorrow afternoon at three o'clock."

Sidney's heart sank.

The judge started looking at documents on his desk. "I've reviewed the pleadings in this case, and I believe we can dispense with opening statements and proceed with the petitioner's witnesses. Do you both agree?"

"Yes, your honor," Clancy said.

"Yes, your honor," Jennifer agreed.

"Petitioner calls Dr. Richard Demille to the stand," Clancy

said.

"Your honor," Jennifer stood. "The Petitioner's disclosure certificate indicates that witnesses Demille and Redington will establish that my client, Ms. Marcum, has had a lesbian relationship with the deceased Dr. Charlotte Gray."

Sidney looked over at Justin, who seemed to ignore her.

Jennifer continued. "In an effort to save the court's time and expense, we will stipulate to the fact that my client had an intimate relationship with Dr. Gray for five years. Therefore, we believe there is no reason to call these witnesses."

Justin just stared at the back of his father. He never acknowledged Sidney's desperate need for eye contact with her son. "Mr. Clancy?" the judge asked.

"We accept that stipulation, however these witnesses will also establish that Dr. Gray lived with Ms. Marcum and Justin, at her Brielle, New Jersey home."

"So stipulated, your honor," Jennifer said.

"Clancy?" the judge asked.

"We accept the stipulation assuming that counselor's definition of intimate means lesbian, your honor."

"Mrs. Warren?"

"So stipulated," Jennifer said.

"We accept the stipulation," Clancy cockily smiled at Michael. He moved a couple pages forward in his notebook. "The petitioner calls Miss Lynette Floras to the stand."

Moments later, Lynette walked through the doors in back of the courtroom and was escorted to the stand where she was sworn in.

"Please state and spell your full name and address for the record."

"Lynette Floras. L-Y-N-E-T-T-E, F-L-O-R-A-S. I live at 567 Beach Way Drive in Point Pleasant Beach, New Jersey."

"Miss Floras, are you familiar with the respondent, Ms. Marcum?" Clancy asked.

"Yes."

"How do you know her?"

"I worked for her as a nanny and housekeeper," Lynette answered.

"For how long?"

"From when JP…Justin was about six months to about three months ago."

"About twelve years?"

"Yeah."

"While you worked for Ms. Marcum, did you live at the house?"

"Never permanently. But when Ms. Marcum would travel, I would stay at the house."

"Did that happen often?"

"Oh, all the time. Ms. Marcum was a very busy lady with her business. Someone had to stay with Justin."

"So Ms. Marcum ranked her business over her son?"

"Objection your honor, leading and argumentative," Jennifer objected.

"I'll withdraw the question." Clancy continued, "Miss Floras, did Ms. Marcum ever talk with you about the amount of time she spent with Justin?"

"Oh yeah. She used to say there weren't enough hours in the day to give him the attention he deserved."

"Did Ms. Marcum ever choose going to work when she should have been caring for her son?"

"Objection," Jennifer interrupted. "Speculation, calls for a conclusion beyond this witness's scope."

"Overruled," Judge Hastings said. "The witness may answer the question."

"On more than one occasion. Once, she chose to go to a party and was out most of the night. Another time, she left in the middle of the night to meet Anastasia somewhere in Connecticut."

"When you say *Anastasia*, you mean the singer, correct?"

"Yeah."

"When Ms. Marcum left for Connecticut in the middle of

the night, you were with him, right? I mean she didn't just leave him unattended. Did she?"

"When she drove off to Connecticut, I couldn't get to her place for a couple of hours. So she had a complete stranger come in to sit with JP."

"Over the course of the twelve years with Ms. Marcum, did anyone else ever live at that house?"

"Yeah, Charlotte Gray. For about the first five years I worked there."

"This was her lover?"

"Objection," Jennifer said. "Lack of foundation."

"Sustained," the judge said.

"Miss Floras, do you know what kind of relationship Dr. Gray and Ms. Marcum had?" Clancy asked.

"I don't know what kind of relationship they had. I know they were very close. Sidney inherited all of her assets when Charlie died."

"Charlie...you mean Charlotte?" Clancy asked.

"Yes, I'm sorry, Charlotte."

"And she died. When?"

"Oh, about seven years ago."

"During the twelve years you worked there, did you ever see or hear her talk about gentlemen callers?"

"Never," Lynette answered.

"Other than Dr. Gray, did Ms. Marcum have frequent women visitors at her home?"

"Oh yeah, all the time...mostly Natalie Springer and Anastasia."

"I understand you were present when Ms. Marcum brought her son home from the hospital, after he had the accident on the boat last year."

"Yes, I was."

"Did you ever discuss the accident with her?"

"Yes."

"Would you tell the court what you remember about that

conversation?"

"Oh, Ms. Marcum blamed herself for the accident. She said she wasn't paying close enough attention to him, and she did not have her eye on him."

"Do you know where the accident took place?"

"Apparently he was cleaning the boat at the dock. He fell, hit his head then fell in the water. Thank God Anastasia was there. I understand she was the one who rescued him."

"So Ms. Marcum told you she wasn't watching him while he played on the boat?"

"That's correct."

Sidney's heart broke as she listened to Lynette testify.

"I have nothing further, your honor," Clancy said.

"Counsel, you may proceed," Hastings said.

Jennifer stood to cross-examine her. "So it's your testimony that in twelve years, Ms. Marcum left her son twice?"

"Yes."

"And both times JP was left with adult supervision?"

"Yes."

"But you think that's unreasonable, Miss Floras?"

"I think she had her priorities wrong."

"The evening you spoke with Ms. Marcum about JP's accident, you testified that `Ms. Marcum blamed herself...she wasn't paying close enough attention to him.'"

"Yes."

"Is it possible that Ms. Marcum was just being hard on herself? Let's face it, accidents happen."

"Objection, speculation," Clancy said.

"Overruled," Hastings said.

"No," Lynette finally answered.

"Miss Floras, did you ever see Ms. Marcum hit Justin?"

"No."

"Did you ever see Ms. Marcum spank Justin?"

"No."

"Did you ever see her abuse him?"

"No."

"Did Justin ever go hungry?"

"No, but it was my responsibility to feed Justin."

"No further questions, your honor."

"Redirect, Mr. Clancy?" Hastings asked.

"No, your honor."

The witness was excused and Clancy called his next witness. "We call Ms. Anastasia to the stand."

Sidney's heart skipped a beat when she heard the name.

Anastasia was escorted into the courtroom and directed toward the stand. Sidney and Anastasia could not help from making eye contact as she was sworn in.

Clancy started, "Please state and spell your full name for the record."

"Anastasia, A-N-A-S-T-A-S-I-A."

"Anastasia what?"

"Anastasia is my legal name as well as stage name."

Sidney heard paper rustling behind her. When she turned, she saw people jotting down notes. *The press.* Sidney wrote a note to Jennifer. *"The press is in the back. This was leaked."*

"Anastasia, do you know Ms. Marcum?"

"Yes."

"And how is it that you know her?"

"Sidney used to be my personal manager and friend."

"She used to be your friend? You two aren't friends anymore?"

"Yes, we're friends."

"Ms. Anastasia, do you know what this hearing is about?"

"I believe it's to decide primary custody for Sidney's son, JP."

"How do you know that? Did you talk with Ms. Marcum about the hearing?"

Anastasia's eyes diverted to Sidney. "I did."

"And what was said during that conversation?"

"I asked why she subpoenaed me."

"You did? What did she say?"

"She told me she had not subpoenaed me, but that her ex-husband must have."

"So, you received a subpoena, directing you to come to court today?"

"That's correct."

"Do you understand that the subpoena came from my office?"

"Yes."

"What else did you speak with Ms. Marcum about?"

"Objection."

"I'll withdraw the question. Did you and Ms. Marcum discuss why Michael would have subpoenaed you to testify?"

"She said Michael believed I would have information regarding a boating accident."

"Did she tell you how you should testify today?"

"Absolutely not."

"Did you tell her what you would say today?"

"No."

"How well do you know Justin Whitman?"

"JP?" Anastasia glanced at him and smiled. He returned the smile. "I think I know him pretty well."

"Do you consider yourself a friend of his?"

"I do."

"What do you do with Justin?"

"I don't understand the question."

"You're friends. What type of activities do the two of you do? Play cards?"

"We've sailed together. We've water skied together, fished, crabbed, listened to music together, and yes, we have played cards. Then there have been times when we've just talked."

"Have you ever been alone with Justin? Or have your visits with him always been in Ms. Marcum's presence?"

"I've been alone with him."

"So Ms. Marcum trusts you to care for her son?"

"Yes, I guess so."

"And you consider yourself a friend of Sidney Marcum's?"

"I do."

"A good friend?"

She hesitated. "A good friend."

"Let's talk about the day of the boating accident. The way I understand it, Justin was playing alone in Ms. Marcum's speedboat. Is that correct?"

"No. That's not correct."

"It isn't? He wasn't alone in the boat?"

"He was the only person in the boat. But both Sidney and I were watching him from the shore."

"So you and Ms. Marcum were watching him from the shore. How far away were the two of you from Justin?"

"I don't know."

"If you were to guess, how far would you say?"

"I don't know."

"Can you tell us if you were closer to five feet or fifty feet away?"

"I don't know."

"Okay. What was the weather like that day?"

"Initially it was nice, then later it became overcast—"

"Overcast? When Justin was playing on the boat alone, did it ever get windy?"

"At some point, the wind picked up."

"When Justin was playing on the boat, did it start to thunder and lightning?"

"At some point, it started to storm."

"Did it rain?"

"Not until after the accident, I believe."

"How old was Justin when he was left alone to play on this boat?"

"I've already told you, he wasn't left alone. And he wasn't playing. He was cleaning the boat."

"On the day of the accident, how old was Justin?"

"I believe he was eleven at the time."

"So while the storm came in, was Justin the only one on the boat?"

"When the storm came in, Sidney told him—"

"Ms. Anastasia, please answer the question. 'Yes' or 'no'? Was Justin the only one on the boat?"

"Yes."

"And his mother sat there and allowed it?"

"No."

"No? Did Ms. Marcum pull him out of the boat?"

"She told him—"

"'Yes' or 'no,' Ms. Anastasia. Did Sidney Marcum pull her son from the boat?"

"It's not a 'yes' or 'no' answer."

"Yes, it is. She either pulled him out of the boat or she didn't. So which is it? Did Sidney Marcum pull her son from the boat?"

"Objection," Jennifer interrupted. "Counsel is refusing to allow the witness to answer completely."

"Objection overruled. Ms. Anastasia, please answer the question with a 'yes' or 'no' response," Hastings directed.

"Let me repeat the question," said Clancy. "Did Sidney Marcum pull her son from the boat?"

"No."

"Thank you. While Justin was in the boat, you and Ms. Marcum were talking, weren't you?"

"We were talking."

"So Justin did not have Ms. Marcum's complete attention, now did he?"

"Sidney was pretty focused on where her son was, and what he was doing."

"Ms. Anastasia, my question was-did Justin have Ms. Marcum's complete attention?"

"She was watching him."

"When Justin fell in the water, neither of you saw him fall. Isn't that true?"

Anastasia hesitated. "Correct."

"So neither one of you was watching him. Is that correct?"

"No, that's not correct. Sidney was very focused on him."

"Then how did she not see him fall in the water?"

"I don't know, maybe she blinked."

"Blinked?" Clancy sighed and was showing signs of frustration. "Is it possible that she was looking at you when he fell?"

"I don't know."

"You don't know if she was looking at you?"

"I don't know," Anastasia repeated.

"After the accident, isn't it true that Ms. Marcum confided in you and told you she blamed herself for the accident?"

"We talked about a lot of things. It was an accident. Kids fall."

"Isn't it true that Ms. Marcum blamed herself because she took her eye off him?"

"She was being hard on herself."

"Yes or no?" The tone of Clancy's voice was antagonistic. Anastasia hesitated.

"Objection, your honor, leading question. Additionally, Mr. Clancy is harassing his own witness," Jennifer said.

"Your honor, I ask that Ms. Anastasia be deemed a hostile witness. She's nonresponsive, she's here under subpoena, she's admitted that she's a good friend of the respondent and therefore biased."

"Agreed. Objection overruled. Ms. Anastasia, you must answer the question."

"Let me repeat the question. Ms. Anastasia, isn't it true that Ms. Marcum blamed herself because she took her eye off her son?"

"In my opinion—"

"Yes or no?"

"Yes. But—"

"Thank you. Ms. Anastasia, what was the nature of your relationship with Stephanie Mitchell?"

Sidney's hand clutched Jennifer's arm. "Jennifer, you've got to object."

"We were friends," Anastasia answered.

Clancy repeated the question, "What was the nature of your relationship with Stephanie Mitchell?"

"Objection, asked and answered," Jennifer objected.

Clancy repeated, "A *friend*, is that what you said?"

Anastasia nodded.

"Let the record reflect that the witness is nodding affirmatively. What do you do with your *friends?*" Clancy asked with a chuckle.

"Excuse me? I don't understand your question."

Clancy walked over to the witness box and stared at Anastasia. "Were you and Stephanie Mitchell lovers?"

"Objection, your honor, relevance?" Jennifer shouted.

There was squirming from the rear of the courtroom. The reporters were starting to wake. *Oh, God. This is going to destroy her,* Sidney thought.

Anastasia's heart raced. She glanced at Sidney and the two recognized fear in each other's eyes.

"Your honor, we have evidence to show that Ms. Anastasia and Ms. Mitchell were lovers, and that Ms. Marcum, with this knowledge, still allowed this type of person to socialize with her son. In fact she trusted this type of person to watch her son," Clancy argued.

"I'll allow it." The judge turned to Anastasia. "You must answer the question."

Is today a good day to come out? Anastasia asked herself as she gazed upon the vultures in the rear of the courtroom. "Yes. We were."

There was a disruption from the rear of the courtroom. A couple of reporters left to call in the scoop.

"Are you a lesbian?"

"If you asked me that a year ago, I would have said yes."

"And now?"

"I'm engaged to be married to a man in two weeks. My preference would be with a woman. But I guess I don't discriminate. Does that make me bisexual, Mr. Clancy?"

"I'm not an expert, and I ask the questions here," he answered sarcastically. "So, let's talk about your relationship with Ms. Marcum."

"What about it?"

"Were you lovers?"

"Absolutely not."

"You were not lovers?"

"I said no."

"Your honor, at this time I would like to enter into evidence this photograph marked as Exhibit 18 for identification." Clancy presented the judge with the photograph. He also provided Jennifer with a copy.

Sidney's heart sank when she saw the picture of Anastasia and herself slow dancing together. She knew the picture was damaging.

Jennifer glanced at Sidney and whispered, "Talk to me."

"It was a first-year celebration for Anastasia. It was innocent. The waitress was making advances toward me, and Anastasia stepped in," Sidney whispered back.

"Your honor, may I approach the witness?" Clancy asked.

"Yes."

Clancy brought the picture to the witness box. "Is this you and Sidney Marcum in the picture?"

Anastasia looked at the compromising picture. "Yes, but—"

"In the picture, you clearly have your arm around Ms. Marcum. What are you doing?"

"We were dancing."

"Were you *slow* dancing?"

Anastasia hesitated. "Yes."

"Do you slow dance with women that are *just friends?*"

"No, but—"

"Thank you. Ms. Anastasia, what do you do with your friends?"

"Objection, argumentative," Jennifer argued.

"Latitude, your honor?" Clancy pleaded.

"Overruled," said the judge.

Clancy repeated, "What do you do with your *friends?*"

"I'm sorry, I don't understand the question," Anastasia replied.

"I'll try to be more specific. Do you have sex with your friends?"

"No."

"You obviously dance with them," Clancy said as he held up the photo. "Do you kiss your friends?"

"Depends what you mean by kiss."

"On the lips," clarified Clancy.

"No." Anastasia's voice was angry, and Sidney knew she was upset.

Clancy returned to his table and sorted through various documents. "May I approach, your honor?"

"Yes."

Clancy returned to the bench and dropped something with the judge, then Anastasia. Sidney knew something was wrong before she saw it. Anastasia's face went pale, then she looked over at Sidney. Sidney saw fear in her eyes again.

"Your honor, I've marked this photograph as Exhibit 19 for identification." Clancy made his way to Jennifer and dropped off a copy of the photograph. Jennifer saw the picture first and her face paled as she turned it over to Sidney.

"Oh God," Sidney whispered. She held a the photograph of Anastasia and her kissing on the beach.

"Your honor, at this time I move for the admission of exhibits 18 and 19 for identification."

"Counsel, any objections?" Judge Hastings asked.

"Yes, your honor," Jennifer stood. "First, Counsel has never disclosed these photographs. Second, he has failed to lay the proper foundation for their admission. Third, these photographs are not relevant and even if you feel they are relevant, their prejudicial impact outweighs probative value they may have."

"Your honor, these pictures are relevant," Clancy argued. "We are trying to determine who will provide a better and more stable environment for Justin. These pictures clearly show that

Ms. Marcum will not provide such an environment. She is not a fit mother, she is gay and is inviting other gay women into her household where she intends to raise Justin."

"Mr. Clancy is trying to attack the reputation and character of this witness and my client," argued Jennifer.

"Counsel, that's enough. Mr. Clancy, are you moving to use these pictures for impeachment purposes or for evidence of witness character?"

"Both, your honor."

"I will allow the admissions of these photographs for the sole purpose of inquiring into Ms. Anastasia's character for truthfulness or untruthfulness," Hastings ruled. "Exhibits 18 and 19 for identification are admitted. Mr. Clancy, proceed."

"Ms. Anastasia, would you please tell the court what two people are in this photograph?"

"Myself…and Sidney."

"What are the two of you doing in the photograph?"

"Kissing."

"Are the two of you kissing *on the lips?*"

"Yes."

"Ms. Anastasia, I thought you don't kiss your friends on their lips."

"That is what I said."

"Do you still deny that you and Ms. Marcum were lovers?"

"That's correct."

"And you expect this court to believe this?"

"Objection."

"I'll withdraw the question. No further questions, your honor." Jennifer stood. "Your honor, I'd like to request a ten-minute recess to confer with my client."

"Ten minutes," the judge agreed and court was recessed.

Sidney turned to look for her son. "I need to see JP."

Jennifer said unsympathetically, "Right now I think you need to come with me." Sidney followed Jennifer into a private conference room. Jennifer turned and stared at her client. "You want to tell me what the hell is going on?"

"Oh God, you don't believe me." Sidney knew it must look bad if Jennifer was questioning her.

"A picture of the two of you dancing together hurts, but kissing…this could destroy our defense. Remember? You haven't been involved with anyone since Charlie?" The lawyer felt betrayed.

"Jennifer, we weren't lovers." Sidney started pacing the small room, wondering where to start. "We used to be great friends. Then about seven months ago, she made a pass at me while we were at the beach…and yes, I did kiss her back, if only for a moment. But then reality hit and I stopped it. It didn't go any further. Our friendship has never been the same, and that's the truth, Jennifer."

"Does she know you're gay?" Jennifer asked.

"She didn't up until the Central Park Concert. She fired me the following day."

"Are there any more surprises?" demanded Jennifer. "Is there anything else I should know?"

"No more surprises, and I don't think this matters, but… I told you once that there was someone I liked, but it never developed into a relationship…"

"Yes, I remember."

"It was Anastasia."

"Great."

Court reconvened and Anastasia returned to the witness stand. "Remember, Ms. Anastasia, you're still under oath," Judge Hastings instructed.

"Your honor, may I approach the witness?" Jennifer asked.

The judge nodded and Jennifer approached Anastasia.

"Anastasia, how long have you known Sidney Marcum?"

"Almost two and a half years."

"During your friendship with Ms. Marcum, have you ever seen her to be an unfit mother?"

"Absolutely not."

Jennifer placed the photo of Sidney and Anastasia dancing in front of her. "Anastasia, do you know where this picture was taken?"

"Yes. We were at a club in New Hope. I think it's called The Cartwheel."

"Why were you there?"

"I hosted a party to celebrate my first year with MPI, Sidney's company. We had dinner in the restaurant, and when it was finished we visited the disco."

"Who attended this event?"

"All the employees of MPI along with their partners, and Stephanie and myself."

"You've stated under oath that you don't make a rule of slow dancing with *just friends*. Would you be able to explain why the two of you slow danced?"

"Yes," Anastasia paused and collected her thoughts. "The waitress from the restaurant followed our group to the bar. She was very interested in Sidney and cornered her on the dance floor. I pretended to be with Sidney by cutting in on her on the dance floor. It worked; the waitress went away."

"So it was innocent?"

"Completely innocent."

"Have you and Sidney Marcum ever been lovers?"

"No."

Jennifer pulled out the picture of Anastasia and Sidney kissing. "Anastasia, could you tell the court what happened in this picture?"

Anastasia glanced over at Sidney. "It was earlier this year and the two of us took a walk on the beach. I made a pass at her, she said no, and that was it."

"*You* made a pass at her?"

"Yes, *I* kissed her."

"Did you think she was gay, when you kissed her?"

"No."

"But you kissed her anyway?"

"Yes…," Anastasia looked at Sidney and spoke slowly. "I had fallen in love with her. I took a chance that she could feel the same. But I was wrong. She made it clear she wasn't interested in me."

"The boating accident. Could you please tell the court what happened?"

"It was an accident. JP was cleaning the boat, and when the weather started to come in, Sidney told him to finish what he was doing. The next minute he was in the water. Sidney was upset with herself because she almost lost her son. She wasn't careless. It was *just* an accident."

"Thank you. No further questions, your honor."

"Mr. Clancy, anything else?"

"Just one more question, your honor." The man stood. "Ms. Anastasia, you said under oath that you had fallen in love with the respondent, Ms. Marcum. Correct?"

"That's right."

"Would you lie to this court if you knew it would be helpful to Ms. Marcum, to maintain custody of Justin?"

"No. I would not."

After Anastasia's testimony, court recessed for lunch. Anastasia left the courtroom with the press chasing after her. Sidney was heartbroken when Justin asked her if he could go to lunch with his father. Sidney and Jennifer hid in a conference room over lunch to assess the damage.

By the end of the afternoon session, Michael's character and expert witnesses had portrayed the man as a saint. Friends and associates had testified that he was a selfless, loving father, who only wanted what was best for his oldest son. His contributions to charities were emphasized, including his generosity to New

York Hospital's Emergency Room.

Michael's wife, Beverly, and their son, Michael Jr., showed up for the afternoon testimony. The mother and child sat on either side of Justin, sandwiching the boy.

Two experts testified for Michael. The first was a caseworker who was hired to assess Michael's home life and visited with Justin. She concluded that Michael's home was loving and certainly more traditional than his mother's. She emphasized the importance of a male figure in Justin's life and discussed problems associated with a home life lacking a male role model. The expert also claimed that Justin wanted to spend more quality time with his half-bother.

Michael's last witness was Dr. Lewis. The accomplished psychiatrist's curriculum vitae was six pages long, boasting impressive achievements in the field. Among the issues that Dr. Lewis effectively expressed to the court were: lesbian parents raise gay children; lesbians make love in front of their children; homosexuals are child molesters; children of lesbians suffer from an absence of male role models; homosexuals are promiscuous and have unstable relationships.

Although his comments to the court were not supported by intensive research, some archaic documents were submitted to support parts of his assertions. What made him so effective was his presence. The man was articulate, attractive and spoke with passion.

Sidney was cautious as she approached her son outside the courtroom after court adjourned. Justin was hanging out with his father, Beverly, Michael Jr., and Kyle Clancy, relishing their afternoon victory. "Hi JP, can we talk?"

"Sure, Mom."

Sidney led him away from his father, down the wide hallway, and sat on a bench. "I didn't want you to find out about Charlie and me this way. I was planning on telling you last night, but you didn't come home."

"It's okay, Mom."

"No. It's not okay. I'm terribly sorry if I've hurt you. I've wanted to tell you for a long time. But I...I didn't want to jeopardize losing you. Do you forgive me?"

"Yeah, Mom. It's okay." Justin paused. "Mom?"

"Yes?"

"Do you think it'd be okay if I stay in the city tonight with Dad? That way I won't have to get up so early tomorrow morning, to get to court."

Sidney's heart ached as she heard her son's words. *She wondered if she was losing him.* "I'm staying in the city tonight at your Aunt Jennifer's. I brought you a change of clothes. Would you like to stay with me?"

"I have my own room at Dad's place."

It took every ounce of strength not to burst into tears. She knew she needed to work late on the proceedings anyway, and certainly couldn't with him near. "Of course," she said and stood. "You'll come home with me tomorrow night. Okay?"

"Sure, Mom."

Sidney hugged her son. "I do love you, JP." *More than you know.*

"Love you too, Mom." He quickly detached himself from her and they walked back toward the small group waiting for Justin. He rejoined them, and Sidney ducked into a nearby bathroom.

She approached the mirror in the bathroom. Gently she wiped tears in her eyes with a tissue to erase signs of her torment.

"Are you okay?" Jennifer asked as she came out from a stall.

Sidney hesitated. "I think I'm losing him."

"This case is far from over, Sidney."

"He doesn't want to be with me. Even if I win and continue custody, he doesn't want to be with me."

"He's had a difficult day, Sid. Things will be better tomorrow. Let's get out of here. We've got work to do."

Chapter 29

Sidney and Jennifer worked into the early hours of the morning. Jennifer knew she had to change her approach to the case.

"I think I should put you on first," Jennifer said.

"Why?"

"You need to tell this judge you haven't been with anyone since Charlie. Our whole defense has hinged on this. That point is essential for your expert's testimony to be effective. If there's any doubt in this judge's mind about you and Anastasia, I want it stopped first thing tomorrow."

"You don't think her testimony cleared it up?"

"People have perjured themselves for a lot less than being in love with a person. Those photographs were very damaging to us." Jennifer was rearranging witnesses on her pad. "You need to drive that message home with the judge, then we'll put our character witnesses and our expert up there."

"How bad is it, Jennifer?"

She sighed. "We've got an uphill battle, and it's not going to be easy. But I'm not going to give in, and I have a couple tricks in my bag, too."

When Sidney and Jennifer arrived in court the following morning, Sidney was not surprised to see Justin sitting behind Michael again. She kissed him. "Good morning, sweetheart."

"Good morning, Mom."

Natalie greeted Sidney with a hug. "How you doing? You look like hell."

"Thanks. It's been a long night."

"What happened in here yesterday?" Natalie asked. "The press is having a field day with Anastasia."

"Oh, God. I completely forgot. I've been so wrapped up in this, it slipped my mind that she came out yesterday."

Jennifer interrupted them. "Natalie, the witnesses are being sequestered. You're going to have to wait in the witness room. I'm going to call you after Sidney. We're going to be starting in a couple of minutes, Sidney, and I need to go over some questions."

Natalie reached for Sidney's hand and squeezed it. "Good luck."

"Thanks."

"Your honor," Jennifer stood. "Before we begin, I would like to ask the court to consider closing the proceedings to the press. We feel it's in the best interest of Justin that the proceedings are closed to the media."

"Agreed," Judge Hastings said. "Any member of the press is asked to leave."

It's too bad this didn't happen yesterday, Sidney thought as she watched the reporters clear the courtroom.

"Your honor, we call Sidney Marcum to the stand," Jennifer said.

Sidney went to the witness chair where she was sworn in. Before she sat, she heard the courtroom door open, indicating someone had either entered or exited. She was surprised when she saw Anastasia.

"Please state and spell your full name for the record," Jennifer directed.

"Sidney A. Marcum, S-I-D-N-E-Y, M-A-R-C-U-M."

"How long ago did you and Mr. Whitman divorce?"

"About thirteen years ago."

"After you divorced Mr. Whitman, when was your next intimate relationship?"

"About a year after the divorce."

"Who was it with?"

"Charlotte Gray."

"And how long did this relationship last?"

"About five years."

"How would you characterize this relationship?"

"It was wonderful. It was loving, caring—"

"Was it stable?"

"Absolutely."

"Why did it end?"

"Charlie was killed in an automobile accident."

"When you say *Charlie*, do you mean Charlotte?"

"That's correct; Charlie was her nickname."

Anastasia sat in the courtroom listening to Sidney's story unfold. It was only then that she realized Charlie was a woman.

"So you had a stable, same-sex relationship for five years. And it ended tragically. Then what? Who did you have your next intimate relationship with?"

"I haven't had a relationship."

"You have not had an intimate relationship in seven years?"

"That's correct."

"Were you and Anastasia lovers?"

"No."

"Do you characterize yourself as gay?"

"I do."

"If your last relationship was seven years ago, why do you still characterize yourself as gay?"

"It's who I am."

"But you haven't had an intimate relationship in seven years. Couldn't you just as easily call yourself heterosexual and celibate?"

"I wouldn't be honest with myself if I thought of myself as heterosexual. Being gay isn't just about having sex."

"But you haven't had sexual relations with anyone, man or woman, since your deceased partner?"

"That's correct."

"Okay. Celibacy is tough to comprehend, especially because you're an attractive woman. Can you tell the court why you haven't had any relationships since Dr. Gray?"

"A couple days after Charlie died, I had a memorial gathering at my house. Michael showed up toward the end of the gathering. He said he had heard that Charlie died and was disappointed because he was close to being able to prove that I was gay." Sidney diverted her eyes to Anastasia, momentarily. "Michael warned me that when I got into another relationship, he would catch me, and prove that I was gay. He threatened to take JP away from me, because he would never allow his son to be raised by a lesbian."

"So you took this threat seriously?"

"Absolutely. I had just lost a once-in-a-lifetime partner. I wasn't about to lose my son, and I vowed to myself that I wouldn't take any chances."

"So you haven't had any intimate relationships since Dr. Gray."

"That's correct."

"Over the course of the seven years, have you ever met anyone that you may have wanted to get to know better, but didn't because of Michael's threat?"

Sidney was surprised at the question, and could not help looking at Anastasia. "Yes."

It was then Anastasia realized why she got mixed signals from Sidney.

"So you sacrificed your personal life for your son?"

"Yes."

"Your honor, I have no further questions at this time," Jennifer said.

Clancy stood. "May I approach the witness, your honor?" The judge nodded.

"You expect this court to believe you haven't had sex in seven years?" Clancy smiled.

"That would be correct."

"What do you think we are, fools?"

"Objection," Jennifer said.

"Sustained."

"You expect this court to believe that you haven't had sex in seven years?"

"That's the truth...so yes, I expect you to believe that."

"Tell me Ms. Marcum, are you a lesbian?" Clancy asked.

"Yes. I am a lesbian."

"Do you consider yourself an honest person, Ms. Marcum?"

"I do."

"Do you consider yourself an ethical and a moral person?"

"I do."

"Isn't it true that when you demanded a divorce from Mr. Whitman, you concealed the fact that you were carrying his child?"

Sidney's heart beat faster. "Yes."

"Yes? Do you admit that you misled Mr. Whitman?"

"Yes."

"Do you admit that you were dishonest?"

"I did what I—"

"Do you admit that you were dishonest?" He repeated the question.

"Yes."

"Isn't it true that you would do just about anything, including perjury, to keep your son in your custody?"

"No."

"Isn't it true that you and Anastasia have been lovers and the two of you will do anything, including perjury, to keep your son?"

"No."

"No? No further questions."

"Mrs. Warren, do you have any other questions?" Judge Hastings asked.

"Yes, your honor," Jennifer stood. "Was your relationship with Michael Whitman loving?"

"Objection," Clancy argued, "beyond the scope."

"Your honor, Mr. Clancy opened the door to this line of questioning."

"Agreed. You can proceed, Mrs. Warren."

"Sidney, was your relationship with Michael Whitman loving?" Jennifer repeated the question.

"I believe, initially, it was."

"And then what happened?"

"I think both of us became involved with our careers…and we grew apart."

"Was your relationship abusive?"

"Yes."

"Emotionally abusive?"

"Yes."

"Physically abusive?"

"Objection, your honor. Beyond the scope. Additionally, counsel is leading the witness," Clancy objected.

"Overruled, I'll allow it," Judge Hastings said.

"Sidney, was your relationship with Michael Whitman physically abusive?"

Sidney moved uncomfortably in her seat. "Yes."

"Did you ever require medical attention from injuries you suffered from Michael?"

"Yes."

"Could you give me an example of medical treatments that

were required?"

"I received treatments for broken bones and lacerations."

"Did you ever require plastic surgery?"

Sidney was surprised that Jennifer knew about the surgery. "Yes."

"What was repaired?"

Instinctively, Sidney's hand moved to her face. "My face, near my eye."

"You have a scar under your right eye. Is the scar from that injury?"

"Yes."

To Anastasia, the testimony put a different light on Sidney's reactions. She recalled the day Sidney blew up during the photo shoot on the beach.

"Sidney, how did you meet your former partner, Dr. Gray?"

"She was the attending physician in the emergency room of New York Hospital. One evening I went there for injuries I received from a fight with Michael."

"So she treated the injuries you received from Michael?"

"Yes."

"Can you tell the court what injuries you were treated for at *that* time?"

Sidney squirmed in her seat. She had never discussed Michael's violent nature with Justin and this was not the way for him to learn about his father. "I believe I had a couple of broken ribs, concussion…and a laceration to my face."

"Was that the extent of your injuries?"

"I think so, but it was such a long time ago."

"Sidney, I actually have the emergency room report regarding your injuries that evening. Would reviewing the report refresh your memory?"

Sidney stared back at Jennifer. "That's not necessary."

"Then what other injuries did you sustain from that confrontation with Michael?"

Sidney remained silent, and glanced over at Justin. "I don't know."

"Your honor, permission to approach the witness?"

"Granted."

Jennifer placed the document in front of Sidney, then repeated the question. "Sidney, what other injuries did you suffer because of Michael's abuse that night?"

Sidney remained unresponsive.

"Read the comments at the bottom of the ER report to refresh your memory." Jennifer pointed to the words.

"No," Sidney finally said. Then she moved away from the microphone and whispered, "Jennifer, leave it alone."

"I can't." Jennifer continued, "Please read the comments."

"Objection, your honor," Clancy interrupted. "Relevance."

"Your honor, Mr. Clancy is attempting to show that my client is an unfit mother, on the sole premise that Ms. Marcum was engaged in a stable, loving, same-sex relationship over seven years ago. Secondly, Mr. Clancy has attacked her credibility, alleging she is dishonest, because my client concealed the fact that she was pregnant when she divorced Mr. Whitman. Ms. Marcum is not a dishonest person. I am trying to show this court why Ms. Marcum did not make the facts known. And lastly, your honor, if this court considers reversing custody, then this court is obligated to evaluate what type of man Mr. Whitman really is, and what type of person would be responsible for Justin's full-time nurturing."

"Your honor, this is highly improper—"

The judge interrupted. "Overruled." He turned to Sidney. "Ms. Marcum you're instructed to read the comments on the report and answer the question."

Sidney looked at Justin in the rear of the courtroom. He appeared to be listening intently. Anastasia had placed her arm around his shoulders. Sidney's eyes blurred as she studied the report. She closed her eyes, shedding the tears. "Rape victim."

Clancy turned to Michael and the two were in discussion.

Jennifer handed Sidney a tissue. "Sidney, what started the

fight between Michael and you the evening you were taken to New York Hospital?"

Sidney wiped the tears from her face, paused to pull herself together, then spoke slowly. "For years I feared Michael's temper. I was scared to death to become pregnant; I feared for a child's safety. So I practiced birth control without his knowledge. That evening, he found my diaphragm and became enraged."

"What happened?"

"He beat me."

"And?"

"And…he raped me."

"After he beat you and raped you, did he take you to the hospital?"

"No. He went to a political dinner. I managed to get to the lobby and into a cab. The driver took me to the hospital."

"Did you go back to him?"

"Yes. I didn't have a choice. I had tried to leave him previously, on two other occasions. But each time, his…subordinates would find me and bring me back to him."

"What made you aggressively push for a divorce when you did?"

"I found out I was pregnant, and I knew I needed a quick divorce before Michael found out about the baby. The last thing I wanted was for the baby to grow up in a violent household. I also believed if Michael knew I was pregnant, he would never grant the divorce."

"So you concealed the pregnancy from your husband and your attorney?"

"Yes."

"After you were divorced, and Justin was born, you contacted Michael to let him know he was a father. Correct?"

"That's correct."

Jennifer turned to the judge. "Your honor, I have an affidavit executed by Charlotte Gray. This document was executed about ten years ago. It explains how the ER report was generated and controlled by Dr. Gray, until which time, she turned the affidavit and report over to me. It supports all the assertions made concerning Mr. Whitman, including the rape."

"Objection, your honor."

"Counsel, side bar now," the judge instructed.

Both Jennifer and Clancy moved to the judge's bench. Sidney remained on the witness stand. As she gazed out into the courtroom, she realized that Justin and Anastasia were gone. She never saw Anastasia take Justin from the room when the attorneys went off the record. Sidney was shaken. All she could think about was her son. *God, he didn't need to learn this.*

The sidebar conversation got louder.

"Go settle this," the judge instructed.

"Excuse me?" Clancy interrupted. "We want full custody."

"Mr. Clancy, if the two parties can't reach a mutually agreed upon settlement, and I have to continue this hearing tomorrow, Whitman will be lucky to keep visitation rights. I haven't read this ER report, nor this affidavit, because they haven't been introduced as evidence yet. Do you want me to read them now and rule on their admissibility? Don't you think this is a good time to get this thing settled? Go settle this! Neither of you can leave until it's done!"

"Court will be in recess the remainder of the day," the judge announced.

Jennifer walked to the stand where Sidney sat. "I'm so sorry." But the only thing on Sidney's mind was her son. "I need to find JP," she said as she stepped down from the stand.

Natalie entered the courtroom and approached Sidney. Although she had not listened to Sidney's testimony, she knew her friend was upset. "JP is sitting with Anastasia outside the courtroom, down the hall. Are you okay, Sid?"

Jennifer grabbed Sidney's arm. "I know this is hard, Sidney, but I need five minutes of your time, then you can take JP and go home." She turned to Natalie. "Would you check on JP? If he's not okay, we'll be in the witness room. Otherwise, tell him that

Sidney will be out in five or ten minutes."

"Okay," Natalie agreed and left.

Still holding Sidney's arm, Jennifer brushed up against Clancy. "You find a conference room. I'll be available in fifteen minutes."

Michael was fuming. "What the hell is going on?"

Jennifer guided Sidney into an empty room where sequestered witnesses waited during proceedings. She sat Sidney down and poured her a glass of water. Jennifer knew that Sidney was shocked by the turn of events. "Sidney, the judge has made it clear that we need to settle this today. He's instructed that we stay until it's worked out."

"Why?"

"It happens. It's an easier way out for the judge. We have the upper hand. Sid, I need to know what would be acceptable to you, and you can go. Just keep yourself available by phone."

"I want primary custody."

"Anything else?"

"I don't want to live the rest of my life looking over my shoulder, worrying about who I'm socializing with," Sidney said.

"Michael's visitation?"

"Every other weekend, no holidays. I won't settle this unless I have primary custody, Jennifer. Do you understand?"

She nodded, then smiled and took Sidney's hand. "I'm so sorry about what happened in there. I didn't want to go this way, but I didn't feel I had a choice."

"I didn't know Charlie made an affidavit."

"She didn't want you to know." Jennifer squeezed Sidney's hand. "Go get your son, and let me do what you pay me for."

"Thank you, Jennifer, for everything."

When Sidney left the witness room, she found Scott waiting for her. He escorted her down the hall to where Justin waited with Anastasia and Natalie. When Justin heard the footsteps approaching, he looked up and saw Sidney. He ran to her. His eyes were red; it was obvious that he had been crying. The two hugged. Sidney was afraid to let go of her son, until he spoke. "I love you, Mom."

"I love you too, Justin." She pulled away so she could look into his eyes. "Let's go home." Sidney held Justin's hand as they turned toward the others. She hugged her two friends. Anastasia was noticeably absent. "Thank you for all your support. Where did Anastasia go?"

"I don't know, she was just here," Natalie replied.

Anastasia left the building in tears. She realized that it was the compromising photographs taken of the two of them that had threatened Sidney. *Sid could have lost JP. How can I ever forgive myself?*

Sidney did not talk to Justin until they reached New Jersey. "Justin, I'm sorry. I never meant for you to learn what you did this way."

"I knew about you and Charlie, Mom." Justin seemed older than his years.

"You did?"

"Yeah, I'm not stupid. To be honest though, I thought you and Anastasia were lovers."

"You did?"

"Yeah."

"How did you find out about Charlie and me?"

"When I was younger, Dad used to ask questions about her, I never thought much about it. Then as I got older, I figured it out. It's okay Mom. Some people actually consider being a lesbian- cool." Justin hesitated. "Mom, when you found out you were pregnant, did you consider aborting? I mean after all, I wouldn't have blamed you. You must have hated me."

Sidney reached for her son's hand. "Never once did I consider aborting. And I never once hated you. You're the best thing that has ever happened to me." She paused. "JP, it was you who gave me the strength to leave your father. Who knows? If I never got pregnant, I may have never left him."

"I hate him for what he did to you. I never want to see him again."

"Sweetheart, the judge has strongly suggested that we settle this."

"What does that mean?"

"It means nobody is going to be one hundred percent happy. Your father will still have some visitation rights, and I hope to have primary custody. I won't settle for anything less."

"But what if I don't want to see him again?"

"You're feeling a lot of bitterness right now. What happened between your father and me was a lifetime ago. What he did to me was wrong, but if he didn't…hurt me, I never would have met Charlie, I never would have gotten pregnant, and I may never have left him. He may not be the man you thought you knew, but don't exclude him from your life. Okay?"

"Why did you tell him about me, anyway?"

"I don't think I could have, if it wasn't for Charlie. That was harder than leaving your father. But she helped me see that you are his son, and he had every right to know."

Mother and son talked openly all the way home. During their conversation Sidney realized Justin was no longer a boy, but a young man.

Chapter 30

When Justin and Sidney arrived home, there was a message from Jennifer on the answering machine. "Hi Sid, it's me. I'm leaving court now and heading home. It's two o'clock, give me a call. It's good news."

Sidney immediately called Jennifer's house. "Hello," Jennifer answered.

"Give me some good news."

"Michael gets JP one weekend a month and no holidays," Jennifer started. "You maintain primary custody. We promise not to initiate a civil or criminal action against him regarding the rape. We won't disclose the information about the rape, but we'll control the evidence. This way the press won't destroy him."

"What about looking over my shoulder?" Sidney asked.

"He's aware that we control the hospital report and affidavit, and if he starts anything again, he knows we'll use them next time. I'll keep the evidence in a safe place, and it will be your insurance policy. Trust me, Sid, he's not going to give you any more trouble."

"How do you feel about it?"

"I feel good. I think it's a good settlement for you."

As Sidney smiled, she felt the tension leave her body. "Thank you Jennifer, we owe you big time. Do you need me in the morning?"

"No, I can take it from here. How's JP?"

"I think he's okay. We're going away for ten days. I've already made the arrangements. If you need me, leave a message at my office."

"Where are you going?"

"I'm not telling anyone," Sidney said.

"Well, have a wonderful time, Sid. God knows you deserve it."

Sidney seemed to be her old self as she explained to Justin the new custody agreement. "Now, go to your room and pack a bag for warm weather. The two of us are going away for about ten days." Although Sidney did not like the idea of taking Justin out of school, she didn't want him around for the press fallout. "I have your school assignments for the rest of the week, and next week. So pack your books."

"Where are we going?" JP asked.

"It's a surprise. If we hurry, we'll be able to make the last flight this evening. So go pack, and let's try to get out of here by seven, okay?"

Sidney retreated to her room and quickly packed a bag for herself. She carried her bag downstairs and put it in the Jeep. When she returned to the house, she flicked on the television, for the news, then went to the kitchen to prepare a couple of sandwiches, she hadn't eaten anything that day.

As she prepared the sandwiches, she listened to the anchorman discuss world events for the day. Then, "In local news, what do billionaire Michael Whitman and Anastasia have in common? Find out next."

Sidney's heart skipped a beat. She left the kitchen and settled in front of the TV. The commercial seemed to last forever, then the news returned.

"Beginning yesterday in family court, testimony was taken in the custody battle initiated by Michael Whitman against his former wife, Sidney Marcum, over their son Justin. We have Blake Stewart at the courthouse to give us an update regarding how the custody hearing is going. Blake, would you tell us what you've learned so far?"

A field reporter was shown standing on the steps of the courthouse. "Yes, Steve, as you're aware, yesterday Michael Whitman pulled his wife into court demanding full custody of their child. Whitman claimed that his ex-wife, Sidney Marcum, is a lesbian and an unfit mother. Yesterday Whitman subpoenaed Anastasia, who admitted under oath that she had been engaged in a long-time lesbian relationship."

"Blake, what is the business relationship between Ms. Marcum and Anastasia?"

"What I know is this—Sidney Marcum is the owner of MPI, an artist management company. The same management company that represented Anastasia." Pictures of Sidney and Anastasia were flashed on the screen. "Ironically, Anastasia hired Sidney Marcum a couple of years ago when her career plummeted because of rumors that she was gay. From what I hear, Steve, Ms. Marcum is one of the best managers in the industry and was responsible for Anastasia's remarkable comeback over the last two years.

"This morning, day two of the trial, Judge Hastings cleared the press from the courtroom. We have not been allowed in court today. We do know that Anastasia returned to court today, but we don't know if she was called to testify again. Hours ago, the judge instructed both sides to come to a settlement and since that time, information is hard to get. Nobody is talking."

"I understand Anastasia is to be married to Brett Pillar in less than two weeks," said the anchorman. "Have your sources heard anything about what impact this information can have on that?"

"No, Steve. We have not been able to reach Brett for comment."

"Any speculations regarding what this is going to do to Anastasia's career?"

"We contacted Dale Peterson, Anastasia's current manager, but he would not comment. My guess is that this is not going to be a career booster."

"Do you know where the child Justin is?"

"Yes, sources have indicated that Ms. Marcum has taken him to their Brielle, New Jersey home, but that is all I have right now. I'll keep you posted as things develop. This is Blake Stewart reporting for WABS."

Sidney knew the repercussions this would have on Anastasia's career.

As Sidney turned off the television, she heard Justin behind her. "Anastasia's going to be hurt by this, isn't she?"

Sidney had not realized Justin was listening to the broadcast. "I hope not, JP, but it doesn't look good." She went to the phone, then turned to Justin. "Honey, could you put your bag in the Jeep? I'd like to be out of here in ten minutes."

"Sure."

Sidney picked up the phone handset and hesitated. She pressed the speed dial and seconds later the answering machine picked up. She was about to hang up, but knew she was running out of time. "Anastasia, it's Sid. It's going on seven o'clock. I just saw the news...I'm so sorry. JP and I are leaving tonight; we won't be back until late next week. I'm picking up messages at the office. Please call if there's anything I can do...or if you just want to talk."

On the other end of the line, Brett sat listening to Sidney's voice being recorded. He listened to the message again, then pressed the erase button.

Sidney and Justin had barely enough time to get to Newark Airport, park the Jeep, and make it to the terminal to catch the nine o'clock flight to Miami. In Miami, they spent the night at the Hotel Intercontinental, and in the morning they boarded a cruise ship.

It was Friday by the time they were settled in a hotel room in Bermuda. Sidney called her office for the first time since Tuesday. "Hi Michelle, it's Sid."

"How are you? How's JP?"

"He's doing well. How's it going there? Do I have any messages that need my attention?"

"You have eleven messages from the press. Do you want them?"

"No. But what are you telling them?"

"Just that you're out of the office and we can't reach you. That's what I'm telling everyone."

"Good."

"Where are you?"

"It's better that you not know. That way you don't have to lie, right?"

"Sure."

"Any other messages?"

"Two. Jennifer called, she said, 'Everything is good. Call when you get back to town.' And...Anastasia called also."

"What did she say?"

"She asked you to call her. Do you have her number?"

"Yes."

"When are you coming back?"

"I don't know," Sidney lied. "See you later. Bye."

Sidney hung up the phone, then picked it up again, hesitated and placed the call. A male voice answered on the third ring.

"Hi. I'm trying to reach Anastasia. Do I have the wrong number?"

"Well it depends. Who's this?"

Sidney recognized his voice. "Hi Brett. This is Sidney Marcum, how are you?"

"Fine."

"Is Anastasia there? I'm returning her call."

"No, she's out right now. She's with her new manager. They're brainstorming what to do about all this bad press. Hey, I never knew you were Whitman's old lady. Then again, I guess there are a lot of things about you I didn't know."

"How's the press treating her?" Sidney asked.

Brett laughed sarcastically. "Are you kidding?"

"Brett, I'm...away. I want to keep JP away from the press. I'm kind of out of touch right now. I haven't seen the news since Tuesday night."

"Oh. The press is digging her another asshole. And you know in her condition, she really doesn't need this stress."

"What condition?"

"She's pregnant. She doesn't need to put up with this shit." He sounded angry. "We saw you at the fundraiser a couple days before the hearing. Why didn't you warn her?"

"Brett, I'm sorry. I didn't think Michael would pull her into this." Sidney knew how much Anastasia wanted to have children. "Congratulations." She knew she should have been happy for them, but there was a part of her that ached.

"Right."

Sidney could detect the bitterness in his voice. She knew he loved Anastasia and could not blame him. "MPI will do whatever she needs to help her out, assuming she'll let us."

"Sidney, I think you've done enough. She'll be fine after the wedding, then people will realize she's not...you know, one of you."

"Brett, let her know I returned her call. Have her call and leave a message at my office when I can call her back. That's if she still wants to talk. I'll be checking messages daily."

Giving Anastasia the message was the last thing he was going to do.

After her telephone conversation with Brett, Sidney felt

terrible. Her mood was visibly affected. Later that afternoon Justin asked, "Is everything okay, Mom?"

Sidney didn't want to bother Justin with her concerns, but she also knew the press was doing a job on her own reputation. *She knew she needed to talk with him about it before they returned.* "I called home. The press is having a field day with Anastasia. I'm feeling...responsible."

"You do like her, don't you?" her son asked.

Sidney was surprised at the question. "Of course I like her."

"You know what I mean."

"JP, Anastasia is marrying Brett Pillar next week," she said flatly.

"But you do like her, don't you?"

Sidney was surprised by how intuitive her son was. She wondered if he new she was in love with her. "Yes, I like her."

"Have you called her?"

"I have. But we need to talk."

"About what?"

"The fact that I'm gay has been made public. Your friends and teachers and classmates are going to know. What do you think about that?"

"I think I have the best mom in the world," Justin answered. "What else matters?"

Sidney spent the rest of the trip trying to convince herself that Anastasia was better off staying away from her. *As painful as it was, she knew that Anastasia's marriage to Brett, and being pregnant was the best thing for her career. And Sidney knew how much Anastasia valued her career.*

Sidney wasn't surprised when she didn't hear from Anastasia the rest of the week.

Chapter 31

On Thursday night, Justin and Sidney returned to New Jersey, exhausted from traveling. Justin went right to bed, while Sidney unpacked. It was close to midnight when she checked the answering machine. There were many hang-ups, three messages from the press, and then her world seemed to stop when she heard Anastasia's voice. "Sid it's me, please call."

Sidney debated. She didn't know when the message was left. It was very possible Anastasia had called before she spoke with Brett. She picked up the phone and hesitated. Anastasia was getting married in three days. The last thing she'd want would be to hear from me, she thought. She also knew it was likely Anastasia was already in California where the wedding was planned to be held.

She gently rested the handset in its cradle. *It's close to midnight. I'll call her tomorrow.*

Sidney was pleasantly surprised when Pat, her new housekeeper, arrived at the usual time the following morning. "How was your trip?" she asked, as she brought some groceries into the house.

"Wonderful!" Sidney had wondered if Pat would return, after the way the press had crucified Sidney. But Pat went about her business as if nothing had happened. "I'm planning to go to the office this morning, but I should be back midafternoon. I think JP will be sleeping in; we got back late."

"I brought some breakfast makings. I figured pickings would be slim. I'm planning on doing food shopping today. Would you like anything special for dinner?"

Sidney was curious. "Pat, before I left for vacation, there was a lot of publicity about me. Did you catch any of that?"

"Every day," the older woman answered.

"Are you okay with that?"

"It's not my business, Ms. Marcum."

Sidney smiled. "I hope I get that response from most people."

It was close to eight o'clock when Sidney left the house for work. Before she got on the parkway, she stopped by the post office to pick up the mail that was being held.

Michelle and Nelson greeted her when she reached her office. Both seemed somewhat distant. "I didn't expect to see you until next week," Nelson said.

"Sorry to disappoint you. I just plan to go through my mail and make some phone calls." She turned to Michelle. "If you can continue to tell people I'm out, I'd appreciate it."

She closed the door of her office, leaned against the back of it, then exhaled. *I guess that could have been worse.*

Minutes later there was a knock at the door and Natalie entered. "How are you?" Natalie asked as she embraced Sidney.

"Good."

"JP?"

"He's great. We've been in Bermuda. I wanted to get him away from the press."

"Smart."

"I understand they've made Anastasia's life miserable."

"Pretty much. The rumor is that Anastasia and Brett's wedding plans are for convenience and her public image. Have you heard what they're saying about the two of you?"

"Anastasia and I?"

"Yeah."

"No. What?"

"Well, word on the street is that you and Anastasia had a torrid affair and you dumped her. That's when she fired you."

"I'm disappointed I missed it."

"Have you talked to her?" Natalie asked.

"No. I haven't seen her since court."

"You haven't told her how you feel?"

"No."

"When the hell are you going to start living, Sid?" Natalie was upset.

"Nat, she's getting married on Sunday. She's pregnant. Leave it alone, please."

"Pregnant?" Natalie paused. "I still think you should talk to her, before it's too late."

"I plan to return her call this morning."

Before Natalie left she hugged Sidney again. "I'm glad you're back."

Sidney called Anastasia's home. When the answering machine came on, she hung up without leaving a message. *I wonder if she's already left for California.*

She started going through the business mail on her desk, then she turned her attention to the box of personal mail she had brought with her. Sidney sorted through the mail separating it into piles of junk, bills and personal. Before long she came across an envelope that made her heart skip a beat when she recognized the handwriting. She rested the envelope up against the stapler on her desk and stared at it, until she gathered up the nerve to open it.

Sidney,

I need to talk with you. I have left you messages, but I haven't heard back from you. I need to know if there is any chance that you feel what I feel, or has there been too much damage?

Sidney, I've been in love with you forever it seems. Before I marry Brett, I need to know if it's too late for us? I'm sorry my carelessness compromised your defense in court. Can you ever forgive me?

Brett and I still have kept our plans to marry on Sunday, October 23. I plan on leaving that Friday for California. If I don't hear from you by Thursday, I'll assume there has been too much damage or you don't feel what I feel, and I will marry Brett.

Anastasia

Sidney dropped the letter on her desk. She picked up the phone and called Anastasia again. This time she left a message, "It's Sidney. I'm in the office. Please call."

As she rested the phone in its cradle, it hit her that it was Friday. She looked at her watch. *I wonder what time her flight* is. She called Anastasia's cell phone, which she only used for emergencies and history had proven that she rarely had it on. While she was expecting to get voice mail, instead a digital message indicated the number had been disconnected. Sidney called Michelle on the intercom. "I need Dale Peterson's phone number, do we have it?"

"Whose phone number?"

"Anastasia's new personal manager, Peterson. Do we have his number?"

"No, but I think Natalie does."

"Find out and get him on the line quickly, please."

Michelle knew something was wrong, she stuck her head in Sidney's office. "Natalie went down to the lobby to get the mail. Is there anything else you want me to do in the meantime?"

"I need to find out when Anastasia is leaving. I was hoping her manager may know her schedule."

"Anastasia's at the airport now," Michelle said.

"How do you know that?"

"She just called, she was looking for you. I told her you weren't in…like you told me."

Sidney's heart sank. "Do you know what airport she was at?"

"It's probably Newark, but I'm not positive."

Within minutes, Natalie had returned and telephoned Peterson. "She's flying United out of Newark, into LAX. But her flight is at 1:15 P.M.," Natalie informed Sidney.

Sidney looked at her watch. "That gives me barely an hour."

"You can do it, but you need to leave right now," instructed Natalie. Sidney hesitated. "This is something you need to do, Sid. I'll call the airport and have her paged. Do you want me to leave your cellular phone number for her to call you?"

"Yes." She grabbed her coat and left.

Sidney was nervous all the way to the airport. *She didn't know what she was going to tell her.* Then there was a car pile-up from an accident and she was delayed an additional twenty minutes. *I'm not going to make it on time.* She checked to see she missed a call on her cell phone. She hadn't. Sidney called her office and spoke with Natalie. "I'm in a traffic jam; I don't think I'm going to make it on time. Did you leave a message at the airport?"

"Yeah, they're paging her. The message is for her to call your cell phone. So we better get off. But no matter what, Sid, go to the airport, no matter how late you think you are."

It was 1:35 by the time Sidney arrived at Newark Airport. She drove up to passenger drop off and left her car at the curb. She ran into the airport and searched the monitors for the United flights. Her heart raced as she searched for the Los Angeles flights. She stared at the monitor, reality hit and her heart sank. The plane had left on time.

As she turned to leave, she heard the airport announcements to travelers. "Will Mr. Harrington, Mr. Bob Harrington, Mrs. Roberts, Mrs. Lisa Roberts...Anastasia, Ms. Anastasia please pick up a white courtesy phone for a message?"

Anastasia never got the message.

Chapter 32

Sidney headed south on the turnpike and continued toward home. Numbed by the fact she had missed Anastasia, she discarded the notion of calling her in California. It was too late, she decided. Everything happens for a reason. She felt like she had been on a rollercoaster ride since the hearing. Receiving Anastasia's letter earlier had brought a bit of hope and excitement to her. It had been so long since she had permitted herself to love, and to be loved. For a moment she had been hopeful, now she felt vulnerable. She hated this feeling and knew the only way to rid it was simply to let Anastasia go.

By the time she merged onto the Garden State Parkway, the rain had started. The light drizzle continued to the shore exits, then it stopped and the fog rolled in. Visibility was poor as she pulled off the highway and headed toward her home. She glanced at her watch; it was close to three o'clock. She opted to drive to her favorite beach rather than home, *hoping a walk could calm her before seeing Justin.* She retrieved the raincoat she had in her trunk for emergencies. As she walked the long lonely beach, she wondered if she had made a mistake. The ocean usually had a calming effect on her, but today, the turbulent tide seemed to foster her emotions. As she walked down the beach she wiped away tears. She headed up by the dunes and sat on the damp sand. She didn't care.

The fog seemed to have increased since she arrived and she no longer could see the water. She sat blindly on the sand, listening to the turbulent waves thrashing against the shore. From her pocket, she removed Anastasia's note and read it again. Tears fell on the note, blurring the ink. She crushed the paper and threw it toward the water. The wind quickly caught the note and blew it out of sight.

Her mind raced as she listened to the waves beat on the eroding sand. She was desperately trying to convince herself that things worked out for the best. *She had custody of Justin, Anastasia was going to have a baby and her marriage to Brett would give her something she never could. Her marriage could potentially earn back her career. That was one thing Sidney could never do authentically. It is amazing the sacrifices people make to protect their careers… or their families.* But no matter how hard she tried to convince herself, she found no comfort.

The words were barely discernible to her ears. "Do you hate me so much that you couldn't even call?"

Sidney thought she was losing her mind and hearing things. Then about twenty feet away, she saw a silhouette which told her she wasn't alone on the beach. Without warning, the figure was swallowed in the fog. Instinctively Sidney stood.

"Who's there?" Sidney called. She headed to where the image disappeared.

"You you think so little of me that you wouldn't even call me?" Anastasia emerged from the fog, stopping a few feet from Sidney.

Sidney felt like she was back on the rollercoaster. Her heart racing as she approached Anastasia. "I thought you were on a plane."

"And you just let me go." Anastasia's voice cracked.

"I've been out of the country. I just got your letter a few hours ago. I tried to catch you at the airport, but I missed your flight.

"I couldn't get on the plane."

"Anastasia...I can't explain how sorry I am I wasn't honest with you about being gay."

"I understand better now. But it hurts that you didn't trust me enough to tell me."

"It wasn't you I didn't trust," Sidney said. "I didn't trust myself."

Anastasia, obviously hurt, continued. "How come you didn't have the decency to return my call? I know you got my message at the office. Michelle told me."

Sidney moved, now only feet away, she could see the pain in her eyes. "I did. call. I called the night of the hearing and left a message on your answering machine. Then I spoke with Brett last week. Congratulations, by the way."

"Congratulations...on what?"

"Your pregnancy."

"I'm not pregnant! Where the hell did you get an idea like that?"

Sidney didn't know what to say. She just stared back at her.

"Who told you I was pregnant, Sid?"

"Brett."

Anastasia was taken back. "He knew I was in love with you," Anastasia started. "But I can't believe he'd blatantly lie to you... and to me."

Sidney inched closer to Anastasia. She couldn't believe she was standing in front of her. Tears welled in her eyes from gratitude. She looked into her striking eyes; from the time they first met they had always been oddly familiar to her though she didn't understand why. There were so many unanswered questions. Sidney brushed a lock of hair away from Anastasia's face. She felt her soft cheek with the back of her hand, drawing Anastasia's lips to her own and they kissed. It was a kiss reminiscent of when their lips caressed on the same beach, only months earlier rousing feelings that had been long forgotten and lay dormant.

This time, it was Anastasia who backed away, and Sidney needed to clear the air. "It was hell pulling away from you last spring when we kissed. I knew then I was in love with you…and while I couldn't love you…" Tears rolled down her cheeks, "I never stopped loving you."

"Can you love me now?"

Sidney smiled. There was a sparkle in her eyes; one that had burned out years earlier. "If you let me. This hearing has given me a new life. I can start living without the mask of pretending to be someone I'm not." She paused. "I'm terribly sorry about the repercussions this has had on your career."

"Don't be. I've learned a hard lesson about what's important in life. I want to be true to myself and those I love. No more tales of being someone I'm not."

Sidney smiled at Anastasia and took her hand in her own. She wasn't sure what their future held, but was excited that they could live without pretending to be someone they weren't. No more Facades, she thought. I wonder when people will be able to live without fearing the consequences of who they love.

As they turned into the fog, Sidney asked. "Have I ever told you I've felt like we've known each other before?"

Anastasia smiled. "We have."

Author's Note

In every person's life there are events or situations which move us to new heights. Often, those events aren't circumstances which bring us warm-fuzzy feelings. Many times it's adversity in life which triggers our greatest accomplishments.

Those closest to me know I haven't always been a writer. In fact, I never aspired to be one. But there was an event in my life which provoked me in such a way that I felt I needed to do something, and surprisingly what emerged was the genesis of "*Façades*," my first novel. The event I am referring to is Colorado's infamous Amendment 2, the anti gay and lesbian initiative from the '90s.

At the time, I admit I didn't have the fondest feelings toward the group responsible for creating such a stir Colorado. Today however, I look at that situation differently. Today, I realize these events moved me in such a way that I opened myself to new interests and gifts. There are many people who were hurt by Amendment 2 and many moved on to do things that have made a difference in the community. For me, without living through those dark moments, I may never have been called to go deeper, of which I am extremely grateful.

There are many messages in "*Facades*." The lesson for me is simple, while it is hard to send love and kindness to those who may be unkind to us, when doing so something greater emerges.

Publications from
Bella Books, Inc.
Women. Books. Even Better Together.

P.O. Box 10543
Tallahassee, FL 32302
Phone: 800-729-4992
www.bellabooks.com

THE GRASS WIDOW by Nanci Little. Aidan Blackstone is nineteen, unmarried and pregnant, and has no reason to think that the year 1876 won't be her last. Joss Bodett has lost her family but desperately clings to their land. A richly told story of frontier survival that picks up with the generation of women where Patience and Sarah left off.
978-1-59493-189-5 $12.95

SMOKEY O by Celia Cohen. Insult "Mac" MacDonnell and insult the entire Delaware Blue Diamond team. Smokey O'Neill has just insulted Mac, and then finds she's been traded to Delaware. The games are not limited to the baseball field!
978-1-59493-198-7 $12.95

WICKED GAMES by Ellen Hart. Never have mysteries and secrets been closer to home in this eighth installment of this award-winning lesbian mystery series. Jane Lawless's neighbors bring puzzles and peril—and that's just the beginning.
978-1-59493-185-7 $14.95

BEACON OF LOVE by Ann Roberts. Twenty-five years after their families put an end to a relationship that hadn't even begun, Stephanie returns to Oregon to find many things have changed... except her feelings for Paula.
978-1-59493-180-2 $14.95

NOT EVERY RIVER by Robbi McCoy. It's the hottest city in the U.S., and it's not just the weather that's heating up. For Kim and Randi are forced to question everything they thought they knew about themselves before they can risk their fiery hearts on the biggest gamble of all.
978-1-59493-182-6 $14.95

HOUSE OF CARDS by Nat Burns. Cards are played, but the game is gossip. Kaylen Strauder has never wanted it to be about her. But the time is fast-approaching when she must decide which she needs more: her community or Eda Byrne.
978-1-59493-203-8 $14.95

RETURN TO ISIS by Jean Stewart. The award-winning Isis sci-fi series features Jean Stewart's vision of a committed colony of women dedicated to preserving their way of life, even after the apocalypse. Mysteries have been forgotten, but survival depends on remembering. Book one in series.
978-1-59493-193-2 $12.95

1ST IMPRESSIONS by Kate Calloway. Rookie PI Cassidy James has her first case. Her investigation into the murder of Erica Trinidad's uncle isn't welcomed by the local sheriff, especially since the delicious, seductive Erica is their prime suspect. 1st in series. Author's augmented and expanded edition.
978-1-59493-192-5 $12.95

ABOVE TEMPTATION by Karin Kallmaker. It's supposed to be like any other case, except this time they're chasing one of their own. As fraud investigators Tamara Sterling and Kip Barrett try to catch a thief, they realize they can have anything they want—except each other.
978-1-59493-179-6 $14.95

APPARITION ALLEY by Katherine V. Forrest. Kate Delafield has solved hundreds of cases, but the one that baffles her most is her own shooting. Book six in series.
978-1-883523-65-7 $14.95

ROBBER'S WINE by Ellen Hart. Belle Dumont is the first dead of summer. Jane Lawless, Belle's old friend, suspects coldhearted murder. Lammy-winning seventh novel in critically acclaimed mystery series.
978-1-59493-184-0 $14.95

LOVE WAITS by Gerri Hill. The All-American girl and the love she left behind—it's been twenty years since Ashleigh and Gina parted, and now they're back to the place where nothing was simple and love didn't wait.
978-1-59493-186-4 $14.95

HANNAH FREE: THE BOOK by Claudia Allen. Based on the film festival hit movie starring Sharon Gless. Hannah's story is funny, scathing and witty as she navigates life with aplomb—but always comes home to Rachel. 32 pages of color photographs plus bonus behind-the-scenes movie information.
978-1-59493-172-7 $19.95

END OF THE ROPE by Jackie Calhoun. Meg Klein has two enduring loves—horses and Nicky Hennessey. Nicky is there for her when she most needs help, but then an attractive vet throws Meg's carefully balanced world out of kilter.
978-1-59493-176-5 $14.95

THE LONG TRAIL by Penny Hayes. When schoolteacher Blanche Bartholomew and dance hall girl Teresa Stark meet their feelings are powerful—and completely forbidden—in Starcross Texas. In search of a safe future, they flee, daring to take a covered wagon across the forbidding prairie.
978-1-59493-196-3 $12.95

UP UP AND AWAY by Catherine Ennis. Sarah and Margaret have a video. The mob wants it. Flying for their lives, two women discover more than secrets.
978-1-59493-215-1 $12.95

CITY OF STRANGERS by Diana Rivers. A captive in a gilded cage, young Solene plots her escape, but the rulers of Hernorium have other plans for Solene—and her people. Breathless lesbian fantasy story also perfect for teen readers.
978-1-59493-183-3 $14.95

AN EMERGENCE OF GREEN by Katherine V. Forrest. Carolyn had no idea her new neighbor jumped the fence to enjoy her swimming pool. The discovery leads to choices she never anticipated in an intense, sensual story of discovery and risk, consequences and triumph. Originally released in 1986.
978-1-59493-217-5 $14.95

CRAZY FOR LOVING by Jaye Maiman. Officially hanging out her shingle as a private investigator, Robin Miller is getting her life on track. Just as Robin discovers it's hard to follow a dead man, she walks in. KT Bellflower, sultry and devastating...Lammy winner and second in series.
978-1-59493-195-6 $14.95

STERLING ROAD BLUES by Ruth Perkinson. It was a simple declaration of love. But the entire state of Virginia wants to weigh in, leaving teachers Carrie Tomlinson and Audra Malone caught in the crossfire—and with love troubles of their own.
978-1-59493-187-1 $14.95

LILY OF THE TOWER by Elizabeth Hart. Agnes Headey, taking refuge from a storm at the Netherfield estate, stumbles into dark family secrets and something more... Meticulously researched historical romance.
978-1-59493-177-2 $14.95

LETTING GO by Ann O'Leary. Kelly has decided that luscious, successful Laura should be hers. For now. Laura might even be agreeable. But where does that leave Kate?
978-1-59493-194-9 $12.95

MURDER TAKES TO THE HILLS by Jessica Thomas. Renovations, shady business deals, a stalker—and it's not even tourist season yet for PI Alex Peres and her best four-legged pal Fargo. Sixth in this Provincetown-based series.
978-1-59493-178-9 $14.95

SOLSTICE by Kate Christie. It's Emily Mackenzie's last college summer and meeting her soccer idol Sam Delaney seems like a dream come true. But Sam's passion seems reserved for the field of play...
978-1-59493-175-8 $14.95

FORTY LOVE by Diana Simmonds. Lush, romantic story of love and tennis with two women playing to win the ultimate prize. Revised and updated author's edition.
978-1-59493-190-1 $14.95

I LEFT MY HEART by Jaye Maiman. The only women she ever loved is dead, and sleuth Robin Miller goes looking for answers. First book in Lammy-winning series.
978-1-59493-188-8 $14.95

TWO WEEKS IN AUGUST by Nat Burns. Her return to Chincoteague Island is a delight to Nina Christie until she gets her dose of Hazy Duncan's renown ill-humor. She's not going to let it bother her, though...
978-1-59493-173-4 $14.95